SWEET HEART

PETER JAMES

ORION

An Orion paperback

First published in Great Britain in 1990
by Victor Gollancz Ltd.
This paperback edition published in 2018
by Orion Books,
an imprint of The Orion Publishing Group Ltd
Carmelite House, 50 Victoria Embankment
London EC4Y 0DZ

An Hachette UK Company

9 10

A CIP catalogue record for this book is
available from the British Library.

ISBN 978 1 4091 8129 3

Printed in Great Britain by Clays Ltd, Elcograf S.p.A

MIX
Paper from
responsible sources
FSC® C104740

www.orionbooks.co.uk

ACKNOWLEDGEMENTS

Research is essential to my novels and there are many people who in the writing of *Sweet Heart* generously gave me much more of their time and their knowledge than I ever asked of them. They include Eleanor O'Keeffe of the Society for Psychical Research, David and Anne Anderson who so kindly and enthusiastically allowed their beautiful home to be the model for Elmwood Mill, Jan Newton, David Venables and Bill McBryde of the Official Solicitor's Office, Simon Fraser of Fraser & Fraser, Vicki and Polar Lahaise, Mick Harris of Brighton Police, Ren Harris, Marie Helene Roussel, Linden Hardisty (who improved my tennis too!), Canon Dominic Walker OGS, The Venerable Michael Perry of 'The Christian Parapsychologist', Dr Duncan Stewart, Robert and Felicity Beard, Ian Wilson of Dean-Wilson, Sarina LaRive, Sue Ansell, Jill Bremer, Dr S. Domoney who successfully churned my stomach, Veronica Keen, and many more.

A special mention is due to my unflagging secretary, Peggy Fletcher, and my equally unflagging agent, Jon Thurley, and editor Joanna Goldsworthy. And to my mother, and to my sister, Genevieve, for their constant support, and to my wife, Georgina, who redefined the boundaries of patience.

To Tim and Renée-Jean

'I prithee, sweetheart, canst thou tell me
Whether thou dost know
The bailiff's daughter of Islington?'
'She's dead, sir, long ago.'

(Ballad)

FOREWORD
by Peter James

The question authors get asked more than any other – and one many dread because we all get asked it so frequently – is, 'Where do you get your ideas from?' I did hear one author telling the inquisitive fan during a bookstore signing that he got them from a corner shop in Oklahoma . . .

I find, to my joy – and love of serendipity – that ideas come from just about anywhere – a chance remark, a newspaper article, something that pops into my mind when I'm out running – and very frequently from a story I get told while I'm out with the police researching for my Roy Grace novels. And sometimes, ideas find me . . . Mostly, I bank them all away, storing them up for that rainy day. But just occasionally an idea hits me so strongly that I can't shake it off, can't file it away, can't get it out of my mind. It's when that happens that I know this has to be my next book. This is what happened with *Sweet Heart*.

It was a period of my writing career when I was exploring supernatural themes – an area that always fascinated me, and still does. I was delving through the archives of the Society for Psychical Research in Kensington, researching premonitions and precognition for my previous novel to this one, *Dreamer*, when I stumbled across an extraordinary story.

An Australian woman, of English ancestry, had a frequently recurring dream throughout her childhood and adult life in which she saw an English country house, both the façade and rear, followed by people digging in woods close by. She had never been to Europe, so presumed that it was a house she might have seen in a movie, or a murder mystery on television, or in a magazine or an illustrated book, and which had imprinted itself on her unconscious memory.

In her forties, she came to England with her husband for the first time. They rented a car and toured around. One Sunday afternoon they were driving through Wiltshire countryside when she suddenly yelled at her husband to stop the car. Startled, he did so. On the far side of the road was the entrance to a small Tudor mansion.

'That's the house I always see in my dream!' she declared.

'You mean it's one just like it?' he queried.

She was adamant. 'No, that's the house – let's drive up!'

Her husband looked at her, horrified. 'It's 3 p.m. on a Sunday, you can't just drive up to someone's house and tell them you've seen it in a dream!'

'Sure we can,' she retorted. 'We're unlikely to ever come back here again, what's the worst that can happen? They tell us to sod off, right?'

So, they drove up and she knocked on the door. An affable old boy answered, and to her husband's acute embarrassment, she introduced herself by saying, 'Look, you might think I'm crazy, but do you have a sunken garden at the back, with a brick archway over a stream and stone steps leading up to woods?'

He looked at her oddly. 'No,' he said, 'We don't – not anymore. But we used to until around forty years ago, when we re-landscaped some of the grounds.'

He was intrigued enough to invite them in and hear more of her story. Then, taking a couple of spades, she led the way into the adjoining woods. She described how the moment she entered the woods, even though there was no apparent path, she knew exactly where she had to go. After around ten minutes they came to a clearing and she said, 'We dig here.'

They dug for several minutes and then she struck something metallic. An hour later they had unearthed a treasure trove of religious artefacts. Eventually these were traced back to a local monastery from which these artefacts had been taken and hidden by the monks to safeguard them during Henry VIII's Dissolution of the Monasteries, between 1536-1541.

She had absolutely no idea how she knew this information and was so deeply freaked out that she never wanted to delve further, and I understand she returned to Australia soon after.

But it got me thinking. Could people really have past lives? And carry them in our genetic memory? It set me off on a fascinating research journey, in the course of which I met a number of people who had astoundingly convincing and credible stories.

Another question I'm regularly asked is whether I ever get scared in the course of my research or writing – and the answer is yes, often! I had a real woo-hoo moment while I was writing this book. Now, I'm giving a very slight *spoiler alert* so read on from here after you've finished the book!

The beautiful old mill house that Charlie and Tom find and fall in love with in Sussex is real. I came across it on a ramble with our dogs, and the moment I saw it, I knew this was the right location to set the bulk of my story. I approached the owners and they turned out to be fans of mine – and could not be more delightful or helpful. They showed me all around, allowed me to photograph the rooms and surroundings and said I could come back anytime.

In the story, Charlie begins to realise more and more strongly that she might have lived in this house in a previous life. But there is a key difference: there was a barn on the hill above the house in the one she imagines, in my story. There is no barn beside this house, in reality.

When I was nearing the end of the novel I went back to the house for a refresher visit, to check my details. The owners said, 'You've never really told us anything about the story.' Over a cup of tea, as I talked them through it and got to the point about the barn, they both looked astonished. The husband jumped up, ran out of the room and returned with ancient plans of the house and environs. He pointed out the location where a barn had been, and which had burned down in 1890. It was on the exact spot I had described in this book . . .

Peter James
2018

Chapter One

The dog scampered under the rotting gates.

'Peregrine!' the woman called. 'Peregrine! Come back at once!'

No one ever went in there, except for a few local tradesmen who privately admitted it gave them the creeps. Not even her dog, which was nosy and inquisitive and was always going in places he shouldn't, had ever gone in there before.

'Good boy! Come back!'

But her voice was drowned by the weir below. She waited a moment. 'Come on!' she called once more. 'Peregrine!'

Most of the days of her life she walked the dog down the lane, across the iron footbridge and up into the woods, always speeding her pace a little past the property and rarely even looking down at the derelict mill below, with the garden and house beyond with its strange old recluse.

She pushed open one of the tall gates and peered down the drive. Her Yorkshire terrier was running up the steps to the house. Without stopping at the top he nosed his way in through the front door, which was ajar.

'Peregrine!' she bellowed, appalled. 'Come back here! Peregrine!' She hurried down the drive.

The roar of water from the weir made the silence of

the house all the more menacing, and the gravel that scrunched under her feet felt as if it must have been put there to make a silent approach impossible. She stopped at the bottom of the steps, perspiring from the heat of the late summer morning. The house seemed larger from here, rising up the bank above her.

'Peregrine!' her voice was more conciliatory now. 'Peregrine!'

The terrier was barking inside the house, a steady insistent yapping, and she sensed eyes watching her from behind one of the dark mullioned windows; the eyes of the old woman with the hideously burned face.

She climbed the steps and stopped at the top to catch her breath. The dog yapped away inside. 'Peregrine!' she hissed, peering past the oak door into the gloomy hallway.

Then she noticed the milk stacked on the doorstep — five bottles, and a carton of eggs. Newspapers and letters were scattered over the floor inside the door. The house seemed still, felt still. She pressed the bell, but heard nothing; she tried again but it was dead. She rapped the brass hoop of the tarnished knocker, gently at first then harder, the full thud echoing, the dog's barking becoming even more insistent.

She pushed the door open wider with difficulty, the perished draught excluder jamming on the mountain of post, mostly junk mail, that had built up on the oak floor. She stepped in.

The hallway was small, dark, with a low ceiling and stone walls, and smelled unpleasant, of something that had gone off. There was a staircase ahead with a passageway beside it, and doors to the left and right of her. A sinister winged bust stood on an ornately carved table, and her reflection stared back through the dust on a spangled mirror on the wall. The dog was in the gloom at the end of the passageway; she could hear him barking, but could not see him.

'Hello?' she called up the stairs. 'Hello?'

She glanced around, seeking movement, a shadow, and noticed the framed photographs covering the walls. Photographs of elegant women in fine dresses. Except their faces had been carefully burned away, leaving their elegantly coiffed hair, forties and fifties styles, around charred holes. She looked closer, startled. Horrible; the old woman was even barmier than she'd thought.

They gaped down at her, the walls of the passageway solid with them, all faceless. The terrier was pawing and scratching at the door at the end.

'Come here, damn you!' she whispered.

He turned to her, whined, then pawed again at the door. She knelt, grabbed his collar furiously, then felt a shadow fall over her shoulder. She spun round, but it was just the front door moving restlessly in the breeze. The smell was stronger here, vile. The dog whined again and tugged, as if it were trying to tell her something. She wanted to go, to get out of here, but the dog's insistence bothered her. She let go of him and knocked on the door with her knuckles. The dog yapped furiously.

She turned the handle, the door opened and the terrier bolted through. The smell rushed out. Strong, pungently strong. A stench of sour milk, unflushed lavatory and meat that had gone badly off.

'Struth.' She pinched her nose with her fingers. She heard flies buzzing and saw a whole haze of them as she walked in, and heard another sound, too, a faint rustling like expensive silk.

The room felt alive, yet at first there did not seem to be anyone in here. An old drying rack hung above the Aga; an ashtray filled with lipsticky butts lay on the table; an open tin of stew with hair growing out of it sat on the draining board. The fridge door was ajar. That explained the smell, she thought, relieved.

Then she saw the old woman's legs.

At first she thought that she was breathing. She was lying face down through the doorway into what looked like a boiler room. The muscles of her legs were moving, and her mouth and left eye, which was the one she could see, were moving too. So were her hands. Her neck rippled like a wheatfield in the wind.

She staggered backwards in shock and retched, but the horror held her throat so tightly nothing came out. The dog stood in front of the corpse barking excitedly. She slammed into the doorway in her panic, then ran down the passage, out through the front door and down the steps.

She could feel them on her own flesh, feel them rippling, chewing, as she hurried back up the drive, brushed them off her thighs, off her wrists, millions of imaginery white wriggling maggots tumbling on to the gravel as she hurried home to the telephone, gulping down the air, trying to flush out her lungs, hurrying because she could see in her mind the old woman staggering out through the door after her, maggots writhing, dropping from her eye sockets, her cheeks, her hands, like white rain, and could hear her screeching, 'Leave me alone! Let them be. Let them eat. It's only my body, my foul scarred body. My prison. They're freeing me. Can't you see, you old cow? They're freeing me!'

4

Chapter Two

Charley's bike had fallen over earlier in the day and the pedal now caught the chain guard with an irritating clack ... clack ... clack as she pedalled in her sodden clothes, head down against the fine June rain that hung like orange gauze over the sodium streetlights. A stream of cars sluiced past, then a lorry, too close, its filthy slipstream shoving her like an unseen hand in towards the kerb; she swerved.

A thumping beat of music rose up through the rain as a river boat, draped in bunting and lit up like a Christmas tree, churned through the inky water of the Thames and slid out of sight beneath her.

She rode across the roundabout, then up into the quiet of the Tonsleys and turned left into the Victorian terraced street, past the silent parked cars, smart GTIs and BMWs and a couple of Porsches. When they had first moved here, fifteen years ago, it had been a run-down area with derelict cars and mostly elderly people. As first-time buyers with no capital it had been all they could afford. Now it was Des-Res London, with sand-blasted façades and smart front doors and satellite dishes pinned to the rooftops like badges of an exclusive club.

As she dismounted she saw Tom's car parked a short way down the street and felt a beat of excitement. She still looked forward to seeing him at the end of each day; looked forward to seeing him as much as she had when they had first met, twenty years before, when she'd been sixteen; more, she thought sometimes. Especially after some of their arguments, increasingly frequent these days, when she was frightened she might come home to find a note on the table and his clothes packed and gone.

Rain lay on the dark pavement like varnish. She wheeled her bicycle up to the front door, unlocked it and parked the bike on the oak flooring of the hall.

Ben greeted her with a rubber dummy of Neil Kinnock's head in his mouth. 'Hallo, boy!' she said, kneeling and rubbing the golden retriever's chest vigorously with both hands. 'Good to see you boy! Yes it is! No, don't jump!' She shut the door. 'Hi!' she shouted. 'Hi!' Tom called from upstairs.

Charley shook water out of her hair, pulled off her cape, slung it over the newel post and glanced in the mirror.

'Shit!' Her streaky blonde hair was partly matted to her head and neck and partly sticking up in spikes, and her mascara had run down her right cheek. She pulled a face at herself, a charging Apache warrior expression, then prodded her hair with her fingers. 'Not great, huh?' she said to the retriever.

A trickle of rainwater ran down inside her pullover as she went upstairs, followed by Ben, and down the corridor into Tom's den.

The room was dark, cosy, lit with a single pool of light from the Anglepoise bent over the tidy desk. Tom was studying a sheaf of documents bound together with looped pink ribbon. He looked round. 'Hi.'

He was wearing a navy V-neck pullover over his striped shirt and had removed his tie. A tumbler of gin and tonic was by his right hand. He had open, un-cluttered good looks with a hint of brooding temper simmering below the surface that rarely flared with other people, only with herself. A temper that could frighten her with its sudden rages, with the distance it put between them, frighten her because it could stay, like unsettled weather, for days. The way it was now.

'Working late?' she said, walking over and kissing him on the cheek.

'Someone has to earn the money.'

'Hey!' she said. 'That's not fair.'

He stared back down at the documents.

She watched him, flattened. 'Did you play squash?'

'No, had a crisis with a client. Husband's grabbed the kids — had to get an injunction. How was your day?'

'OK. I went to acupuncture, helped Laura in the shop, then we saw *Shirley Valentine*.'

'We've already seen it.'

'Laura hadn't. Anyone call?'

He yawned. 'No. How was the acupuncture?'

'Unpleasant; as always.' She sat on his lap and crooked her arm around his neck. 'Don't be bad tempered.'

He put his hand against her stomach. 'Does your acupuncturist think it's going to work?'

She shrugged. 'Yes, he does.'

'At thirty quid a go he would.'

She looked at his clean, manicured nails. He had always been meticulous about his appearance; even when they had no money at all he had always managed to turn out looking smart. She stole a glance at her own nails, bitten to the quick, and wished she could find the willpower to stop. He used to chide her about it constantly, now he only did when he was irritated by something else.

He wriggled. 'God, you're sopping!'

'The forecast was wrong.'

'I don't think you should be biking.'

'That's daft. Helps keep my figure.'

'Your figure's fine. Cycling's not very relaxing in London and you're meant to be relaxing.' She felt a twinge of anxiety as he yanked open a drawer, pulled a book out titled *Infertility* and tapped it. 'It says here that too much physical exercise worsens infertility problems. It dries everything up inside, or something. I'll read it out, if you like.'

Please don't let's row again tonight, she thought, standing up and walking across the small room. She gazed at the bookshelves, at the toy Ferrari she'd put in his Christmas stocking, at a copy of *Inner Gold*. She picked up a Rubik cube and gave it a gentle twist; dust flew off.

'Did you discuss it with the acupuncturist?'

A car hooted in the street outside; the cubes rotated with a soft crunch. 'He had some pretty crackpot theories,' she said.

'So do you.'

'They're not crackpot.'

'What about the crap therapy thing you went to with Laura. Rebirthing?'

'Rebirthing was good.'

'Great,' he said. 'One session of rebirthing and no sex for two months.' He rocked his drink from side to side, rattling the ice. 'You don't make babies without screwing — or didn't anyone tell you that?'

She was silent.

'You ought to get on and do this regressive hypnotism you keep talking about. You'll probably find you were a nun in a previous life.'

'Laura says —'

'I'm not interested what Laura says.' He drank some of his gin. 'Do you really discuss our sex life with your friends?'

8

Three yellows lined up down one side. She twisted the cube again. 'Don't you discuss it with yours?'

'There's not much to discuss. We don't have a sex life these days, we have scientific experiments. When did you last *enjoy* sex?'

She put the cube back on the shelf, walked over and kissed him again. 'Don't be like this, Tom. I always enjoy it. It's just that' — she bit her lip — 'time's running out.'

Tom's voice became a fraction gentler. 'Darling, everyone says you didn't conceive before because you worked too hard, because of tension. That's why you gave up work. No one said you have to give up sex.' He took her hand and squeezed it. 'Listen, there's a house I like the look of. The particulars arrived today.' He flipped open a file with a wodge of estate agents' particulars.

As she looked at the coloured photograph in the centre a fleeting sensation of familiarity rose inside her, then sank away like a shadow underwater. The photograph was fuzzily printed and the view of the house was partially obscured by shrubbery. Tudor, more a large cottage than a house, the lower half red brick and the upper plaster with wood beams. It had small mullioned windows and a steeply pitched roof tugged down over it like a hat that was too large. It seemed tired, neglected and rather melancholic.

ELMWOOD MILL, ELMWOOD, SUSSEX. A delightful 15th-century mill house in outstanding secluded position, with outbuildings including the original watermill and large brick barn. In need of some modernisation. About 3 acres. For sale by private treaty or auction at a date to be agreed.

'I think I — I've —' Her voice tailed away.

9

'You've what?' Tom said.

She shook her head. 'Nothing. I — I thought for a moment I knew the house.'

'What do you think of it?'

'It's very pretty.' She glanced through the particulars. 'Doesn't say a price — it's probably way out of reach.'

'I rang them up.' He smiled triumphantly. 'They're asking two-fifty, but they might take two twenty-five.'

'How come?'

'It's a complete wreck.'

'Just what we want!' she squealed, and Tom was suddenly touched by her glee and enthusiasm, by something that seemed rekindled inside her. A drop of rain water fell on his cheek, but he barely noticed. Even soaking wet she smelled nice. She always smelled nice; it was one of the things that had first attracted him to her. Her face was pretty with an impish toughness behind it, and there was an element of tomboy in her that had always appealed. Her body was slim, but strong and she could look dynamite in a mini and just as good in jeans. She wasn't beautiful, but she had a raw animal sexiness about her that was part of the chemistry between them. It had barely dimmed in all the time they had been together. Until now.

He should be patient and understanding, he knew; he should be sympathetic and caring. Instead he felt chewed up inside. He was guilty about his resentment against her childlessness (when maybe it was his fault — or at least partly his fault). Moving to the country. That was what they had both decided to do. Get out of London, out of the Big Smoke and the Big Hassle. It would be different in the country. It would come right there.

'I've made an appointment for tomorrow. There's some-one else keen, apparently,' he said. 'Three o'clock. OK?'

10

She nodded and looked down at the photograph. The sense of familiarity returned.

'Have you fed Ben?' she asked.

'Yup.'

'And Horace?'

'Rats, I forgot.'

'You never remember Horace.'

'Teach Horace to bark and I might.' He yawned and closed the file. 'I must get on.'

'How was the lasagne?'

He was already reading his documents. 'Fine.'

She went downstairs. Ben ran after her and over to the front door. 'Sorry, boy, I'm, not going out in that rain. I'm going to have a hot bath. You can go into the garden on your own.' She walked through to the kitchen and unlocked the back door. 'OK, boy!'

Ben sat down and sighed like an old man.

'God, you're a wimp!' She went to the dresser. 'Hi Horace, you don't mind getting wet, do you?' She pressed her face against the glass bowl. The magnified red carp swam over and watched her as if she were a good movie, mouth opening and shutting. 'Had a good day, have you?' She opened the lid of its food. 'How do you feel about moving to the country, Horace? It's a shitty old place, London, don't you think?' She dropped a pinch of food in and it spread through the water like a cloud of fallout. The fish swam unhurriedly to the surface and took its first glum bite.

Elmwood Mill.

Something stirred deep in her memory. Like a forgotten name on the top of the tongue it hung there, tantalising her, then slipped away.

She went upstairs and into the bathroom. As she turned the taps and water splashed out she felt, for some reason she did not understand, afraid.

Chapter Three

The property was by a lake at the end of a mile-long lane that sloped continuously downhill. They had passed only three other houses, the last over half a mile distant. Charley saw the green and white estate agent's board through the trees beside a crumbling brick wall which had jagged glass cemented along the top. Daylight glinted through the slats of the rotting wooden gates.

The appointment was for three o'clock. The car clock said 3.44.

'He must have buggered off,' Tom said.

Charley let Ben out. The golden retriever hurtled clumsily past her, shook himself, then bounded over and cocked his leg against the wall. Eight months old, still a puppy. They had got him when she'd given up full-time work.

The car ticked and pinged and smelled of hot oil. She stretched, feeling flat suddenly, and silently annoyed at Tom for picking her up so late. Always something. For over a year they'd been house-hunting, and every time something was not right. The rooms were too small or the neighbours were too close or someone else got interested and the price went too high. Both of them knew, but rarely spoke, of their need for a fresh start.

12

Black clouds like locomotives shunted through the blue sky. Gusting wind tugged at the roots of her hair. The foliage, lush from a long spell of heavy rain, bent in the wind and the sodden grass sparkled under the coarse sunlight. Moisture seeped into her shoes.

The lake stretched like a grubby carpet between the walls of trees around it, slapping its creases out against the banks. A solitary upturned skiff lay on a patch of grass in front of them under a faded sign nailed to a tree. 'PRIVATE. NO FISHING. MEMBERS ONLY.' Beyond it was a metal footbridge over a weir, and a path leading up into the woods.

A flock of starlings flew overhead. She felt the chill of the wind, more like March than June, and hugged her arms around herself. She heard the rattle of branches, the woodsaw rasp of a crow, the roar of water from the weir. Behind the sounds was an odd stillness after the bustle of London. Strange not to hear any traffic, or voices.

There was a sharp clank as Tom pushed the gate open, the metal bolt scraping through the gravel of the drive. He was unchanged from court, in his pinstriped suit and Burberry mackintosh. They must look odd together, she in her jeans and baggy pullover and bomber jacket.

Then her heart skipped as she stared down the sweeping drive at the cluster of buildings nestling in the hollow a hundred yards away, between mossy banks that rose up into the woods on either side. The house — a different view from the estate agent's photograph — a brick barn, and a dilapidated wooden water mill.

There was little sign of life. The windows were dark. Water tumbled from the weir into a brick-walled sluice pond below them. It frothed angrily around the motion-less wheel and slid in a fast narrow stream through the

13

garden, under an ornamental wooden bridge, past the barn and into a paddock beyond.

Excitement thumped inside her, although the house was smaller than she'd thought it would be, and in worse condition. Shadows boxed on the uneven roof as the wind punchballed the trees; an L-shaped single-storey extension seemed as if it might collapse at any moment on to the coal bunker and an oil tank beside it in a bed of nettles. Then she stiffened.

Something was missing.

She stared around, noticing something new all the time. A bird bath, a shed, a wheelbarrow, a hen run. Two uprooted oak trees leaned against one another on the front lawn, their branches interlocked like fighting dinosaurs.

The hollow had once been the river valley, she realised, before the river had been dammed to make the lake. Apart from the grass, which looked as if it had been cut, it was wild. There were some rhododendron bushes, a few desultory clusters of wild flowers, a small orchard.

Something was missing.

Her eyes were drawn to a level patch of scrub grass halfway up the bank above the barn, between the mill race and the woods. Her armpits were clammy; she felt dizzy and held on to Tom's arm.

'Are you OK?' he said.

Strands of hair thrashed her cheek. A bird chirruped.

The slapping of the waves on the lake. The tumbling water of the weir. The wind in the trees. The quiet. It was touching something, stirring something, like snatches of an old tune.

'Charley? Darling?' He shook her arm. 'Anyone home?'

'What?' She came back to earth with a jolt and felt disoriented for a moment. 'Sorry, I was just —' She smiled. 'It's wonderful.'

'Don't get your hopes too high. There's someone else interested, and we might hate the inside.'

'We won't!'

Ben tore down the drive and loped across the grassy bank.

'Ben!' she shouted.

'It's OK, the house is empty.'

'Why don't we phone the agent and tell him we're here now?'

'Let's go and have a look first.'

The sluice pond was deep and cold. Slime coated the wall. The thunder of water grew louder as they walked down and she felt a fine spray on her face.

'We'd be wanting to pee all the time,' Tom said.

Further on clear water flowed under the ornamental bridge and Charley thought how on warm summer evenings they could have supper, the two of them, by the stream. Bring her mother down on fine days. Convert the barn and maybe Tom's father could live there. If Tom and his father could stop hating each other.

The house seemed larger as they neared it, partly because it sat up above them. The front was the pretty view in the particulars. Elizabethan, one end slanted and the other square. The plaster of the upper floor was crumbling, the wooden beams were rotten and the brickwork of the ground floor was uneven. The windows were small and differing sizes.

They heard a car door. Ben ran back up the drive, barking. A man hurried in through the gates, short and purposeful, a blue folder tucked under his arm, hands and feet pointing outwards like a penguin. He paused to pat Ben, and was rewarded with muddy pawprints on his trousers. He hove to in front of them, puffing, a plump, dapper man in polished black loafers with shiny pens in his breast pocket and alabaster skin.

'Mr and Mrs Witney? I'm sorry, so sorry to have kept you.' He leaned slightly backwards. Wind lifted the hair off his bald pate.

'We were a bit late ourselves,' Tom said.

'Ah yes, tricky to find the first time.' A Rotarian badge glinted smugly in the lapel of his grey suit. 'Budley, from Jonathan Rolls.' His fleshy fingers gave Charley's hand a sharp downward tug, as if it were a bell-pull. 'Moving out of London?'

'Yes.'

'Something like this comes on the market once in a decade.'

'Windows look bad,' Tom said.

'Reflected in the price. So little's been done for years.' He gave his signet ring a twist. 'Dates a long way back — to the Domesday Book. Been added to since, naturally.'

Charley stared up the mossy bank at the level patch of scrub, at the woods, at Ben playing happily, then at Tom, trying to read his face, but it was blank, giving nothing away.

'Wonderful place for children,' Mr Budley added.

Charley caught Tom's eye.

Tom tied Ben to the boot scraper at the bottom of the steps and they followed Mr Budley. The front door was oak with a tarnished lion's head knocker. The wind billowed Charley's jacket.

'How long has the house been empty?' Charley asked.

'Only about nine months. Miss Delvine passed away at the end of last summer,' Mr Budley said.

'Here?' said Charley. 'In the house?'

'Oh no, I don't believe so.'

'I always think it's a bit creepy when someone's actually died in a house,' Charley said.

'You know who she was, of course?'

'No.'

'Nancy Delvine.' He said the name in a reverential hush.

Charley repeated it blankly and glanced at Tom. He shrugged.

'The couturier,' Mr Budley said, making them feel for a moment they'd let him down. 'She was very famous in the forties.' He leaned towards them and lowered his voice. 'She made for royalty.' He allowed them time for this to sink in before pointing to a brass plaque above the door with a crude etching of a sun. 'The original fire insurance plaque from 1711. Steeped in history, this house.' He placed the key in the lock and turned it as if he were opening a pearl oyster.

The tiny entrance hall was strangely silent and smelled like a church. There were closed doors with iron latches to their right and left, a narrow staircase ahead, a dark passageway to the right of it. A winged bust stood on the hall table under a pockmarked mirror.

Mr Budley pressed a light switch. There was a sharp metallic click. Nothing happened. The grimy lampshade was fixed to the low-beamed ceiling above Charley's head. She could have changed the bulb without standing on tiptoe.

'The mains power,' Mr Budley said. 'It keeps tripping. The box is in the cellar. We might as well start there.'

They walked along the passageway, Tom's metal-capped shoes echoing on the bare boards. The walls, panelled in oak, were badly in need of a polish and seemed to press in on them. Dozens of picture hooks and nails stuck out of the panelling. Mr Budley stopped beside a door and noticed Charley's expression.

'Valuable paintings. Couldn't be left in an empty

house — the insurance.' He opened the door. Thick pipes ran above it. 'It's steep,' he warned, switching on a tiny torch.

Charley felt a draught that smelled of coal and damp as she followed him down the wooden staircase into pitch darkness. He shone the beam of his torch on a dusty electricity meter, then on a metal box with a large handle and a row of ancient ceramic fuses. There was a crackle and a flash of sparks, then a weak light filled the room.

Charley shrieked and clutched Tom. A group of bald, naked shop window mannequins on pedestals stared at them.

'Miss Delvine did some of her work here in the house.'

'God, they gave me a fright!' Charley looked warily around the rest of the cellar. The floor was brick, and uneven. There was a wine rack, a wooden wheelchair and a cast-iron safe. Beyond an opening in the far wall was pitch darkness.

Tom turned to the mannequins. 'All right class, sit down.'

Charley giggled uneasily. The mannequins gazed stonily.

'This lever—' Mr Budley pointed. 'There's a built-in voltage trip. For some reason the circuit keeps overloading.'

'Seems pretty primitive,' Tom said.

'Needs rewiring.'

The first floor landing was lit by two candle bulbs in a gilded sconce on the wall. A pot stand with a dead plant sat in a narrow recess. The floor was on a slant, as was a window with tatty chintz curtains overlooking the rear garden. With the timber beams and low ceiling it felt like being on an old ship.

'Has anyone done a survey?' Tom asked.

'No. Not yet,' said Mr Budley, 'but there's no problem. Houses like this might tilt a bit but they're solid as rocks. I'd rather be in a house like this when the bomb drops than in any of the modern ones on our books.'

The master bedroom reminded Charley of a country house hotel they had once stayed in. It had beamed plaster walls and a huge carved oak bed with a grimy counterpane the colour of parchment. There was a maple wardrobe, a matching dressing table with a silver hairbrush and a comb and crystal bottles caked in dust. The room smelled strongly of rotting fabric and more faintly of musky perfume.

'East,' Mr Budley said. 'This room gets the morning sun.'

'Good size,' Charley said. 'Plenty of space to build in some fitted cupboards. It's got a nice feel to it, this room.' She stared out of the leaded-light window. The view across the lake was stunning.

'Is the furniture going?' Tom said.

Mr Budley nodded. 'If there's anything you are interested in I'm sure a price could be discussed.'

Behind them was a tiny door through which even Mr Budley had to duck. 'The ensuite bathroom is one of the features of the house,' he said. 'Wonderful taste, quite what you'd expect of a woman like Nancy Delvine.'

It was in hideous bright pink with gold-plated taps. There was an unpleasant carbolic stench, and mildew on the carpet.

'Here we have the airing cupboard and the upstairs lavatory. And this is the smallest spare room, ideal for a young child.' Mr Budley walked on ahead. 'This one is a much better size,' he said as he went into a room at the end of the landing. 'Miss Delvine's workroom,' He announced. 'To think she made garments for royalty actually here in this —'

19

His voice stopped suddenly. His eyes darted round at the treadle sewing machine, at the work surface under the window covered in cuttings of fabrics, bits of chalk and a pattern weighted down by large scissors, at the desk with a sketchpad and a vase full of crayons. There were two tailor's dummies, one bare with 'Stockman 12' stencilled on its midriff, the other partly covered in tattered black taffeta. Sketches were pinned haphazardly around the walls. A showcard of a model in a boa-trimmed hat, white gloves and an elegant dress had a large printed caption at the top: 'CHOSEN BY VOGUE'.

The room felt cold, icily cold. Charley pulled her jacket around her. A bunch of brown paper pattern cards swung gently on a butcher's hook hanging from the picture rail.

'This would make a good study, Tom,' she said. She went to the window. Her eye was drawn to the patch of scrub grass on the bank behind the barn. 'Were there stables here, Mr Budley?'

'Stables?' Mr Budley said. 'No, I — I don't believe so. You could build some, of course.' Hurriedly he ushered them out.

The kitchen was in custard yellow, the ceiling stained uneven ochre with nicotine and the light shade was full of dead flies. There was an Aga. Blackened and ancient in an ugly tiled recess, but an Aga.

'Nice to have breakfast in here,' Mr Budley said.

There was a deep enamel sink, a wooden draining board and dreary fitted cupboards. The floor was brick, which Charley liked. A slatted clothes rack was suspended from the ceiling on a pulley and cord system, a ragged tea towel draped over it. She pulled the cord. There was a creak and the rack wobbled precariously.

'Saves you hanging the laundry out on a wet day,' said Mr Budley.

'It might be nice to keep some of these old things, mightn't it, Tom? Make a feature out of them.'

'Keep the whole house as it is and save a fortune.' Tom winked at Mr Budley, and blew his nose.

'You could,' Mr Budley agreed. 'You could indeed.' He threw open the dining room door with a weary flourish. 'The mill owner was an important man in the community. This is reflected in the size of the reception room.'

It was larger than she expected, with a refectory table that had ten chairs and could have seated more. The beamed walls were wattle and daub, they were informed. There was a recess by the fireplace with a kneehole writing desk and chair. It would be good to have friends for dinner in this room. She pictured them around the table, the fire roaring.

They crossed the hallway. 'The drawing room,' Mr Budley said. His ebullience seemed to have left him.

The room must have been a fine one once and was dominated by the huge inglenook. The curtains across the French windows at the far end diffused the sunlight, and the rich warm glow masked much of the grime and faded colour. There was a peach-coloured sofa with shell-shaped cushions and several matching chairs, a cocktail cabinet that could have come from a state room of an ocean liner and an elegant chromium magazine rack.

It felt strange walking across the floor. Very strange. She had a curious sense of familiarity, and as she opened the curtains of the French windows she felt she had seen the same view before. The bank rose up to the right, the grass rippling in the wind. A chestnut horse was grazing in the paddock beyond the wooden fence. The feeling faded and left her wondering where it reminded her of.

Mr Budley was studying his watch, 'I — ah — have

clients waiting at another property. Would you think me terribly rude it I left you to see the grounds on your own? Or do you wish to go around the house again?'

Tom looked at Charley, then turned back to the estate agent. 'How much interest have you had? You mentioned someone might be offering this week, didn't you?'

Mr Budley glanced over his shoulder as if worried he was being spied on. 'Confidentially, I think an offer of two hundred and thirty would secure this.'

'It needs everything doing,' Tom said.

'Oh yes. No denying.' Mr Budley raised his hands. 'But with everything done it would be worth four to five hundred thousand, at least, with development potential — so much potential. Where can you find a property like this, so close to London yet so quiet? It's really very underpriced. If my wife and I were younger we'd buy this, no hesitation. How often can you buy beauty?' His eyes darted nervously again.

'I'll call you tomorrow,' Tom said.

'You'll make the right decision. I can tell you are people who make right decisions.'

They followed the agent down the steps and Charley held on to Ben as he hurried off up the drive.

Tom puffed out his stomach and covered his mouth with his hand. 'Nancy Delvine lived here!' he said, mimicking Mr Budley.

'Gosh? Really?' she mimicked back.

'Have you ever heard of her?'

'No.'

Charley let Ben go. He bounded towards the stream. A crow swooped down low over him.

'But you used to be in the rag trade.'

'So I don't think she can have been very famous.'

'Well,' Tom said, 'what do you think?'

'I think Mr Budley's a creep.'

'I don't imagine he comes with the house.'

Charley was silent for a moment. 'It's a wreck.'

'We wanted a wreck!'

'Do you like it?' she said.

'I love it! It's absolutely wonderful. I want to live here!'

'I like it too. It's just —'

'Just what?'

'I'm not sure about being so isolated.'

'Christ, we're much safer here than living in the middle of London.'

'I'll probably get used to it,' she said.

'We've got those people interested in Wandsworth so now's the chance. This place is a terrific buy, and if we end up not liking it we'll sell it at a profit in a year or two's time. But we're going to love it.' He clapped his hands together. 'It's what we need — a new beginning.'

'Yes,' she said uncertainly.

A shadow flitted on the ground in front of her. For a fleeting moment she thought it was the crow. Then she heard Tom's shout, saw him leap towards her, saw his hands raise up, felt them shove her sharply backwards. There was a crash on the ground beside her as though a table had been dropped, and a stinging pain in her leg.

She turned, white-faced, shaking. A large slate tile lay where she had been standing, shattered like a pane of glass. Blood dribbled out of the gash in her jeans leg and ran towards her ankle. Tom grabbed her wrist and pulled her further away from the house, out into the middle of the drive.

'You OK?' he said, tugging out his handkerchief and kneeling down.

She looked at the roof, then at the slate, her heart hammering. She winced as Tom pressed the handkerchief over the wound.

'Lethal,' he said. 'Christ, if that had hit you . . .'

23

She nodded silently, staring up again. 'Just the wind,' she said. Another shadow zigzagged towards her and she stepped back out of its path. But it was a sparrow, coming down to take an insect from the lawn.

Chapter Four

Charley opened the door of the cubicle and carried out the two small specimen jars. They felt warm and slightly tacky. Tom followed sheepishly, his cheeks flushed.

The row of people sitting in the low leatherette chairs looked up from their magazines and murmured conversations. Couples, husbands and wives in their twenties, thirties, even in their forties, with nervous faces, anxious faces, desperate faces, clutching their empty jars, waiting their turn, hopefuls all.

She walked selfconsciously down the carpeted corridor and knocked on the door marked 'Laboratory'.

'Come in.'

A young woman sat behind a small desk, writing on a pad with a fountain pen. The name on her lapel said Dr Stentor. She had short blonde hair, was about twenty-six years old and rather hearty. Charley handed her the jars.

'Well, these look jolly good, don't they?' she said in a booming voice. 'Did you manage the split ejaculate?'

Tom gave a single embarrassed nod. He hated this. He had turned up today, reluctantly dutiful, the way he might have attended a distant relative's funeral.

Dr Stentor tilted one of the jars so the grey fluid slid down the side. 'You got the first spurt in here?'

'I'm afraid some of it' — Charley blushed — 'got spilt.'

Dr Stentor squinted in the jar. 'Well, gosh, don't worry. There's enough here to fertilise half of England.' She gave an accusatory glance at Tom. 'That's if they're all right, of course. Jolly good, have a seat.'

They sat down while she went into another room. The telephone rang, three warbles in succession, then stopped. The office was bare, functional, greys and reds. A framed certificate hung on the wall.

'Is it today, your regression hypnosis thing?' Tom said.

'Yes.' Charley saw his smirk. 'Laura —' she began.

Tom raised his eyebrows. 'Laura what?'

'She knows someone who was having problems conceiving. She went to a regressive hypnotist and discovered she'd seen her children murdered in a previous life. She got pregnant very soon afterwards.'

'Tosh!'

'No harm in trying it.'

Tom took out his diary and checked a page. 'No. No harm.'

They sat in silence for a moment.

'What do you feel about the house, Tom?'

'Positive. You?'

'I like it, but it's a big undertaking and I'm still worried about it being so remote.'

'I think it's great it's remote. Peace and quiet! Who the hell wants neighbours?'

She looked at him uncertainly.

'Listen,' he said, 'if we lose our buyer it could be months before we get another chance of anything. At least let's make an offer.'

'OK.'

Dr Stenor returned and sat opposite them. 'Well, it's gone up. Around forty million. Perhaps the boxer shorts are helping.'

'I'm ...' Tom gritted his teeth. 'I'm still dunking them in cold water every day.'

'That's obviously helping too. It is possible for you to conceive with this sperm count. You only have one tube open, Mrs Witney, and it's not brilliant, but there is a chance. If you want to try an implant again we'd be very happy to do it, though we're booked until November. I'll send a report through to your doctor,' she went on. 'I wish there was some magical solution I could offer. Good luck.'

They took the lift down, the smart, plush, carpeted lift. 'It's encouraging isn't it?' Charley said, trying to break the awkward silence between them.

'Encouraging?'

'At least your count's gone up.' She took his hand and squeezed it. 'I feel fine about the house. I'm sure I'll like it. Will you call the agent?'

'Yes,' he snapped, pulling his hand away and digging it into his jacket pocket. 'I said I would.'

'I'll call him if you'd prefer.'

'I said I would.' He hunched up his shoulders and leaned against the wall of the lift like a sulking child. 'I'm not so sure about it now.'

'Why? Two minutes ago you couldn't wait.'

He shrugged. 'I have people come to me every day who've moved house because they thought it would save their marriages.'

'What's that meant to mean?'

He said nothing and she wished she had not asked the question, because she knew exactly what it meant.

Chapter Five

The engine roared gruffly as they accelerated. The black bonnet sloped upwards in front of her, its chromium radiator cap glinting coldly in the moonlight. The exhaust biffed twice as he changed gear, and the note of the engine became smoother.

The dull white lights of the instruments flickered and the thin needle of the speedometer jerkily moved past sixty ... seventy ... seventy-five. The thrills of the speed, of the night, tingled insider her. She felt indestructable as the car raced past sentinel hedgerows, the headlights unfurling a stark chiaroscuro world of light and shadow through the narrow windscreen.

It was like being in the cinema, except it was happening, she was part of it. She could feel the vibration of the car, the inky cold of the wind thrashing her hair around her face, could see the steely dots of the stars above, and smell the tang of wet grass that hung in the air, the perfume of the night.

She was afraid there would be a click, the ride would stop and she'd have to put another penny in the slot. She chewed the gum; the minty flavour had gone, but she still chewed ... because he had offered it to her ... because the girl in the film they had just seen had chewed gum ... because ...

'Who is in the car with you?'

The voice was American, a long way away. It belonged to another time.

The note of the engine changed again, the road dipped then rose and her stomach rose with it. Trees, telegraph poles, road signs flashed past. He braked harshly, the wheels locking up, the car snaking, the tyres yowling as they came into a sharp left-hander. She gripped the grab handle on the door, then relaxed as he accelerated again and sank back deep into the seat. Her body and the car and the road and the night seemed fused into one; the pit of her stomach was throbbing and she could not stop the smile on her face. She turned away, embarrassed, not wanting him to see, wanting to keep her excitement private. His hand left the wheel and squeezed her thigh, and she felt the wetness deep inside her.

Tonight. It would be tonight.

His hand lifted away and there was a grating crunch as he changed gear, then the hand came back, bolder, began to slide her skirt up until she felt his cold fingers on her naked flesh above her stockings.

'Oh,' she breathed, feigning shock, and wriggled slightly because she felt she should react, that she should not seem too keen.

Tonight. She was ready.

'Do you know his name? Can you tell me his name? Can you tell me your name?'

They squealed through a bend and the road widened into a long straight stretching out ahead like the dark water of a canal. The engine was straining and there was a loud protesting whine from somewhere beneath her as his fingers slid about her wetness and pulled away reluctantly as he put both hands back on the wheel. She heard the clunk of the gears and the note of the engine soften. The thrill was accelerating within her, some wild animal instinct aroused, a careless abandon.

His hand came back, one finger probing deep, and she parted her legs a little to give him more room, pressing against the leather seat, blinded by her hair in her eyes. She changed the angle of her head and her hair whipped away behind her.

'Where are you? Do you know where you are?'

The finger slid out and they went into a long curve that threw her against the coarse tweed of his jacket, the tyres squealing like piglets, then the road straightened and she wanted the finger back in again.

She was intoxicated with a raw energy. They snaked through another bend, almost flying now; a rabbit sat in the beam of the lights and the car thudded over it.

'Stop, please stop!'

'You what?'

'Stop. You hit a rabbit.'

'Don't be a stupid cow!' he shouted.

'Please. It may be in pain.' She imagined the rabbit lying in the road, its head twitching, legs and back smashed into the tarmac, fur and blood spread out. 'Please stop.'

He stood on the brakes and she lurched forward, her hands slamming against the dash, the tyres howling, the car snaking crazily. They stopped with a jerk, then reversed. She stared at the black lane behind them, and could see nothing.

'It were just a stone, yer silly cow,' he said. 'Just a stone. We didn't hit no rabbit.'

'I'm glad,' she said.

He turned towards her, kissed her, his hand slid up her thigh, the fingers probed inside, parting her, opening her wider. She smelled burnt rubber, leather, heard the rumble of the exhaust, the knocking rattle of the engine, felt the tweed of his sleeve brush her face. Their lips pressed together, their tongues duelling hungrily, the rubbery ball of her chewing gum rolling around. She tilted her head away, dug her fingers in her mouth and plucked it out. As their lips met again she reached with her left hand towards the window, scrabbling to find the winder. The finger thrust even deeper and she moaned softly, her hand finding the dashboard, the glove locker, and she pushed the gum hard under it out of sight.

The finger worked up and down and strange sensations of pleasure exploded through her body. Her left hand was now on the flannel of his trousers, feeling the heat of his leg. It slid slowly across into the dip that was even warmer, and squeezed the bulging stiffness.

She fumbled for the metal tag of his zipper, pulled it. It stuck. She tugged at it and it opened and she slipped her hand inside, felt the soft cotton, something damp, then she was holding his hard flesh, large, huge, smoother than she'd imagined. She ran her thumb over the top, felt something slimy, slippery, traced her finger along the shaft.

He blew air down her neck and rolled over on to her, tugging her knickers down. She lifted her bottom, helped him, heard the buckle of his belt free.

The thingie.

No time.

His hands slid up her bare skin, under her bra, fondled her breasts clumsily, then gripped her ribs and began pushing his hardness inside her, shoving, thrusting it in, forcing it in. Too big for her; it wasn't going to fit. She thought it was going to split her apart, then it went deeper, rising right in her, thrusting up and down. Her stomach was juddering.

Oh. Oh. Oh. She was gasping. Oh. So good, So good. She pulled at his shoulders, touched his face, his hair, tugged his ears, feeling him further in, further in, pumping. A million pumps working inside her, his breath in her ear, his tongue, panting.

She screamed. Then again. She exploded, howling in wild ecstasy into the night.

Then silence.

Saw his eyes, close, staring, his lips smiling. Except they weren't his lips. It was a woman. Looking down at her.

'Charley? You OK?'

A soft American voice.

'You OK? You were pretty far gone, eh?'

Charley said nothing. Her whole body was burning with embarrassment and perspiration trickled into her hair.

The American woman's face was large like the rest of her, and heavily made up. It was encased in a shock of rusty hair, and clusters of silver balls the size of Christmas baubles hung from her ears. She was smiling encouragingly.

'Who were you, Charley? Who were you with? *What were you doing?*'

'I —' There was a minty taste in Charley's mouth. 'I was chewing gum,' she said.

She was lying on a bed. A red bulb burned overhead in a paper globe. She heard faint strains of a musical instrument which sounded like a sitar. The woman's tongue curled inside her painted lips like the stamen of a rose. Flavia. Charley remembered her name now. Flavia Montessore. She stared around the large dim room. Tapestries on the walls. Bookshelves. Sculptures. A rather grand, ornate room, eastern feeling.

'You were making love, right?' Flavia Montessore asked.

Charley hesitated, then nodded.

'That's terrific!' Flavia beamed. 'You know something? You're my first ever orgasm!'

Charley's hands were beneath the blanket covering her. She found she was still wearing her underwear.

'Don't look so worried,' Flavia Montessore said. 'You were having a good time. Going into past lives can be fun!'

'I — I've never had an erotic dream before.'

Flavia Montessore shook her head and the earrings jangled. 'It wasn't a dream, Charley, it was happening.' She had green eyes and bright green mascara. Her fingernails were green too. 'You were there. It was real. You regressed. You were reliving it. Boy, were you reliving it!'

'It was just a dream.'

'You were in a deep trance, Charley. You weren't dreaming. You were reliving something from a past life. Tell me about it, it'll help you remember too. Where were you?'

'I was in a car.'

'What sort of car?'

'A sports car.'

'What period? Nineteen twenties?'

'No. Later.'

'Do you know the make?'

'I was inside it all the time. I didn't see the outside. I don't know what it was.'

'Where were you? Which country?'

'England,' she said reluctantly. 'I was in the country-side.'

'Can you remember your name?'

'No.'

'The man you were making love with. What about his name?'

'I don't know.'

'You were chewing gum. What flavour was it?'

'It was Wrigley's Doublemint. I can still taste it. I took it out of my mouth and put it under the dash-board.'

'How old were you?'

'Young. My teens.'

'Have you ever been regressed before?'

'No.'

33

'You're a good subject. I think you could remember a great deal if we worked on it. When I come back from the States this winter I'd like to do some more work with you.'

'I thought past lives were hundreds of years ago, not this century,' she said.

Spangles of light danced in Flavia Montessore's earring. 'There are no rules, Charley. Some people have gaps of hundreds of years between lives, some thousands. Some have only a few years and some come back immediately. It depends on your karmic situation.' She smiled again.

Charley was finding it hard to take her seriously. She had always found it hard to believe in the idea of reincarnation, in spite of Laura's enthusiasm. The hypnotist's heavily made-up face reminded her of a seaside fortune teller. Deep inside was a feeling that she had somehow been tricked, conned.

Chapter Six

'This would go well.' Charley shook the silk square out to show its full design, then draped it around the woman's shoulders. The woman held it by the corners as if it were a grubby sack and stared at herself in the mirror. Her face was taut, like her hair. Charley winked at Laura. Laura gave her a cautionary frown.

'Cornelia James?' The woman looked down at the corner for the signature.

'Of course, madam,' Charley said.

'Does rather suit me, wouldn't you think?'

'Absolutely. And it gives you two outfits.' Charley removed the scarf with a conjuror's flourish. 'Without it, a simple day dress.' She draped the scarf back around, arranging it more strikingly. 'With it, you dress up. Perfect for a cocktail party or the theatre. You'll find it wonderfully cool to wear when it's hot.'

'And you think this blue really is my colour?'

Charley performed a ritual walk of approval, like a Red Indian round a totem pole. 'It definitely suits you. Your husband'll love it.'

'Boyfriend,' the woman said.

'He'll love it too.'

She paid with a platinum card that matched her hair and swept out into the Walton Street drizzle, the rope-handled carrier bearing the emblem of Laura's boutique rubbing against the crocodile scales of her Chanel handbag.

Laura closed the door behind her and tossed her imaginary hair back from her face, still not used to the fact that she'd had it cut short. She was attractive, with rather boyish features, and her cropped brown hair made her look even more masculine. A rack of linen jackets swayed in the draught behind her. The summer displays looked bright but uninviting against the June rain.

Charley clipped the American Express slip into the till. 'Lady Antonia Hever-Walsh, my dear, no less,' she said. 'What a cow.'

'She's a good customer,' Laura said tartly.

Charley wondered what had happened to Laura's sense of humour recently. She was normally far ruder than Charley about customers she did not like, which was understandable, since she had to put up with them for six days a week while for Charley, helping out in the boutique was a hobby.

A horn blared from the stationary traffic in the street. Someone under a red umbrella peered in through the window, then hurried on. Ella Fitzgerald's voice drifted from the speakers; Charley did not think it suited the gloomy afternoon.

'It wasn't a dream, Charley, your regression. No way. It would definitely have been a past life.'

'It was bloody embarrassing, I tell you. Having the only erotic whatever-it-was of my life in front of this woman.' Charley entered the sale in the ledger and flicked back a couple of pages. 'You haven't had a bad couple of weeks. Perhaps you've turned a corner.'

'Flavia Montessore's famous. She's rumoured to have regressed Nancy Reagan. She practices all over the United States. She's one of the top regressive hypnotists in the world.'

'How can you tell something's a past life and not a dream?' The traffic crawled forward. A warden walked

36

past with her satchel. 'Didn't you say you were a Crusader in one life? How do you know it's not some story you read when you were a child and have forgotten about?'

'Because it was too vivid. There was detail I couldn't possibly have got from reading a school book.' Laura began to straighten out the pile of clothes Lady Antonia Hever-Walsh had tried on and discarded. 'I know people who've spoken languages they've never learned under regression.'

'And screwed people they've never met?'

Laura hooked the straps of a skirt onto a pine hanger. 'I've never got laid in regression.' She slipped the size cube over the hook.

'I wasn't in the past at all,' Charley said.

'You said you were in an old car.'

'Not that old. I'd say it was post-war.'

Laura was silent for a moment. 'The window's wrong. I think we should change it.' She hung the skirt on the rack. 'You don't know much about your past, do you? You don't know anything about your real parents, about your ancestors?'

'My real mother died in childbirth,' Charley said; the thought always disturbed her.

'How did your real father die?'

'He died of a broken heart.'

'*What?*'

'It's what my adoptive mother's always told me,' Charley said defensively.

'Do men die of broken hearts?'

'They can do.' Broken heart. Throughout her childhood that explanation had seemed fine, but the scorn on Laura's face made her doubt it and she wanted to change the subject. 'You know what I think the regression thing was? It was a horny dream, that's all. Tom and I have had sex once in the last two months,

37

after we got back from seeing the house for the first time. These things come out in dreams, don't they?'

'What's your acupunturist hoping to achieve by making you celibate?'

'He's trying to get the balance in my body sorted out so I'll be more receptive. Don't laugh, Laura. You're the one who suggested acupuncture.'

'They have weird ideas sometimes. Want some coffee?'

'I'm not meant to have any. Another of his things.'

'Tea?'

'That's a no-no too. Have you any juice?'

'Aqua Libra?'

'Sure. Have you ever heard of a couturier called Nancy Delvine?'

'Nancy Delvine? Rings a bell. Why?'

'She lived in Elmwood Mill.'

'Elmwood Mill? Oh, the house, right! Any news on it?'

'We should be exchanging on Wandsworth this week, and if we do we'll exchange on Elmwood.'

'Excited?'

'Yes.'

'You don't sound it.'

'I am. It's just — it's a big change.'

'I love the countryside. I'd move there if this place wasn't such a tie.' She went into the little room at the rear of the shop and emerged a few minutes later with a mug of coffee and a glass. She handed the glass to Charley and stirred her coffee.

'Flavia Montessore's worried about you,' she said at last. 'She rang me before she went to the airport this morning. I didn't really know whether I should tell you or not.'

'What do you mean, worried?'

'I don't know. She wasn't very precise. She said she

was picking up some bad vibes.'

'What about?' Charley said, suddenly alarmed.

'She thinks she ought to give you more regression when she gets back.'

'Sounds like a good con-trick.'

'She's not like that. She only regresses people she genuinely believes have had past lives.'

Charley smiled. 'The way I could only sell a dress to someone if I genuinely believed it suited them?' Like wallpaper over a crack, her smile masked her unease. She walked over to the window. Shapes passed outside blurred by the rain sliding down the glass. Blurred like her own past.

The unease had begun when she'd awoken on Flavia Montessore's bed. It had stayed with her through the night and throughout today. As if sediment deep inside her had been stirred and would not settle.

Chapter Seven

Charley changed the flowers in the vase in her adoptive mother's room, as she did every week. It was all she could do for her.

She shook the water from the stems of the carnations and dropped them into the waste bin. The sun streamed in through the window. It was hot in the room. Stifling. Charley paid the nursing home extra for the view over the park, a view her mother had never noticed and was unlikely to.

The white-haired woman lay silently in the bed that she refused to leave these days, the regular blink of her eyes every thirty seconds or so virtually the only sign that she was alive.

'Your favourite flowers, Mum. They look lovely, don't they?' She touched the cold cheek lightly with the back of her hand and held the roses up. There was the faint twitch of an eye muscle. Until a few months ago her mother might have uttered some incoherent words, but now Alzheimer's disease had claimed even those.

Small and functional, the room contained few of her mother's possessions. A couple of armchairs from her flat, a chest of drawers and the television that was never on. Two three-winged picture frames were on the bedside table, one showing Charley taking her first bath, Charley with a monkey on Brighton seafront, Charley in her wedding dress grinning exuberantly and Tom, subdued in a morning suit. There was a faint tang of urine, and stronger smells of disinfectant and fresh laundry.

Charley lifted the roses to her nose. Their scent brought a memory from childhood of her adoptive father pruning the bushes in the garden, and then another: they were in his greenhouse and he picked a ripe tomato and gave it to her. She bit into it and the seeds squirted on to his shirt and down her dress and they both laughed.

He had died when she was seven, of cancer. She remembered his eyes best, his large watery eyes that always looked so gently at her, eyes she could trust implicitly. They had looked out from his skeletal figure as he lay dying, and they looked out now from the other frame beside the bed.

Sadness welled for the frail woman who had worked so hard for many years to look after her, and was rewarded with Alzheimer's for her efforts.

All their money had gone in caring for her father, and after his death they had moved from the house to a flat. Her mother had etched a living making soft toys at home for a company in Walthamstow, and Charley had gone to sleep to the whirring of the sewing machine in the living room. In the holidays she had earned them extra money, sitting on the floor packing hair bows into plastic bags for the same company. There was a white van that came round twice a week to bring work and collect it. Their lives were run by the van's timetable.

After her mother had been admitted to the nursing home Charley had gone to clear out the flat in Streatham. She had listened to the rumble of traffic outside and the bawling of a baby on the floor above as she sifted through the drawers, pulling out tights that smelled faintly of perfume, a Du Maurier cigarette tin filled with hairpins, a brown envelope stuffed with early love letters between her adoptive parents. She had been

41

searching for something, she wasn't sure what; some small affirmation of her past, some hint about her real parents, maybe a newsclipping of a death notice, or an obituary. But there was nothing.

She arranged her roses, their crimson and white petals like satin in the brilliant sunlight.

'Pretty, aren't they, Mum?' she said, then sat and held her mother's limp, bony hand, gripping it tightly, trying to find some warmth in it, wishing she could again snuggle into her arms.

Life seemed sad, finite and pointless when you could fit a person's possessions into a suitcase or a trunk or a crate. When you could simply pack away a life. A life that had probably once, like her own, been filled with hope and endless possibilities (expressed in the love letters), and gone nowhere.

She blinked away her tears. 'We're moving, Mum,' she said brightly. 'We've bought a house in the country. Elmwood Mill. Doesn't that sound romantic? It's got an old mill in the garden, and a real millstream, or race as it's called, and a barn, and an Aga in the kitchen, and we're going to have our own hens. I'll bring you eggs. Would you like that?'

Her mother's hand was trembling; it seemed to have gone colder, clammy.

'What's the matter, Mum? You needn't worry — it's only forty-five minutes on the train. I'll still see you just as often.'

The trembling was getting worse.

'You can come and stay with us. We've got plenty of room. How about it?' She looked at the old woman, alarmed. She was shaking, her face had gone even whiter and perspiration was streaming down it. 'It's OK, Mum, don't worry! It's no distance away at all! It won't take me any longer to get here from Elmwood than from Wandsworth.'

The door opened and a nurse came in, a beefy girl with a bucktoothed smile. 'Would you like some tea, Mrs Witney?'

'My mother seems a bit feverish,' Charley said standing up.

The nurse hurried over, felt her pulse then pressed the back of her hand against her forehead. 'She's on some new medication. I'll ask the doctor to come in.'

Charley lowered her voice. 'I think I've upset her. I told her we are moving to the country and maybe she thinks it means I won't be visiting her so often.'

The nurse gave her a reassuring smile. 'No, I really don't think she's able to register anything these days. I'm sure it's just a chill or a reaction to the medication. We'll get the doctor as quickly as we can.'

The nurse hurried out and Charley waited anxiously. In the park a woman was pushing an infant in an old black pram; the traffic rumbled and hooted. Charley turned. Her mother's eyes were closed, the trembling was subsiding. She was sleeping.

Chapter Eight

They moved on Wednesday 12th September.

Charley felt an air of unreality about the drive down from London. All her life she had wanted to live in the countryside, yet she could not quite tune into the fact that today, unlike the half-dozen previous occasions when Mr Budley had loaned them the key, she was no longer coming as a visitor.

The Citroën's engine drilled loudly, the air of the baking late summer day barely cooling her face through the sunroof. She overtook a tractor then slowed as she crested the hill, glancing in the mirror, waiting for the removals' pantechnicon to catch up. Tom's Audi, in front, slowed too.

'ELMWOOD. TWINNED WITH BEIZE-LES-AIX.' A groundsman was rolling the cricket pitch. A kid came out of a newsagents drinking a Coke and behind him a Wall's Ice Cream sign rocked in the breeze. She was already familiar with the mini-roundabout next to the petrol station, the sight of the church ahead up a steep lane and the bustling high street to the right, with bric-a-brac on the pavement in front of an antiques restorer. She'd seen a promising-looking butcher and found a good farm shop.

A mile past the village Tom turned off the main road and drove in through the gateway at the end of a cluster of farm buildings. Several signs were fixed in a line down one gatepost: MANOR HOUSE. THADWELL'S BARN. ROSE COTTAGE. ELMWOOD ANGLING CLUB. The bottom one, rotted and barely legible, said ELMWOOD MILL.

The pantechnicon loomed in Charley's mirror and she turned into the cloud of dust kicked up by the Audi. The little Citroën banged through a pothole with a jar that threw her up against her seat belt and she cast a worried glance at the cardboard box on the passenger floorwell.

The track dipped steeply, then levelled out past a large modern red-brick house in a garden that was still maturing. A blonde-haired woman in wellington boots and a bikini strode out of a loose box towards a Range Rover. In the garden was a swimming pool surrounded by stark white busts on Grecian columns. Naff. Tom had christened it Yuppie Towers.

There was a stagnant pond, then a wooden barn neatly converted into a house with a dilapidated corrugated iron workshop adjoining it that jutted out to the edge of the track. An elderly saloon car was parked on the hard, and through the open doors of the workshop she could see a pair of feet underneath a jacked-up car. The trail of dust from the Audi stung her eyes. The pantechnicon laboured behind.

There was one more building, a stark grey stone cottage with a white picket fence and a neat garden. An old bicycle leant against the wall and an ancient Morris Minor sat in the driveway. The track narrowed and dipped again, the tall straggly hedgerow on each side pressing in on the Citroën like the brushes of a car wash. She felt a twinge of claustrophobia. The hedgerows had grown rampantly in the past three weeks. A bramble clawed at the window and the aerial twanged and juddered.

A cow stared down over the hedge beside an old

45

bathtub that was its trough, then the light dimmed as the sun was blotted out by the interlocked branches of the woods rising up on either side. Among them cables swung between the telegraph poles that followed the track. Charley bit a nail. She'd seen too many movies about isolated houses where the wires had been cut.

She pulled her finger from her mouth. Ben whined. Remote. It was beginning to feel too remote. 'OK, boy! Nearly there —' She hesitated. 'Nearly home!'

Home.

It had been strange last night, with the carpets rolled up and the curtains down. Sad. Sad that a house could be your home one day and belong to a total stranger the next. Gone. Too late to turn back. The bridges were burnt. Tonight 14 Apstead Road would have new people under its roof, new voices, new laughter, new tears. They'd probably change the colour of the front door and pave over the front garden, and she and Tom would drive by in a couple of years and scarcely be able to pick out the house.

A trail of cuttings of leafy branches and brambles littered the track around the next bend. The hedgerow was cut in a neat flat-top style. In the next dip a short man in a tweed cap lowered his power trimmer and pressed himself into the hedge to let her pass. She waved an acknowledgement and Ben barked at him.

Tom was heaving a cool box out of the boot of the Audi as she pulled up and the pantechnicon inched its way through the gate pillars. As she climbed out of the car she heard the steady roaring of the weir and the mill race tumbling over the wheel. Ben ran around excitedly.

She opened the lid of the cardboard box and peered in. The perforated cling-film was still in place over the neck of the bowl, and Horace was swimming around happily enough. She felt a surge of relief. She had been frightened the fish might die during the journey. She wanted no omens.

The engine of the pantechnicon clattered then faded, and there was complete silence except for the sound of rushing water. The breeze died and the still air was hot in the sun; sheep bleated in the distance and there were two faint blasts from, possibly, a shotgun. A bird trilled. Her feet scrunched on the gravel. Ben began barking again.

A metal door slammed. Voices. A bumble bee zoomed towards her and she flinched. Tom called out, 'Any of you guys like a beer?'

She walked to the bank of the stream. Only about three feet wide and maybe a couple of feet deep, it was easily jumpable. The water moved swiftly, clear and fresh, and the bed was lined with pebbles and rounded stones. The shadow of a bird strobed across.

'Cor, it's all right, innit?' someone said. A beer can opened with a hiss. She looked at the other side of the bank, at the patch of scrub grass.

Stables.

The feeling remained each time she had come, nagged her from a dark recess of her mind that was just out of reach, taunting her.

The executors of Nancy Delvine had taken every light bulb, even the one in the cellar.

'Bastards!' Tom said angrily, and drove off to the village in search of an electrical shop. The removals men took their lunch break and sat by the stream with their sandwiches.

Charley carried Horace into the house and placed him safely on the draining board. 'Like your new home?' She screwed up her face at the custard yellow. 'Think we'll change the colour scheme. Any preferences?'

She walked around the house, her plimsoles squeaking on the bare wood. Without furniture, the rooms seemed smaller, lower-ceilinged and dingier. Light rectangles marked the walls where pictures had hung or cupboards had stood. They reminded her of a film about Hiroshima her mother had taken her to see as a child; it had shown shadows on the walls that were the remains of people who had been vaporised when the bomb dropped.

She climbed the steep staircase to the attic. Shafts of light from the one small window picked their way through the dust which hung as thick as sleet, tickling her nose and throat. There was a faintly unpleasant smell of something decomposing. It was hot and uncannily quiet. The only sound was the sharp ping ... ping ... ping of a single drop of water every half second on to something metallic. The room was empty, the boxes of junk under dust sheets had been cleared out. She walked across to the window, the hardboard floor sagging then springing back into place with a dull *boomf*, shedding small eddies of dust into the air.

Most dust came from human skin.

Weird. Weird thoughts coming into her head. Maybe it was part of moving. Moving was the second biggest trauma of married life. Or third. Something like that, Tom had told her.

There was a fine view out of the window over the lake and beyond. Maybe a couple of miles across the woods and down the valley on the far side, were the roof and chimneys of a large house.

It was going to be OK. Tom was right. It was beautiful here. Beautiful and peaceful.

A shadow moved across the wall, as if someone had walked behind her. She turned, but the attic was empty. It must have been a bird passing the window, she thought. Except the shadow had come from a different direction. She felt a prickle of unease and stepped to the left, then right, to see if the shadow could have been from herself.

A rattle above her head, like dice, startled her, then she heard the chirp of a bird. A man shouted, his voice faint. Another replied.

Boomf.

She looked round as the floorboard made a sound as if someone had trodden on it. Probably just springing back into place after she had walked over it, she realised, but she left the attic quickly.

As she went on to the first floor landing a thud echoed around the house. It was followed by several more in rapid succession.

Door knocker.

She hurried down the stairs. A tall man was standing at the front door wearing grimy overalls over a frayed collar and a ragged tie. He was in his early forties, she guessed. He had an unkempt beard and there were streaks of grease on his high gaunt cheeks. His straw hair looked as if it had been battered by a hurricane. She liked his face instantly. It had both a salt-of-the-earth trustworthiness and a hint of fiery nobility that reminded her of Russian aristocracy. His eyes were sharp, penetrating, but warmth and a hint of mischief danced in them like winter sun.

'I'm Hugh Boxer, your neighbour from up the lane. Thought I'd pop by and say hallo.' His voice was easy and cultured.

She held out her hand. 'Charley Witney.'

He wiped his grimy paw of a hand down his trouser leg and shook hers with a solid, positive grip. 'Welcome to the lane.'

'Thank you.' She smiled. 'Which is your house?'

'The barn. Thadwell's Barn.'

'With the old cars?'

49

His eyebrows were like miniature bales of straw, and his face crinkled as he smiled back. 'Some people in the country breed animals — I prefer cars. They don't need milking.'

She laughed. 'I think the barn — house — looks great.'

'Not bad for a cowshed, is it? Actually, the other thing I came to see you about was the car. I wondered if it would be OK to leave it for a day or two.'

'The car? I'm not with you, I'm afraid,' Charley said.

'Nancy Delvine's old Triumph Roadster. I bought it from the estate. It's in the barn, behind the straw bales.'

'I didn't know there was a car there. Is it something very rare?'

The removals men were unloading a sofa from the lorry.

'No,' Hugh Boxer said, 'not exactly. There are a few around. Ever watched *Bergerac*?'

She nodded.

'One of those. I don't think its been on the road for thirty years.'

'Do you collect them?'

'Sort of.' His eyes studied her more seriously for a fleeting moment, as if they were probing for something. It made her feel uncomfortable.

The removals men were humping the sofa up the steps behind him.

'It'll take me the best part of a day's work to move the bales. I'll try and do it sometime in the next week.'

'There's no problem. We're not using the barn for anything.'

They stepped aside. An arm of the sofa thumped into a doorpost. 'Where's this to go, missus?'

She pointed through to the drawing room. 'Anywhere in there.'

'I'll get out of your way,' Hugh Boxer said. 'If I can

be any help any time, anything you want to know, just give a shout.'

'That's kind of you ... Oh, who's the chap trimming the hedge in the lane?'

'Gideon. We all employ him. He'll be along to see you, I should think.'

'We were told.'

'The George and Dragon's the best pub for food. Turn right out of the lane and it's a mile straight on.'

'Thanks. You must come and have a drink when we're straight.'

'Have you got a lot to do?' he glanced past her into the interior of the house.

'Plenty.'

'Nice house. I always thought it was rather attractive.' He hesitated, as if he were about to say something else, then he turned away. She followed him down the steps and Ben bounded up. 'Hallo, chap!' he said, pausing to pat him. 'You're not much of a guard dog, are you?' He gave Charley a cheery wave, and strode off.

The barn had double doors, both halves rotten and held shut with bricks. She tugged one open. Something small scuttled across the concrete floor and disappeared into the shadows. There was a smell of straw and oil. The ancient sit-on lawnmower they had bought from the executors was in front of her, its grass collector unhooked and propped against the wall beside it. It was about the only thing they had wanted that the executors had been willing to sell at a reasonable price.

Halfway across the barn was a wall of straw bales, and a narrow gap to the right which she had not been through before. As she approached she could see an old work bench under a high window. She squeezed through into what appeared to be a derelict workshop.

It was dark, with one grimy window filtering out most of the light.

In the middle of the floor was a tarpaulin, old and heavily coated in dust, the shape of a car silhouetted beneath it. Her heart rose into her throat; there was something about it that made her hesitate. A sleeping monster that should not be disturbed.

There was a scratching sound in the rafters and a trickle of dust fell. Rats? Bats? The wall of straw towered over her. More shapes came into focus out of the gloom. An old metal table. A garden roller with its handle broken.

Leave it, a voice in her head whispered.

I'm not going to be spooked by my own damned barn!

She lifted a corner of the tarpaulin. It revealed the dull pitted chrome of a bumper and a black wing with a sidelight mounted on top. She tried to peel it back further, but it was heavy. She walked sideways, tugged it over the bonnet and saw the upright radiator sandwiched between two massive headlamps. There was a chromium cap on top of the radiator and a small round badge on the front with a coloured globe of the world and 'Triumph Motors' in tiny letters.

She stepped backwards, tugging the tarpaulin across the bodywork and over the canvas roof. Finally it came free and slithered into a crumpled heap on the floor. Her nostrils filled with a smell of metal, musty canvas, stale oil.

The car looked familiar.

Because of *Bergerac* on television. She had seen the detective series, knew the model. She circled it. A bulbous sports convertible with running boards and a stubby nose. There was a narrow window at the back of the roof, and two glass panels in the boot where the dickey seats were. The black paint was thick with dust and the tyres were flat. A cobweb was spun across a corner of the windscreen, and a tax disc was visible behind it. She leaned closer and could just make out the faded lettering. *Nov 53.*

She pressed down the passenger door handle and pulled; the door opened with a cracking sound, as if some seal of time had been broken, and the smell of old leather and rotting canvas rose up from the interior, engulfing her.

The silence was complete. She had a feeling of being an intruder. She squeezed in through the passenger door and sat on the bench seat. It was hard and upright. Knurled black knobs protruded from the wooden dashboard on metal stalks. Two round, white dials were mounted in the middle, the speedometer on her side. The large spoked steering wheel was almost touching her right arm, the tiny column change gear lever sticking out from it like an antenna. She pulled the door shut with a dull clunk and felt very enclosed, the roof inches above her head, the screen just in front of her nose.

She pushed herself further down in the seat and sat for a moment, uncomfortably aware of the silence. She could see the outline of the bonnet through the dust on the windscreen and the radiator cap at the end. She touched a knob on the dashboard, then gripped it in her fingers and twisted it; it was stiff and for a moment would not move. She twisted it harder, and the windscreen wiper blade lifted an inch and broke several strands of the spider's web. She let go of the knob, startled, and the blade dropped down. The spider ran up the screen and she could almost sense petulance in the motion. She put her hand on her lap guiltily.

She was trembling. The seat creaked, crackled, a spring twanged.

A spring released itself somewhere inside her too.

She knew this car. Not just from seeing one in the

television series. She had been in one like this before, travelled in it. She was certain it was the same make of car in which she had made love in her regression.

She could remember everything: the roughness of his tweed jacket, the gruff roar of the engine, the wind thrashing her hair, the harsh ride on the uneven surface, the engine straining, the biff of the exhaust as he changed gear, the minty taste of the gum in her mouth.

She remembered the erotic sensation of the finger inside her. The car slithering to a halt. The smell of burned rubber, fresh leather, the rumble of the exhaust, the knocking rattle of the engine, the bonnet shaking, vibrating, the tweed of his sleeve brushing her face, his mouth over hers, their lips pressed together, kissing hungrily. The rubbery ball of chewing gum she had plucked out of her mouth and pushed under the glove locker.

There was a crack like a pistol shot.

She sat up with a jerk, dripping with perspiration, a deep feeling of fear in the pit of her stomach. She shook her head but her hair, matted with sweat, barely moved. Rivulets ran down the back of her neck, her armpits; she was shaking. The car seemed to be shrinking around her, the air getting scarcer as if something was sucking it out.

She scrabbled for the door handle and as she did she realised she was holding something in her hand, something small and hard.

She stumbled out, grazing her leg on the top of the sill, but barely noticing. She stood and stared at the small hard object in her hand, took it over to the window, but it was too dark to see.

She hurried through the barn and outside, squinting against the dazzle of the brilliant light. She looked down. About half an inch across, dark grey and pitted like a miniature shrivelled brain. A tiny strip of wood veneer was stuck to one side.

It was an old dried piece of chewed gum.

Her hand shook, making the gum dance like spittle on a griddle. Then it fell. She looked down, tried to spot it, knelt, sifted through the gravel, rummaged her hands backwards and forwards. Over by the house she heard a shout, the sound of metal banging, the scrunch of feet; a laugh. She carried on rummaging, making a widening arc, but it had gone, swallowed by the pebbles the way the sea swallows a footprint in the sand.

A voice called, 'Mrs Witney? Hallo? Need to know where you want these packing cases!'

'Coming!' she shouted.

Hundreds of people chew gum in cars. Thousands. Millions. There was nothing special about finding gum in a car.

Nothing special at all.

Chapter Nine

Tom and Charley dined outside on the sheltered patio at the rear of the house, on a Chinese takeaway and a bottle of champagne, and watched the red ball of sun sink down behind the paddock, leaving its heat behind it in the dusk.

The days were getting noticeably shorter; in a few weeks the clocks would be going back, but now, in the balmy evening, winter seemed a long way away.

The grazing chestnut mare turned into a silhouette and slowly faded to black. Stars appeared in the metallic sky, bats flitted and the lights of planes coming into Gatwick winked.

They picked at the last grains of rice and strands of noodles and wrote a list of things to be done.

Later, in bed, they made love. But in a strange way it was more like a rite than a spontaneous act of passion. It reminded her of when they had made love on her wedding night after two years of living together. Both of them had been tired, flaked out, but they knew it ought to be done. Consummation.

They had consummated the move tonight for their own secret needs, hers to be held and to hold; to hold something real, to feel Tom, to feel life after the weirdness of the discovery, first of the car in the barn then the chewing gum. Reality.

She wondered what his need was. Wondered what

went through his mind when he made love to her so mechanically, so distantly. Who did he think about? Who did he fantasise she was?

The noises came after, through the open window. The noises of the night. Real darkness out there.

She could taste the minty gum in her mouth.

Ben padded restlessly around the room, growling at squeals, at shrieks, at the mournful wail of vixens.

It was two o'clock. She slipped out of bed and walked across the sloping wooden floor to the curtainless window. The new moon powered a faint tinfoil shine from the lake. Somewhere in the dark a small creature emitted a single shriek of terror, several more in fast succession, then one final shriek, louder and longer than the rest; there was a rustle of undergrowth, then silence. Mother Nature, Gaia, the Earth Goddess was there dealing the cards, keeping the chain going. Life and death. Replenishment. Recycling the living and the dead equally methodically.

Serial murderers were out there too. In the inky silence.

Tom had taken two weeks' holiday for the move, but he had to go to London in the morning. A wife had poured paint stripper over her husband's new car and had blinded his racing pigeons. Tom brought home stories of cruelty every day. Sometimes Charley thought there were few acts committed in the world crueller than those under the sanctity of marriage.

The water slid relentlessly over the slimy brickwork of the weir, crashing down into the dark spume of the sluice. It seemed to echo through the stillness, unreal; it all seemed unreal. She was afraid. She wanted to go home.

She had to keep reminding herself that she was home.

* * *

57

'Blimey, what you running here? A space station?' The Electricity Board man's eyes bulged from a thyroid complaint and there was sweat on his protruding forehead from the heat outside. He tapped his teeth with his biro.

'What do you mean?' Charley asked.

Footsteps from the hall above echoed around the cellar. Somewhere a drill whined. She looked at the man irritably. She was tired.

He held the printed pad so she could see the markings he had made. 'The quarterly average for the past year here has been five hundred units. This quarter it's gone up to seven *thousand*.'

'That's impossible. It's been empty for a year and we only moved in yesterday.' She watched the metal disc revolving. 'Is the meter faulty?'

'No, I've tested it. It's working fine. See how slowly it's going? You're not using much juice at the moment.'

'If there's a short circuit, could that —?'

'Must be. You've got a leak somewhere. You'd better get an electrician to sort it out. It's going to cost you a fortune otherwise.'

'We're having the house rewired. They're meant to be starting today.'

She was not sure he had heard her. He was checking the meter once more with a worried frown.

The Aga was smoking from every orifice, and Charley's eyes were smarting. A new telephone was on the pine dresser next to the answering machine, its neat green 'Telecom Approved' roundel hanging from a thread. The phone was red to match the new Aga — when they could afford it. For the time being, her hope of replacing the existing solid-fuel one was item 43 (or was it 53?) on the list of priorities she and Tom had written out last night. 'Central Heating' was at the top and 'Snooker

Room In Barn' was at the bottom (item 147). During the next twelve months, if they found nothing disastrously wrong with the house, they could afford up to item 21, 'Window Frames'. If Charley went back to full-time work, eventually, it would help. (Item 22, 'Double Glazing'.) For the time being the sacrifices were worth it. It was a good investment. On that point, Mr Budley, the estate agent, was right.

The telephone engineer poked his head round the kitchen door. 'Same place as the old one in the lounge?'

'Yes, with a long lead,' she said, scratching what felt like a mosquito bite on her shoulder.

'The cordless one in the bedroom?' He had an attachment clipped to his waist with a large dial on it.

She nodded and coughed.

The engineer looked at the Aga. 'Needs plenty of air. Leave the door open until the flames have caught. Me mum had one.'

'Open? Right, thank you, I'll try that. I'm making some tea, or would you prefer coffee?'

'Tea, white no sugar, ta.'

She opened the oven door as he suggested and backed away from the plume of smoke that billowed out. She picked up the kettle and turned the tap. It sicked a blob of rusty brown water into the stained sink, some of which splashed on to her T-shirt, hissed, made a brief sucking noise and was silent.

Bugger. The plumber, she realised, had just asked her where the stopcock was. She flapped away smoke. With that and the sun streaming in, it was baking hot. They needed blinds in here (item 148, she added, mentally).

There was an opened crate on the floor labelled in her handwriting 'kitchen'. Crumpled newspaper lay around it and the pile of crockery on the table was growing. A flame crackled in the Aga. She peered into the goldfish bowl. 'Hi, Horace, what's doing?' she said, feeling flat.

Ben padded in and gazed at her forlornly.

'Want a walk, boy?' She stroked his soft cream coat and he licked her hand. 'You've had a good morning's barking, haven't you? The builders, the electrician, the telephone man and the plumber.'

She filled the kettle from the mill race, which looked clear enough, and boiled the water twice.

The smoke from the Aga was dying down and the flames seemed to be gaining ground. While the tea was steeping she admired the flowers Laura had sent, the three cards from other friends and a telemessage from Michael Ohm, one of Tom's partners, which had arrived this morning.

There was no greeting from Tom's widower father, a London taxi driver who had desperately wanted his only son to be a success, to have a profession, not to be like him. When Tom had succeeded his father resented it in the way he resented everything he did not understand. He had lived in Hackney all his life, in a house two streets from where he was born. When Tom told him they were moving to the country, he had said they must be mad.

Ben bounded on ahead up the drive. The builders were unloading materials from a flatbed truck, and an aluminium ladder rested against the side of the house. A squirrel loped across the gravel into the shade between the house and the barn. Charley could hear cattle lowing, the drone of a tractor, the endless roar of the water and a fierce hammering from upstairs.

At the top of the drive she felt the cooling spray. The weir foamed water, but the lake was flat as a drumskin. Mallards were up-ended near the shore and somewhere close by a woodpecker drilled a tree.

She crossed the iron footbridge, looking down uncomfortably into the circular brick sluice pond. It reminded her of a mineshaft. On the other side of the bridge there were brambles and the remains of a fence which needed repairing. It was dangerous and someone could trip and tumble in. She walked quickly and turned to wait until Ben was safely past.

The path was dry and hard and curved upwards, left, climbing through the woods above the lake. The undergrowth grew denser and the trees were slender, mostly hornbeam, birch and elms. A large number were uprooted, probably from the winter storms or maybe the hurricane of eighty-seven. They lay where they had fallen, leaning against other trees or entombed in the creepers and brambles and nettles of the wild undergrowth.

Traces of a nightmare she had had during the night remained in her mind: a horse rearing up, opening its snarling mouth to reveal fangs chewing a piece of gum the size of a tennis ball, breathing hot minty breath at her then laughing a whinnying laugh. She had woken and tasted mint in her own mouth.

Chewing gum. In the car. It —

Her train of thought snapped as Ben stopped in front of her and she nearly tripped over him. He began barking, a more menacing bark than normal, and she felt a flash of unease. The bark deepened into a snarl and something moved ahead on the path.

A man hurrying, stumbling, very agitated, holding a fishing rod with a bag slung over his shoulder. He was wearing an old tweed suit with leather patches on the sleeves and gum boots. There was a strip of sticking plaster above his right eye, and a solitary trickle of sweat ran down his face like a tear. He was about sixty, tall and quite distinguished, but his state of anxiety was making him seem older. Ben's snarl grew louder. She grabbed his collar.

61

'I wonder if you'd mind terribly nipping down and telling Viola I'll be a bit late,' the man said without any introduction. 'I've lost my damned watch somewhere and I must go back and look for it.'

'Viola?' Charley said blankly.

The man blinked furiously. 'My wife!' he said. 'Mrs Letters.'

She wondered if he was a bit gaga.

'I must find my watch before someone pinches it. It has sentimental value, you know.'

'I'm sorry,' Charley said. 'We've only just moved in.' Ben jerked her forwards.

'Rose Cottage, up the lane! I'd be very grateful. Just tell her I'll be a bit late.' He raised a finger in acknowledgement, then turned and hurried back up the path.

Charley continued holding Ben. He was still snarling and his hackles were up, his eyes flickering with colour.

'What is it, boy? What's the matter?' She pulled him and he followed reluctantly. She waited until the man was well out of sight before she dared release him.

Rose Cottage. She had seen the name on the board at the entrance to the lane. It must be the stone cottage. Ben ran on ahead sniffing everything happily, his growls forgotten.

She came out of the shade and the sunlight struck her face, dazzling her. Ben cocked his leg on a bush. The potholed ground was dry and dusty and the hedges buzzed with insects. A swarm of midges hovered around her head and there was a strong smell of cows, an acrid smell of bindweed and the sweeter smell of mown grass.

The roof of the cottage came into view through the trees and a dog was yapping. A car door slammed, then a woman's voice boomed like a foghorn.

'Peregrine! Quiet —!'

Charley rounded the corner. The ancient Morris Minor estate was parked in the driveway of the cottage behind the picket fence and beside it was an old woman who had a cardboard groceries box under one arm and was holding the leash of a tiny Yorkshire terrier with the other.

Ben leapt forward playfully but the terrier replied with another volley of yaps. Charley grabbed Ben's collar and made him sit.

'Are you Mrs Letters?' she shouted above the terrier's yapping.

'Yes,' the woman shouted back. She was a no-nonsense country type in stout brown shoes, tweed skirt and rib-stitched pullover. Short and plump, she had a ruddy, booze-veined blancmange of a face and straight, grey hair which was parted and brushed in a distinctly masculine style.

'We've moved into the Mill. I'm Charley Witney.'

'Ah, knew you were coming sometime this week.' She glared at the dog and bellowed in a voice that could have stopped a battleship, 'Peregrine!' The dog was silent and she looked back at Charley. 'Viola Letters. Can't shake your hand, I'm afraid.'

'I have a message from your husband.'

The woman's expression became distinctly hostile and Charley felt daunted. She pointed towards the valley. 'I just met him and he asked me to tell you that he's lost his watch and he's going to be a bit late.'

'My husband?'

'In a tweed suit, with fishing tackle? Have I come to the right house?'

'Said he'd lost his watch?'

'Yes — I —' Charley hesitated. The woman was more than hostile; she was ferocious. 'He seemed rather confused. I think he may have hurt himself. He had a strip of elastoplast on his head.'

The terrier launched into another spate of yapping and the woman turned abruptly and walked into the house, dragging the dog so its feet skidded over the paving slabs. She closed the front door behind her with a slam.

Chapter Ten

The gardener turned up in the afternoon, small and chirpy with a hare lip, and tugged the peak of his cap respectfully.

'I'm Gideon,' he said with an adenoidal twang, 'like in the Bible.'

Charley smiled at him. 'You've done a good job with the hedge.'

'I wanted it to be nice for when you arrived,' he said, obviously pleased with the compliment. 'The old lady, she never wanted nothing done.'

'Why not?'

'I dunno; never saw her, 'cept rarely. She left me the money for cuttin' the hedge and the grass out the back door.'

'Didn't she ever go out?'

'Nope. Had everything delivered.'

'Why did she do that?'

'She were what you call a recluse. Mind, I'm not sorry. I know I'm not Robert Redford, but she really didn't look that great.' He glanced at the house. 'Is there's any jobs in the garden you want doing?'

There were plenty.

They walked around together, and agreed on a plot between the hen run and the paddock fence for the kitchen garden. The soil was moist and sandy, he told her, pretty well everything would grow. They could buy spring cabbage and broccoli plants, and he had some leeks to spare. They would be eating their own vegetables before the winter was over, he said.

She bluffed her way through a discussion about hens, helped by a book she had read called *Poultry Keeping Today* which she'd borrowed from Wandsworth library. Gideon knew where to buy good layers, but the run needed fixing first to make it fox-proof and he'd get on with it right away. He charged three pounds an hour and she paid him for the work he had done on the hedge. Eight hours, which sounded about right.

She tried to get him to tell her more about Nancy Delvine, but he did not seem to want to talk about her. He'd only seen the woman twice in ten years, and that was enough. Why, he would not say.

The first call Charley received, after the engineer had tested the equipment and gone, was from Laura.

The engineer had been right about the Aga. It had heated up and the smoke had gone. The musty smells of the kitchen faded a bit and the dominant one now was from the cartons of the Chinese takeaway in the rubbish sack. She had spent the last three hours opening crates, unpacking and moving furniture around. It would have to be moved again for the decorators and the carpets, but at least it was beginning to look vaguely like home.

'The flowers are wonderful,' Charley said, caressing the petals of a pink orchid.

'Got your green wellies out yet?'

'It's too hot.'

'You're lucky you're not in London. It's sweltering. No one's buying any winter clothes. How did the move go?'

'Fine. Great. You must come to Tom's birthday a fortnight on Saturday. We're going to have a barbecue, if it's warm enough.'

'Any dishy bachelors around?'

'Actually there's a rather nice chap down the lane.'

'Really?'

'I have a feeling he's single. If he is, I'll invite him.'

'Tom's going to be thirty-eight, isn't he?'

'And not very happy about it. Someone told him middle age starts at forty.'

'He doesn't look middle-aged.'

Hammering echoed around the house. 'Laura,' Charley began. 'Do you know when Flavia Montessore is going to be back in England?'

'In the autumn sometime.' Laura sounded surprised. 'Why?'

Charley toyed with the green tag hanging from the phone. 'I — I just wondered, that's all.' There was a clatter outside the window and the rungs of an aluminium ladder appeared. 'You know I said I was in a car?'

'Bonking. Yes.'

'I was chewing a bit of gum. I took it out of my mouth and stuck it under the dash —'

A pair of legs climbed past the window.

'I found . . .' Her voice trailed off, and she left foolish.

'Found what? Charley, what did you find?'

The ladder was shaking. 'The autumn. Do you mean October? Next month?'

'She usually calls me. I'll let you know.'

Rude, Charley thought, suddenly. Mrs Letters. Rose Cottage. Very rude to slam a door.

'If you want to see someone sooner I know a very good man called Ernest Gibbon. He does private sessions.'

She'd gone out of her way to give Mrs Letters the message, and she'd turned her back and slammed the door. Rude. Except it hadn't felt rude at the time, just odd. The woman had seemed upset. Upset by something more than a husband being late.

'I can give you his number,' Laura said. 'He's in south London.'

'Is he as good?'

'He's brilliant. Give him a try.'

'I might,' she said distractedly, and wrote the number down on the back of an envelope.

Tom arrived home in the evening and changed into a T-shirt and jeans. He thought three pounds an hour was fine for the gardener, but he would look after the lawn himself. Part of the fun of moving to the country was to work in the garden, he said.

He went in the barn and managed to get the huge old mower started, then sat on the seat and drove it with a terrible racket across the gravel and up the bank. It farted oily black smoke and the engine kept cutting then racing, jerking him about like a circus clown. Finally there was a loud bang and the engine stopped and would not start again. Tom climbed off doubled up with laughter and she felt, almost for the first time, that everything was going to work out.

'Let's find a pub,' Tom said. 'I fancy a beer and a steak.'

'The chap up the lane said the George and Dragon was the best for food.' She brushed hairs back from his forehead, and the evening sun danced deep in his slate blue eyes. He didn't look thirty-eight and she didn't feel thirty-six; she felt twenty-six, or maybe sixteen, when she'd first seen those eyes, gazed up at them from the sticky carpet where she'd fallen sloshed in the pub and seen them grinning down at her. 'Hallo, Joe Cool,' she'd said to the stranger, and then passed out on his shiny Chelsea boots.

The George and Dragon was an old coaching inn and the glass panel in the door displayed its credentials: 'Relais Routiers', 'Egon Ronay', 'Good Pub Guide,'

'Good Beer Guide'. The thin licensing strip across the lintel proclaimed the proprietor to be Victor L. Lubbin.

A roar of laughter froze as they went in. A bunch of labourers around a table glanced up then one said something and the laughter resumed. A solitary fruit machine stood against a wall. It winked its lights, flashed its signs, changed its colours and repeated a scale of musical notes every few seconds, its sole audience an old English sheepdog which lay on the floor eyeing it sleepily like a bored impresario at an audition.

The room had a low ceiling, yellowed from age and smoke, and massive timber beams. Ancient farm implements had been hung on the walls along with a dartboard. There were old-fashioned beer pumps and an unlit inglenook. Beside the dartboard were notices advertising a jumble sale, a steam traction rally, Morris Dancing — 'Morfydd's Maidens'.

A knot of three people stood at the far end of the bar. One Charley recognised, the tall frame of Hugh Boxer, their neighbour, raising a stubby pipe as a greeting. 'Hi!' he said.

He was wearing a crumpled checked shirt, a knitted tie and had an amiable smile on his bearded face, though there was the strong, authoritative presence she had felt before. The grease smears had gone and his hair had been tidied a bit.

Charley introduced Tom, and Hugh Boxer ordered them drinks and introduced them to the couple he was with. They were called Julian and Zoe Garfield-Hampsen, and lived in the red-brick house with the Grecian columns around the pool at the end of the lane. Yuppie Towers. Julian Garfield-Hampsen was tall, with a booming voice and a ruddy drinker's face. He wore a striped Jermyn Street shirt with corded cufflinks and smoothed his hand through his fair hair each time he spoke. He was probably about the same age as Tom, but he looked ten years older.

'How super to have another young couple in the lane!' Zoe said. She had a small, reedy voice and spoke slowly and precisely, which made her sound like a schoolgirl in an elocution lesson. She was the woman Charley had seen walking out of the stables in her bikini and wellington boots. 'Julian and I have always simply *adored* Elmwood Mill,' she added.

'We love it,' Charley said.

'It's super! The only thing that put us off buying it is it sits so low down and doesn't get much sun in the winter.'

'Spritzer.' Hugh Boxer handed Charley her glass. 'And a pint of Vic's best sludge.'

'Cheers.' Tom held his dark bitter up to the light, studied it for a moment, drank some and nodded approvingly at the landlord.

The landlord, a stocky, dour man with thinning black hair, made no response for a moment. He turned to take a tumbler from the small aluminium sink, then said, in a dry Midlands accent, 'Cricketing man, are you?'

'I used to play a bit,' Tom said surprised.

The landlord wiped the tumbler with a cloth. 'Sunday week,' he said. 'Ten o'clock, Elmwood Green. We've a charity match against Rodmell and we're two short.'

'I'm a bit rusty. I haven't played for a few years.'

'Bat or bowl?'

'I used to be a bit of a batsman, I suppose.'

'Put you down for opening bat?'

'Well I wouldn't — er —' But the landlord had already started to write his name on a list. 'Witney? With an *H* or without?'

'Without,' Tom said. 'I haven't got any pads or kit.'

70

'You get roped into everything down here,' Hugh said. 'They'll have you on every committee going within a month.'

'Viola Letters is doing the tea,' the landlord continued. 'I expect she'll be in touch with you, Mrs Witney.'

'Oh, right,' Charley said, taken aback but smiling.

'Do you do food at night?' Tom dug his fingers hungrily into a large bowl of peanuts on the bar.

'Restaurant's through there.' The landlord pointed. 'Last orders for food at nine forty-five.'

Tom shovelled more peanuts into his mouth. They had half an hour.

'Julian played last year, but he's hurt his shoulder,' Zoe said. 'How many children do you have?' she asked Charley.

'None, so far.' Charley's face always reddened at the question. 'We — we hope to start a family here.'

'Super!' The expression on Zoe's face said, *At your age?*

The Garfield-Hampsens had three children. They were called Orlando, Gervais and Camilla. Julian (Joo-Joo) was in computer software. Zoe evented-and-thinged on horses. Everything was *super*.

Charley caught Hugh Boxer's eye. 'Is that your lovely Jaguar outside? Tom's been ogling it since we first saw the house.'

'Tell him to pop in any time if he sees the workshop door open. I'm working on a beautiful old Bristol.' He tapped his pipe against the rim of an earthenware ashtray. There was something cosy about the sound. He dabbed his forehead with the back of his massive hand. 'It's close tonight.'

She felt the sticky heat too. 'It's clouding. The forecast is thunder.'

He struck a match and took several long sucks on the

71

pipe, then shook the match out. There was still grease under his nails.

'Is that your business, old cars?' Charley said.

He drew on his pipe and fired the smoke out through his nostrils. It rose up in a thick cloud around him. 'No. I'm a ley hunter,' he said, and took a sip of his whisky, cradling his glass in his hand.

'Ley hunter?' She caught the twinkle in the eyes; morning sunlight on an icy pond. Beneath the ice there seemed to be immense depth.

'Hugh's frightfully famous. He's our local celebrity,' said Zoe.

He waved his pipe dismissively. 'It's not true. Don't believe it.'

'It is!' She turned to Charley. 'He's been on television, radio, and in all the papers. He had a whole half page in the *Independent* with his photograph. They called him Britain's leading authority on ley lines.'

Hugh puffed on his pipe as if he were not part of the conversation.

'And he's had two books published.'

'What are their titles?'

The smoke smelled rich and sweet. Charley liked the smell of pipes.

'I shouldn't think you've heard of them,' Hugh said. '*The Secret Landscape*, and *Dowsing — the Straight Facts*.'

'He's absolutely brilliant. The books are fascinating.'

Tom and Julian Garfield-Hampsen were talking about property. 'We're trying to get permission to extend,' Julian said, and Zoe's attention switched to them.

'Were they bestsellers, these books?' Charley asked.

He sucked on the pipe again. 'No.' he grinned and raised his straw-bale brows. 'It's a very specialised subject. I don't sell many, just a few copies.'

'Is that how you make your living?'

'I earn my crust at the university. I lecture.'

'Which one?'

'Sussex.'

'I thought you didn't look like a garage mechanic. Do you lecture on ley lines?'

'No. Psychology. Ley lines are my hobby — for my sanity.'

'And old motor cars?'

'Anything old. Old cars. Old buildings. Old landscapes.' He shrugged, and looked closer at her, more penetratingly. His voice lowered and his face suddenly seemed more gaunt. 'Old spirits.' He tamped his pipe with his stubby thumb. He bit his nails too, she noticed with surprise. His eyes lifted from the pipe back to her. They stared intently. It was as though they were searching for something, as if they were trying to rub away an outer layer and peer through.

'What do you mean, old spirits?'

'Past lives. I can always tell someone else who's had past lives.'

'How?'

'Just by looking at them.' She felt something cold trickle through her, pricking at her like an electrical current.

'You mean reincarnation?'

He nodded.

'You believe in that?'

'Don't you?'

'No, I don't believe in it. I don't think it's possible.'

'I don't believe in divorce,' he said quietly. 'But my wife still left me.'

There was a silence between them.

'I'm sorry,' she said at last.

He smiled, but she saw the pain beneath the mask.

'Do you believe in regression?' she asked, sipping her spritzer.

73

'Regression hypnosis?'

'Yes.'

He took a match out of the box. 'There are a lot of meddlers, amateurs. Anyone can announce he's a hypnotist and set himself up in business.'

'The Triumph in our barn,' she said avoiding his eyes. 'How old is it?'

'The original log's missing. I'll have to check the chassis and engine numbers. They started making them in forty-eight.' He struck another match. 'Have you met Viola Letters yet, the grand old dame of the lane?'

There was a single flash of lightning. Conversation in the pub flickered for a brief instant then resumed.

'In Rose Cottage?'

He sucked the flame into the bowl of his pipe. 'That's her. Keeps a hawk-eye on what goes on.'

There were three more flashes.

'Do she and her husband not get on too well?'

He looked puzzled, then faintly amused. 'I didn't know they communicated.'

Charley felt her face reddening. 'What do you mean?'

Thunder crashed outside.

Hugh swirled his whisky around in his glass, then drank some. 'She's a widow,' he said. 'Her husband's been dead for nearly forty years.'

Chapter Eleven

The sky was clear again the next morning and the air felt fresh after the storm. Water dripped from the trees, an intermittent plat ... plat ... plat, and wisps of mist hung over the lake. It was just after eleven.

As Charley walked alone up the lane she heard a rumble ahead of her, and a tractor came around the corner towing an empty trailer. She stepped into the brambles to let it pass, and smiled up at the driver, an elderly wizened man. He stared fixedly ahead and drove past without acknowledging her. She watched him rattle on down the dip, surprised.

The Morris Minor was in the driveway and the Yorkshire terrier started yapping before Charley had pushed the gate open. She went hesitantly up the path. A ship's bell was fixed to the wall beside the front door. She searched for a knocker but could not see one, so she jangled the bell. The yapping intensified and a voice the other side of the door quietened it.

The door opened and Viola Letters stood there, half kneeling, holding the terrier by its collar, in the same stout shoes as yesterday, a tweed skirt too thick for the heat and an equally thick blouse. She looked up at Charley warily.

'I've come to apologise,' Charley said. The old woman's eyes were peering over the top of her cheeks like a crab staring out of wet sand, and the dog's eyes were black marbles sparkling with rage. 'I'm desperately sorry. I wasn't playing a trick. I didn't know your husband was dead.'

She pulled the dog back. 'Would you like to come in?' Her voice sounded like a deeper bark.

Charley stepped into the hall and the dog glared at her in an uneasy silence.

'Close the door. He'll relax then.'

Charley did so and the dog yapped angrily.

'Kitchen!' Mrs Letters dragged it into a room at the back, gave it a gentle slap on the bottom and shut the door on it.

'Sorry about that. He's normally fine with visitors. Getting a bit cantankerous in his old age,' her mouth opened and shut as she spoke like a secret door in the folds of flesh.

'He can probably smell our dog.'

The woman looked at her, suspicion returning to her face. 'You're Mrs Witney, you said.'

'Yes.' Charley noticed a strong waft of alcohol. 'I'm afraid I made a terrible mistake yesterday. I don't know how it happened, I must have misheard completely what the man said.'

Viola Letters was silent for a moment. 'Can I offer you a drink?' she said then.

There was a smell of linseed oil and polish in the house. It had a cared-for feeling, the walls painted in warm colours with contrasting white woodwork. There were fine antiques and almost every inch of wall was covered in paintings, mostly seascapes and portraits, and a number of amateurish landscapes in cheap frames.

Charley followed Mrs Letters through into the drawing room. A copy of the *Daily Telegraph* with the crossword filled in lay on a small Pembroke table. Viola Letters pointed her to a small Chesterfield. 'Gin and tonic?' she barked. 'Whisky and dry? Sherry?' She said everything in a raised voice, as if she was trying to make herself heard above an imaginary din.

There were Persian rugs on the floor and the tables were covered with lace tablecloths weighted down with silver snuff boxes, ivory animals and photograph frames. On the mantelpiece was a sepia photograph of a bearded Edwardian in naval uniform, his chest adorned with decorations, and on the floor, by the brass coal scuttle, was a small military drum.

'Actually, I'd love a soft drink, some mineral water or tap, please.' She had a strange metallic taste in her mouth, which she had noticed before.

'Water?' Viola Letters said the word as if it was a disease. 'Nonsense! Sun's almost over the yardarm. Pinkers? Scotch? What's your poison?'

'Perhaps just a small sherry?' Charley said, not wanting to offend her. She sat down.

'Expect we could rustle one up from ship's stores,' Viola Letters said, going over to a mahogany cabinet.

Something brushed against Charley's leg and miaowed. She lowered her hand to stroke it. She tickled between its ears and the back of its neck, then looked down. An eyeless socket in the side of the cat's face was pointing at her.

'We're a tight ship here, our little community. If I can be of any help just give me a call or pop over any time. There aren't many of us down here. I try to keep watch. We don't get too many strangers, but it's going to be a bit worse from now on: some fool journalist has written this up in a book of country walks. It's a public footpath down over the lake. Did you know?'

'It doesn't look as if it's used much.'

'It will be. We'll have hordes of bloody ramblers all over the place, I expect.'

There was something about the old woman that

seemed vaguely familiar, but Charley was not sure what. 'How long have you lived here?' she asked.

'Since nineteen fifty, but I'm not classed as a local. They're odd, the farming community. They don't trust anyone who moves here. You have to be born here. There are two farmers who won't even nod good morning to me, and I've seen them most days for the past forty years.'

'I saw one on my way today.'

'Most peculiar.' She lowered her voice. 'Interbreeding — a lot of that sort of thing round here.' She raised her voice again. 'You're Londoners?'

'Yes.'

'Well, you'll find country life a bit different. If there's anything you need to know — doctor, vet, what have you — just shout.'

'Thanks. I wondered if it's possible to get newspapers and milk delivered.'

'I'll give you the number of the dairy. There's a jolly good newsagent in Elmwood who delivers — darkies, of course, but one can't help that.'

The cat rubbed its eyeless socket against Charley's leg. She tried not to look at it.

'Nelson! Buzz off!' Viola Letters marched across the room clutching a massive schooner filled to the brim. 'There you go.' She went back to the cabinet, poured herself a tumbler of neat gin, splashed in some angostura and sat down opposite Charley. 'Cheers.'

'Cheers.' Charley sipped her sherry.

'Your husband's not a naval man, I suppose?'

'He's a lawyer. He specialises in divorce.'

There was a silence. In the kitchen the terrier began yapping.

Mrs Letters looked at her carefully. 'Sorry if I seemed rude yesterday, but you did give me the deuce of a shock.'

78

Charley sipped some sherry for courage. 'I must have misheard — got the wrong address — name —' Her voice tailed off.

The crab eyes slid up above the cheeks. 'No. I think you did see him, the old love.' She leaned forward, her face lighting up. 'Are you very psychic, dear?'

'No, I don't think so.'

Viola Letters fetched a photograph in a silver frame from another room and showed it to Charley. It was black and white, a tall, serious man, standing to attention in the uniform of a naval officer. The face was clear, and the resemblance to the man she had seen yesterday was strong. She had to look away, suddenly, as his stare began to make her feel uneasy. Sherry slopped over the rim of her glass on to her hand.

'It was the sticking plaster that convinced me,' Viola Letters said, reseating herself. 'Before he went up there he caught his forehead on a shelf, just above his right eye.'

Charley shivered. That was where the plaster had been.

'We were meant to be going to a luncheon and he'd gone fishing, promising to be back early. It seems he lost his watch. It had belonged to his father who'd been presented with it after the battle of Jutland and was of great sentimental value. He'd been a commander too.' She drank a mouthful of gin and swallowed as if it were fuel. 'He'd asked someone to pop down and tell me, just like you did, that he'd be late.' She blinked twice and smiled wanly. 'He was a fit man, never had any problems with his ticker before. I found him on the bank a couple of hours later. The doctor said he must have been dead for at least an hour by then.'

Charley felt icy mist swirling inside her. 'Has — anyone — ever — seen him — before?'

'No. About a year afterwards I went to see one of

79

these spiritualist people — a medium — but nothing came through. I hoped to find out if there was anything he had wanted to say.' She gulped some more gin. 'That thunderstorm yesterday,' she went on. 'Perhaps it was something to do with the atmospherics . . . Still, it's jolly good to have some young blood in the lane,' she said, trying to brighten her face, to swallow her tears. 'We have a charity cricket match Sunday week, for the NSPCC. Don't suppose you could bake a couple of cakes?'

'Yes, of course.' She wanted to keep the conversation about Mrs Letter's husband going, but could not think what to say.

'Have you met everyone else in the lane?'

'I think so.'

'Delightful couple at the top in that rather vulgar house, Julian and Zoe Garfield-Hamsden. And Hugh Boxer, my neighbour in the barn. He's a dear. A brilliant man but a bit loopy.' She tapped her head. 'All these university professors are. Spends half his time wandering round with a couple of coat hangers looking for ley lines or some rubbish. Cheers!' She drained her glass.

'You have some nice paintings,' Charley said to fill the silence.

'My husband did several of them. He loved this part of the world and painted a lot locally.'

'I thought they looked familiar.'

'There's one that would interest you upstairs. I'll get it in a minute. It's a very nice one of Elmwood Mill.' She studied her glass, the crab eyes blinking slowly.

'Did you know Nancy Delvine?' Charley asked.

'No. Not at all.'

'What did she die of?'

'A stroke.'

'Had she been in hospital for a long time?'

'Hospital, dear?' The old woman looked at her. 'No, it was in the house. I found her. In the kitchen.'

Charley's mind raced aimlessly. She remembered the elusiveness on the estate agent's face. *Here? In the house?* Mr Budley's voice. *Oh no, I don't believe so.*

'Was she married?'

Viola Letters stood, rather hastily Charley thought. 'Can I get you a top up?'

'No, thank you. I've still got —'

The woman took the glass out of her hand. 'You haven't got a drop in that, not a drop.' She refilled Charley's glass and brought it back to her, brimming.

Charley gazed at it in horror. 'It's really a bit —' But the old woman had already set it down beside her and was on her way back to the cabinet. 'Thank you.'

Viola Letters splashed angostura into her gin and stirred it noisily. Charley's nose dipped involuntarily towards her sherry. She was feeling decidedly blotto.

'Dick loved the countryside. He was quite a sensitive old thing really, although they used to say he was tough in the Navy. I'll go and get that picture.'

Charley heard her walk up the stairs then across the floor above. The terrier yelped again, sorry for itself rather than angry now. She thought of the face in the photograph, the man yesterday in the woods. Tom had laughed at her dismissively, told her what she had told Viola Letters — that she must have mistaken what the man had said. But she had known in her heart she could not have mistaken everything. Not the name Letters, and the watch, and the address.

She hadn't told Tom about the gum. She knew he would have been even more scornful about that.

Viola Letters came back into the room holding a small framed painting. 'This is it.'

Charley took the painting. It was an oil of Elmwood Mill viewed from behind the bridge. The quality was good, clear, the detail immaculate. She studied the house and the mill, noticing its roof was in better condition than now. The picture blurred suddenly and she screwed up her eyes, trying to focus. Something was wrong, odd, different.

'When did he do this?' she asked, her voice trembling.

'Golly, now you're asking. He died in nineteen fifty-three, so before then, of course. Before the fire.'

Charley stared again, the picture shaking so much in her hands it was hard to see clearly. She tried to compose herself, to concentrate, brought it close to her face, stared harder, harder, at the building on the level patch of ground beyond the barn, the other side of the mill race, halfway up the bank. A large smart stable block.

The stable block that was missing.

Chapter Twelve

Beldale Avenue reminded Charley of the street in Finchley where she'd spent her early childhood, before her adoptive father had died and they'd had to move. A quiet south London backwash of unassuming semi-detached houses with pebbledash walls. Tidy. Orderly. Two delivery men were unloading a new washing machine from a yellow van. A mother pushed a baby in a pram. Three children raced each other down the pavement on BMX bikes.

She was surprised by the ordinariness. She had been expecting something different, although she did not know what. Something more secretive, sinister.

Number 39 had soup-brown walls, secondary double glazing and an almost smugly neat front garden presided over by a ceramic gnome with a grin on its face like an infant that has just dumped in its nappy. An old estate car was parked outside sagging on its springs, the rear window plastered with faded pennants of English counties.

As she ground through the traffic, Charley resented being in London again. She parked on the shaded side of the street and locked the Citroën with the windows open and the roof partially rolled back for Ben, who barked in protest at being left.

Tom had been as dismissive about Mrs Letters's husband as about everything else. It was Charley's mistaken identity, Viola Letters's wishful thinking, an imagined resemblance to an old faded photograph. 'Ghosts glide down corridors of houses late at night, rattling chains. They don't wander through woods at eleven in the morning carrying fishing rods,' he had said.

He had been equally dismissive about the stables. All old houses had stables, he had said. Elmwood Mill was bound to have had some.

They had worked on the house together over the weekend. Between them they had finished stripping the walls of the bedroom and decided on the colour. Tom had favoured Wedgewood blue. Charley thought that might feel cold in winter. They agreed on magnolia, then started on the largest spare room, which had been Nancy Delvine's workroom and would now become Tom's study. They had decided to leave the downstairs until after Tom's birthday party.

A curtain parted above her and she hesitated, tempted to go back to her car and drive off. It was Laura who had persuaded her to come. Or maybe she had persuaded herself. She did not know. Fear rippled through her, fear and curiosity and something else she did not understand. She felt clammy, too, and had the metallic taste in her mouth again. Her watch said 12.05. She was five minutes late.

Ernest Gibbon had not sounded how she had expected over the phone. No drama, no Flavia Montessore theatricals. He had not sounded anything much at all, other than a man who had been interrupted in the middle of the cricket match on the television. She had phoned him on Friday afternoon after speaking to Laura, and had been surprised he had been able to fit her in straight away on Monday morning.

The bell rang with a single chime and a tall, ponderous man in his late fifties opened the door. He was accompanied by a smell of boiled cabbage which made her nausea worse.

'Mr Gibbon?' she said.

He had a hangdog face, with droopy flesh that disappeared each side of his chin into mutton chop sideburns, and limp black hair that was centre-parted and a little too long, giving him a Dickensian air. He looked down at her through eyes distorted by the dense lenses of his tortoiseshell glasses. His dark suit had seen better days and his tartan tie was knotted too tightly, making the points of his shirt collar stick up slightly, and in spite of the heat he wore a cardigan. She glanced out of habit at his shoes. Her mother had told her you could always judge a man by his shoes. He was wearing wine-coloured corduroy carpet slippers.

'Yes. Mrs Witney?' he intoned in a flat, soporific voice that had no trace of emotions; he might have used the same tone to comment about the weather or to concur with a complaint about the punctuality of trains.

He held the door until she was inside, then closed it firmly. Unease rose inside her as he slid the safety chain across.

The hallway had a bright orange and brown patterned carpet; a porcelain spanish donkey in a straw hat was on a copper trolley in front of her. On the wall above it was a wooden crucifix.

'I'm afraid it's at the top.' She detected a faint wheeze after he spoke, as if he had a slight touch of emphysema, and as they climbed the staircase the wheezing became more distinct. 'Come far, have you?'

'From Sussex.'

Wooden plates with scenes of Switzerland relieved the grim Artex stair walls. He paused on the landing to get his breath. On this floor the house had a tired old smell, a milder version of the way Elmwood smelled at the moment, and it depressed her. Her stomach fluttered uncomfortably and she felt increasingly nervous, part of her wanting to pay him now, pay him for his time and go, forget about it.

He walked a few paces down the landing, opened a door and put his head in. 'My client's turned up, mother. You'll have to make your own tea. I've put your lunch out in the kitchen for you, and locked the front door if you have to answer it. See you later. Cheerio.'

Psycho. There was no mother. It was all an act.

Christ, calm down!

Ernest Gibbon climbed the next flight, the stairs creaking under his heavy plod, and then a third into a spartanly furnished attic room with the same orange and brown carpeting as the rest of the house. There was a divan with a microphone on a stalk above it, an office chair on castors and an untidy stack of hi-fi equipment and wiring. It was hot and stuffy.

'Lie down on the couch, please,' he said. 'Make yourself comfortable. Take off your shoes, loosen anything that's tight.' His instructions sounded as if he were reading out a shopping list.

She pushed off her white flats. 'Could we have the window open a little?'

'You'll find you'll cool down soon enough. Your body temperature will drop very low.' He went out and came back with a folded blanket which he put on the divan. Everything at the same unhurried pace. He walked across to the window, drew the flimsy curtains and the room darkened.

'Have you ever been regressed before, Mrs Witney?'

She stretched out, feeling awkward, regretting she had taken off her shoes because it made her feel more vulnerable. The pillow was lumpy. 'Yes, once.'

'My fee is thirty-five pounds if we're successful, fifteen if we're not. One in eight fail to regress. It will take two hours and we should get two or three previous lives on the first occasion. They are normally between thirty or three hundred years apart.' Another shopping list.

She glanced up at the microphone over her face masked in grey foam rubber. The divan smelled of vinyl.

'I tape each session and give you a copy. It's included in the price. Make yourself comfortable. It's important you are comfortable as you are going to be staying in the same position for a long time.'

Psycho. She felt a flash of panic. The mother was a rotting skeleton. He was going to ... then she heard the sound of a lavatory flushing below and relaxed a little.

'Is there anything you'd like to ask me before we begin? I can see that you are nervous.' He busied himself with his recording equipment, sorting out a tangle of wires. 'It is natural to be nervous. Going back into past lives means that we are opening up Pandora's boxes deep inside us.'

'Do all people have previous lives?'

He continued untangling the wires. 'Jesus Christ existed before he came to earth. He told us, "Before Abraham was, I am." The Bible has many mentions. Christianity is founded on life everlasting. In my Father's house there are many mansions. In our own lives are buried many past lives.' He pulled out a jackplug and pushed it into a different socket. 'Our present carnations are part of an ongoing process. Some people have deep traumas carried from previous lives. When they understand the cause, the traumas go.' He removed the wrapping on a new cassette, wrote slowly on the outside, then looked up at her. 'Do you have a particular trauma? A fear of anything?'

'Heights, I suppose.'

'You probably died in a fall in a previous life. We'll find it.'

The simplicity of his comment made her suspicious. It was too pat.

He pushed the cassette into the machine. 'Do you have a special reason for wanting to be regressed, Mrs Witney?'

'I — I've been getting a feeling of *déjà vu* about somewhere.'

'You feel as if you've been there before?'

She hesitated. 'Yes.'

He adjusted a flickering sound level light. 'Sometimes we access trace memories passed down through genes. Sometimes we transcend time. Sometimes we connect into the spirit world. The important thing is to feel free. Relax. Enjoy yourself. If there is anything uncomfortable or threatening you must tell me.'

'Why?'

The hypnotist pressed a button. There was a click and a loud whine. His voice and her own repeated: '. . . or threatening you must tell me.' 'Why?'

He pressed another button and she heard the shuffling of the tape rewinding, then another click. He stooped to inspect the machine. 'Because you'll be reliving all that happens. It will feel very real. Pain will feel real. Danger will feel real. It will be real.' He stood up. 'Comfy, are you? Get your hands comfy too.'

Charley wriggled around and he gently laid the blanket over her. 'I shall be putting you into an altered state of consciousness. You won't be asleep, but it will seem like it. When you come out you'll feel like you do after a nice Sunday lunch; lazy and relaxed.' He allowed the merest hint of a smile to show on his face for the first time, and it made him seem more human, made her feel safer. He walked ponderously over to the door and turned a dial on the wall.

The overhead light went out and a much dimmer red light came on. The hypnotist coughed and sat in the chair beside her. A train went by in the distance and he paused as if waiting for it to pass, then leaned towards her.

'Tell me your first name.'

'Charley.'

'I want you to look at the microphone. Concentrate on the microphone. Blank everything out of your mind except the microphone, Charley.'

She stared at it for a long time, aware of the silence, waiting for him to speak, waiting for something to happen. The silence continued. The microphone slipped out of focus, turned into two, then back into one. She wondered how long she had been looking at it. A minute? Two minutes? Five? Another train went by.

'Velvet, Charley. I want you to think of velvet, soft velvet all around. You are in a tent of velvet. Your eyes are feeling heavy. Everything is soft, Charley.' His voice droned, the tone unaltering. 'You are safe.'

She tried to imagine being in a cocoon of velvet.

'How old are you, Charley?'

The banality of the question surprised her. She glanced at him, saw the frown of disapproval, then looked back at the microphone. 'Thirty-six.'

'Close your eyes now. Think back to your thirtieth birthday. Can you remember what you did on your thirtieth birthday?'

She racked her brains. Thirty. Yes, she could remember that one, would never forget it. She opened her mouth, but it was difficult to speak; she had to strain to get the words out; they came out slowly, sounding slurred, almost as if someone else was speaking them.

Tom had taken her to dinner to a new Italian restaurant in Clapham to celebrate. They'd had a row, one of their worst rows ever, and Tom had stormed out of the restaurant, leaving her to pay the bill. She could feel the burning embarrassment now, six years later, could see the faces of the other diners, a woman with long blonde hair studying her disdainfully from across the restaurant as if she was an exhibit in a zoo, whispering to her dinner companions and the whole table chortling with laughter. Then it got even worse. When she opened her handbag and found she had not brought her purse. The manager had not let her leave, had locked the restaurant door and stood guard over her while she called Tom.

'Did he come back?'

'Yes.'

The microphone seemed to nod at her sympathetically.

'Go back in time, Charley. Go back to your twenty-first birthday. Can you remember your twenty-first birthday?'

Her eyelids drooped. She forced them open. Slowly they closed again and she felt herself sinking down through a soft darkness towards sleep. 'Camping.' The word seemed heavy. It rolled out of her mouth and dropped away into an abyss. 'Tom and I. In Wales. The Brecon Beacons. It rained and the fire wouldn't light. Had champagne ... a bottle of champagne in the tent. We were giggling and it collapsed. That's when he proposed to me.'

'Go back to sixteen now, Charley. Feel sixteen.'

Silence.

'You are sixteen. Look down at yourself, tell me what you are wearing.'

'A red miniskirt. White boots.'

'How is your hair?'

'It's long.'

'Do you like being sixteen?'

'Yes.'

'Why?'

'Because I'm going out with Tom.'

'Are you going out tonight?'

'Yes.'

'What are you going to do?'

Charley began to tremble. 'There's something bad.'

'What do you see?'

'Sharon Tate. People murdered. It's horrible.'

'Are you there?'

'No.'

'What are you doing?'

'I'm reading a paper. We're going out. To a movie.'

'What are you going to see?'

'*Easy Rider.*'

'Is Tom your boyfriend?'

'Yes.'

'When did you meet him?'

'On my birthday.'

'On your sixteenth birthday?'

'Yes.'

'Let's go back to your sixteenth birthday. Can you remember it?'

'Yes.' Her voice sounded slurry.

'Are you having a party?'

'In a pub — with Laura — other girlfriends, to celebrate. I'm really pissed.'

'What are you drinking?'

'Cuba Libre. He's laughing at me.'

'Who?'

'The fella. With the Beatle haircut.' She giggled. 'He thinks he's so cool. Joe Cool! He's laughing at me. I'm feeling sick now, going to be sick.' Her head spun.

Silence.

'Go back to your tenth birthday, Charley. Can you remember your tenth birthday?'

Images of childhood drifted past her, flashed at her briefly and floated away like roadsigns at night. Packing bows into plastic bags, her mother stitching stuffed toys, the television on loudly. *Emergency-Ward 10.* Vietnam. Hancock. Alf Garnett. *Juke Box Jury.*

Bonanza. Peyton Place. Kennedy was shot. Churchill was buried. Screeching Chinamen burned books. Man landed on the moon. She could smell the carpet of the sitting room floor where she lay for hours, dressing her doll, tending it, making it better when it was ill, the doll that needed her, depended on her, rolled its eyes obediently, gratefully. Florence Doll. Princess Margaret married Anthony Armstrong Jones. Florence Doll got married too. The ceremony was even grander. Florence Doll married Binky Bear who was the Head of the World.

'Your tenth birthday, Charley.'

The memory was indistinct. She was becoming aware of the room, aware of the hypnotist, and felt a trace of disappointment. She lay in silence for a moment. 'I think I'm awake,' she said.

'Your tenth birthday, Charley,' he repeated.

Damp animal smells filled her nostrils. 'The zoo. London Zoo ...' Her voice trailed off. She floated in silence again. She opened her eyes. The microphone was a blur and her whole body seemed weighted down with sandbags.

'Can you remember your fourth birthday?'

'*You careless girl! You stupid, stupid, careless girl.*'

'He's shouting at me.'

'Who is shouting at you?'

'My dad.'

'Why is he shouting at you?'

'I rode — bicycle — I got a red bicycle — into a bush. He's going to spank me and lock me in my room. My mum's crying. She's telling him it's my birthday, but he's still going to lock me in. It's the pills he's on. Mum says the pills for his illness make him angry.'

Tiredness drained her. Time faded. She was floating. It was pitch dark. She was scared. She tried to wake. She could not. She tried to sit up. Nothing moved.

'Relax, Charley.'

Her body and the darkness seemed to merge together.

'We're going back now, Charley, we're going back a long way further.' His calm voice drifted around her, seemed to fill her like air. 'We're going to go back now to before you were born. You are floating in darkness, floating in space, in the void, all is calm, peaceful, you have no worries, Charley, you are in spirit now, free, weightless, free of life.'

Dark silence carried her.

'You are in spirit now. You have a complete set of memories. The clock is running backwards. You are free to search for a memory in all time.'

The darkness swirled.

'Think about your previous life now, Charley. Remember your death. Remember how you died.'

Fear tightened around her. She began spinning, helpless, spinning in draining water, faster and faster like an insect being drawn down to the plughole; she was fighting, flailing, arms slithering, spinning faster still, being sucked down, down.

Then she was in brilliant white light. Sunlight, beating down, hard, tormenting her, sunlight pressing her against the hill, trying to crush her into the hill, to stub her out on it. Sadness filled her. An immense weight of sadness, and despair.

'Where are you?'

'On an 'ill.'

'How old are you?'

'I dunno.'

'What's your name?'

'I dunno.'

'Do you have brothers or sisters? Parents?'

'I dunno.'

'Do you recognise the hill?'

'No.'

'What's the colour of your hair?'

She pulled some strands out with her fingers. 'Brown.'

'Are you working? At school?'

'I dunno. I don't want to be here.'

'I presume you've had education? Where did you go to school?'

She looked up. She could see clouds through the trees. Tears were sliding down her face.

'Why are you crying?'

The ground was soft under her feet, too soft. She was sinking in. She stepped forwards and her left foot came free with a squelch. Her right foot was stuck. She pulled and it came out of her shoe, leaving that behind. She knelt down, put her hand into the boggy mud and pulled. 'My shoe. I'm wearing the wrong shoes. I oughter be in boots.'

'Why are you crying? Where are you?'

'Dunno.'

'How old are you? Tell me how old you are. When was your last birthday?'

'Dunno.' She pushed her foot back into the shoe, and stumbled on. Something bit into her hand, something sharp, hard-edged, something she could not let go. She fell and there was a sharp pain as it cut into her palm; she transferred it to her other hand, a small metal tin, and stood, forcing herself upwards, pushing the sky off her back as if it was a tent that had collapsed on to her. Something rattled inside the tin. Above she heard running water, splashing, cool water and she forced herself to go on, into trees, squelching on upwards.

'What are you carrying?'

The voice was distant in the sounds of the woods. She paused and stared around at the darkness of the trees. A rabbit was watching her. A crow. There was sudden complete silence as the chatter of the birds stopped. As the water stopped. It felt as if the whole animal kingdom was watching her. The track forked here, and she knew the way was to the right. She went on through thick bracken which crunched under her feet.

The rock loomed out of the trees, blurred through the tears that filled her eyes and streamed down her cheeks.

She reached the base of the rock, and the path was dry here, easier to walk on. As she carried on up around it she saw another rock, a strange upright rock indented in the centre, shaped like a heart.

She climbed towards it, puffing from exertion, sobbing gently. The huge granite rock at the edge of a small bluff looked as if it could topple over at any moment.

The track went underneath the overhang then around the back of the bluff on to the top. The rock looked heart-shaped from this side too, although less distinct, and even bigger than from below. It was a good eight feet high and six feet across. She knew it well. It was covered in carvings, initials, and she knew them too. *P loves E. Chris l. Lena. Mary-Wilf, Dan-Rosie. Arthur Edward loves Gwennie. D loves BJ.*

'Do you recognise any of the initials?'

She swallowed, stared down at *D loves BJ*, and squeezed the tin harder between her hands. Then she walked to the shrubbery behind the rock, knelt down, and for a while was blinded by her tears.

She scraped away the dead leaves and began to scoop a hole in the damp sandy earth. When it was nearly a foot deep, she laid the tin in, scraped the earth back over and spread the leaves out on top.

'Why are you burying it?'

She stood up and patted the earth down with her foot, then walked on through the shrubbery and down a steep bank towards a small waterfall. She began to feel spits of water on her face, her arms, her legs, and as she got closer, holding out her dirty hands, the spits turned to a fine continual spray that got heavier and wetter until she was standing in the waterfall itself, the fine spray drenching her, tiny needles of water coming harder and harder, so hard they were hurting now.

She tried to move away, but crashed into a wall. She spun round. Her face stared back from a mirror. 'Room,' she mouthed, but it was strange. Her face in the mirror did not move.

'I don't like this room,' she said.

'What room are you in?'

'I don't like this room. I don't want to be here.'

'Where is it?'

'I don't like it. I don't want to be here. Please, I don't want to be here. Please take me out.'

A figure loomed in the mirror behind her.

'No!'

The mirror exploded into spidery cracks. A jagged shard landed at her feet.

'GET ME OUT! GET ME OUT! OUT! PLEASE GET ME OUT!' She hammered with her fists. Terror throttled her, strangled her voice. 'OH QUICK, OUT! PLEASE GET ME OUT! PLEASE! OH PLEASE!'

A face looked at her anxiously. 'Charley. Wake up now. It's all right.'

The terror still surged. She was thrashing wildly.

'Charley, it's all right.'

The strange face. The centre parting. Mutton chops. Eyes like pinheads through the thick lenses. He disappeared. There was a click. Bright light flooded around her, then his face was over her again.

'It's all right, Charley. You are safe.'

She felt as if she was lying in the water. Rivulets ran down her face, over her neck, her shoulders, her stomach. She pulled her hands out and pushed away the blanket and immediately felt cooler. She lay still, exhausted, and looked up into the myopic eyes. 'What—?' It was an effort to speak. 'What happened?'

'Your past life. You were reliving something unpleasant, some bad experience,' he said gently. 'That's a good thing. It is only by reliving bad experiences in previous lives that we free ourselves of the traumas we have in this carnation.'

There was a choking lump of fear in her throat. 'It was awful,' she said. 'Horrible. It didn't make any sense — like a bad dream.'

'It wasn't a dream. You were in a past life.' He looked at his watch. 'I'm afraid we'll have to stop there. We've run over, and I have another appointment. I'll give you the tapes.'

'I thought . . . I thought I had two hours.'

'It's three o'clock,' he said.

'Three? Impossible! Nearly three hours? I've only been a few minutes — ten minutes — it can't be —'

'It takes time, going into past lives; you were there a long time.'

She shook her head, bewildered, and tried to move, to get up, but she felt completely drained.

'We need to have another session,' he said. 'We should not leave it like this, with the wound open. We need to find out more.'

She stared at him, her mind jumbled.

'You were talking in quite a different voice. We need to find out who you were, what you were burying in the tin. We need to know what terrified you.'

'Why?' she mouthed. It came out a squeak of terror, like a hunted creature in the woods at night caught out in the open, away from its nest, its lair, its mother.

'Our past lives are part of our psyche, Charley. When we regress to them we stir that up, transcend the time bands. We don't want you start having trace memories, or suddenly being frightened and not knowing why. You may find that a lot of your fears now relate to this incident in your previous life. If we can see what happened, find out what caused it, it might help you.'

'And if we don't?'

'We shouldn't leave it,' he said. 'Not like this. I don't think that would be wise.'

He smiled with a smugness that disturbed her. She shivered as fear coursed through her veins.

'I still don't understand.'

'You will,' he said. 'You'll understand.'

Chapter Thirteen

'We've met before,' she said. 'In a previous life.' She tilted her glass towards her lips and stared into his eyes. 'We were lovers.'

He blushed, glanced away, then back; she was still staring. He raised his own glass and grinned. 'When?'

'It's lovely wine,' she said, the words running into each other.

'You're only thirty-eight once.'

'Are you sure?' She clinked her glass against his.

Charley watched Tom and Laura in the shadows of the hurricane lamps, at the end of the two tables they had joined together, and wondered what they were talking about so deeply. Laura in a white jacket, with a large quartz brooch, leaning towards him, her elbows on the table. Beautiful. She looked beautiful and Charley felt dowdy in comparison. She had been putting on weight since the move, just a little, and it annoyed her.

Smoke from the barbecue drifted over the table and Bob Dylan's voice sang softly from the speaker Tom had run from the drawing room. He always played old records on his birthday.

'Bats bonk upside down. Did you know that?' She heard Richard Howarth's voice, dimly, through the chatter.

'You're very brave, entertaining so soon,' said

Michael Ohm, sitting on her right. His Zapata moustache seemed to be getting thicker each time she saw him, as if to compensate for the widening bald patch in the centre of his head. He pushed his red-framed glasses back up his arched nose. One of Tom's partners. Trendy. Lawyers were starting to look like architects. Architects were looking like bankers. Change. Life shifted silently beneath you like sand.

She shivered. The heat of the Indian summer day had gone and a damp chill filled the darkness. People were putting on pullovers. Rubbing their hands. They would have to move inside soon.

Richard Howorth, Tom's best man, was here and his girlfriend, Louisa, an interior decorator. John Orpen, Tom's accountant, and his wife, Sue, were trying to prise conversation out of an extremely drunk Julian Garfield-Hampsen. Charley had suggested inviting Hugh for Laura, and Tom had thought it a good idea to invite Julian and Zoe as well; she was glad he was keen to make friends with the neighbours.

Laura was ignoring Hugh. Matchmaking for her was always difficult. She did not seem to know what she wanted herself. She had chucked away a marriage that could have been salvaged without ever really explaining to Charley why, and had fought fiercely for custody of her two girls, yet sent them to boarding school because she needed to concentrate on her shop.

Michael Ohm wiped soup from his moustache. 'How do you find it here compared to London?' he asked.

'Strange,' Charley replied. 'But it's nice getting to know Mother Nature. We actually had our own eggs for breakfast this morning — well, egg — but it's a start. We're planting all sorts of vegetables. Some of the local shops are hysterical. The grocer in the village sells only one kind of bread — sliced white. Can you believe it?'

'Geller is a con man! He's a complete fraud!'

100

The outburst came from Hugh Boxer at the other end of the table. He sat up in his chair, shoulders hunched inside his crumpled linen jacket, his eyes blazing fiercely, black crevasses scoring the gaunt skin of his face.

'How can you say that?' Zoe Garfield-Hampsen piped heatedly in her little girl voice, her breasts almost popping out of her low-cut dress in indignation. 'I've seen him with my own eyes. I've seen him do it!'

One hurricane lamp flickered, died for a second, came on again roaring fiercely, then Bob Dylan stopped abruptly in mid-chord; the table dimmed. Charley looked at the house. The lights had gone out. Then both the hurricane lamps went out as well, plunging them into darkness. She felt a blast of cold air as if a freezer door had been opened behind her. Someone howled; a ghostly wail.

'Mains trip,' Tom said. 'I'll do it. Won't take a sec.' There was the sound of a glass smashing. 'Ooops, bugger,' he cursed.

John Orpen clicked on his lighter and lifted the glass lid of the hurricane lamp in front of him. 'The wick's too low.' He relit it and turned it up.

Bob Dylan started singing again, several lights in the house came back on together and everyone cheered. Tom reappeared. 'We've had the place rewired,' he said, 'but they've done something wrong.'

'The trip's probably been set too sensitive,' Michael Ohm murmured.

'The soup was absolutely brilliant,' Sue said. 'Can you give me the recipe?'

Charley stood and began clearing the table.

Laura followed her into the kitchen with an armful of plates which she balanced precariously on the stack Charley put down. She looked at the clothes rack on the pulley and tugged the cord. The rack rose up and down,

101

then wobbled above them. Charley noticed she looked sloshed, and was surprised: Laura rarely drank much.

'S'beautiful place. You're so lucky! I'm incredibly envious!' She pulled the cord again, mildly irritating Charley, and the rack rose up and down with a creak. 'So tell me, how did it go with Ernest Gibbon? What did you think of him?'

Shadows from the rails of the rack swung across the floor as Charley loaded plates into the dishwasher. 'I thought he was a creep.'

'He's sweet!' Laura slurred indignantly. 'S'lovely man!'

'Tom's listened to the tapes — bits of them anyway. He says he was feeding me with thoughts.'

'He'd never do that. He's got a terrific reputation.'

'It struck me as a good con. He leaves you feeling terrified, so you want to go back to find out what happens next.'

Laura tugged the cord once more. 'No, I don't think he's like that.'

There was a wailing screech then a bang like a clap of thunder in the room.

Laura jumped back and crashed into the fridge.

Charley stared in shocked silence at the clothes rack; it was lying on the floor between them.

'Sorry,' Laura said, looking lamely at the cord. 'Forgot to hook it back.'

Tom turned the pork chops and sausages over on the barbecue. Fat spat and sizzled on the red coals. He prodded a couple of the jacket potatoes, gave each of the sweetcorns a half turn, blinking against the searing heat and the smoke, stood back unsteadily and had a gulp of his wine. He could see the glow of the lamps and the shadowy figures at the table fifty or so yards away, but the darkness and the booze made it hard to make out much more.

A pair of hands slipped around his waist. 'Hi,' she said, quietly, simply. He smelled her perfume, felt the light pressure of her hands.

'Not quite done yet,' he said, turning round.

Laura's eyes were locked on his, her mouth smiling quizzically in the faint glow of the coals. 'I like looking at you,' she whispered.

He smiled, embarrassed.

'I often see you across a room at a party, looking at me. I like it when you look at me.'

Her fingertips brushed against his, then her fingers curled around his, squeezing them gently. He glanced over towards the table. Shapes, just shadowy shapes; he and Laura would be shadowy shapes too. He hoped.

Laura stretched up on tiptoe and placed her lips against his, soft lips, much softer than Charley's, he thought, before pulling back, taking her wrist and leading her behind a tree. They kissed, longer this time, and he pressed her against the tree, filled with a sudden urge of drunken lust. He slipped his hand inside her jacket, inside her blouse, ran his fingers over her breasts while she ground her pelvis against his growing hardness. He drew away and squinted mischievously at her. 'What are we doing?'

'Having a snog.' She smiled petulantly then grasped the back of his head and kissed him again. His hand wandered under her skirt, over the nylon of her tights and the smooth skin of her stomach, then slid inside her tights and over the bare skin of her buttocks. He started trying to pull her tights down.

She shook her head, still keeping her lips to his, murmuring. 'Uh oh, no!'

He broke away and glanced furtively round the tree. 'We could have a quick knee trembler.'

'No!'

He fumbled with her tights.

'Stop it!' she said. 'I smell burning.'

He turned to the barbecue. Flames were leaping up around the chops. 'Shit!'

'I think I'd better get back and join the party,' Laura said. 'Which way's the loo?'

'The least grotty one's at the top of the stairs, turn left, second door on the right.'

They began to sing happy birthday as Charley brought the cake out. The baker in the village had made it. There was a legal-looking scroll on the top and the wording 'HAPPY BIRTHDAY TOM' visible through a forest of candles. The wind blew most of them out and Tom the rest. There was a roar of applause and raucous shouts of 'Speech!'

His face became a flickering blurr.

She felt a deep sense of unease. The smell of the barbecue disturbed her. Burning embers. The flames licking at the inky darkness. Silence pressed in around her. The smiling faces and the shouts and laughter faded.

She had been here before. Seen flames here before.

She saw the old man stumbling through the woods towards her. The girl climbing up towards the rock with the tin in her hand, crying.

'Penny for your thoughts.'

She looked round, startled. Hugh was sitting in Michael Ohm's seat and was grinning at her.

'Sorry,' she said. She shivered, rubbed her arms. 'It's cold. Do you think we should move inside?'

'Soon.'

'Do you remember what you were saying in the pub, Hugh, about old spirits?'

'Yes,' he said, taking out his pipe. 'OK if I —?'

'I love the smell, she said. 'Have you ever been regressed into past lives?'

'Under hypnosis?'

'Yes.'

He bit the stem and cocked his head slightly, his eyes narrowing. He lowered his voice. 'I told you, there are a lot of amateurs around. Don't get involved.'

'I thought you believed in reincarnation.'

'I don't believe in playing games with the occult.'

'Games?'

Wisps of dry ice were curling through her veins. Hugh was looking around uneasily. 'Sorry about the car,' he said, abruptly changing the subject.

Car. Triumph. Car. Gum. She put her hand out to her glass and it was shaking so much she nearly knocked it over. Her cheeks felt red.

'I ought to pay you a fee for parking,' he said.

'No. Not at all. It's — you can leave it, really.' There was a minty taste in her mouth. Gum.

There was a thud. A clatter. Hugh bent and picked up her fork.

'Oh, thanks —' She wiped it with her napkin. 'Please, leave the car for as long as you like.'

'A few more days would be helpful.' He lit his pipe with an old Zippo. A gust whipped hot ash from it and he clamped his hand over the bowl. 'Have you done much exploring around the area yet?'

'No, not really.'

'This is a very interesting part of the world. It's riddled with old energy lines. Used to be considered quite fey.'

'Witches on broomsticks?'

'That sort of thing.' He grinned and sucked on his pipe. 'Have you been to the Wishing Rocks?'

'Where are they?'

'It's a pretty walk. You go up through the woods the far side of the lake, take the right fork after the marshy bit and carry on.'

'Why are they called Wishing Rocks?'

'They're pagan holy stones — I don't know how they got them up there, unless they were hewn out of the hill — and the locals had a superstition that if you wanted something really badly you took the rocks a present.'

'A sacrifice?'

His pipe had gone out. 'No, not a living sacrifice, but it had to be something personal.' His lighter clanked and he sucked the flame down into the bowl of the pipe. She sniffed discreetly as the thick blue smoke drifted over her head. 'And if you wanted your love to be eternal you engraved your names on the Sweethearts' Rock. If your love ever faded, you took the rock a token and it made everything OK again.'

She was silent for a moment. 'What does that rock look like?' she asked.

'You can't miss it. It's shaped like a heart.'

Chapter Fourteen

Charley slept badly. The cacophony of birds and the roaring of the water and the churning thoughts in her mind kept her awake.

Tom lay awake too, tossing beside her. He got up and went to the lavatory. A while later he got up again, went into the bathroom and came back with a glass that was fizzing.

'You OK?'

The bed sagged as he sat down. 'Jesus. It was quieter in London. Can't we shut those bloody birds up?'

The sky was grey, stormy, and a strong wind was blowing. There was the clatter of a bicycle and tyres scrunched on gravel. Ben ran to the bedroom door, barking.

'Newspapers,' Tom said.

'Did you enjoy last night?'

'Good fun.' He screwed up his eyes.

'You and Laura were talking a lot.'

He stirred the Alka Seltzer with the handle of his toothbrush, drank some and grimaced.

'What were you talking about?'

He was silent for a moment, then mumbled. 'Nothing in particular.'

The window rattled and a gust of chilly air swept across her face. 'The weather's not so nice for your cricket,' she said.

'It might clear up.'

'What are you doing this morning?'

'I thought I'd start stripping the drawing room. There's no point in painting anything while they're messing around with the floorboards.'

Charley yawned and looked around the bare walls and the raw beams and the low, uneven ceiling. It still felt strange in this room, felt each morning as if she were waking in a hotel and not *home*.

'Back to work for you tomorrow,' she said. 'End of holiday.'

Tom nodded. 'Are you in London this week?'

'Tomorrow. I'm going to see mother, and I said I'd help Laura for a couple of hours. The money's useful,' she added defensively.

'It doesn't even cover your train fare.' He went to close the window.

'I've seen some very inexpensive kitchen units. I meant to tell you.'

'Is there any point at the moment? We might as well wait.'

'It's so dreary in there. It's going to be years before —'

He ducked through into the bathroom. The bath taps gushed then the sound changed to the hiss of the shower.

She raised her voice. 'I really wish I was still working.'

'Why?'

'Because I'm fed up not having any money. I'm guilty all the time about spending anything.'

He poked his head through the door. 'It's not forever. After we —' He hesitated. 'You know, have kids, you can go back again.'

'Not to my old job.'

'Your old job was killing you.'

'I liked it.'

She had liked the pressure. Her boss, who designed fashion accessories, had been a workaholic and it was infectious. She was expected in the office at seven and rarely got home before eight. They travelled somewhere in Europe at least once a fortnight, to the States twice a year and occasionally to the Far East, buying, exhibiting, looking. It had been fun. And well paid.

'A couple of new units and a lick of paint and the kitchen'll be fine until we can afford to do it properly.'

'If you put your mother somewhere cheaper, we could afford to do a hell of a lot more now.'

'I hope you remember that one day when your father's old and infirm,' she said angrily.

The first rock loomed out of the woods above her. She climbed over a fallen birch and stopped at the edge of a small clearing to get her breath back. The woods were dark and hemmed her in; they spooked her. Ben stopped, maybe sensing something too, and nuzzled his head against her leg.

She was the furthest she had been up here, beyond the point where she had met the old man, Commander Letters ... or imagined him ... or seen a time warp, a freak of the atmospherics. Or had met someone totally different, an innocent old codger with a fishing rod and had passed on his message to the wrong person.

She was nervous of meeting him again.

A shadow moved in the darkness through the trees, moved steadily, came out to greet her and she shrank back, goosepimples creeping over her flesh, until she realised it was just a bush behind a tree moving in the wind.

Two eyes watched her from under a dock leaf. Then the rabbit turned and scuttled through the undergrowth. Ben did not notice. She patted the dog, felt comforted by his company, by his hair, his warm body.

'Good boy,' she murmured.

The track ahead was through bracken. She climbed on, under the overhang of the rock, past a narrow fissure which reeked of urine and where there was a used condom lying on the ground. Behind, a long way back, she thought she heard a child shout and a woman's voice reply.

Then she could see the second rock a short distance above, and she stopped. There was no mistaking this rock, no saying it was just another rock and maybe ...

Heart-shaped, distinctly heart-shaped. It sat at the top of a short escarpment silhouetted against the boiling sky.

It was the rock she had seen in her regression.

She stared for a long while, trying to remember, to think back to childhood, to the outings in the country she had had with her mother. On Sundays they took a bus or a train to the country. However hard up they had been, her mother had insisted on a weekly treat. Maybe they had come here one Sunday? Or seen it in a film? Television? A book? Hugh said it was an ancient monument, a religious stone. Maybe she'd seen it in a magazine? A documentary?

She bit her lip and climbed a steep narrow gully up through the escarpment, scrambling over several smaller rocks. She reached the top and stood in the open, on a bracken-covered knoll with the heart-shaped rock in front of her and shrubbery behind.

She gulped down air, staring at the view; the buffeting wind made it hard to stand still. There was a panorama across the treetops in every direction except straight ahead which was obscured by the rock. Fields and woods and spires, pylons, farms, several large houses, a glinting swimming pool in the garden of one, a tennis court. She could see part of the lake, and the white columns and conservatory of Yuppie Towers.

The rock was a massive granite lump, with deep cracks and patches of lichen, rising out of a bed of dried bracken. It was covered in names and initials and messages, crudely carved, mostly weathered and barely distinct. P loves E. Chris l. Lena. Kenneth/Elizabeth. Anna l. Lars. Mary-Wilf. Arthur Edward loves Gwennie. D loves BJ.

D loves BJ.

She looked closer.

D loves BJ.

The initials she had stared at in the regression as if she had known them.

She touched the rock; it felt, smooth, cold. Silent. Ben loped around below, crunching through the bracken. Up here was silence. Only the wind. She read the initials again.

Coincidence? Tricks of the mind? Like the chewing gum? The stables? The man with the fishing rod?

D loves BJ.

The tin. The tin she had carried up here in her regression. If that was here too? Her heart was hammering.

Chinese box, Tom had said with a grin. The Chinese box was a delicacy. You buried a tin full of maggots in the earth, with no food. When you dug it up a fortnight later the maggots would have eaten each other and there would be one left, fat, juicy, the survivor. You ate him.

She could remember the spot. There, barely ten feet away in the shrubbery. She went over to the dense undergrowth. Something was glinting. Excitement rose as she parted the bushes then fell as she saw it was just glass from a broken bottle. She cleared it and knelt down.

This spot here.

She stood up and walked away, feeling foolish. She gazed at the view, tried to fight, but slowly she was drawn back, slowly she walked across and knelt again. This time she began to dig with her hands, the sandy soil packing under her nails. Ben arrived and licked her face, thinking she was playing some great game.

'OK, boy, help me dig! Big bones buried!'

He sat and scratched himself.

She dug down several inches, felt something hard which grazed her finger, and she clawed the soil away around it until she could see that it was a piece of flint.

She widened the hole, winced as she scraped her hand on a sharp stone. She dug beneath it, felt the cold slime of a worm stuck to her fingers and shook it free with a grimace.

Stupid, she thought, standing up. Daft. Should have brought a spade. Need a spade. She shook some of the sandy mud from her hands and stared at the small molehill she had made. Her watch said quarter to eleven. A spot of rain struck her face. With her boot, she shovelled the earth back into the hole and trod it flat, then hurried, half walking, half running, back to the house.

It was past twelve when she got back to the rock, her lungs aching, perspiration guttering down her body.

She sat for some minutes listening to the silence, the wind. Blue crevasses were appearing in the grey sky and it was getting brighter. She turned the trowel over in her hands; the rusted old tool was slightly bent and there was a crust of earth on the blade.

She glanced round. Ramblers in orange waterproofs had trudged up the track behind her, but they had turned off at the fork. Her hair thrashed her face. A voice inside her whispered *Go back! Forget it!*

She went to the shrubbery and knelt. Her pulse tugged at the base of her right thumb, as if someone was pinching at the skin. She felt a weird throbbing up her right arm and a tickling at the back of her throat. She glanced around once more, then began to dig.

Half an hour later the sky had brightened a little more. She had dug a crater eighteen inches deep and was wondering whose land this was and whether people were allowed to come along and dig holes. Did it belong to some farmer? The National Trust? Was an irate gamekeeper going to march out of the trees?

Ben had gone off somewhere and she felt very alone. Exposed. The silence was eerie. Forget it, there's nothing. No tin. She rammed the trowel into the earth, more in frustration than an intention to go on digging, and a metallic clank rang out.

She froze.

She raised the trowel an inch and pushed down again. The clank again. Duller.

She began to dig more carefully, feeling her way around the object, then dumped the trowel and used her hands. Something sharp grazed her finger and there was a trickle of blood in the mud. She dug with the trowel again, cutting the soil away on each side.

Then it was free, and she levered out a small mud-caked object. It was light, weighed scarcely more than the earth that was stuck to it. Something inside rattled, rattled again because she could not hold it steady.

She scraped the mud away with the blade of the trowel. Pitted metal showed through. A small square tin, three inches across and an inch deep. In parts the rust had eaten almost through it. She closed her hand around it, felt the edge. She could hear Ernest Gibbon's voice, probing.

What are you carrying? Why are you burying it?

It was this tin she had been carrying. Shiny and newer, but this tin. She was certain. And she was afraid to open it.

She looked into the crater. Two halves of a worm wriggled at the bottom.

Sometimes when you open the tin the maggot's bigger than you think.

The lid was held on by pressure. She tried to pry it off with her hands, but it would not budge. She used the blade of the trowel as a lever and twisted. The edge of the lid curled upwards then came free with a pop and a faint hiss of trapped air and fell into the hole.

A heart-shaped locket lay in the tin.

She stared at it, transfixed. An inch-high enamelled heart, ruby red, with a tarnished gold chain which spilled out and slithered down over her wrist, icy cold. It glinted dully in the sunlight that broke through the cloud. She blinked.

She knew this locket.

Knew that inside it she would find a note, carefully folded. Her head throbbed and her vision became blurry. Slowly, with fingers that felt like hams, she lifted the locket out. There was a tiny hinge and an even smaller clasp which, though rusted, moved under the pressure of her thumbnail. A minute piece of paper nestle inside, yellowed, brittle, folded several times. The wind fluttered it and she shut the locket, scared it would blow away. She felt giddy.

She wet her fingers with spittle and wiped them as clean as she could on her jeans then, shielding it from the wind, she took the tiny square out, and unfolded it. The ink was blurry, smudged, brown with age, and the paper so brittle she was frightened it would disintegrate. The handwriting was just legible.

'Dear Rock, I love him. Please bring him back. Barbara.'

'What are you doing?'

It felt as if a lever had been pulled inside her, switching her blood flow from slow to fast. A small boy was watching her, brown-haired, an earnest freckled face. He was about seven.

'Are you making a wish?' he said.

She nodded and managed a weak smile. A voice called out. 'Timothy! Come on, darling!'

He scampered out of sight. 'Mummy! Mummy! There's a lady up there making a wish!'

Her face was burning red with embarrassment. And guilt. This was someone else's locket, someone else's note. She had no business digging it up, reading, prying.

She refolded it, placed it inside the locket and snapped it shut. Then she laid it in the tin, closed the lid firmly and put it in the hole. She scooped the earth in and stamped it down with her foot. When she turned around, the boy was there again.

'Is that your doggie?' he said.

'Yes.'

'What's he called?'

'Ben.'

'I made a wish here,' he said.

'What did you wish?'

'I wished that the rock would make my daddy better.'

'Did it work?' she said smiling, almost relieved to have company.

'No.' His face puckered. 'He died.'

Chapter Fifteen

Tom hit a four off the first ball.

'I knew he could bat,' said Vic, the landlord from the George and Dragon, as glumly as if he had been clean bowled. 'I can tell a good bat when I see one.'

'Well done, darling!' Charley yelled, applauding the loudest. She stood beside the tea table, watching as the bowler paced out his run, rubbing the ball on the left cheek of his buttock. He started his run, slow, quick, slow, quick. The ball sailed through the air, Tom lunged out, missed, and it passed the wicket keeper.

'Yes! Go!' yelled the batsman the far end, already halfway down the crease. Tom ran, made the far crease long before a fielder ever got to the ball. There was more clapping. Fielders waited as the second batsman took his guard.

Charley felt a spot of rain on her face. The doilies under the cakes on the trestle tables flapped in the wind. Viola Letters's terrier ran in and out of the table legs yapping.

Charley squatted, patted the dog and tickled its chest. 'Hey, chappie, are we going to make friends?' It licked her hand tentatively.

Hugh Boxer came over, padded up, a weathered bat under his arm, cap tugged down over his head, wearing an old-fashioned college cricketing jumper and baggy white trousers. The outfit suited his aura of faded nobility.

'That was a bloody fine hit,' he said. 'Bold shot for an opener. He looks like rather a useful player.'

'He used to be very good.'

'Still is. Thank you for last night by the way,' he said.

'I hope you enjoyed it.'

'Very much. It was a good evening. Laura's a bright girl.' His eyes were probing.

'Yes, she is,' she said. 'I went up to the rocks this morning, the Wishing Rocks.'

'Oh yes?'

'You're right. It's a pretty walk.' She glanced at her nails, which were not completely free of mud, then back at Hugh. 'This custom — of burying things — does it still go on?'

'You might get the odd kid doing it occasionally. I think people have got more cynical about things like that these days.' He stretched down to tighten a strap on one pad.

There was a crunch and a silence on the pitch. The middle stump was bent backwards behind the batsman. Tom was at the other end she saw, relieved.

'I'm on parade,' Hugh said, and grinned.

'Good luck!'

'I'll need it.' He strode out, tugging on his gloves, pads flapping.

There were a couple of hundred people, Charley estimated, crowded around the jumble stall and the tombola and seated on the benches in front of the tiny pavilion. Several families lay sprawled on picnic rugs around the boundary, and two old buffers sat in front of the wooden scoreboard in deck chairs, surveying the match from under their green sun visors.

A batsman stood at a practice net while two others alternately bowled at him. He returned the ball each

117

time with a proficient *snick*. A group of children played their own game with a tiny bat and a rubber ball. Hamburgers and hot dogs sizzled on a griddle, and the banner 'NSPCC CHARITY MATCH' shook precariously in the wind.

''Ow much is the cup cakes?' a child asked.

'Twenty pence,' Charley said.

He handed her a grubby coin, which she dropped in the tin, and helped himself to a pink one.

Viola Letters stood on a milking stool behind a trestle table covered in upturned cups on saucers, and peered into a massive steel urn. There was a half-hearted ripple of applause as Hugh reached the crease, and the unfortunate opening batsman arrived back to face his team mates.

'Bad luck, Johnny!'

'Got me on a Yorker. He used to bowl for Kent, that one.'

Charley watched Hugh and Tom. The ball came hard at Hugh and he blocked it neatly. An umpire called, 'Over!'

Cricket. Lazy days. It brought back good memories. Tom played regularly when they first went out and she had spent happy hours lying with the sun on her back, watching, reading the same page of a paperback over and over, chewing sweet blades of grass.

The urn hissed steam. Viola Letters lifted a huge metal teapot from underneath the table and filled it with boiling water from the urn. 'Be a dear, Charley. Give it a couple of minutes and start pouring.'

Charley staggered under its weight. She put it down on the edge of the table and waited for the tea to steep. Tom hit another run. Hugh hit a four. It was a pretty village green, bounded on two sides by houses, and a wilderness of common land on the other two. She was glad Tom was playing, glad to be here herself, helping with the teas, a part of it. Belonging. She was glad Tom was doing well.

The tin and the locket suddenly swirled through her mind, and fear followed like a wave, crashing through her. The terrier yapped.

'Oh, Peregrine, I'm sorry! I didn't mean to frighten you.' She put her hand down to stroke it, but it scuttled away and yapped again.

Dear Rock, I love him. Please bring him back. Barbara.

It was coincidence: the gum, the stables, the old man. But not the tin.

A cold gust blew through her and she smelt a strange, musky perfume, strong, so strong, as if the woman wearing it were standing next to her; then it was gone like a snatch of smoke whipped away by the wind. She glanced around, wondering where it had come from, then picked up the heavy teapot, holding the handle with both hands, and tilted it towards the first cup.

It happened quickly. Just a jerk, that was all, and the handle became weightless for a fraction of a second as the top of it sheared away from the pot, which swung upside down dumping two gallons of scalding tea straight on the terrier.

She heard the howl almost before she realised what had happened, before the hot metal banged into her legs, before she even felt the sting of the scalding liquid on her own feet.

The dog fell sideways, rolled on to its back, twitching, steam rising around it. Its howl constricted into a tight screeching scream.

Viola Letters dropped to her knees to help it, and it twisted its head, bared its teeth and bit her hand savagely. Then it slithered a few feet across the grass on its belly, tried to stand and fell, howling, snapping at the grass, snapping at one of its legs. It rubbed its face on

119

the grass and most of the skin of its nose came off.

A child screamed.

'Peregrine!' Viola Letters bellowed, desperation in her voice, blood streaming from her finger as she ran after it.

The tiny dog rolled in agony, thrashing one way then the other, frothing, steam rising from its coat, like some grotesque beast from the pit of hell.

The shower was running upstairs, the plumbing creaking, water spurting up the pipes. The kitchen was snug from the heat of the Aga. The wind had died and a steady drizzle fell outside.

The cricket had gone on in the way games always went on, with a barely perceptible change in the tone, as if someone had tweaked the volume control and maybe the contrast knob. The children went back to their own games of cricket, except for a couple of tots who had leaned against their mothers, crying, their thumbs in their mouth.

The dog had been wrapped in towels to prevent it from biting anyone else, but by then it had given up struggling and lay helpless, twitching and whimpering. A girl from St John's Ambulance had bandaged Viola Letters's finger and someone had driven her and the dog to the vet. Charley had offered to go with her too, but Viola Letters had stoically told her to stay and carry on with the teas.

'It's not your fault, old girl,' a man with a handlebar moustache had said to Charley kindly. He held up the teapot, its handle twisted and hanging on by one bent bolt, and pointed at the jagged holes where the top bolts had sheared. 'Metal fatigue. Happens in aircraft.'

Later a tall woman in galoshes announced they had raised three hundred and forty-two pounds and eleven pence for the NSPCC. There was a ragged cheer. Tom had scored forty-two runs and bowled two of the other side out. He was voted man of the match and presented with a pewter tankard, and Charley's eyes had felt moist as pride broke through the cloud of shock and doom.

There were two messages on the answering machine, one from Holly Ohm thanking them for the party, the other was from Tom's squash partner, Paul Lerond. 'Tom, I got your message about cancelling tomorrow. How about Wednesday evening at six fifteen?'

Charley dropped a couple of pinches of food into Horace's bowl and chopped up the ox heart for Ben's supper, wrinkling her nose at the stench of dried blood.

Tom was lying on the bed wrapped in a towel, the Sunday papers strewn around him. The television was on: *Only Fools And Horses.*

'What do you want for supper?'

He combed back his wet hair. 'What have we got?'

'Tons of leftovers.'

'Fine. You look frozen.'

'I am frozen.' She peeled off her clothes, and examined the blotches of brown tea stains on her white trousers. There was a rash of small blisters on her feet from the scalding tea, and a larger one on her heel from where her wellington boots had rubbed earlier in the woods.

She went through into the bathroom. 'Do you think I should call Mrs Letters, or go round?' She stared at herself in the steamed mirror. Her face was sheet white, her eyes like dark beads.

'Call her.'

'If it's died — I —' She bit the skin below her thumbnail. 'Perhaps I should send her some flowers.'

'Or donations to its favourite charity.'

'Don't. That's horrible.'

Fatter. She was definitely getting fatter and losing

121

some of her muscle tone. Her breasts were larger. Maybe that was going to be a perk of growing old? Tom always complained they were too small.

'Bernie the builder said he'd keep an eye on Ben tomorrow. Want to meet up in London?' she said.

'I won't have time. It'll be hectic after two weeks away and I'm playing squash.'

'With Paul?'

'Uh huh.'

There was a roar of laughter from the television.

'There's a message on the machine from him, about cancelling.'

Another roar of laughter, more feverish.

'Oh, ah — yes,' Tom said, his voice sounding rather odd, she thought. 'I forgot. We've got a partners' meeting.'

Her birthmarks stood out tonight, two fine straight lines, each a couple of inches long, one on her stomach, the other on her right thigh. They were red, livid, like weals. They seemed more pronounced than usual. She touched them gingerly.

She heard the rattle of the locket, saw it again, in her mind, lying in the tin. Something inside her rattled too, something dark and cold and ominous. She looked again in the mirror. Her eyes stared back.

Afraid.

She could not sleep. Her mind was alive, crawling, echoing with the pitiful howling of Viola Letters's dog and the image of it thrashing on the grass with the steam rising.

She tried to think of something pleasant, but instead recalled the Chinese box. She could hear the maggots, smell them, wrestling, sweating, climbing over each other with their sharp claws, their concertina bodies heaving, eating through days and nights of never-ending darkness. Eat or be eaten. Their jaws chomping, chomping, each chomp echoing around the tin, a dull boom.

The biggest one had the blunt face of a snarling pug. It was faster, uglier, greedier than the rest. It twisted in the darkness, its body bulging, chopping the rest up until it was surrounded by writhing white shapes that waited, helpless, to be sucked into its mouth until there was nothing left for it to eat, nothing left but to lick the tin shiny clean and wait.

For her.

Inside the folded piece of paper inside the shiny ruby heart inside the tin was a tiny speck of darkness. It was a speck only because it was far away in a dimension she did not understand. A vanishing point on a far horizon. As she opened the tin, opened the heart, unfolded the paper, the speck came at her. Huge, dark, its teeth like rusted blades, fire hurtled out of the dark tunnel of its throat, fierce volcanic flame that stank of Doublemint and melted away the skin of her face.

Tom rolled over and snorted air.

The killings of the night went on out in the darkness, under the light of a moon shrouded in mist. The shrieks, the cries, the crackle of undergrowth. The ecosystem taking care of its own.

Water tumbled down the weir. Boiling water tumbling from the kettle. The howl of Viola Letters's dog joined the screams of the night.

The teeth of the maggot closed, severing her in half below the shoulders. She tossed, twisted, trying to shake the image from her mind.

'Christ, you're restless,' Tom said grumpily. She snuggled up to him, put her arms around him, held him tightly, kissed him, slid her hands down his body.

'Charley, for God's sake! I have an early start. Let me sleep.' He turned away.

She laid her head against the small of his back, smelled his skin, felt its heat, pressed her cheek against him as warm salty tears slid down past her mouth.

Chapter Sixteen

The marigolds had wilted. Charley dropped them in the bin and changed the water in the cut glass vase. 'I'm sorry I didn't come last week, mum, but there was a lot to do in the house. It's in pretty bad condition — worse than we realised. The builders say we should really have a new roof.'

She held the flowers before the blank gaze of the old woman in the bed.

'Michaelmas daisies. They're from the garden.' She arranged the daisies and ferns in the vase by the window. 'We're planting lots of flowers.'

A blind girl with a guide dog walked across the park below.

'Lies death.'

She spun round, but her mother was staring motionless into space. She did not look as if she had moved or spoken. 'What was that?' Charley said. 'What did you say?'

The old woman blinked once and continued her eternal motionless stare.

'Lies death?'

No response.

'Is that what you said, mum?' Charley sat down beside her, took her bony hand. It was the first time she had heard her speak for months. Since before Christmas. 'Lies death, mum? Where does it lie?'

Silence.

She rubbed the old woman's hand. 'What did you mean, mum? Please tell me.'

There was no reaction. Charley waited. Five minutes passed, ten, half an hour. Her mother did not move. Charley stroked her hand gently. 'I went to a hypnotist the other day. To go back into my past lives. Have you had any past lives? Do you believe in that?' She didn't expect a response. There was a faint smell of urine.

'I don't think I believe in it,' Charley said with more conviction than she felt. 'But what was strange was that he made me go back through childhood. I had to tell him what I'd done on my sixteenth birthday, and my tenth. You took me to the zoo, do you remember? I had a ride on a camel. And my fourth birthday. I could remember it in such incredible detail. Daddy spanked me because I rode the bicycle you'd given me into his rhododendron bush. It was a red bicycle, a Raleigh, with whitewall tyres and a white saddle and it had a horn instead of a bell and little fat wheels, and two extra ones on the back for balance. He'd never spanked me before. You said it was his medicine that made him do funny things.'

She thought she detected a faint pressure from her mother's hand, but it might have been her imagination, her own wishful thinking.

'I've been thinking about childhood a lot recently. Maybe because I'm trying so hard to have a child of my own, maybe it's the move. Everyone says moving is pretty traumatic. I've had so many bizarre thoughts. It's noisy in the country, you know? Much noisier than London. Most nights I've lain awake, listening to the animals, watching the moon, thinking about how I used to sit on the floor with you, playing with Florence Doll, packing the bows. I used to feel safe then, with you.' She looked at the bedclothes, at the loose knit of the blanket that heaved gently up and down like the swell of a calm sea. 'I don't feel safe any more.'

As she was leaving she heard the voice again behind her.

'Lies death.'

'I think you should go back to him.'

'I'm frightened.'

Two women stared in through the window of the boutique and pointed at a coat. One said something and the other nodded. They moved on.

'I think this is incredible!' Laura said. She pressed the stop button on the cassette player.

'Sure you do,' said Charley. 'It's not happening to you.'

'Let's hear that bit again.' The tape rewound for several seconds, then Ernest Gibbon's voice:

'Why are you crying? Where are you?'

There was a long silence, while the tape hissed. A girl in culottes opened the door of the shop, changed her mind and went out again.

'Dunno.' The voice was strange, not her own voice. It was a rural working girl's accent.

'Where are you going?' said Gibbon, his voice steady, lethargic.

A minute passed.

'Up an 'ill. There's a rock.'

'Can you describe the rock?'

'Like an 'eart. It's got initials. Like lovers' initials.'

'Do you recognise any of the initials?' said Gibbon.

'D loves BJ. 'E wrote 'em.'

Laura stopped the tape. 'BJ! You said the piece of paper in the locket was signed Barbara, didn't you?'

Charley nodded.

'You see?'

'It doesn't mean anything.'

'It's working, Charley. Don't you see?' Laura seemed irritated.

'See what?'

'Oh, come on! *Barbara J.*'

'Laura, I just dug up someone's locket.'

'Your locket! It's your locket!'

'It wasn't my handwriting.'

A woman came into the shop. She made for a rail of blouses and began flicking through them.

Laura lowered her voice. 'You're not going to have the same handwriting.'

'I don't want to go on any more.'

'Why not? Christ, Charley, you must! Really!'

Charley looked at the customer. 'Can I help you, madam?'

The woman held up a blouse as if it were a mouldy cabbage. 'Hrumph,' she said, hung it back and hoicked out another.

Charley turned to Laura. 'What are you doing after work? Want a quick drink?'

'I — I'd love to, but I've got —' She hesitated. 'Dinner party. I'm having a dinner party.'

'Anyone interesting?' Charley wondered why Laura was blushing. Because she had not invited herself and Tom?

'No, just some friends I haven't seen for a while — people I met on holiday. I don't think you know them.'

'How about Wednesday?' Charley said. 'Maybe catch an early movie. There are several films I want to see.'

'Wednesday? Yes, that sounds great. I'll check my diary.'

The customer held several blouses up to her face, comparing the colours against her skin. She hung them back untidily; one fell on the floor and she ignored it.

'Why don't you want to go on with your regression?'

'Something's telling me to stop, that's why. I had this strange feeling' — she shrugged — 'that I hadn't any business digging it up.'

'But don't you see?' Laura said.

The customer marched over to a row of dresses.

'What has Tom said about the tin?'

'He's sceptical, even more than I am.'

'You're *still* sceptical? Come on!'

'Maybe I imagined it. I don't know. I'm sure there's a perfectly rational explanation.'

'There is.' Laura smiled and looked at her intently. 'You've lived before.'

It was just before seven when Charley turned into the lane. The Citroën bounced through a deep pothole, springing her up and down in her seat.

There were stories of sportsmen who carried on playing to the end of a game with broken legs. The mind was a strange thing. You could carry on, you could believe anything if you tried hard enough; for a while.

The Indian summer was ending. The evening sun shone through the open roof, but the air had an autumnal chill and she felt a coldness that would not go away. Charley knew she believed the discovery of the tin was coincidence the way a footballer believes his broken leg is just bruised, the way a drunk believes he'll feel fine in the morning.

She was frightened.

As she passed Hugh Boxer's house, she heard the sound of a power tool in his workshop. Viola Letters was in her front garden dead-heading her roses. Charley stopped the car, and climbed out.

The old woman came to the gate, her eyes red, a smile mustered on her pallid face and enough gin on her breath to anaesthetise an elephant. Her finger was still bandaged. 'Thanks awfully for the flowers,' she said, 'it was jolly sweet of you.'

'I'm sorry,' Charley said. 'I'm so sorry.'

'Like a snifter?'

'Thanks, but I've got some chores. I must get home. I've been in London.'

'Hardly ever get up there these days. All my old chums are dead or gaga.' She smiled sadly. The cat glared at Charley and kept its distance, as if Charley carried some pestilence. 'It wasn't your fault. I'd noticed the handle was a bit wobbly. I hope you weren't hurt.'

'A few splashes. Nothing. I'm sorry, I really feel awful.'

'You mustn't. I should have thrown the bloody teapot away.' She gazed around her garden. 'The Alexanders have done well this year, don't you think?'

'They're pretty. What's that one?' Charley pointed to a pink tricorn-shaped bud.

'An Admiral Rodney. No relation, I'm afraid.'

There was a silence.

'I — I don't suppose I could rope you in for something else?' the old woman said.

'Yes, of course.'

'It's this Wednesday afternoon. We have a jumble sale in the church hall. Doreen Baxter usually does it with me, but she's ill.'

'I'm meant to be helping a friend with her shop in London on Wednesday, but I could probably change that. I'll give her a call when I get home and ring you back.'

'Very kind of you, dear. Don't worry if you can't.'

'I'm sure it'll be all right.'

Viola Letters blinked. 'Kipling was right you know. Never give your heart to a dog to tear, but we always bloody do.' Her face crinkled as she fought to keep her composure. 'Still. I shan't get another one, not at my age. Wouldn't be fair. Peregrine was thirteen. Kipling said a lot of wise things. Shame he's gone out of fashion.' She mustered a smile again. 'I'd like to invite you and your husband to supper one evening.'

'You must come to us.' Charley ran her finger along the top of the fence. 'I don't seem to be terribly good news for you, do I?'

Viola Letters gave her an odd glance, as if she were about to say something, but changed her mind. In that moment, Charley had the sensation that she had stood at this fence talking like this to the woman before. She looked up at the dark stone wall, at the crenellations against the metallic blue sky, at the small mullioned windows, like the windows of a keep, and the feeling grew stronger.

'I suppose I'd better get on. I'll call you about Wednesday.'

'Thank you, dear,' Viola Letters said, and Charley had the feeling that she felt the same thing. 'And thank Tom for the flowers, will you?'

Charley promised she would.

The phone stopped ringing as she fumbled with her key, and Ben, inside, was barking excitedly. As she pushed open the door, picked up the groceries she had bought on the way home and stumbled into the dim hall, she heard the click of the answering machine. Half the floorboards were up, and lengths of unconnected piping lay around.

A voice in the kitchen echoed around the house. She ran down the passageway.

'... marvellous fun, great food. Great party tricks! Talk to you soon, bye!' It was Richard Howorth. There was a clunk. She dumped the groceries on the kitchen table and rushed over to the machine and lifted the receiver, but he had already hung up. The light winked

131

busily, six messages. Ben was thrashing his paws against her waist.

'Hallo boy, hallo boy! Yes, yes, yes, it's good to see you too!' She knelt and hugged the dog while he splashed her face with licks. 'Have you had a lousy day? Have you? Yes, I know, it's no fun being locked in. Did Bernie let you out? Take you for a walk? Let's go, shall we?'

Ben raced out of the front door and over to a duck that was waddling beside the mill race. The duck took off in panic.

'Ben! Wicked! Wicked boy!' she scolded.

Ben wagged his tail. Long shadows lay across the grass and the drive. It would be dark in an hour. She stared up at the woods. At the hill. The hill with the heart-shaped rock on top and the locket buried in the sandy soil.

A flicker of recognition sparked deep inside her and faded. The roar of the water seemed gentler. The chirruping and trilling and distant cawing of the birds sounded like an orchestra tuning up for the evening's performance. A thrush swooped down near her and pecked at the grass.

She crossed the wooden bridge, pausing to look down into the clear water, brown in the fading light, then climbed up the short mossy bank on to the level patch where the stables had once been. She rummaged around with her feet through the long scrub grass for a sign of stones, foundations, but could see nothing. She sniffed as she thought she noticed a smell of burning, but it had gone, and she walked the width and length, criss-crossed the patch, but there was nothing there, no hint that there ever had been anything other than grass and weeds and earth.

On the opposite bank, across the stream, the house was bathed in a glow from the setting sun. A pile of

132

bricks and building materials lay near the bottom of the steps, covered in plastic sheeting, with two long ladders laid out on the grass next to them.

Up above, at the edge of the woods, was the row of old sheds, a donkey shed, a privy, and an open-sided woodshed. Next to them, running along to the paddock, was the hen run and the kitchen garden.

Cattle lowed and a sheep gave out a single bleat as she walked back over the bridge and along the gravel past the barn. Viola Letters had been so sad. She wished there was something more she could do for the old woman.

The blisters from her wellingtons and the scalding tea made her limp slightly as she climbed the bank. In the paddock beyond the fence two chestnut mares stood silhouetted against the red ball of the sun, and she would have liked to have taken their photograph; except her camera was somewhere at the bottom of a packing case. Time, though. There was all the time in the world for photographs.

The hens clucked and tutted inside the compound that Gideon had fixed. Molly, the white hen, ran in a small circle clucking in fright at Ben. Daisy, white with black speckles, strode out of the henhouse rocking from side to side like a fat lady carrying shopping and pecked at some corn. Clementine, the prettiest, brown with a gold collar, poked her beak through the mesh as if she wanted to have a private word. Ben stared, uncertain still what to make of them.

Charley filled the hopper with feed pellets, ran some water from the stand pipe into the watering can, and filled the drinking bowl. She went to the back of the henhouse, squatted down and unlatched the flap of the nest boxes and slid her hand in. The red bantam they had christened Boadicea gave an outraged squawk and flapped away. Where she had been were two brown eggs, still warm. The other boxes only contained the plaster dummy eggs.

She relatched the flap and went into the run. 'Bedtime, ladies!' She herded the hens into the henhouse, closed the door, carefully shooting the top and bottom bolts, and walked away with a feeling of satisfaction, putting her hand into her pocket and touched the two eggs nestling there. She liked eating their own produce. Early days, but a start.

The kitchen clock said seven forty-five. She put the eggs in the basket on the table, picked up the phone and began dialling.

Chapter Seventeen

Tom lay on top of her, breathing heavily, his chest heaving, heart thumping, sweat running down his body. He rolled gently off, cradling her small shoulders in his arm and ran his fingers through her short razored hair.

She turned to face him, and he wondered what she was thinking. Her eyes looked serious; she opened her mouth, then closed it and studied him further.

He glanced past her at the darkening sky through the window. Going to rain, he thought, watching the winking lights on the roof of Chelsea Harbour Tower in the distance. The room was snug and pretty, white shag carpet, white wicker furniture, all white except for a few green plants; another woman's bedroom; the pleasant unfamiliar smells, different soaps, talcs, perfumes; sensuous; forbidden ground.

He felt the soft skin of her back, his fingers following the contours of her shoulder. 'On Saturday, at dinner, you said we had been lovers in another life. What did you mean?'

She gazed into his eyes. 'I think we've been lovers before. We might meet up in another life and be lovers again.'

Tom wasn't sure what to say. 'I hope you have such lovely skin again,' came out.

She kissed him lightly. 'Charley's a very lucky lady.'

'Oh yes?'

'To have you as a husband.' She pulled away and rolled on to her stomach. He traced a finger slowly down the small of her back and was about to reply, then realised what he was going to say would sound banal.

She kissed him softly on his eye. 'You shouldn't be here. We shouldn't be doing this.'

Tom said nothing.

A compact disc played on the far wall. Tiny columns of blue lights beside it rose and fell in tune with the music, which came out of thick padded speakers. The assured voice of Tanita Tikaram. Meaningless words sung with meaning. Tom heard those kinds of words in his office all day. His mind tuned out of the music and into the traffic noise from the King's Road below. There was a dull ache in his dried-out balls.

Guilt ate him up.

Every day of the week someone like him sat on the other side of his desk in the office. Good-looking guys and ugly guys, smart guys and dumb guys. Nice guys and creeps. He'd never thought that one day he could be in the same equation. Never start something you can't finish was a rule, a maxim, by which he had always lived. You kept order and control over your life that way. The divorce courts were full of people who had started things they could not finish.

A bead of sweat trickled down his back. Laura tidied his hair, tousled it, tidied it. 'Have you ever sensed anything odd in your new house?' she said.

'What do you mean, *odd*?'

'A presence.'

Tom grinned. 'Only this strange rapist at the barbecue.'

'I mean it. You don't think there's anything there?'

'No. Why?'

'When I went to the loo upstairs I sort of — felt something.'

'Has Charley been feeding you some claptrap?'

She slipped out of bed. 'No. I don't know what it is. I don't think I'd particularly want to spend a night there on my own.' She went through into the bathroom. As she closed the door there was a warbling sound beside him that made him jump. It paused, then warbled louder.

'Answer it, Tom, it'll be the plumber,' Laura shouted.

He fumbled, picked up the receiver and pulled it to his face. 'Hallo?' he said breezily. 'Laura Tennent's phone.'

'Tom?'

It was Charley.

He felt as if he was sinking in an express elevator. For a moment he toyed with slamming the phone down. Christ, she'd never know for sure — not absolutely for sure. But it was too late, he had hesitated too long. 'Darling, hi.'

'Tom, what are you doing?'

'Just popped in to have a look at — a letter — rather nasty letter Laura's had. Ah. From Bob.' Bob was Laura's husband.

'Bob?'

'Yes, he's creating a few problems — the house. I'll get her for you. I think she's outside with the plumber.'

'Isn't she having a dinner party?' she said, with faintly disguised hostility.

'Dinner party? No — I. No, I don't think so.'

There was a silence.

'I thought you were having a partners' meeting?'

'I — Laura rang, rather distressed. I —'

'What time will you be home? Are you going to want any supper?'

'Yes, I'm on my way now. Be on the next train, whenever it is.'

The bathroom door opened and Laura came out.

'Hang on, I think I can hear them.' He jammed his hand over the mouthpiece. 'It's Charley,' he hissed. 'I told her I'd popped in to look at a letter from Bob. About the house.'

Laura took the receiver. 'Charley, hi. Dinner party? Oh, yes, I am. It was really sweet of Tom to pop over. I got home and found this absolutely stinking letter from Bob.'

Tom went to the window and stared out. Shit, he thought. Warm air and fumes from the King's Road traffic below wafted around him. A taxi rattled up, a stream of cars, a bus. Shit. Shit. Laura rattled on.

Doing OK, keep it up, girl. Keep it up.

'No, he's on his way now. He's been so sweet — so helpful. Plumbing? Plumbing, did you say? Plumber here? No, I thought you were the plumber phoning.'

Tom's heart sank.

'Want another word with him? OK, see you on Wednesday. No? Oh, all right. Bye!'

She sat down on the bed beside Tom, and lowered her head. Neither spoke for a moment. He put his arm around her.

'How did I do?' she said, turning to look at him.

He stared gloomily back. 'Great,' he said. 'Just great.'

Chapter Eighteen

'Is she a good screw, the bitch?'

Perfectly reasonable explanation. Of course there'll be a perfectly reasonable explanation. Of course.

She forced a smile on her face and tilted her head. 'Hi, darling! How was your meeting?'

Ben looked up at her, puzzled.

It was dark outside now. A cloying blackness pressed against the window panes. Laura had warned her about that, been right about that: the countryside was dark, black, a million times blacker than London.

Laura's flowers were in a vase beside Horace. He drifted in his water, mouth opening and shutting, gawping at the endless movie he watched through the curved glass. Charley wondered if he realised that he saw everything distorted, as if he were watching life through a hall of mirrors reflection. She wondered if she saw it distorted too.

There was a faint smell of laundry in the kitchen, from the dishcloths and socks and underwear and Tom's striped shirts hanging on the drying rack above her. 'How was Laura? OK, was she? I mean she was fine when I saw her, just fine. But that was five o'clock and she couldn't come for a drink because she was hurrying home to organise a dinner party.'

Ben's tail wagged. He dropped the bone he had been chomping on and padded over expectantly. 'Not for you, boy,' she said, staring at the lumps of steak on the chopping board. Nothing. Nothing. Nothing to worry about.

It was really sweet of Tom to pop over. I got home and found this absolutely stinking letter from Bob.

Why the hell shouldn't Laura have had a letter from Bob? Bob was always causing Laura trouble. Perfectly reasonable. Yes-yes-yes. Tom had gone round because ...

Is she a good screw, the bitch?

Charley stood still for a moment. The thought slammed through her; the words; as if someone else were speaking them, whispering them into her ear. They repeated louder, more insistent. She shook her head, trying to clear it. Not Laura. No. Maybe others, but not Laura. Definitely not.

Never.

Friends didn't do that. Not friends who went back twenty years.

The kettle boiled and she poured some water into her mug. She stirred the coffee. Tom's steak was thick, red, huge; she had asked the woman to cut it thick and she had, a massive T-bone. She prodded it and felt squeamish suddenly at the soft slimy texture.

A navy blue sock fell silently on to it.

She looked up at the drying rack. It was motionless. The other sock still hung from one of the wooden rails. Ben let out a low rumbling growl. Her eyes narrowed, her heart was beating a little faster than it should. She picked the sock off the steak and saw that some of the cotton fibres had stuck to the meat.

She didn't feel squeamish any more. It looked good as it was, raw. Flesh. Red meat. Bloody. She wanted to eat it, to cram it into her mouth and chew it raw, like an animal. She remembered, vaguely, a book she had read where a woman had a craving for raw meat.

She picked up her piece of steak, cut thinner than Tom's, and bit a mouthful off it. Her eyes screwed up and bile heaved in her stomach. She leaned forward, spat the chewed meat out into the sink, ran the tap, held her mouth under it, swilled the water around and spat it out.

Ye gods.

Why on earth had she done that? The taste lingered, of blood, flesh, something rancid, something — She gulped at the coffee and spat that out too, then, feeling sick she ran upstairs into the bedroom, through to the bathroom and brushed her teeth.

She leaned against the basin. In the mirror her eyes were red and puffy from crying. Crying because she knew ... knew that he had not gone there to look at a letter from Bob.

Her mouth tasted better, minty. She went into the bedroom, sat down at her dressing table and dabbed some powder on her face, then tidied up her smudged mascara. Anger welled inside her again.

The front door opened and closed and she was surprised not to hear Ben barking. Still absorbed with his bone, she assumed, and tried to prod some life into her hair.

The stairs creaked; Tom's footsteps up it, slow, as if he was tired, or nervous of a confrontation.

Stay calm. Cool. She tossed her head and tried to concentrate on her hair, tried to ignore him as she heard him come in the door, heard him walk across the slanting floor and felt him standing behind her.

Cold air had come in with him. Bitter cold air. The room felt like a freezer. She stared in the mirror.

But could not see him.

She felt the icy breath down her neck and smelled a musky perfume. She spun round.

There was no one. The room was empty.

But a smell of perfume hung in the air. Strong. Shivers ran down the small of her back. It was perfume she had smelled before, knew from somewhere. The room reeked of it, as if someone wearing it was there. Her eyes darted around.

'Tom?' she called out. 'Tom?' She walked across the floor, peered into the bathroom, stared at the bath, at the shower curtain, walked back into the bedroom, stood and listened.

She went out on to the landing. The cold air seemed to follow her. 'Tom?' She sniffed, but there was nothing now, no smell. Goosepimples prickled her. 'Tom? Is that you?'

Slowly, nervously, she went downstairs. 'Tom?'

She walked along the dim passageway, past the cellar door and into the kitchen. Ben was gnawing busily. She stopped, listened again. The door; she was certain she had heard the front door, footsteps up the stairs. Smelled the perfume. She stared at the drying rack, nervous of it for some reason, stared at the single blue sock, then lowered the rack slowly, creakily, paying out the cord and hung back the second sock.

Bright lights flashed against the window. A car scrunched down the gravel outside. Tom's car.

Instead of anger, as she walked down the passageway to greet him, she felt only relief.

Charley gazed through the curtainless window at the black starless night. Tom slept beside her, breathing heavily, smelling clean, squeaky clean, exuding a faint odour of pine shampoo.

She'd cooked him his steak, exactly as he liked it and he'd sat at the kitchen table opposite her and eaten his way through it silently, mechanically, not dining, merely refuelling.

Throughout their marriage there had been many

times before when they had eaten in silence, when Tom had been in one of his moods, moods that had often lasted for days. But tonight it wasn't one of his moods, and Charley wished it was because she understood those, knew that with a mood it was a matter of waiting and everything would be OK again.

Tonight something had changed, in both of them.

She wished they were back in London, in their small house with the streetlights and cars outside and neighbours around, the house where they had begun their married life, where they had made their home. Where they had been happy.

Ben padded around the room, his name-tag jingling from his collar, restless.

There was a cry outside, like a woman in distress. Ben barked and Tom stirred slightly.

Ben whined and pawed at the door.

'Foxes,' Tom grunted. 'Vixens.'

She dozed. Images flashed in her mind, and she could not sleep. She listened to the roar of water, heard the hissing of the urn, the howls of Viola Letters's dog. Howls. Shrieks. Screams.

'Jesus Christ!'

The bed moved, creaked. She opened her eyes. Tom stood silhouetted at the window. Her clock radio said 4.35. Then she realised.

The sound was real.

It was coming from outside. Dreadful panicky squawking, screeching. Ben was barking frantically. Tom pulled on his dressing gown. She ran downstairs after him, into the kitchen and jammed her bare feet into her wellington boots.

They ran across the wet grass, under the streaky back-lit sky, the noise getting worse the closer to the hen run they got, a hideous cacophony of clucking and beating wings and croaking and clattering wire, and a lump swelled up inside her throat. Ben stopped, unable to comprehend what was going on.

At first she was unable to comprehend also. She thought they were panicked, that was all. They were flapping wildly, Boadicea and Daisy and Clementine and Molly, rolling around as if they were drunk, crashing into each other, into the wire, falling over, pulling themselves along the floor of the run by their wings like old people on crutches. It was as if someone was shaking the run like a box. Boadicea rose up in the air, crashed into the netting, fell upside down, her neck twisting, her beak opening and shutting, her legs kicking, two bloody feetless stumps.

Charley clutched Tom's arm. Molly cartwheeled over and over, blood smeared across the white feathers of her stomach. She crashed into the mesh in front of Charley, trying to push her head through as if she was screaming for help.

'Jesus,' Tom said. 'Bastard. Bastard.'

Charley stared in horror at a twig on the ground, a thin grey gnarled twig, except it wasn't a twig, it was the foot of one of the hens. Then she saw another.

All the hens' feet had been severed.

Boadicea tried to stand on her bloody stumps, Boadicea who had been so proud now fell over sideways, chewing at the ground with her beak.

The bile slid up and she turned away and was sick on the ground behind her, her ears filled with the pitiful agony of the clucking and flapping. Tom marched into the run. He knelt and grabbed Boadicea firmly, gave a sudden sharp twist of his hand, there was a crunch and the hen went limp. Blood dripped down.

The cacophony of sound seemed to be getting louder. The wings of a hen thrashed against Charley's face, blood sprayed over her. It was Clementine. Charley picked her up, but she wriggled free and fell to the ground showering blood and feathers. She tried again, holding on harder, and put her hand on the hen's neck. For a moment Clementine was motionless, staring her straight in the eye, her beak opening and shutting as if she were trying to speak. Charley put her down and turned away.

She stumbled out of the run and sat down on the wet grass of the bank, listening to Ben barking and the cries of the hens quieting as Tom worked through them, the same pattern, a flurry of squawking, a crunch, a brief silence. Then a final silence, complete silence, even from Ben, even from the dawn chorus of birds, even, it seemed, from the weir.

Tom sat beside her, his face and dressing gown spattered in blood and excrement and feathers, and wiped his hands on the grass. 'I thought humans were the only creatures that killed for sport,' he said.

The air was full of the coppery smell of blood and the stench of damp feathers and the sweet morning dew. The sky above the lake was streaked with brushstrokes of pink and yellow and grey. She stared at it dully through her haze of tears. It was going to be a beautiful day.

Chapter Nineteen

Charley sat in the morning sun holding her mother's hand as she always did, staring at the flowers in the crystal vase and the oak chest of drawers on which they stood that contained most of her mother's possessions.

A few clothes, some photographs, trinkets, a passport with its one single purple stamp on its blank pages, '10 Jul. 1978, Entrada A Barcelona', the only time her mother had ever been abroad. Charley and Tom had taken her with them on holiday to a villa they had rented in Spain. Her mother hadn't liked it much — too hot, she had said apologetically, and the toilet had a peculiar smell.

'We lost our hens on Monday night. It was horrible. The fox didn't kill them, he just bit off their legs. I wanted to bury them and Tom said that was ridiculous and got angry. He said we'd have eaten them anyway.

'I couldn't do that. I buried them up in the woods, then I bought four chickens from Safeways and put them in the freezer, so he won't know.'

Her mother's nails were getting long, would need cutting soon. 'I think Tom's having an affair. But I can't say anything in case I'm wrong. I'd look a bloody fool.' She hesitated. 'You know who I think he's having it with? Laura.'

Laura. The name stuck in her gullet.

'Did daddy ever do anything like that?'

There was no reaction; they sat in silence for a while.

'What did you mean, mum, on Monday when I was here? You said "lies death". At least, that's what it sounded like. *Lies death*. What did you mean?'

There was a rasp of breath, different to the normal pattern. Her mother was trembling and perspiration was trickling down her face. 'What is it, mum? Are you OK?' A child shouted outside and there was a burst of music from a car radio that was too loud. Her cream gabardine dress was feeling too tight and stuck to her skin. It was always like a hothouse in here, summer and winter.

'I wish we could talk, mum, like we used to. There's so much I need to know from you. So much advice I'd like. I don't have anyone else to ask.'

There was another silence. After a while Charley said, 'Horace is still going strong. My goldfish. Remember him? He's eleven now. Tom won him at a funfair by shooting at ping-pong balls. He was in a tiny plastic bag and we never thought he'd make it home, let alone live for eleven years.' She scanned her mother's face, seeking a glimmer, but saw nothing. She stroked her hand gently. 'Funny how you get attached to things. Even a dumb fish in a bowl can be your friend.'

'Truth,' her mother said suddenly. 'Go back.'

Charley looked at her, startled, but she was staring blankly ahead again. '"Truth", mum? "Go back"?'

There was no reaction.

'What do you mean *truth*?' She leaned closer. 'What truth? Go back where?'

Nothing. Charley listened to the traffic outside. A telephone rang in another room. Her mother still trembled.

'I helped out at a jumble sale yesterday in the church hall in Elmwood. There's an old lady down the lane —

147

Viola Letters — that's an old-fashioned name, Viola, isn't it? She's getting me involved in the local community. A nice old stick. She doesn't have any children either. Been a widow for years. You've been a widow for years too, haven't you? Would you have liked to have remarried? Did I stop you, make it harder for you?'

Charley chatted on, trying to sound jolly through her heavy heart, about the party they were going to on Saturday, colours they had chosen for some of their rooms and the carpets they were going to look at. They thought a rug for the bedroom floor, keeping the bare wooden floorboards either side, would be more in character than wall-to-wall carpeting.

Her mother made no further sounds and gradually the trembling subsided during the next two hours. She was still staring vacantly ahead as Charley left, blowing her one final hopeful kiss from the door.

'Tom, if I wanted to trace my real parents what would the procedure be?'

He dug around disinterestedly in his salad bowl, elbows on the kitchen table, his striped office shirt opened at the collar and the cuffs rolled up. He lifted a forkful of mung beans and alfalfa sprouts and gazed dubiously at it. 'I thought you weren't interested in tracing your parents.'

A light breeze came through the open windows and a late bird twittered. She speared a couple of pasta shells. 'I used not to be. I suppose I am a bit now. I thought if we ever did have children it might be nice for them to know their ancestry.'

'Your parents are dead.'

She ate a mouthful. 'There might be aunts and uncles.'

He chewed his sprouts and screwed up his face.

'Christ, these taste like an old sack.' He had a pallor of grease on his skin from London that a quick dab from the cold tap had not cleaned away. He looked tired, strained. The way she felt. 'Charley, when people are adopted it's usually because there aren't any relatives who can — or want to — care for the baby.'

'I'm not saying I'm going to contact anyone. I think I'd like to know. I mean it's not as if I was the result of a one-night stand or anything like that. My parents were married.'

'Your mother died giving birth to you and your father died of a broken heart. Right?'

'That's what mum always told me.'

'He probably died of something else.' He frowned. 'How would your mum have known that, anyway?'

'That he died of a broken heart?' She shrugged. 'No idea. I've never thought about it.'

'You were adopted within a few days of being born, weren't you?'

'Yes.'

'People who die of broken hearts don't die immediately. And adoptive parents never usually maintain contact with the real parents.'

'Maybe he had a heart attack or something,' Charley said.

'Has your mum ever told you anything about them?'

'Not really. They were young, hadn't been married very long — about a year.' She drank some wine but it made her feel queasy.

'Do you know their name?'

'No.'

'The hospital where you were born?'

'No.' She saw her adoptive mother trembling in her bed.

'If they had a common name, it can be very difficult. I've known it take years — and cost a fortune.'

'What's the procedure?' she said. Her voice was barely more than a whisper.

'You have to apply for your original birth certificate at St Catherine's House in London.'

'Is that a long process?' It seemed as if it were someone else speaking.

Lies death.

Lies.

Lies about her parents' death? Was that what her mother had been trying to say? That she had told lies about their death?

Truth. Go back.

She remembered her mother trembling when she first told her they were moving. Had she started trembling because they were moving?

Or because of where they were moving to?

Go back.

Where?

A fat hamburger slid past, leaking gherkins and ketchup from its midriff like an open wound. It was followed by a plate of bacon and eggs, then a girl tossing her long brown hair in the wind.

'Alpha Temps. Join the smart set!'

Charley stood wedged in the crowd as the escalators carried her upwards like flotsam on a wave.

The rush hour. A few weeks of country living and she was feeling increasingly an alien in London. She stepped out into the daylight, found her bearings and turned right down the Strand.

She had not been back to the boutique, had not spoken to Laura since that Monday night. The thought of Laura at the moment made her uneasy. She was certain last night, when Tom had arrived back late again, that she had smelled Laura's perfume on him.

The words 'ST CATHERINE'S HOUSE' were clearly

visible on the other side of the Aldwych. The building had large glass doors and a sign 'Wet Paint — Use Other Entrance'.

Inside were two enquiry desks, a felt board with several blank forms pinned to it and some steps up to a large modern room filled with rows of metal book-shelves. Although teeming with people, the place had the studious quietness of a public library.

She joined a small queue for the desk marked 'Enquiries only', and waited her turn.

'I'm adopted,' she said, feeling as if she were saying *I'm a leper.* 'I want to get a copy of my original birth certificate.'

The clerk, a small man with a cosy smile, pointed round to the right. 'You'll need the reference number,' he said. 'Those rows there are Adoptions.'

She walked along the brightly lit corridor between the rows of files. It was strange to have your identity hidden behind a reference number. There was a rack of metal shelves against the wall with 'Adoptions 1927 onwards,' printed above.

She half wanted to turn away, forget the whole thing. What if? If?

Lies death. If what her mother had told her had been a lie?

So what if it was? If the truth was different, would it matter? She had met an adopted woman who had traced her parents and discovered she was the product of a one-night stand in the rear of an army truck. But that hadn't made any difference, had not brought her world crashing down. She always said she was pleased she knew, felt more comfortable with life for knowing.

And if she had been the product of a one-night stand she wouldn't have to tell her children, or anyone else (unless, maybe, it had been a duke). And if she was the daughter of a hooker or (please not an escaped loony) a criminal, well, that would be a shock. And maybe a secret. But at least she would know.

'1952. 1953. 1954.'

She lifted the ochre fabric-bound volume out. It was heavier than it looked. She laid it down on the flat writing surface and opened it. The pages were dry and turned with a sharp rustle; she was wary of tearing them. Boone. Boot. Booth.

There were about fifteen Booths, typed on old black typewriter ribbons. She ran her eyes down them, then stopped, feeling a sense almost of embarrassment at seeing her own maiden name there in print.

'Booth. Charlotte Lesley. 12.8.53. No. of entry: 5A0712. Vol No. 388.'

That was all. Somehow she had expected there to be something more, something that might make it feel special. But there was nothing special. The ink was thicker on some entries than others, where errors had been corrected.

She read it several times, glanced at the rest of the Booths, wondering who they were and where they had ended up, wondered how many others had made the same journey here and had stared at the same page and felt the same flatness when they should have been excited.

She took the book back to the clerk's desk.

'You have to fill in one of those.' He tapped a buff and yellow form on the felt noticeboard. 'They're out on the counters. Were you adopted before 12th November 1975?'

'Yes.'

'You have to send one of those to the CA section of the GRO. General Register Office,' he translated, seeing her blank face. 'The address is on the back. They'll send you an adoptee's application form and get in touch with you about counselling.'

'Counselling?'

'It's the law, I'm afraid. You'll have to be counselled. You can fill in the form I've given you here, if you like, and we'll send it off for you.'

She went into a stall, pulled out the antique Sheaffer fountain pen Tom had given her for her birthday, and pressed the nib lightly against the form.

There was a sudden tang of musky perfume. She began to write. The smell became stronger, engulfing her, as if the wearer were leaning over her shoulder. She turned, but there was no one behind her; nothing but the empty stall across the narrow corridor.

Chapter Twenty

The remains of the simple picnic were spread beside them and she lay back contented, her head nestling against his chest, smelling the sweet scents of the flowers and grasses.

His fingers ran through her hair, and the sun beat down between the trees. She closed her eyes and watched warm red spots dancing in the darkness. The chattering of the birds felt lazy, too, and the breeze rustled the leaves like the sea lapping on a shore. The ground seemed to sway a little, and she imagined they were castaways on a raft on a flat blue ocean.

Somewhere in the distance she heard horses' hooves.

The fingers touched her cheek and then her lips, and she bit one gently with her teeth. His stomach rumbled loudly and the baby inside her own belly made a few tiny jerks. She opened her eyes and saw a tortoiseshell butterfly skim the bluebells that were all around them.

He shifted his position and his face was over hers. He kissed her and she could taste the beer and sausage on his breath. She put her hand up to his chin, felt the rough stubble, and stroked it.

'Your name? Can you tell me your name?' a voice said.

He traced a line down her neck, then slid his hand inside her frock, inside her brassiere and began to fondle her breasts. He took hold of a nipple between his finger and thumb and she flinched.

'Ow! Careful! It's sore!'

'Your name? Tell me your name!'

Not far away a horse whinnied.

'Dunno.'

'Who is the man you are with? Your boyfriend? Husband?'

A hand was on her knee, sliding up her thigh, coarse fingers moving up her bare flesh.

'Do you know where you are?'

'Bluebells,' she murmured, irritated by the intrusion, wishing the voice would go away. The branches swayed above her, sunlight dappled through the leaves. A bee buzzed past them, a bird flew overhead, then the man's face blocked out the light as his lips pressed down again, his tongue ran along her teeth and searched hungrily inside her mouth. His fingers slid inside her knickers, tugged their way through her pubic hair. She tightened, pushed his hand firmly back down, said, 'No. The baby. We mustn't.'

'Course we can.'

The hand pushed its way back up.

'No!' She giggled. 'Stop it.'

'Won't do any harm.'

'It will. We mustn't.'

'Don't be a stupid cow.'

'Dick, please.' She closed her knees together. He rolled away from her and she sensed his anger.

She lay still. Her heart felt heavy and she did not know why. She lifted the locket that lay on her chest and stared at it, the heart-shaped stone glinting in the sunlight, ruby red, the gold chain sparkling. Then a shadow fell across the locket. A horse stamped its right foot behind her.

She looked up.

A woman on a chestnut horse, silhouetted against

the sky, stared down at them. She had fine features, handsome but severe, jet black hair tied back below her hat, and an elegant hacking jacket, smart breeches and shiny boots.

The woman's eyes were shadowed by the peak of her velvet riding hat, but they seemed to burn like sun through a mist. She could feel scorn, disgust, and something else — something that made her afraid.

Before she could react the woman had turned and ridden off, but the stare of the eyes remained and burned into her own retinas like sun spots.

Her dress was up over her stomach, and she tugged it down and giggled, a solitary giggle that fell away into silence. 'She must have seen. Why didn't she say nothing?'

He stood up abruptly, brushing the grass from his trousers.

'She was dressed fancy,' she said. 'I ain't seen her before. She must be stayin' at the manor.'

'She's from London,' he said brusquely. 'A lady. She's rented old Markham's place for the summer.'

'The mill?'

'Wants to buy it, I'm told.'

'That's 'er? The one they talkin' about? She ain't no lady from what they say.' The venom in the woman's eyes was vivid. 'Was that Jemma she were ridin'?'

'She's paying good money for me to saddle her.'

'Jemma's *my* 'orse. You promised.'

'After the summer. Anyway, you shouldn't be riding at the moment.'

'They say she's loose.'

'She's a lady,' he said, his voice rising.

'Do you think she's pretty?'

He did not reply and she put out her hand to him. 'Dick, you love me, don't yer?' It was dark suddenly. She was cold, shivering. 'Dick?' Dick?'

She smelled burning. Flames licked the darkness. Flames all around. Horses whinnied. There was a splintering crack above and a burning beam was tumbling down on her.

She screamed. Ran. Another beam fell in front of her, more beams were falling. Flames everywhere. A figure staggered towards her, a human being burning like a torch. She screamed again, turning, running, running into a wall of flame.

The flame dissolved into a red glow.

Eyes looked at her, myopic eyes through thick lenses. Anxious eyes. A voice intoned, 'Charley, wake up now please. You are back in the present. You are no longer in trance. You are back with us. You are safe.'

She saw the sad hang-dog face, the centre parting, the mutton chop sideburns, the cardigan the colour of dried mustard. Ernest Gibbon's crows' feet crinkled into the hint of a smile and his baggy jowls heaved. The microphone in its foam padding peered down at her like an inquisitive bird.

'You are quite safe, Charley,' he said in his soporific monotone. 'You're back with us.'

Tight bands of anxiety seemed to be cutting into her skin. Her heart thumped and her pulses throbbed.

'Dick,' the hypnotist said. 'You called him Dick. Can you remember your name?'

She lay motionless for some while, then shook her head.

'Do you know where you were? Did you recognise it?'

She thought hard before answering, trying to clear her mind, trying to work up the energy to speak. 'Woods near where we live. I think I was asleep — dreaming — just a bad dream. There's a girlfriend who —' She paused, partly from tiredness, partly from embarrassment, and smiled lamely. 'I — I'm jealous of.

157

Probably nothing in it. I keep thinking she's making a beeline for my husband. I think I was dreaming about her.'

'No, you were in a previous carnation,' he said, as blandly as if he were talking about the weather. His jowls heaved up and down as if he were chewing a cud.

A vague smell of cooking was seeping into the room. Meat, potatoes, gravy. It made her feel queasy. Outside she could hear the wail of a siren and rain tapped on the window. Smells and sounds that should have been normal seemed alien.

'What can you remember about the man you were with, Charley?'

'I — I've seen him before.'

'Would you like to tell me when?'

'I told you I was regressed once before I came to you. I think it's the same person.'

'Can you describe him?'

'Quite nice looking. Rugged. He had short brown hair. Stocky, wiry. A bit like — I suppose he looked like that actor Bruce Willis but rougher. He was attractive.'

Gibbon pulled out a large polka dot handkerchief and began wiping his glasses. 'Was he a farmer?'

'Yes.' Her voice tailed off. 'I'm not sure. I think so.'

'Were you living with him?'

'Yes.'

'Did you have a wedding ring?'

'I don't know. Locket,' she said. 'I had the locket, the same locket I found in the tin I dug up. The tin I buried last time —'

He studied her. 'And you were pregnant?'

She nodded.

'Is there anything else you can remember about yourself? The clothes you were wearing?'

She thought. 'A frock. A sort of muslin frock.'

He finished cleaning his glasses, and put them unhurriedly back on, settling them comfortably, adjusting first one side then the other. 'Do you know what time period? Which century?'

'It didn't seem that long ago.'

'How long ago?'

'It felt quite recent.'

'All past lives feel quite recent, Charley.' He breathed slowly, steadily; the wheezing made him sound as if he were asleep.

'It had to be recent,' she said, hope dawning. 'The woman was riding astride. She wore breeches. So I could have gone to the Wishing Rocks and watched someone bury it years ago and have forgotten. Cryptic something, isn't it, when you've forgotten something you've done or read as a child?'

'Cryptomnesia,' he said, with a faintly glazed look, as if he were used to trotting out the same old defence against the same old hoary argument. 'How much proof do you require?' His voice sounded testy.

'I don't know,' she said, deflated.

'Are you frightened?'

'A little.'

'What of?'

'I'm not sure.'

He smiled a smug teacher-knows-best smile. 'Are you frightened of the idea of having lived before?'

'I've always been sceptical about the supernatural. I still don't believe that ...' The self-satisfied smile on his face distracted her, irritated her.

'Don't believe or don't *want* to believe?'

She said nothing.

'People who come to me are often full of traumas they don't understand. These are caused by unpleasant happenings in previous carnations. Once people understand the reason for the trauma, the trauma goes.' His dreary voice could as easily have been reading out the instructions on a washing machine. 'You want to have children, and are not conceiving. Now in this previous carnation we find you have been pregnant and some trauma has occurred — something which frightens you so much you can't face it and I have to bring you back out. It could be the memory of this trauma that's blocking you from conceiving.'

The words stirred something. A tiny frisson of doubt tapped its way down her corridors of nerves.

'I've regressed many thousands of people, Charley,' the hypnotist continued. 'There are others who have found some sort of evidence to prove their regressions have not just been cryptomnesia, names in books ... landscapes ... But to go out and find an object, a buried object ... This hasn't happened before, you see. We need to continue, to have another session. It's very important.'

'Do you think we might find more buried treasure?' she said more cheerily than she felt. He did not smile back.

'It's not the locket, Charley. It's what we've dug up inside you. It's the connection.' His face tightened into trembling concentration. 'There's something in your past that ...'

'That what?' she prodded, his expression making her nervous.

'That's more than a memory.'

'I don't understand.'

'It's — it must be something malevolent you've done in that carnation and I believe you have brought it with you, into this present life.'

'Brought what with me?'

'It's that we need to find out.'

'I don't want to go on any more.'

'I don't think it's up to you to decide,' he said.

160

'What do you mean?' Anger arose at the smug, weird man. Creep.

'You could bury the locket back on the hill, but you can't bury this back in your mind. You see, it's very strong. We had better make another appointment.'

You bastard, she thought. This is all a trick; a great con. 'I'll think about it.' She opened her handbag and took out her purse. 'Thirty-five pounds?'

He shook his head and waved a hand dismissively. 'Give it to a charity. I support Guide Dogs for the Blind.'

She stared at him in amazement. 'Why?'

'Because I don't want you to think I'm a confidence trickster.' He smiled another teacher-knows-best smile, then stood up wearily and walked towards the door.

Chapter Twenty-One

'Surprise him! Greet him at the front door in a sexy negligee with a glass of his favourite drink in your hand and music playing. Give him a candlelit dinner of his favourite foods; pamper him at the table; cherish him. Don't break the spell ... leave the washing up till morning!'

Charley glanced around the crowded train compartment, trying to keep the cover of the magazine as low in her lap as possible so that no one could see the lurid teaser that had made her buy it at the bookstall.

HOW TO KEEP YOUR MAN TURNED ON!

The train rattled south, rain streaking the windows, through Gatwick Airport, backpackers waiting on the platform like refugees, past the hangars, the parked aircraft. A Jumbo was coming in overhead and she watched it until a tall warehouse blocked her view, regretting they'd cancelled their holiday in Greece because of moving; holidays were the only times these days she and Tom seemed to get remotely close.

She had played the tapes of her regression over and over when Tom had not been around, not wanting him to know she had been again, had spent more money. Each time she played them, part of her grew a little more sceptical and part of her a little more afraid.

She had worked in the boutique today, but had not seen Laura who had gone to France for two days, buying. They had not seen each other since her phone call to Laura which Tom had answered; when they had spoken on the phone a couple of days ago, Laura had chatted gaily; too gaily.

She had left the boutique at four, leaving another part-timer there, and gone to the nursing home to visit her adoptive mother. She had told her she had started the procedure for finding her real parents, and had half expected some angry reaction, but that had not happened. If anything (although she knew she might have imagined it) she thought she noticed a small expression of relief.

Sussex countryside was sliding by, and darkness was falling fast. A good-looking man in his mid-twenties was eyeing her. Being eyed always made her feel good, boosted her confidence. Right now it needed boosting.

Then she wondered if he had seen the cover of the magazine, if that was why he was smiling.

Her heart felt heavy again. She and Tom had made love once since they'd moved in, on the first night. For a long while they had only made love once a month, but that had been deliberate, on the instructions of her acupuncturist. The acupuncturist Laura had recommended, whose needles hurt like hell (even though Laura insisted they didn't), who assured her she would become pregnant very quickly.

Nothing wrong ... nothing wrong ... nothing wrong. Her brain beat to the rhythm of the train, to the rhythm of the specialists they had seen over the years.

Nothing wrong, nothing wrong, nothing wrong.

She had ditched the acupuncturist, the funny little man with his strange ideas on celibacy and body balance and energy, and the pungent herbs he burned from time to time and applied against her body. '*What are you trying to do? Conjure up a baby from black magic?*' she had said jokingly to him once, but he had not been amused.

Now she wanted to make love with Tom, wanted it more than at any time in years, and he was not responding.

On Sunday he'd gone off for the day, told her he had to go to the office to deal with an urgent problem. On Sunday night he'd smelled of Laura's perfume.

The rooftops of Haywards Heath appeared and the train slowed. She stood up and lifted the smart Janet Reger bag down from the luggage rack. It weighed nothing, and for a moment she was worried the negligee had fallen out. She opened it and peeked in. She could see the black lace and the receipt and her Access slip lying loosely down the side. £145.

She began to smile as she stepped off the train and joined the queue at the ticket barrier. Tom would be mad as hell. Good. He hadn't lost his temper for ages. Maybe it was time. Sometimes their lovemaking was at its most tender after Tom had come out of one of his tempers.

Outside the station a line of cars waited, engines running, wipers shovelling away the rain, dutiful wives in their Volvos and Range Rovers and Japanese runabouts with their *Baby on Board* stickers and children's faces pressed against the windows.

She felt a twinge of sadness, as if there was some cosy family club from which she was excluded, barred.

It was nearly a quarter to eight as she turned into the lane. She'd had to go to Safeways in Lewes to get steaks, and she'd bought scallops there as well. His favourite foods, as the article in the magazine had told her to do.

Scallops, steak, then vanilla ice cream with hot fudge sauce.

And sod the cost.

The memory of Apstead Road, Wandsworth, was beginning to fade. The new woman in there had rung up a couple of times relaying phone messages, but she hadn't been very communicative, hadn't said how much they loved the house. In fact, she'd sounded a little pissed off. Maybe they'd found damp or rot, though Charley knew there was nothing much wrong, apart from the leak in the roof of the utility room which she'd kept guiltily quiet about. It only leaked in heavy rain. It was probably leaking now.

Headlights came out of Yuppie Towers. It was Zoe in her Range Rover. 'Charley, hi!' She wound her window down and made a face against the weather. 'We're going to the George tomorrow. Do you and Tom feel like joining us?'

'That would be nice, thanks — if he's down in time.'

Zoe shielded her face with her hand. 'See how you feel. Got to pick up the kids. Bye!'

Charley drove on down the lane. Hugh's workshop doors were battened tightly shut, and a television flickered through the drawing room window of Rose Cottage.

She felt lonely as she drove down the steep hill, under the shadowy arches of the trees of the wood. Tom was playing squash and wouldn't be home until after nine. Her headlights picked out the green hull of the upturned skiff, and the sign 'PRIVATE. MEMBERS ONLY. NO FISHING', nailed to the tree. They'd seen a few people fishing at the weekends, and one or two in the early evenings. There was a small card in the window of the grocery shop in Elmwood village with details of a name to phone for membership.

The surface of the lake was spiked by the rain, and an arc of grubby froth slopped against the bank. There was straw lying on the gravel and she looked at it, surprised for a moment, then remembered that today Hugh had been moving the old car out. The rain increased, stalactites of water hurtled down from the sky and shattered in tiny sprays on the ground. She sprinted with her carrier bag for the front door. She could hear Ben barking. 'OK, boy!' she shouted as she went into the hall and switched on the light. Then she stopped, staring at the hall table.

It was lying on its side in the middle of the floor, the mail scattered around it.

Ben? Had he knocked it over? She peered down the dark passage. There was a tremendous bang behind her. She spun round. The wind had slammed the front door shut.

Christ. Her nerves were shot to pieces. She switched the passageway light on, and, water running down her face, her clothes drenched, went into the kitchen. Ben barrelled out, jumping up. 'Did Bernie look after you again? Take you for a walk, did he? Let's go, outside!'

He loped down the passageway. She followed and stared uneasily at the table in the hall. How had it fallen over? Surely Bernie, or the other builders, or the plumber or electrician would have had the nous to pick it up? Clumsy fools. She would speak to them about it in the morning.

She let Ben out; he ran down the steps and cocked his leg on the polythene sheeting the workmen had left over their materials. She grabbed the groceries from the boot of the Citroën and rushed back in, Ben following.

A buckshot volley of rain struck the windows. Wind yowled down the inglenook and something scuffled about inside it, rapping against the chimney breast.

166

Twigs of a bird's nest dislodged, she thought, breathing out a little as whatever it was fell and rattled against the sides. The wind moaned like breath against a bottle top.

Ben pattered along the passageway unconcerned, his collar jingling. She heaved the heavy table upright and examined its sturdy legs. They were fine. It hadn't fallen over of its own accord, and no one could have knocked it over without noticing.

She heard a scrape upstairs, and froze. She looked up the dark stairwell, listening. Ben drank from his bowl with a loud slurping. There was another volley of rain. A clank.

Kerwumph.

Just the new boiler. Water flowing through the pipes. The plumber wanted to leave it on for a few days, to check the system. It must be on low because there was a damp chill in the house. She replaced the mail on the table, another wodge of redirected letters from London, bills, circulars, a handwritten enveloped which she opened; it was a belated thank you from the Orpens.

She carried the groceries through into the kitchen and put them on the table. It was warm in here from the Aga. The red light on the answering machine was static; no messages. The goldfish drifted around in its bowl. She fed Ben, then boiled some water and took out the mug Tom had given her a few years back with 'Happy Xmas Charley' printed on it. She heaped in a larger spoon of coffee than usual to try to stop herself yawning, poured in the water, then put the steaming mug down on the table and emptied the scallops out of the white plastic bag into the sink.

Ben let out a low, rumbling growl.

'What is it, boy?'

A blast of cold air, colder than a midwinter draught, engulfed her.

167

Ben barked at the ceiling, back at her, then at the ceiling again. The drying rack swayed. The chill passed as suddenly as it had come, leaving her hugging her arms around her body.

'Shh, boy!' she hissed, trying to keep her voice low, like a child keeping its eyes tightly shut in the dark. Her hand went to her mouth and she bit at the skin on her thumb, staring at the ceiling, at the drying rack, at the pulleys, listening, listening. She could hear nothing.

She picked up the mug, sipped, and jerked it away from her mouth with a start: the coffee was stone cold. It was the right mug — Happy Xmas Charley.

Ben sniffed the floor and the skirting board, making a whining sound. She touched the side of the kettle. It was hot. She lifted the lid and steam rose out. She dipped her finger in the mug to make sure she was not mistaken, but it was cold, so icy cold she could not leave it there. Nuts. Going nuts. Must have filled it from the cold tap. She frowned, tried to think clearly, but her mind felt fogged. Poured from the kettle. Surely she had. Surely —?

Ben growled. He was staring down the passageway, the hackles rising down his back. She felt the hairs on her own body rising too. He padded out of the kitchen and she followed. He stopped at the foot of the stairs, glared up and growled again.

'Tom?' she called out, knowing he wasn't there. 'Hello?' Her voice had risen an octave.

Ben's gums slid back, his ears lifted. She switched on the light and the stairs became brighter.

Kerwumph.

The boiler again. She picked up her carrier bag and climbed the stairs, trying not to move too slowly, not to seem scared, but slow enough so she could hear if — *if?*

168

If anything was there?

She reached the landing. The bulbs in the sconces threw their shadowy light along the walls. The floorboards creaked and the beams seemed to creak too, like an old timber ship sailing through a storm.

The doors were all shut and she went into each room in turn. Nothing, nothing, nothing. Each time she turned the light off and shut the door with a defiant slam. She checked the attic too, quickly, attics always spooked her, then went down into their bedroom.

She thought vaguely that something seemed to be missing; it seemed tidier than usual. She checked the en suite bathroom, then lifted the black silk negligee out of the carrier, went to the dressing table and held it up to her neck.

As she did so she noticed the envelope lying flat on the table weighted down by her hairbrush. It had not been there this morning. It was marked simply 'Charley', in Tom's neat handwriting.

She picked it up, and it fell from her trembling fingers back on to the table with a slap. She tore it open with her index finger.

Darling,

I love you very dearly, but it doesn't seem to be working out too well down here.

I need a few days on my own. I'm sorry I haven't been brave enough to say it to you face to face. You've got a cheque book and credit cards and there's money in the account, and £500 cash in the drawer under my socks. I'll give you a call.

Sorry if this letter seems clumsy, but you know I've never been very good at expressing how I feel. I need to think about my life and what I really want.

I know it's going to hurt you. It hurts me too,

169

more than I can write and you don't deserve to be hurt. I've taken a few things I need.

Love you,

Tom

Chapter Twenty-Two

Sunlight streamed in the window, as Mr Budley had solemnly told them it would, and she felt good for a moment, for a brief moment, smelling the sweet air and listening to the early morning chit-chit-chit of the birds before the memory lying asleep inside her began to stir.

There was a smell of burnt paper in the room.

She sat up, disoriented and drenched in sweat. Tom's pillows beside her were still plumped, undented, his side of the bed undisturbed. A swell of gloom rolled through her.

Darling, I love you very dearly.

She had dreamed it. It was a bad dream. Everything was fine. Tom was in the bathroom shaving, brushing his teeth.

'Tom?' she called out. There was no answer. Her hands were stinging and she pulled them from under the sheets and looked at them. Her eyes widened.

They were caked with mud and covered in lacerations.

A cut ran right the way down one finger and there was muddy, congealed blood around it. The skin was scraped off the top of three of her knuckles. More cuts criss-crossed the backs of her hands. They were hurting like hell. She turned them over. More cuts on the palms. Tension pulled her scalp. Ben? Had Ben attacked her? Never. A dream. Just dreaming. Just —

She swung her legs out of bed, put them on the wooden floor and then blinked in astonishment as she noticed her feet. A squall of undefined fear blew through her veins. Her feet were caked in mud, dried mud packed between her toes, spattered up her legs. She leaned over, touched them. The mud was damp; some came away on her finger. Her nightdress was filthy too, mud-spattered, sodden and streaked with blood.

She tried to think, think back to last night. Sitting at the dressing table; she had been sitting at the dressing table. Then — nothing. Blank.

A muscle twitched inside her throat. She stared hopelessly around the room as if somewhere in it she might find an answer. Dressing table. Hours. Crying. Maybe she had broken something, a mirror, a glass, was that why —? She shook her head. The mud, where had the mud —? Her hands and feet so sore, painful.

She looked at the dressing table, and it was then she noticed the small muddy object next to her hairbrush.

She staggered over. Rusty tin showed through the mud. She put her hand out slowly, hesitating, as if she were reaching out to a poisonous insect, and picked it up.

Something inside it rattled, slithered, clanked. She scraped away the mud with her raw fingers, ignoring the pain, until she could see enough to know what it was, to be certain what it was.

She waited, afraid, numb, then she pressed her thumbs up against the lid of the tin. It came off with a quiet pop, and there was the heart-shaped locket nestling inside. The same locket she had dug up then reburied at the Wishing Rocks.

Ben came over and stood beside her. The locket rattled as her hands shook. She put the tin down, knelt and patted the dog, squeezed him, put her arms around and hugged him, needing to feel something real, alive.

His coat was wet. His paws were wet too; wet and muddy. He wagged his tail. 'Good boy,' she said absently. 'Good boy.' She stood up. Her head was muzzy; the locket was muzzy too, a blurr. She lifted it out of the tin and the tarnished chain slithered down her wrist. She pressed the clasp, and prised the heart open.

A trail of fine black powder fell out. At first she thought it was earth, finely ground earth; then slivers of blackened paper floated out, zigzagged to the floor.

Dear Rock, I love him. Please bring him back. Barbara.

Someone had burnt the note.

The TCP stung her hands. The paint stung her eyes. She dunked the roller in the flat tray of paint, pressed it against the wall, ran it up, down, covering a little more of the lining paper on the panels between the oak beams with cream paint. Because she needed to do something. Anything.

'You oughter do the ceiling first.'

Laura. Bitch Laura.

She'd rung Laura, got her answering machine at her flat, got her answering machine at the boutique, rung Tom's private line which had not answered, rung his main number then hung up as the telephonist answered. Was he in Paris with bitch Laura?

'Otherwise it goin' run down the walls, innit?'

Bernie the builder stood in the doorway in his grubby overalls and his single gold earring, grinning cheekily.

'Ceiling? Yes — I — I should, I suppose.'

Bernie ran his hands over the lining paper. 'Not bad. You could turn professional. We'll give you a job any time.'

She forced a smile.

'Yeh, s'orl right it is, for an amateur!' He rubbed his finger on the crack between two joins. 'Got an overlap, want to avoid overlaps. Makes the paint bumpy.'

'I don't think it matters on these walls.' Her voice sounded weak. She squeezed her hands together, trying to stop the pain.

'Christ, wot yer done to yer hands?'

'Glass. I broke — some glass.'

He glanced at the beams. 'There's some good stuff you can put on those, bring their natural colour right back. Can't remember the name. I'll ask Pete.' He tugged his earring. ''Bout your table.' He jerked a finger towards the hall. 'The one what you said was knocked over. I remember the second post come, and I stacked it neat on the table.'

'Who was here after you left?'

'There wasn't no one. I locked the dog in the kitchen like you said.'

'The plumber wasn't still here?'

'No.'

'Are you sure?'

'He went early.'

'Did you see my husband when he came?'

'Yeah, 'bout three. Going off on a business trip. Orl right for some, innit? Where's he gone? Somewhere exotic? Leaving you to do the work, that's typical men, that is.'

There was a rap on the knocker. Ben barked. Charley wiped her hands on a rag and went to the front door.

Gideon stood there, well back, looking edgy. He touched his cap. 'I'm afraid I won't be coming any more, Mrs Witney.' He handed her a grubby envelope. 'That's me hours for the last week.'

She took it, surprised. 'It's not because of the hens, is it? We don't blame you for the hens, Gideon. It's not your fault. You did a good job with the fencing.'

He shrugged and avoided her eyes. 'I thought it would be different with 'er gone, but it's not.'

'What do you mean?' Mechanically she opened the envelope.

'I'd rather not say, if you don't mind.'

'I'd rather you did say.'

His edginess increased. 'You won't have no problem finding anyone,' he said as she took the handwritten sheet out. 'Eight and a half hours last week.'

'Have you been offered more money somewhere else? I'm sure we could perhaps give you a raise.'

He shook his head, and gazed at his boots. 'No, that don't come into it.'

'I don't understand. What's the problem?'

'I've made up me mind. I really don't want to say.'

'I'll get my purse,' she said, bewildered and angry.

She stood by the hall table and sifted through the morning post. There was a formal buff envelope addressed to herself and she opened it. Inside was a short letter, a leaflet entitled 'Access to Birth Records — Information for adopted people', and a form. She read through the leaflet, glanced at the form, then folded it back into the envelope, a thin stream of excitement, of hope, trickling through her gloom.

The electrician came down the stairs, a short chalky man with a goatee beard.

''Scuse me, Mrs Witney. Are you usin' any unusual electrical apparatus in the house?'

'Unusual? In what way unusual?'

'Something not domestic. Very high powered.'

'The man who came to read the meter said too much power was being used. He thought there was a short circuit somewhere. Didn't my husband tell you?'

'We haven't found no short anywhere. We've rewired and tested it all.' He tapped the small screwdriver clipped to his shirt pocket as if to underline what he had said, then tried to work a splinter out of his finger.

175

'There's somethin' being used here that's too powerful. Some of the new wiring we've put in is starting to melt.'

'*Melt?*'

He tugged a bit of the splinter out with his teeth. 'I've checked your appliances. They're fine. I'm goin' to have to replace some of the new wirin' I put in.' He shook his head. 'Something's funny. I'll give the Electricity Board a bell, make sure there's no underground cables round here.'

'Is there anything else that could be causing it?'

'Like what, do you mean?'

'I don't know. Damp, heavy rain.'

'Electricity can be affected by a lot of things. I'll keep looking.'

'Thank you.' She went into the kitchen, put the kettle on, sat down at the table and studied the application form for her birth records. She picked up a biro.

The form blurred; her mind blurred. She began to write, to fill it in, determined, oh yes, determined. She wrote in big letters, huge letters; twice the biro scored the paper, and she had to stop and press it back down around the punctured hole.

The kettle boiled, clicked itself off and the form came back into focus. She stared wide-eyed at what she had written. Except it was not her handwriting.

The lettering was bold, large, scrawly.

'LEAVE IT ALONE, BITCH.'

'Hello?'

Hugh Boxer stood in the kitchen doorway, holding a plant the size of a small tree. She turned the adoption form over, trying not to look obvious.

The top of the plant was bent, and leaves straggled in all directions; it was as untidy as Hugh's hair. 'A little thank you for keeping the car in the barn,' he said. 'And a sort of welcome-to-the-neigbourhood present,' he added.

LEAVE IT ALONE, BITCH.

Her insides churned. She stood up unsteadily. 'It's lovely. What is it?'

He looked down at the plant as if trying to remember what he was meant to be doing with it. His face was streaked with grease and he was wearing grimy dungarees over a frayed collar and tie. 'It's got a Latin name, and there's special food in a pack you have to give it. Red meat, or something.'

She smiled faintly and touched one of the leaves. It was soft and furry. 'Thank you, it's lovely. That's really nice of you.'

'What have you done to your hands?'

'Oh, it was — glass. Just scratches.' She looked away from his questioning stare. 'It's a beautiful plant.'

'I'll put it down for you somewhere. It's heavy.'

'The table will be fine.'

'It needs light,' he said.

'Maybe it'll like the view,' she said, trying to muster cheeriness.

He grinned, 'Particularly partial to views, I'm told.' His eyes fell lightly on her and she noticed his almost imperceptible frown.

'I was going to make some coffee.'

'Great, thanks, but don't let me —'

'It was going to be instant but I'll do proper in your honour.'

Company. She did not want him to see her misery, but wanted him to stay, to talk. Something was comforting about him — about his face, his manner, she was not sure what. He seemed even taller in here, barely had any headroom below the ceiling.

She put the adoption form on the windowsill and weighted it under a perspex picture frame of various snapshots of herself and Tom; Hugh put the plant on the table. There was hammering directly above them.

He wandered over to the dresser. 'I like goldfish.' He leaned over Horace's bowl and opened and shut his mouth, apeing the fish. Charley smiled, trying to prevent the welling tears. He made her feel sad. Sad because he was nice.

The blade of his frayed tie swung out of the top of his grimy boiler suit and dipped into the water. He left it there as the fish swam up to it. 'He likes my tie; this is obviously a sartorially aspirational goldfish.'

'You can take him anywhere,' she said, then had to turn her face away so he did not see the trickling tears. 'Do you always wear a tie?' she asked, her voice cracking as she spooned coffee into the percolator. She dabbed her eyes with a dishcloth.

'Yes.' He squeezed water from the end of his tie. 'Old habit. My father was always obsessed with respectability.' He smoothed the blade out and tucked it back inside his dungarees. 'He was one of those Brits you'd come across in the middle of the desert. It could be a hundred and forty in the shade and he'd still be wearing a tweed suit and a shirt and tie.'

'What did he do?'

He rummaged his hand through his hair. 'He was an archaeologist. A sort of real life Indiana Jones, but not as dashing. Obsessed with the Holy Grail, spent a lot of his life digging up tombs.'

'And always in a tie?'

'He was worried people would think he was a bit potty, so he liked to appear respectable. He believed people would trust a man in a tie. Poor bugger was always trying to raise money for this expedition or that, trying to convince people.' He touched his tie. 'That's probably why I always wear one. Wearing a tie is in my genes.' He grinned. 'Prisoners of our past, you see.'

178

'Did he ever find anything?'

'Oh yes. Not what he was looking for, but he made a few discoveries.'

Discoveries. Digs. She wondered whether his father had ever dug up a locket. Spots of tiredness danced in her eyes, fluttered in front of her.

'Are you all right?'

She nodded.

'You look pale.'

Genes. Parents. People always took their parents for granted, and the little traits they adopted. She wondered what traits her own parents had had, whether her father had always worn a tie, too. What perfume had her natural mother worn? Details like that had never occurred to her before. 'I'm a bit tired. It's hard work decorating.'

'I hope I didn't leave too much mess moving the car out. The straw was pretty rotten. It must have been there for years.' The hammering got worse above them. He glanced at Tom's pewter tankard on the dresser. 'How's Man of the Match?'

'Oh, he's —' She felt as if a cloud had suddenly slid over her sun. 'Away, on business.' The tears threatened again and she poured the coffee into the pot, holding the percolator clumsily, trying not to close her fingers too tightly around it. 'How is Viola Letters?' she asked, opening a cupboard and taking out a biscuit tin.

'She's OK. She rather doted on that dog. I'm not crazy about Yorkies, but it didn't deserve what happened to it.' He pulled the cord of the drying rack. The rack raised and lowered a few inches with a squeak, then he went to the sink and looked out of the window. Two swans drifted on the flat water. 'Fine view.'

'Gideon's not coming any more,' she said.

'Oh?'

'He wouldn't tell me why. I think he's upset about

179

the hens — thinks we blame him.'

'He's not going to do the lane at all?'

She shrugged. 'I don't know. He rather took me by surprise.'

Hugh carried the tray of coffee and biscuits out to the small patio at the rear of the house. They sat on hard benches at the oak table. Ben wolfed down a digestive biscuit, then stretched out on his stomach on the flagstones beside them. Charley scratched an insect bite on her neck.

'Nice to be able to sit outside in October,' Hugh said, heaping a spoon of sugar into his coffee. 'Make the most of it. How's your friend Laura?'

'Oh, she's well,' Charley answered, too quickly.

He stirred his coffee, the spoon clinking. A bird in the woods above squeaked like a plimsole on linoleum.

'Hugh, at our barbecue you said you had evidence of people being reincarnated, but you did not believe in regressive hypnosis. Do you really believe in reincarnation?'

He pulled his pipe out of a pocket and checked the inside of the bowl. 'I don't disbelieve all regressive hypnosis. There have been some convincing cases.'

There was a tinkle from inside the house that could have been breaking glass or something being dropped on a sheet of metal. They both glanced up, for a second, then she looked back at him. There was an expression of concern on his face that disturbed her. 'It's what I said. I don't believe in playing games with the occult.' he added.

'You think regression is playing games?'

'It depends how it's treated. On who's doing it. Regression itself is valid. And very dangerous. There are a lot of hypnotists around who treat it as a game — and that's even more dangerous.' He stared into her eyes.

180

LEAVE IT ALONE, BITCH.

She blinked; her eyes felt raw; she wished he would stop looking at them. She touched her cup and the heat hurt her cuts. 'What is the danger?'

'Hypnotists are like mediums. They put people into altered states of consciousness, try to reach out to different planes, different dimensions, and contact things that don't necessarily want to be contacted, or even want to be disturbed. Things they don't have any business disturbing.' He clicked his lighter and held his hand over the flame, shielding it from the breeze.

Coldness seeped through her. 'What do you need in order to prove you have lived before?'

'Evidence.'

'What sort of evidence?'

He tapped the burning tobacco down in the bowl with his thumb. 'Like knowing something happened during a previous life that no one else living knows. Something you could not possibly have known any other way, unless you had lived before.' He raised his eyes. 'It doesn't have to be anything enormous. In a way, small things are more convincing because they are less likely to have been in the history books.'

Small things.

Like a locket.

A locket that no one knew was there?

'Can it help people to resolve traumas? That's what I was told.'

'You mean someone's afraid of water in this life because they drowned in a previous one?'

'Yes, that sort of thing.'

'Learning how to swim stops people's fear of the water, not finding out that they drowned in the Spanish Armada.' He picked up a biscuit, broke it in half, then quarters. She wondered if he was going to make a

181

diagram; instead he dunked each piece in his coffee and ate it.

He spoke between bites. 'I think regressive hypnotism has all kinds of dangers. It tampers with thoughts and emotions that are dormant in the mind, usually dormant for a good reason because the mind has managed to put them away. You risk stirring them up.'

She put her arms around her chest and hugged herself. A sharp breeze blew and a brown leaf rolled past.

'Anything that involves dabbling in the spirit world is dangerous,' Hugh said. 'It's not just people who have memories. Places have them too.' His eyes fixed on hers again and she looked away.

She sipped her coffee and nearly spat it out, a wave of nausea sweeping through her. Puzzled, she lowered her nose and sniffed. It smelled of good coffee, but the taste in her mouth was vile. 'Places have memories?' she said.

'I think they do. You know the way you get atmospheres in houses? What happens over a period of time affects how places feel. If there's been some great tragedy or sadness in a house, quite often it — or a room in it — will feel depressing, maybe even cold as well.' He shrugged. 'It may be quite scientific. Perhaps the atomic particles in the walls retain trace memories, like videotape, and some people can accidentally tune in and trigger off replays. That's one of the theories for ghosts — that they are replays.'

Hugh looked up at the house, his eyes flicking from window to window, first floor then ground floor, back at her, back at the house.

He offered to carry the tray into the kitchen, but she insisted she could manage. As he was leaving he said quietly, deliberately quietly, she thought, as if he did not want someone to hear him, 'Be careful.' He patted Ben and walked off through the garden and up the drive.

She took the tray into the dim boiler room and through to the kitchen.

Something crunched under her feet.

Horace's bowl was not on the dresser and for a moment she wondered who had moved it. There was another crunch. She looked down. The floor was covered in water, broken glass, tiny coloured pebbles, strands of weed.

She was barely conscious of the china pot sliding across the tray, jerking against the latticed edging before it tumbled out of sight and exploded at her feet.

Horace?

Her eyes scanned the floor, her heart straining on its mountings, searching the shards of glass and china for the small fleck of gold. Please be all right.

Be flapping around. Please.

She put the tray on the kitchen table and was about to drop to her knees to look under the dresser when her eye ran down a black rivulet of coffee that had pushed its way through the debris, carrying Horace with it for a few inches until he jammed between a leg of the table and the severed spout of the pot. His tail waggled in the remains of the coffee and for a fleeting moment she thought the fish was still alive.

'Horace,' she mouthed, scooping him up in her hand. He was motionless, already stiffening, the eyes sightless, mouth open. Light, so light, he felt like the tinfoil wrapper of a sweet.

There was another volley of hammering and the dresser shook, the crockery rattling inside. She put the plug into the sink, ran the cold tap and laid Horace in the water, watching as he swirled around on the surface, hoping any moment he might wriggle and dart down to the bottom.

But he continued swirling on the surface, rising with the water. She picked him out. The water was cold and hurt her fingers. The fish had become stiffer still.

The hammering continued and the wooden rack rocked on its pulleys, squeaking, and she rocked on her feet, cradling Horace, making a high-pitched creaking noise herself as she tried not to cry over a dead fish.

She buried him in a plastic bag on the same bank in the woods where she had buried the hens, and placed a small stone over the tiny mound of earth.

She walked back down the bank and the horses grazing in the paddock reminded her of the smart horsewoman in her last regression who had stared down at her so contemptuously. And the unease she had felt.

Lies death. Truth. Go back, her mother had said.

Go back where?

There must be someone, someone who would know. She racked her brains, thinking back. Her adoptive mother had no relations alive now. Perhaps she had confided in a friend? Irene Willis. She might have confided in Irene Willis. Hope flared and faded. Irene Willis had died of cancer four years ago.

She went into the kitchen.

LEAVE IT ALONE, BITCH.

She stared at the form she had defaced, still tucked beneath the perspex picture frame. Nuts. Talking to myself. Sleepwalking. I dig lockets out of the ground in the middle of the night. I write instructions to myself.

Rebirthing. Weird rebirthing she had done with Laura, where they had tried to teach her to be positive about herself, where they gave her things she had to say in front of the mirror for half an hour a day.

'It is safe for me, Charley, to feel all my cleverness and all my feelings.'

'I, Charley, am loved and wanted as a woman.'

Laura. Bitch. Cow.

She sat at the table and breathed deeply, choking back a sob, stared at the empty space on the dresser where Horace's bowl had been and at the damp on the floor. She fidgeted, waiting for as long as she could, waiting for the phone to ring.

For it to be Tom.

Upstairs, music blared from the builders' radio. She turned the pages of the morning papers, her eyes sifting listlessly through the columns, a meaningless blur of black print and photographs, IRA bombers, a divorcing billionaire, a starlet on a bike, a wrecked car. Then she stood up and wandered aimlessly around the house.

In their bedroom she picked up the locket and toyed with the idea of writing a note herself. *Dear Rock, I love Tom. Please bring him back. Charley.*

She dropped the locket in the tin, put it at the back of a drawer and closed it. She went into the small room which would have been ideal for the cot for their first child, and looked out of the window, at the barn and the mill and the woods; it was starting to cloud over. It clouded in her mind, too, and she began crying again.

She went down into the kitchen, composed herself, picked up the phone and dialled Tom's private line. It was engaged. She waited, just in case he was trying to call her, then rang again. It was still engaged. She rang his switchboard, but hung up as soon as the operator answered.

It was weak to call him. He wanted time, space, whatever, to think things over. It was what he said in his letter. Fine. Let him think things over. She'd think things over too. She was not going to be weak. No way. Somehow, she determined, she was going to cope, to be strong, calm.

* * *

She was not so calm when she saw Laura through the glass front of her boutique holding up a dress for a customer. She walked in, seething.

'The shape is terribly flattering. Try it on. You really —' Laura's voice died as she saw Charley.

Charley stood near the window and flicked through a rail of dresses.

'The cut on these is tremendous. So many dresses like this aren't good over the hips.'

Charley moved on to a rail of blouses.

'And, of course, if you accessorise with a scarf, and maybe a pair of gloves —'

Charley sat down at the till and tapped digits out on the calculator, multiplied them, divided them, square-rooted them. Another customer came in, touched the collar of a jacket, flipped over the price tag and went out again. Laura glanced nervously at Charley, then turned her attention back to her customer. But the conviction had gone from her voice and she was losing her.

'I'll think about it,' the woman said, and left.

Charley tapped another row of digits on the calculator.

'Hi!' Laura put on a smile the way she might have put on lipstick.

'What the hell's going on, Laura?' Charley said, without lifting her eyes from the display of digits.

'What do you mean?'

'Come on!' Charley said, warningly.

Laura shrugged. 'I'm sorry, Charley.'

'Sorry? You're sorry? Is that all you can say?'

Laura turned away and fiddled with a showcard. 'What do you want me to say?'

Charley stood up. 'Bitch. You fucking bitch.' She stormed across the shop, yanked the door open,

186

marched out into the street and along the pavement. She kept on walking, angry at herself now, angry for being weak and going there, for doing exactly what she had determined she would not do.

Chapter Twenty-Three

She became aware she was walking through darkness; except it was not darkness, not shadow. She was walking between two tall hedgerows, down a crumbling lane. She stumbled on a loose stone. 'Darn!'

'Where are you?'

'Lane.'

'What is your name?'

'Dunno.'

'How old are you?'

'Dunno.'

'Tell me what you are wearing.'

'A frock. It's sort of cream with a pattern.'

'How long is it?'

''Alfway down me legs.'

'What shoes are you wearing?'

'Brown. Heels are too high. I shouldn't be wearin' heels.'

'Why not?'

'Cos I'm expectin'.'

'Who is the father?'

'Dick.'

'You sound frightened. What are you afraid of?'

'Dunno. It feels bad. Bad.'

She passed Thadwell's Farm, with its cobbled yard and the tractor and haycart in the tumbledown barn, and on past the stagnant pond.

A man she recognised was sitting in the lane in front of Rose Cottage, painting at an easel. He was well groomed, very correct looking, and stood up politely as she approached.

'Good afternoon,' he said in a crisp military tone.

'Good afternoon,' she mumbled in response.

'Who are you talking to?' said a voice in the background, a voice she no longer recognised.

'Jolly nice one, isn't it?' said the man.

He was in the Navy, she seemed to remember.

She reached the gate and stopped. She stared down at Elmwood Mill. A horse in the stables whinnied, as if it recognised her. Horse. A black cloud engulfed her. She took a packet of Woodbine cigarettes from her bag and lit one.

'You are bothered by the horse. What is bothering you?' said a faint voice, distant, like a radio that had been left on in another room.

'Jemma's my 'orse. She's got my 'orse. He promised me.' Her voice was breaking up; she was crying. She took a nervous pull on her cigarette, then opened the gate, and paused, searching for the dog, listening; she stared down at the kennel. No sign of it. She began to walk down the drive, scared, weary, the infant weighing heavily in her belly.

The car was there. His car. The black Triumph with its roof down, parked carelessly in front of the barn. The horse whinnied again and she gazed through eyes fogged with tears at the smart stables and saw the head of a chestnut mare looking out.

Everything was fresh, in good condition. The barn was newly roofed, the doors recently painted. The woodwork of the house was bright. She threw away her cigarette and walked across the gravel and up the steps, where she hesitated, daunted. She looked at the bell, at the polished brass lion's head knocker, then at the bell

189

again. She pushed the button.

There was a solitary deep bark from inside the house and the door was opened almost immediately, as if she were expected. A woman stood there, tall, elegant, aloof, in a hacking jacket, breeches and riding boots. Her black hair hung down across one side of her face with studied carelessness. She pursed her lips and glared witheringly, with fierce burning eyes.

'I told you not to come back here,' she said coldly.

'Please, I just want to see 'im. Please let me see 'im.'

The woman smiled, a cruel smile filled with menace. She turned, walked across the hall and opened a door. She clicked the fingers of her right hand once, and mouthed one word: 'Prince.'

The mastiff came into the hall and stared in hostile recognition; he lowered his head, his gums slid back and he snarled.

She backed away, turned and ran, almost falling down the steps, heard the dog snarling behind her. She felt a searing pain as his teeth bit into her leg.

'No! Get off!' she screamed, windmilling her arms and kicking out. The dog shook her leg in his massive jaw, like a bone. She lost her balance and, cradling her belly with her hands, crashed down the rest of the steps on to the drive.

The dog was over her. 'No! Get off! Get 'im!' she screamed, trying to roll away. 'Oh please get 'im off! No! Dick! No! The baby! Don't harm my baby!'

Above her she could see the face of the woman in the hacking jacket, watching, arms folded.

She clambered to her feet and tried to run, but the dog went for her leg again and sent her back on to the gravel. She screamed in pain.

'Prince, stop. Prince!'

The dog let go.

She lay there, weeping, her leg and hands in agony,

and saw Dick, in baggy trousers and collarless shirt, his face puce with rage. 'Clear off, I told you! Clear off! I don't want you coming back. Out!'

She looked up at the woman who was staring at her as if she was nothing. Nothing on earth, just absolutely nothing.

'You hear?' he shouted. 'You hear what I said? Next time I won't call him off.'

She climbed to her knees. 'Help me. You got to help me. Please, you got to help me.'

They stared in blank silence.

'Help me!' She was shouting now. 'You got to help me!'

Their faces faded.

A distant siren. Wind rattling glass. A chair creaking. Someone wheezing.

'You're all right, Charley. You are all right. You are safe. You are free in time. Stay with it. Move forward a little, move forward.'

She opened her eyes, saw Ernest Gibbon's face, almost without recognition. She closed them heavily again. She felt herself sinking into darkness.

There was roaring of water in her ears.

It was dark; night; the weir thundered. There was determination in her step. She had something in her left hand that was heavy and slimy. She walked on the grass, the wet dewy grass beside the gravel. The dog growled.

'Shh,' she hissed. She was trembling; afraid of the dog; afraid he might not be chained. The mill race flowed darkly. The dog growled again and she tried not to be scared, tried to think only of the hatred she felt. He barked and the chain rattled in the iron hoop. She looked at the silent silhouette of the house, expecting at any moment a light would come on or a torch beam would flash across at her.

Swift. Had to be swift. The barn loomed ahead. She flashed her torch straight on the kennel and the glint of red of the mastiff's eyes glared back at her. He snarled and strained at the end of his chain. Her heart pumped fast; the snarl seemed to fuel her anger, made her strong, suddenly; stronger than the dog.

'Prince! Shh!' her hissing voice commanded.

He hesitated at her tone, hesitated at another smell. The smell of the bone which she held out towards him as she called him softly, 'Good boy! Here, boy!'

She held it high, just out of his reach, and as he tried to jump up, his jaws snapping, the chain pulled him back and he lost his balance. She stepped forward, holding the bone even higher so he had to stretch his head up, exposing his neck.

As he took the huge bone greedily in his jaws, she sliced the serrated blade of the knife she held in her right hand as hard as she could across the centre of his throat, pushing with all her weight, feeling it biting in, razor sharp, cutting through flesh and muscle and bone.

There was a punctured sigh, and the dog seemed to sag. Blood sprayed over her hands, her clothes, her face. The mastiff made a gargling sound. There was a squeak of air, like a whistle. He whined, the bone fell out of his mouth and he coughed, lurched sideways, his paws collapsing, and fell forwards making sharp rasping sounds, blood spewing out of his mouth, flooding around his chest, his paws. The rasping sound began to die down.

She ran over the bridge across the mill race up the embankment to the woods; a prickly bush tore at her. She stopped, her heart thumping so loud she could hear it echoing around the woods, around the night, could hear it echoing a million miles away. She threw the knife into a clump of bushes, heard the rustle as it dropped. Somewhere close by an animal squeaked.

192

They could find the knife in the bush. Stupid. The lake. Why the hell not throw it in the lake? She tried to switch the torch on, but it slipped out of her blood-soaked hand and fell into the undergrowth. She knelt down, scrabbled for it, then was paralysed with fear as she sensed something behind her.

She turned. A light had come on in the house. The bedroom light. Someone was at the window, a shadow behind the curtain. The curtain parted; there was a creak as the window opened.

Except it wasn't a window; it was a mirror. She was staring at her face in a mirror, and a figure was looming behind her, blurry, indistinct. She smelled smoke; burning wood; straw.

Charred flesh.

She saw the eyes, just the eyes. Raw through the blackened skin. There was a loud bang. The mirror exploded into spidery cracks. A jagged shard fell away, landing at her feet, and she screamed as the figure moved towards her.

The darkness became red. A red light. Ernest Gibbon's face, myopic through his thick lenses; his jowls heaving up and down as if there were tiny motors inside operating them. She was drenched in sweat.

'It's happened again,' he said. 'The same every time.' He sat for a while, wheezing, studying her with the faint disconcerting trace of humour she had noticed last time. 'We need to get beyond it. The answer is beyond it.'

'There's a parallel,' Charley said. She felt drained.

'Oh yes?'

'My real-life relationship with my husband and my relationship here with this man — Dick. Don't you think that's too coincidental?'

'People often come back and go through the same situations as in previous carnations. Some people believe it is because they failed in the way they dealt

193

with the situations before.' He removed his glasses and wiped them with a spotted handkerchief. The surrounds of his eyes looked naked. 'Who is this unpleasant woman? Do you know her name?'

'No.'

'Could she be the person who comes up behind you in the mirror?' He put his glasses back on.

'The person in the mirror looks hideous — disfigured — the face is burnt.'

'Is it a man or a woman?'

'I don't know.'

'How would you feel if I did not bring you out when that figure comes up behind you next time?'

She felt a current of fear. 'What — what would happen if you didn't?'

He thought for a moment. 'You might find you are able to deal with it. We should try. I think it would be dangerous not to try.'

'Dangerous not to try?' she repeated.

He nodded like a sage. 'When we open up the subconscious like this, there is always a danger of spontaneous regression.'

'What do you mean?'

'I try to do everything here in a controlled way. If you are getting uncomfortable or frightened, I can bring you back out, quickly. If you were to start regressing on your own, somewhere away from here, and the figure in the mirror took hold, then —' He shrugged.

'Why should it? It's only something in my memory.' She saw uncertainty in his eyes and that scared her. She wished she were not here, had not started this. She wished she had more faith in the man.

'I don't know why it should, Charley. I don't know if it is just memory. It's what I said last time. It's very strong.'

'But you didn't tell me what it was.'

The teacher-knows-best smile was fainter, had lost some of its confidence. 'I don't know what it is. I haven't come across this particular situation before. I don't know anyone who has. I'm going to do some research, to see if there is anything to compare, some other case history.'

'I thought you were meant to be an expert,' she said, more acidly than she intended.

He looked at her and blinked slowly, seriously. The smile was gone. 'In man's understanding of the supernatural, Charley, we are all amateurs.'

Chapter Twenty-Four

She walked along the station platform among the throng of commuters returning home from work, from London mostly, the smart and the shabby, the eager and the despondent, home to *her indoors*, to *she-who-must-be-obeyed*, to *the little woman, the little man*, home to noisy kids and empty dark houses, home to the loved, the hated, the infirm, the dying, the dead.

And the reborn.

If you kept coming back, you didn't die. You merely changed. You got reconstituted. Recycled. Even your knowledge, your experiences, got recycled.

She filed through the ticket barrier then walked, her shoes clattering on the concrete of the steps, down into the tunnel. The train moved off, rumbling above them. Did everyone else around her, all the hurrying people, have past lives? Had they come back many times too, back to this life each time they died, the way they came back to this station night after night?

If? If it was there? What then?

The thought spurred her to walk faster, to run up the steps the far side, out into the blustering wind of the clouded grey evening, almost to sprint across the car park to the little Citroën with its two-tone paintwork.

Her hands still hurt, but she barely noticed as she climbed in, started the engine and switched on the radio out of habit. There was a roar of laughter. Frank Muir was telling a story. Not now, she could not cope with humour now. She pushed in a tape. Rachmaninov, solemn, sombre, old, too old. She felt the violin string as if it were sliding down her own tight nerves and she punched the tape out and drifted into her thoughts again.

She drove out of Haywards Heath on to the country road, pressing the accelerator to the floor, wishing the car would go faster, almost willing it to go faster. To get home.

To find out.

The car lurched as she came into a bend too fast, the tyres squealing, saw a car coming the other way, the driver looking at her alarmed, thought for a moment she was going to hit it but somehow the Citroën hung on. Then the bend went the other way and she swung the wheel, foot stabbing at the brake, cut the corner and narrowly missed a cyclist who swerved, fist waving in the air. Christ, slow down. She gripped the wheel, felt her face steaming.

The sky was blackening as she pulled up in front of the barn. It looked like a storm was on the way.

She climbed out of the car and closed the door, crossed the bridge over the mill race and ran up the banked slope on the far side and into the woods, following the route she had taken in the regression. A gust of wind rattled the branches and spots of rain were coming down.

She trod through some bracken on to the mossy earth and looked up at the trees, the tall, thin hornbeam trees growing crookedly out of the wild undergrowth. Their branches were tangled, some of them supporting uprooted trees from past storms which lay across them like spars, lay where they would stay until they rotted, until they went back into the earth. Biodegradable. As humans were.

In the regression it had been dark, but she knew the way. There was a small indent in the ground, a ditch in front of a thick bramble bush that was covered in rotting blackberries. She went a few yards to the left and through a heavy undergrowth of bracken. A bird jumped in the branches of the trees above, chirping like a dripping tap. A distant dog barked. A tractor droned. The woods were darkening around her, melting the trees, closing in on her.

She was panting and shaking, covered in a clammy sweat. She did not want to be here any more, wanted to turn, run to the house and close the door on the night, close the door on the bramble bush that seemed to be drawing her in, that seemed to be growing as she looked at it, spreading around her ankles, rising up her legs. Switches were clicking inside her, changing the speed of her blood, re-routing it, churning it, pumping it over blocks of ice, sucking out the heat, refrigerating it.

She crawled underneath the bush, pushing up the branches, the thorns catching at her clothes, then something caught her eye. At first she thought it was a rotting strip of wood, or a flat root.

A stone. Might be a stone. Hoped it was a stone. It seemed to rise out of the brambles at her, bringing the bush with it. She scrabbled towards it on her hands and knees, oblivious to the stinging pain of the brambles, and she gripped the handle, gripped it as if it was the lever that would move the world, then backed out and stood up, pulling branches up with her, letting them rip through her clothes, through the skin of her arms.

She turned it over in her hands, touching the cold, rusted metal. A knife with a bone handle black with age and weathering, and a long serrated blade eaten with rust.

The knife she had carried in her regression. The knife with which she had killed the mastiff.

She felt pain in her finger, as if she had been stung, and looked down. A thin line of blood began to appear from the tip of her index finger down to the first joint. She dropped the knife, jammed her finger in her mouth and sucked hard. The cut had gone right down to the bone.

It seemed as if the thousand eyes of the falling night were watching her. The wind tugged at her hair, her thoughts tugged at her mind.

She bound the cut with her handkerchief, her mind racing, trying to find an answer that was better than the one she had.

She had killed a dog. With this knife. In another life.

She pulled herself free of the brambles, her linen dress ruined, and stumbled down through the woods towards the lake. An explanation. There had to be an explanation. Something.

A drop of water struck her cheek, then another. She reached the bank, heard the lap of a wave, saw the lake black and sloppy under the rising wind. She stared down at the knife, frightened it might cut her again, a deeper cut than her finger.

She made sure there were no anglers, then threw it as hard as she could out into the lake. Far enough and deep enough so she could not wade out in her sleep and get it back. It rolled over in the air, barely visible, then fell into the water with a plop like a rising trout. Gone. It no longer existed.

It had never existed.

She went towards the house, squeezing her finger through her handkerchief, thinking, hoping, trying to convince herself that maybe she'd cut it on a thorn; not a knife. You didn't find knives under bushes. No one *ever* left a knife under a bush.

She took her handbag out of the Citroën and stared at the barn wall where the mastiff had been chained in her regression. She walked over, her feet dragging through the gravel, and scanned the wall. In the falling darkness it blended in with the bricks and she took a moment to spot it. She went closer, put out her hand and touched the hoop. It had almost rusted away; a chunk flaked off and crumbled into dust in her fingers.

Mad. Going mad. I have lived previous lives.

I killed a dog.

It was raining harder, but she hardly noticed as she stood gazing at the barn; the barn with its bats and spiders and the old car which it had held, like a secret. And which in turn had held its own secret. The chewing gum.

She looked down, just in case, although she knew she would never find it because it was not there, had never been there; it had been her imagination, like everything else. That was all.

She unlocked the door of the house and stepped into the tiny dark hallway, switched on the light and closed the door behind her.

The wind had stopped howling, the mill race was silent. It felt as if time had stopped.

'Ben! Hello, boy!' she called out. 'Ben?' She walked down the passageway, into the kitchen. Silence. 'Ben?' The red light of the answering machine winked frenetically out of the gloom. Rain spattered against the windows.

She jerked open the boiler room door, saw the dim blue flame of the boiler 'Ben?' She switched on the light.

He was cowering against the far wall, whimpering, his hair standing up along his back as if it had been brushed the wrong way.

She ran over, knelt beside him and put her arm around him. 'Boy? What's the matter?' He was shaking and a puddle of urine lay beside him. 'It's OK, boy, it's OK.' She stroked his head and rubbed his chest.

The boiler sparked into life and she jumped. The flame roared, the air hissed, the sound of metal vibrated. 'What is it? Aren't you well? Why are you shut in here? Was it one of the workmen? Let's get you supper.'

She went into the kitchen, took his meat out of the fridge and put it with some biscuits in his bowl by the basket. He stayed cowering in the boiler room, watching her, then slowly, warily, came out. The answering machine continued its winking. The windows shook, a volley of rain struck the glass. The drying-rack swayed in the wind, its pulleys creaking, its rails casting shadows like prison bars.

She cleaned up Ben's puddle and patted him again. He began to eat. She pressed the message play button on the answering machine, heard it rewind and went over to the sink and washed her hands carefully. She rinsed her finger under the cold tap, worried about the rust on the knife, trying to remember when she'd last had a tetanus jab. Her hands looked awful, felt awful; every time she moved a finger the skin parted on a wound, layers of it pulling apart.

The answering machine finished its rewind and began to play. There was a bleep, then a hiss, then a message-end bleep, and another hiss. She frowned. The bleep again. Another hiss. Silence. Hiss. The shuffle of the tape in the machine. Another bleep. Wind shook the house, shook the shadowy bars of the drying rack across the table. Ben looked up at her, then down at his food. He was still trembling.

Bleep. Hiss. The tape shuffled. The wind hosed the rain against the house. Bleep. Hiss. Again, as if someone demented was phoning, someone who refused to speak, who just listened, listened.

Tom. Was it Tom, phoning then hanging up, not having the courage to speak? She turned the volume up, listened to see if she could hear any background sounds, an office, other people talking, to see if she could tell where the caller was.

Ben's ears pricked and he let out a deep rumbling growl. All she could see in the window was her own reflection against the blackness. There was a final long bleep, the messages-end one. A cold draught of air blew through the old tired glass. The house was vulnerable, easy to break into, easy if someone wanted to —

She picked up the phone, listened to the hum of the dial tone and felt reassured, but she wished they had curtains, blinds, anything. Someone could be out there, looking in, watching. Ben half-heartedly chewed a chunk of meat.

She took the cassettes of today's session, which Ernest Gibbon had given her, out of her handbag and put them on the kitchen table. At least Tom wouldn't see them, wouldn't be able to get angry about her spending money.

There was antiseptic and dressings under the sink; she anointed the knife cut and bound it with Elastoplast. Ben shot into the hallway and started barking. The doorknocker rapped, flat dull thuds. She hurried down the passageway. Through the stained glass panel in the front door she could see a short figure in yellow. 'Yes?' she called out. 'Who is it?'

'Viola Letters,' shouted a muffled voice.

Charley opened the door, holding Ben's collar. The plump diminutive figure of her neighbour was parcelled in sopping yellow oilskins, sou'wester, red wellington boots and held a large rubber torch. She looked as if she'd just stepped out of a lifeboat.

'I say, frightfully sorry to bother you on a night like this,' she barked in her foghorn voice. 'You haven't by any chance seen Nelson, have you?'

There was a spray of rain, and Charley smelled the

alcohol fumes on the old woman's breath. 'Nelson? Your cat? No, I haven't I'm afraid.' She stepped back. 'Please, come in.'

'Don't want to make your hallway wet.'

'Would you like a drink?'

'Well, if you —' She strode forwards. 'Rage, roar, spout — always reminds me of King Lear this sort of a night,' she barked. 'Damned bloody cat. Been gone over a day now, not back for his food. Never usually wanders very far — can't see much having the one eye.' Ben trotted up to her with his chewed rubber Neil Kinnock head in his mouth. She patted him. 'Thank you, chappie. Dreadful bloody man, Kinnock, but very kind of you.'

'What can I get you?'

'Rather feel I'm barging in.' Viola Letters squinted at her and began tugging the knot of her sou'wester.

'No, not at all. I'm not doing anything. Whisky? Gin? We've got most things.'

'Went to Evensong on Sunday,' the old woman said, following Charley into the kitchen. 'Have you met that vicar chap? Damned good mind to write to the bishop about him. He's off his trolley. Either that or he was sloshed. Gin and tonic, dear, no ice.' She tugged off her wet overclothes and Charley hung them on the rail on the Aga.

'He was rabbiting on about organic farming; said that if Christ came back today he wouldn't be a priest, he'd be an organic farmer. Said it was better to have the odd maggot you could see, and pluck it out, than to eat a ton of invisible chemicals. Some analogy to casting out the moneylenders. Beyond me.'

Charley poured a large dollop of gin. 'I'm afraid we don't go to church.' She unscrewed the tonic cap; there was a hiss.

'Can't blame you, the way it's going. Quite mad.

Barmy.' She took the glass. 'Cheers!'

Charley poured herself a glass of white wine. 'Cheers,' she replied and sat down.

Viola Letters looked around. 'You've done a lot of work here,' she commented.

'It needs a lot more.'

The old woman sipped her gin and tonic. 'I gave my poor boy his breakfast yesterday morning, and I haven't seen him —' She stopped in mid-sentence as her eye caught the perspex photograph holder on the window-sill. There was a montage inside which Charley had made up from various holiday snaps: Tom in a suede coat and herself in a camel coat, looking very early seventies, in front of the Berlin Wall. Tom at an outdoor café in dark glasses, the two of them in the cockpit of a yacht in Poole harbour. A shot of herself having a go (her one and only go) at hang-gliding. Tom on a beach in scuba gear. The two of them amid a drunken gaggle of friends around a restaurant table.

Viola Letters blinked and leaned closer, then pointed a finger at the picture of Charley and Tom in front of the Berlin Wall. 'That's you?'

Charley nodded. 'Yes. I've changed a bit since then.'

She gazed at Charley, then dug her pudgy fingers inside the neck of her jumper and pulled out an eyeglass, closed one eye and studied the photograph.

She looked back at Charley. A strange wariness appeared in her crab eyes. 'It's uncanny, dear. Most uncanny.'

Charley felt edgy.

Viola Letters dabbed her forehead. 'I — if you don't mind dear, I'm really not — don't think I'm feeling very well.' She put her half-full glass on the table and glanced at the ceiling, as if she had heard something.

'Can I get you anything?' Charley said. 'Would you like me to call a doctor?'

'No. No, I'll be all right.'

'I'll walk you home.'

'No — I'll —' She stood up. 'I think it's just — bit of a chill.' She looked at the photograph again.

It had been taken by another tourist, an American. He'd had difficulty with the camera, kept pushing the wrong button and Tom had got exasperated. Strange the details one could remember over the years. That was taken before they married, when she was about nineteen. She could remember the American. He looked like Jack Lemmon with a beer belly.

'What is it that's uncanny?' she asked.

The old woman put on her wet oilskins and pushed her stockinged feet into her wellingtons. 'The resemblance,' she said. 'I'm sorry. It's really given me a bit of a shock. I'll be better tomorrow.'

'What do you mean, resemblance?'

Ben growled, his head tilted upwards, and the old woman's eyes slid up to the ceiling again, then at Charley, and she managed a weak smile. 'Nothing really, dear. Me being silly. The brain's not so clear as it was. It's just that you —' She paused. 'Perhaps another time, dear. Pop round and we'll have a chat about it.'

'I'll come tomorrow,' Charley said. 'See how you're feeling. I could get you something from the chemist.'

'It's only a stupid chill,' Viola Letters said, knotting the sou'wester strap under her chin. 'It's this damned change in the weather. Boiling hot one day, then this!'

'Is it someone who you know who I look like in the photograph? A resemblance to someone you know?'

They stopped by the front door and the old woman shook her head. 'No, I — I'd prefer to talk about it — another time.' She leaned forward, dropping her voice almost to a whisper. Her mouth became a small, tight circle. The eyes slid down out of sight, then peeped warily at her again. 'The first time we met, when you came with that message from my late husband. Did I tell you I'd had that same message before? On the day he died?'

'Yes,' Charley said. 'You did.'

'That photograph of you — there's a most extra-ordinary resemblance to the girl who brought me the message. I thought for a moment it was her.' She opened the door. 'Another time, dear. We'll talk about it another time.'

Chapter Twenty-Five

That photograph of you — there's a most extraordinary resemblance to the girl who brought me the message. I thought for a moment it was her.

Viola Letters's voice sounded crystal clear. As if she were in the room. Sunlight streamed in. Her finger hurt and her head ached. She climbed out of bed and walked to the window.

The storm had died sometime around dawn. Birds were out in force, thrushes and sparrows and blackbirds and robins prospecting for worms. Water dripped from the trees. The weir and mill race seemed louder this morning.

That photograph of you —

It was half past seven. The workmen would be here soon. She put on her towelling dressing gown and moccasin slippers and went downstairs.

As she bent to pick up the newspapers she heard a rustling sound coming from the kitchen, a crackling like shorting electricity. There was a smell of burning plastic. She ran down the passageway.

'Ben!' she yelled in fury.

But it was too late. Ernest Gibbon's two cassettes were lying on the floor, their casings split, the thin tapes unspooled, crumpled, twisted around the table, around the chair legs. Ben was having a great time, rolling in the stuff, burrowing, rustling, scrunching it up, tangling it further all the time.

'Ben!' her voice stormed out, deeper and louder still. 'Wicked!'

The dog stopped and looked at her. He stood up, brown tape draped around his head like a wig, and shook himself. The tape fell free and he slunk out.

She stared at the mess. How the hell had Ben knocked the cassettes off the table? She knelt and began to scoop the tape up into bundles, wondering whether it was still usable. But it was twisted, creased, knotted. Hopeless. She stuffed it into a garbage bag and tied the neck, ready for it to go to the large bins at the end of the lane. Then she noticed the smell of burning plastic again, getting stronger. It was coming from the Aga.

The lid of the hot plate was up and the picture frame of their holiday snaps, or what was left of it, was lying on the flat top, soggy, melting. The photographs inside were frosted globules of washed-out colour.

As she snatched out her hand to rescue it the frame burst into flames and she jumped back as filthy black smoke rose, twisting savagely upwards. She grabbed a dish cloth and whacked it. Bits of molten plastic and burning photographs scattered around the kitchen. One tiny piece landed on her hand, clung to it, burning, and she shook it and rubbed it against her dressing gown. Patches of lino were melting. She ran the tap into the washing up bowl, lifted the bowl out and poured it over the burning plastic on the Aga, then dowsed the rest of the tiny fires.

She opened the windows, coughing, her throat full of the filthy cloying smoke. The remains of the frame hissed and sizzled on the oven. She scraped it off with a metal spatula, dropped it into the sink and ran the cold tap. More steam rose and the blackened perspex curled as if it had a life of its own. The charred photographs inside it curled too.

* * *

The new application form for her birth certificate had arrived in the post. She read through it as she ate her muesli, chewing with no appetite, leaving the newspapers untouched beside her on the kitchen table.

The stench of the burned plastic and wet charred paper hung thickly in the room, and the floor was damp from where she had washed it down. The new wound on her hand ached along with the others. She finished her cereal and was having another go at scraping the remains of the perspex off the top of the Aga when the phone rang. She answered it mechanically, almost absently.

'Yes, hello?'

'Charley?'

It was Tom.

She slammed the receiver straight back down and sat, quivering, as it rang again. Three rings, then the answering machine clicked and Tom spoke as the tape revolved.

'Charley? Darling? I want to speak to you, please pick up the phone.' There was a pause. 'At least call me back. I'm in the office all day.' Another pause 'Darling? ... Charley?' Then the sound of the receiver being replaced.

'Go to hell,' she said.

She made the workmen their morning tea and walked with Ben up the lane to see whether Viola Letters was better. To see if the old woman would explain why a photograph had freaked her out so much.

Charley was pleased she had hung up on Tom, pleased she had been strong. She wondered how long she could stay strong.

The curtains of Rose Cottage were still drawn, which surprised her; it was after eleven. There was a mournful miaow and Nelson, the one-eyed cat, was rubbing itself against the front door.

'You're supposed to be missing,' she told it.

There were two bottles of milk on the step and the *Daily Telegraph* stuck out of the letter box. Charley closed the front gate behind her, tied Ben to the fence and ordered him to sit. She rang the brass ship's bell. There seemed something idiotic about it, she thought, as the clang rang out. Nothing happened. She rang it several more times, then rapped on the door as well.

She looked at the cosy yellow Neighbourhood Watch sticker in the frosted glass pane beside the door, then pushed open the letter box and peered through. She could see the carpet, the stairs and a picture on the wall. Everything looked very still.

She walked around the side of the house. There was a fine view from the rear beyond the fence at the end of the neatly tended lawn, over the valley and woods. The cat followed her, miaowing insistently.

A fan vent in the kitchen window was spinning. She could see a tray, laid with a crystal glass and an unopened bottle of wine, a napkin in a silver ring, *Country Life* magazine, a peach and a knife on a small plate. She rapped on the glass pane of the back door, gently at first, then louder. 'Hello? Mrs Letters!' She called, then hesitated. Maybe she was asleep and did not want to be disturbed?

She walked to the front again and stared at the grey stone wall and the crenellations along the roof. Wrong. Something was wrong. A high-pitched whine cut through the still of the morning. Hugh working on one of his cars, probably. She untied Ben and went up the lane.

Hugh's Jaguar was parked in his yard and the doors of his corrugated iron workshop were open. He was bent over the engine of the Triumph, which was sitting, minus its wheels, on metal jacks. A bright light hung down from the ceiling above him, its bulb inside a wire mesh cage. The place smelled of oil and old leather, and there were acrid fumes of burnt electricity.

She gritted her teeth against the banshee din.

There were two other cars crammed into the small area, both under dust sheets. Tools and bits of motor cars lay on the floor, the work top, the shelves. There were boxes, tins full of nuts and bolts, loose spark plugs. More tools hung from racks. Old wheels, tyres, were propped around. The bonnet of a car was suspended on wires from the roof girders and there were several metal advertising signs fixed to the walls, Woodbine cigarettes, Esso Extra and battered licence plates, mostly American.

The noise died. There was a clank and something metal rolled along the grimy concrete floor. Hugh lifted his head out of the engine compartment and saw her. 'Hi!' He gave her a welcoming grin and laid the tool on the ground. The two halves of the hinged black bonnet sat up in the air like claws behind him.

'How's it going?'

'I got the head off.' He wiped his forehead with the back of his oily fist and nodded at the engine compartment.

She peered in; car engines always baffled her. She saw a tangle of wires, rubber tubing, several thin metal rods sticking up beside elliptical holes in what looked like the main part of the engine.

'Considering she hasn't been run for years, she's not too bad. I need a couple of gaskets, and I might get her started up. Take you for a spin.'

She smiled thinly, feeling the odd recognition stirring again.

Chewing gum.

'How much do you know about its history?' she asked.

'I'm going to try and trace the provenance. I don't

211

think Miss Delvine was the original owner.'

No, she wasn't, Charley wanted to say. *His name was Dick.*

Her fingers felt as if they were touching ice.

Touching an old knife.

'I've written off to the licensing people in Swansea.' His eyes stared at her, penetrating, a deep curiosity in them, and she looked away uneasily.

'Have you seen Viola Letters today?' she said.

'No. She came round yesterday evening searching for her cat.'

'She came to me as well. She wasn't well. I've just been to see her. The cat's on her doorstep, and it doesn't seem like she's got out of bed. I hope she's OK.'

'Maybe she's asleep. Taken some pill. All that booze she knocks back, I should think a couple of aspirins and she goes critical.'

Charley smiled.

'Let's try phoning her.'

They went into his house, Ben was invited too. In contrast to the neat exterior it was a ramshackle chaos, mostly of books and manuscripts, among them, she noticed to her surprise, a row of James Herbert novels. The walls were hung with old framed maps; there wasn't much furniture, and what there was looked masculine and slightly dilapidated. Comfortable, in a lived-in sort of way, none of it would have looked out of place in a student room at a university.

He picked up the phone from under a pile of papers on his massive desk, rummaged through a book for Viola Letters's number and dialled. He let it ring a dozen times, then redialled.

There was still no answer.

'I'll pop by later on and see if she needs anything,' he said. 'Actually, while you're here, I was wondering if you and your old man would like to come and have supper on Saturday, if you're not doing anything.'

She blanched. 'I — we'd — he's away — business. I don't know when he's coming back.'

'So you're on your own?'

She nodded.

He was quiet for a moment. 'I'm going to the pub this evening. Why not come? There'll be a few people there.'

'I —' Cheery faces. No, no thanks, couldn't face it, could not face lying about Tom. Could not face —

Being alone in the house. Waiting for Tom to call. Tom could go to hell.

'Thanks. That would be nice.'

A police car was parked on the grass bank by the upturned skiff, and two policemen were standing on the footbridge with a local farmer she vaguely recognised, peering down into the sluice pond. She walked through the gate pillars, wondering what they were looking at.

Then she saw it herself. For a moment she couldn't make out what it was. A carrier bag blown by the wind, maybe?

It was wrapped around one of the blades of the mill wheel, flapping like a trapped animal in the water that surged over it.

Bright yellow.

Her heart came up into her mouth. Yellow. She began to run. Ben ran with her, thinking it was a game. Yellow.

Viola Letters had been wearing a yellow sou'wester last night.

It was a yellow sou'wester that was wrapped around the blade of the mill wheel.

Then she saw the huge chunk that was missing from the bank the other side of the footbridge. The path and the shrubbery had gone, collapsed into the sluice pond, leaving raw earth like a wound from which the dressing had been ripped.

The yellow sou'wester flapped again.

Charley screamed.

Chapter Twenty-Six

The man from the Water Board cranked the small round handle at the side of the wheel; the rods and gears it was attached to were rusty and creaked. One of the policemen cranked the opposite handle. The two corroded steel gates moved slowly, inches at a time, until they locked together.

Charley was aware of the new silence, as if a tap had been turned off. A bizarre silence.

The last of the water slid down the slimy concrete blocks of the weir and the level began to sink rapidly down the circular wall of the sluice pond.

The man from the Water Board knelt, peered over the edge of the bank and took out a measuring stick. 'Four inches,' he said. 'The level's high. It'll rise that in an hour. I can give you forty-five minutes then I'll have to open the sluice again.

Charley barely heard them talk as she stared over the parapet at the slime rising around the brick walls and the dark shapes becoming visible below the surface.

Be an old sack. Please be just an old sack, or plastic sheeting.

The top of a gas cooker appeared first; but by then the shape beside it was clear to them all, and their expressions tightened as the water fell further and they gazed at the dark sludge and the body wearing yellow oilskins and red galoshes that lay face down in it, between the mangle and the bicycle and the rusted bedstead.

'To look for her cat? You think that's why she went up there?' Constable Tidyman's notebook was in front of him on the kitchen table. His face was puffy, the smooth skin, on the turn from youth to middle age, streaked by red veins. He had the eyes of a small bird.

The kitchen still smelled of molten plastic. Through the window she could see two policemen stretching white tape around the weir. A Scenes of Crime officer was walking around with a camera, taking shots.

'Yes. She seemed in a bit of a state about it.' Steam from her tea rose. She saw Viola Letters sprawled in the sludge, arms outstretched as if she had been dropped from a great height. She had not been able to watch her body being hoisted out.

The policeman tapped his pen on his notepad, his nose twitching at the lingering unpleasant smell. Hammering echoed around the house and there was the whine of a drill. 'You saw her last night?'

Charley nodded.

'What time?'

'About nine o'clock.'

'And you gave her a drink?'

'A gin and tonic.'

'A large one?'

The question disturbed her; he was trying to lead her somewhere and that angered her suddenly. She didn't fall, for Christ's sake! It was a landslip. She contained her anger. 'No.'

'Do you think she might have been tipsy when she left?'

'No.'

'Had she been drinking before she came here?'

'I wouldn't know.'

216

The beady eyes stared at her accusingly. 'The dam wall was not maintained properly. Water must have been seeping through, undermining the path. It only needed one heavy rainfall to sweep it away.'

Charley shook her head numbly. She did not like the way the policeman had suddenly changed tack, as if he were determined to lay the blame on her.

'The wall is the Water Board's responsibility. I understood that it's checked every year,' she said.

The policeman heaped a spoon of sugar into his tea, stirred it, then tapped the spoon dry on the rim of the cup, more taps than were necessary. 'Did her cat stray often?'

'I don't know. We've only been here a few weeks.'

'Do you suppose there'd be any other reason why she might have gone up there?'

'No, I —.' Her brain fogged.

I wonder if you'd mind terribly nipping down and telling Viola I'll be a bit late. I've lost my damned watch somewhere and I must go back and look for it.

The voice of Viola Letters's husband rang around inside her head, and she felt her cheeks getting hotter. Constable Tidyman leaned forwards, as if he had picked up a scent.

'Was there anything odd about Mrs Letters's behaviour last night?'

Yes, officer, she was very distressed by a photograph. Unfortunately it got burned this morning.

'She wasn't feeling very well. I did offer to walk her home.'

The first time we met, when you came with that message from my late husband. Did I tell you I'd had the same message before? On the day he died?

'Is there something else you'd like to tell me, Mrs Witney?'

'No. No, I'm sorry. I feel very upset; she was a nice

217

woman; she was kind to me.'

The beady eyes did not leave her. 'I understand she lost her dog recently.'

The eyes drew her like magnets. Bored into her. She nodded.

'Accident with a kettle?'

'Teapot,' she mouthed.

'Another accident,' he said.

She bit her lip. Tidyman looked solid in his serge jacket with its polished chromium buttons. He looked like a man who enjoyed afternoon cake in front of the telly and a pint with his mates, a man who was happiest dealing with shotgun licences and lost property. He asked a few more questions, finished his tea and prepared to leave. She let him out of the front door. At the top of the drive two men were loading a large black plastic bag into a white van. The Scenes of Crime officer was changing a lens on his camera. Water was tumbling down the weir once more.

Some people thought death was OK, they could accept it, some religions thought it was OK too. She could not. Death of people she knew always affected her badly. Death was evil. It disturbed her, disoriented her, as if the world had been given a half rotation so that instead of looking up at the sky she found herself looking down into an abyss.

She wondered sometimes what it felt like to die; what Viola Letters had felt plunging down the bank, into the water, being sucked under the water. Some man on a television programme about death, a jolly, earnest fellow whose name she had forgotten, said drowning was quite a pleasant way to go, actually.

It hadn't seemed very pleasant from where she'd stood at the top of the sluice.

It hadn't seemed very pleasant when they'd put Viola

Letters's body into what looked like a bin-liner.

The application form for her birth certificate was missing from the table. She searched the kitchen but it was gone.

She thought back to last night, to when Viola Letters had come into the kitchen. The cassettes had been on the table then, the old woman had noticed them. Had she moved them? The frame? Her mind was fuzzy; her sense of recall seemed to have gone. ·

Another time, dear. We'll talk about it another time.

That had gone too.

Hugh picked Charley up at half past seven in his elderly Jaguar saloon which felt solid and rather quaint. The ignition was on the dash and there was a starter button. She groped around for the seat belt.

'Afraid there aren't any.'

'Oh, right,' she said, feeling slightly foolish, as if she should have known there wouldn't be. There was a low whine from the gear box as they moved off and a gruff roar as he accelerated up the drive. The instruments flickered, the speedometer bouncing around the dial without settling.

The beam of the headlights picked up the white tape that cordoned off the sluice pond and the weir, and was staked across the footpath with a large sign in front, 'POLICE DANGER'.

She said nothing until they were past the old woman's cottage. 'Lovely car.'

He smiled. 'She's getting a bit tatty.' He changed gear, then slowed for a pothole outside the driveway of Yuppie Towers, stopped at the end of the lane then pulled out on to the road. He drove gently, rather sedately, as if he were nurturing the car along, respectful of its age, tilting his head for a moment and listening like a doctor to the note of the engine. She found herself comparing his driving to Tom's frenetic pace.

'Where's your hubby gone?'

Hubby. Sounded cosy. The acid in her stomach rose as steadily as the sluice water had fallen. 'He's — in the States.'

'Does he travel a lot?'

Never. 'Yes. Quite a lot.'

'He does international law?'

'Yes, a bit. Child custody and things.' She was uncomfortable at lying.

'Do you mind being on your own?'

'No, it's fine,' she said too hastily. 'I suppose I'm more used to being on my own in a city than in the country. I don't think I've quite got used to it yet.'

'You haven't had a very good start.'

'No,' she said. 'I haven't.'

The pub was quiet; she was glad not to see Zoe and Julian and to have to listen to how well the girls had ridden and how *sooooooper* Elmwood Mill was and weren't she and Tom simply *adoring* it?

Two wizened men sat at the bar with their own personal tankards, one smoking a pipe, the other tapping his cap which was by the ashtray in front of him. Hugh nodded at them and the one tapping his cap nodded back without interest. A youth was playing the fruit machine and a plump girl in her late teens sat eating a packet of crisps behind him. The fruit machine bleeped and there was a clatter of money.

Hugh ordered her a drink and exchanged a few words with Vic, the landlord, about Viola Letters.

'That path been goin' f'years. Any fool could a see'd it,' the old man with the pipe said to Vic.

Vic nodded, his dark funereal face ideally suited to the gloomy atmosphere.

Charley sat on a bar stool. Tom had rung again, left another message sometime in the afternoon when she had been out, gone for a long walk with Ben, tramping across the fields. She had not rung him and she was pleased, took a certain bitter satisfaction in playing his voice back. It would not last, she knew that; it came in waves, and when she was at the top she was fine, but each time she sank down into the trough she wanted to pick the receiver up and dial him and hear his voice telling her all was fine, he was coming back.

She thought of Viola plunging with the landslip into the water. Was it the cat that had made her go up that path in the darkness? Or her husband? Had she gone to try and communicate?

'Charley must have been the last to see her,' Hugh was saying.

'That path been goin' f'years,' the man with the pipe repeated. 'F'years.'

Hugh handed Charley her spritzer and clinked her glass lightly with his beer tumbler. 'Cheers,' he said.

'Cheers. Thank you.' She sipped the drink; it was cold and rather sharp. Vic walked down the bar and began to tidy some glasses.

'How are you feeling?' Hugh said.

'Pretty shitty.'

'Blaming yourself?'

'I offered to walk her home. She wouldn't let me. If I had insisted ...' She was silent for a moment. 'She didn't have any children, did she?'

'No.' Hugh was wearing a battered jacket, crumpled shirt and a vivid red tie with vertical stripes that reminded her of toothpaste. He ran his eyes across her face, searching for whatever it was he looked for.

Right now, she was not missing Tom. She was glad to be alone with Hugh, to have a chance to talk.

'Hugh. If — If I told you I had proof I have lived before, how would you react?'

The serious expression on his face did not alter; he

221

studied her a little more intently. 'What sort of proof?'

'Didn't you say that to prove you have lived before you need to know something that happened during a previous life that no one else living knows? And which you could not possibly have found out any other way, unless you had lived before?'

'Yes,' he said. He took his pipe from his jacket pocket.

'You said it could be something small.'

He rummaged in another pocket and pulled out a leather tobacco pouch.

'I have two things.'

He unzipped the pouch and pushed the bowl of his pipe in. 'Tell me.'

She told him: about her background; everything she could remember about her regression sessions; about the stables, Viola Letters's husband, the Triumph and the chewing gum, about the locket, and the note inside it, the inscription on the rock and the knife.

She did not tell him about digging the locket back up again, and burning the photographs; nor that Tom had left her. She did not want him to think she was nuts and dismiss everything as her imagination, because she was not nuts, not really — well, maybe just heading a little that way. But not the whole hog.

'D loves BJ?' He tapped his teeth with the stem of his pipe. 'Do those initials mean anything to you?'

'His name is Dick.'

'And what's yours in these regressions?'

'I don't know.'

Hugh struck a match and lit his pipe; the blue smoke drifted towards her.

'You're adopted and don't know your real parents?'

'I'm trying to find out now.'

'So cryptomnesia would be the most likely explanation.'

'Cryptomnesia is things one knew as a child and have forgotten, isn't it?'

'Totally forgotten, as if they never existed.' He sucked on his pipe. 'Memories of the ages one and two, for instance. Very few people can remember anything at all, without the help of hypnosis.' He peered at the bowl and prodded the tobacco with his finger. 'Maybe you were down here with your natural parents, before you were adopted.'

'I was adopted at birth.'

'Are you certain?'

'That's what my mother's always —' She stopped.

'Mothers often shield their children from bad memories. Is there any chance she's been shielding you from something?'

Lies death. Truth. Go back.

She glanced around. One of the old men at the end of the bar was staring at her. She looked back at Hugh; out of the corner of her eye she saw the old man tug the sleeve of his companion and mumble something.

'Surely if — if I had been in this area with my natural parents — or my adoptive parents — I would have some memories?'

Hugh took the pipe out of his mouth and twisted the stem around, adjusting it. 'You do have some memories. You knew where the stables were. You knew where the locket was buried, where the knife was.'

She nodded.

'You're pretty certain your adoptive parents were always in London. Do you think it might be possible that your natural mother was from around here? That you spent your first year or two here before being adopted? Or maybe, if you were adopted at birth, your adoptive mother has some connections here?'

'I suppose it's possible,' she said. 'But wouldn't I have remembered more than this?'

'You're remembering more all the time. You lost your natural father, then your adoptive father. That's a heavy trip for a small child. You've coped with it by burying it away. You needed a hypnotist to dig it up.'

'I thought philosophy was your subject, not psychiatry.'

He tamped the tobacco in the bowl with his finger. 'I'm playing devil's advocate, that's all.' He shrugged. 'There's usually an explanation for these things. If your mother won't tell you — or can't — what about any of her relatives?'

'There aren't any alive.'

'Friends?'

'No. I should have started this ten years ago.'

'You don't know your real parents names?'

LEAVE IT ALONE, BITCH.

'I'm hoping to get them.'

'It still might not help much, but it may tell you where they're from.'

She drained her glass and ordered another spritzer and a pint for Hugh. Just memories. Across the room the fruit machine made a demented wailing sound and sicked up a bucketful of coins. Memories. The minty taste of the chewing gum. The woman on the horse. The locket. Blood gouting from the mastiff's neck. She looked down at her hands, scratched and cut to ribbons. Wounds were memories. Wounds made the body remember that certain things were painful and not to do them again. Her mind was full of wounds. They hurt too much to belong to someone else.

She could see from Hugh's expression that he knew that as well.

They ate in the small restaurant at the back of the pub. Charley picked at her prawn salad, wishing she had not ordered it. The prawns disturbed her, something about them seemed too intense, the fishy flavour, the texture. It felt like eating maggots.

A low mist smudged the beam of the Jaguar's headlamps as they drove back down the lane, just after eleven. Rose Cottage slid by, dark under the marbled moonlight. A tiny red dot winked by the front door.

Hugh braked. She climbed out unsteadily, more drunk than she'd realised. Nelson miaowed mournfully. Hugh stood beside her. She opened the gate. The engine of the Jaguar ticked behind them. 'Nelson!' he said. 'Good boy!'

The cat miaowed again and the cry echoed through the night.

'I'll give him some milk,' Hugh said.

'I've got dog food, if he'll eat it. What's going to happen to him?'

'I'll tell the police in the morning,' Hugh said. 'They'll probably take him to a home or something. Unless you'd like him?'

'I don't think Ben would. You don't want him?'

'He gives me the creeps.'

Nelson wailed again, his solitary eye glowing.

'I'll run you down.'

'I can walk.'

'It's no problem. All part of the service.'

As he pulled up behind her Citroën a feeling of gloom enveloped her; she didn't want to be alone, did not want to go into the house alone. She stared through the windscreen at the dark shapes of the night.

'I keep thinking about Viola Letters all the time.'

'You mustn't blame yourself.'

'Would you like some coffee?'

'I ought to get back. I'm behind on my writing.'

'What are you doing at the moment?'

'Oh, I'm kicking around with the philosophical aspects of ghosts.'

She raised her eyebrows at him. 'What's that to the layman?'

He smiled. 'Maybe a quick coffee.'

She opened the Jaguar's door and the weak interior light came on and made the night beyond the windscreen even darker. The house seemed to be tilting in different directions above her. Lights burned inside; she had left plenty on, had not wanted to come back to darkness.

Hugh got out and closed his door. The weir roared, the water tumbling as if it had never been disturbed. The moon was sliding slowly through the sky, making the same journey it had made a million billion times before she'd ever been born and would go on making aeons after she was dead.

'Weird things, stars,' Hugh said.

'Do you know them all?'

'Ghosts,' he said. 'I always wonder how many of them are ghosts.' He pointed up with his pipe. 'You're not seeing the stars as they are now, you're seeing them as they were hundreds of years ago, millions of years ago; some of them don't exist any more. You are looking at light they emitted, images of themselves. That's what I think a lot of ghosts are. Images of dead people, like video replays.'

Ben barked as Charley unlocked the front door. They walked down the passageway and into the kitchen. She switched the light on and was startled by a sharp crackle from the switch. The light flickered, then steadied. 'There's some problem with the electrics, still,' she said.

'I thought you'd had it rewired.'

'We have.'

Ben was jumping excitedly and she let him into the garden. She filled the percolator with water and took a coffee filter out of a pack. Hugh stared around the room and up at the ceiling with a worried frown. The

226

answering machine winked and she wondered if there was another message from Tom. She hoped there was. Sod him.

'Do you really believe in ghosts, Hugh?'

He prodded inside the bowl of his pipe. 'Yes. I believe in ghosts, but I don't know what they are. I don't know whether ghosts have any intelligence, any free will, whether they can actually do anything other than keep appearing in the same place, going through the same movements, like a strip of film replaying. I'm not sure whether a ghost could really harm someone, apart from giving them a fright by manifesting. That's part of the thesis in my book.'

'Have you ever seen one?'

'No.'

'Would you like to?'

'Yes. Would you?'

'No.' She let Ben in and sat down at the table. 'I'd be really freaked.'

'I don't think it's that frightening. We talk about reality and the supernatural as being two different things. But they aren't.'

'How do you mean?' The percolator gurgled and spat; a steady dribble of coffee fell into the jug.

'We know what corpses are, but I don't think we know what death is. I don't believe in death any more than I believe in life.'

'You don't think Viola Letters is dead?'

'They pulled her corpse out of the sluice pond.'

'But her spirit is the thing that matters?'

'Bodies matter too. All the cells in them, all the tiny particles, the atomic particles and the sub-atomic particles. Genes. Electricity.'

'Electricity?'

'The particles in our bodies have electro-magnetic charges. When our corpses break down, either through

227

cremation or burial, it all goes back into the earth one way or another, gets recycled. Each particle keeps its memory, like a tiny piece of a videotape. It's possible that you and I are made up of particles which have been in hundreds of other people. You might have particles that have been in Einstein, or Michelangelo, or Boadicea.'

'Or a mass murderer?'

'We don't necessarily get reconstituted as human beings. We might — or bits of us might — come back as humans, bits as dung beetles. Might even come back as a tree and get made into a table.'

'Or an encyclopaedia.'

Hugh grinned and relit his pipe.

She tried to fathom out his argument. 'You said the other day that places could retain memories of things that had happened.'

'There is a view that if there has been an intense emotion in a place then somehow the electro-magnetic particles in the atoms in the walls have absorbed this — and either some people, or certain atmospheric conditions, cause the replay effect.' He shrugged. 'That explains a large percentage of ghosts.'

Charley put two mugs on the table. 'Sugar?'

'Thanks.'

'What about the others?'

He rolled a spent match between his fingers. 'Intelligent ghosts? They seem to use the same electro-magnetic energy, but they need other energy too. They take the heat out of rooms, which is why rooms go cold; they draw energy off people; they even draw it off the electricity in a house.' His eyes glanced around the room again, over at the switch, up at the light bulb.

She noticed him. 'What — what do ghosts do with this energy?' she said.

'They can't do very much themselves. They are

energy forces but they don't have voices or bodies or limbs. They can move objects around — poltergeist activity — and they can manifest, but if they want to do something they have to do it through a human — or maybe sometimes an animal.'

'How?'

'By using their physical energy.'

She stared into her coffee; dark brown, swirling, like the sluice pond; like the sludge; the old woman lying face down. 'Can ghosts make people do things?'

'It's possible. There is evidence.'

'Viola Letters was going to tell me something. Last night, when she was here, she saw an old photograph of me that she said reminded her of someone. She got quite distraught — wouldn't finish her drink — and left.'

'What did she say?'

'She said she'd explain another time.'

'That was all?'

'She said that on the day her husband died, someone brought her a message. A girl. She said in the photograph that I looked like that girl.'

'Can I see it?'

'It — I — burned it.'

'Why did you do that?'

He looked harder at her, and she felt her face reddening. 'I don't know.'

He did not take his eyes off her while he spoke. 'Sometimes people do get spooked by photographs; the camera catches someone at a particular angle, in a certain light, and they look like someone else.'

'Do you really in your heart believe it is possible people can be reincarnated, Hugh?'

After a long while he nodded. 'Yes, I do.'

'I used to believe death was the end,' Charley said. 'It was easier that way. Do you think we come back time

229

after time and go through the same things?'

'Life's not some slot machine in an arcade with a sign that flashes up saying "I'm sorry, you have been killed. Would you like another go?" But we might get put through the same tests each time, get faced with the same situations until we've learned how to cope.'

Charley felt for a fleeting instant as if she had pushed her fingers into an electrical socket. She was startled by the shock, by the jolt to her mind. 'Do you think that the past can repeat itself?'

Hugh smiled. 'You needn't worry; you're not pregnant, are you?'

She shook her head.

'The character in your regression is pregnant. So it's different, isn't it?'

'Yes,' she said reluctantly.

'Even if your husband has left you.'

She sprang upright in the chair, her eyes opening wide in astonishment. 'How? How do you —?'

'Am I right?' he said.

She sank down on her elbows, squeezing her eyes tightly shut, felt the tears trickle down her cheeks. 'Yes.'

'You're going through a lot.'

She sniffed, and felt angry suddenly, angry at herself, at the world. 'And no doubt I'll have to go through it again in some other bloody life; and again; and again.'

Hugh poured more coffee into his cup. 'I don't think we're doomed to go on forever round and round in the same spot, like some goldfish in a bowl.' He frowned. 'Where is your goldfish?'

'Dead.'

'I'm sorry.'

'You needn't be. It's going to come back as the next Pope.' She blew her nose. 'I'm sorry. I didn't mean to be trite. I just find this whole thing so freaky. These regressions. I really don't want to go on with them.' She sipped her coffee. 'Do you think I should go on with them?'

His eyes rested on hers, probing, still probing. He shot a brief glance around the room, then leaned closer and lowered his voice. 'I think you're close to discovering something; it could be very important, because you are intelligent and articulate and willing to talk about it.' He was quiet for a moment then added, 'I also think you are in danger. Quite serious danger.'

'Danger of what?'

He said nothing.

'Danger of going mad? Is that what you mean?'

'The paranormal,' he said. 'The supernatural. Occult. Whatever you want to call it. It's always dangerous to dabble.'

Chapter Twenty-Seven

She drove to the George and Dragon the next morning, trying to work out what time Hugh had finally left. Four? Half past? Must have been even later than that because it had been starting to get light.

They had talked through the night. About life after death. About religion. About themselves. Talked as if they had known each other all their lives. Hugh had a son who lived in Canada with his ex-wife and she was surprised; it had not occurred to her that he might have had a child. He hadn't seen the kid for two years; a custody fight slogged on. Tom might be able to help him, she said. Tom. She had mentioned Tom as if he was some third party, a casual acquaintance.

It was strange when Hugh left. Letting him out of the front door into the dawn chorus, the way she used to let Tom out of the front door of her mother's flat when they were dating. They used to come back after a night out and cuddle on the sofa until they were sure her mother was asleep, then they'd make love, trying to be quiet and ending up giggling, terrified her mother would wake. Sometimes they dozed, and when he left it would be first light and the milk floats would be starting their rounds.

She had felt comfortable with Hugh last night; so comfortable that if, instead of opening the door for him, they had gone upstairs to bed it would have seemed just as natural.

Get a grip girl, she thought. Fancying other men already. They say it doesn't hurt if you are shot, not for a few moments until the shock and the numbness wears off. Then it hurts. Maybe she was still in shock, still numb? No. Then a seething pang of pain twisted inside her at the thought of Tom and Laura waking up together, and Laura making him breakfast.

The pub was empty. Vic the landlord was behind the bar reading the *Sporting Life*. The fruit machine was silent, its lights off; a faint smell of coffee cut through the background odour of beer ingrained in the walls and the beams. The room was cool.

She stood patiently in front of Vic as he ringed a selection in a horse race. Then he looked up at her and smiled like a man caught leafing through a dirty magazine in a newsagents.

'Any good tips?' she said.

'Not usually.'

'Those two old boys in here last night, sitting just there.' She pointed. 'Who are they?'

'Regulars,' he said. 'Arthur Morrison and Bill Wainwright.'

'Which was the one with the pipe?'

'Bill Wainwright.'

It had been the other one who had stared at her the most. 'Do you know where Arthur Morrison lives?'

'On Crampton's farm. Saddlers Cottages.'

'How would I find those?'

'Simple enough.'

The sign was less than a mile down the road. Charley turned on to a rutted farm track which went across an open field, past a large barn and through a farmyard. A black and white dog ran out and barked at the car. A few hundred yards further was a row of dilapidated brick cottages and she pulled up outside the end one, behind an old van, and climbed out.

The garden was scrubby, overgrown and largely filled with rusted junk. An old black bicycle was propped against the wall and hens clucked somewhere round the back.

She stood, her head stinging from tiredness. For a brief instant she felt she had been here quite recently, and wondered if it was with Tom when they were looking for a farm shop, or maybe Gideon when they had bought the hens.

Arthur Morrison. Arthur Morrison with his wizened glum face and half his teeth missing who sat in the pub sipping his beer from his private tankard. Staring at her. That stare.

She walked down the path, stood in front of the faded blue front door and looked for the bell. She could not see one. There was no knocker either, so she rapped with her knuckles and winced with pain from the raw wounds that were only just starting to scab over.

Silence, then she thought she heard the shuffle of feet and the clink of crockery. She knocked again, using her car key this time. A curtain twitched in the window beside her.

In the farmyard the dog barked. The door opened a few inches and a face peered out of the gloom inside, a shrivelled, suspicious face that looked even older than last night, his scalp visible through his hair like a stone floor through a worn carpet. A smell of age came out of the door with him; of mustiness, tired furniture, tired people; decay.

'Mr Morrison?' Charley said, trying to smile politely.

His expression became increasingly hostile, his gnarled hands trembled. Yet through the hostility and shaking she saw sadness welling in the small yellowing eyes; sadness and tears.

'Go away,' he said, his voice quavering. 'Leave us

alone. Go away. We don't want you here.'

He stepped back smartly and shut the door.

Tom came home that night. It was late, past midnight, dark, and Charley was sleeping lightly, fitfully, when the door clicked. Ben barked.

'Hi, darling.'

Her heart trembled as she heard him walk across the floor, felt him sit on the bed, take her hand. His hand was cold, as if he had been out walking in snow, and she squeezed it.

'I'm sorry,' he said.

'That's OK,' she murmured sleepily.

He leaned over and she smelled strong, musky perfume on him, smelled his breath, which was foul and stank of smoke, not cigarettes or cigars but of burnt straw and wood. He kissed her.

His lips were hard and cold.

She recoiled in shock. The smell of burning and perfume got stronger, more pungent, filled her nostrils. The cold, hard lips pressed into hers, as if they were trying to grind them to pulp. She tried to pull away, pull back, but his arms gripped her around the neck, pulling her in towards him, tighter, tighter.

She shook her head, cried out, heard Ben snarling, cold pins and needles stabbing her body. The room was freezing. She smelled his breath, foul, the ghastly burned smell; the pressure of his hands was getting tighter, tighter. She tried to get out of bed, then realised she was out of bed, was standing up; smashed into something.

His hands tightened more. 'Tom!' Her voice emerged as a gargled cry. She thought her neck bones were going to snap. It was getting harder to breathe, Ben's barking was deafening. She kicked out, but her feet were barely touching the ground. She was breathing in short gasps, standing on tiptoe. She threw her hands up, spun round,

235

fell forwards, cracked her head against something; fell sideways. The pressure around her neck got worse. She stared wildly, looking up, but could only see the moon through the window.

The moon.

The window.

The window was in the wrong place.

Then she was aware of the silence. Of the breeze of cold air. The fierce grip around her neck.

Not hands. It was not hands around her neck; it was something soft that felt hard, was cutting into the skin. It was all right if she stood upright, stood upright on tiptoe and did not move, then it was just all right, just bearable.

The grip around her neck tightened.

It was silk. She tugged at it. The smells had gone. Something silk was knotted around her neck. She stood on tiptoe, as high as she could and tried to loosen it. She found a knot and tugged, but it was too tight. She stumbled and the knot choked her again. Ben barked in fury.

'Help me.'

She put her hands up above her head, felt the silk stretched taut. Where the hell am I? I want to wake up now. Please wake up.

But she was awake. She knew that. She was awake and dangling on the end of a silk noose. Someone had tied it around her neck. Someone in the room.

Her eyes were becoming accustomed to the moonlit gloom. She could see the bed, empty; the archway to the bathroom; Ben. She was standing with her back to the wardrobe. She tried to move away, but the noose around her neck jerked sharply. She clawed at it with her fingers, tried to loosen it but it was getting tighter all the time and she was shaking in panic, gasping for air, having to force herself up on tiptoe to breathe.

She pushed her hand out behind her, found the wardrobe door handle and pulled it. It swung open, thumping her, and she stepped back a few inches, grabbed at the dresses she knew were behind her, felt the polythene covers, heard the rustle of the clothes, the clatter of the hangers. She ran her hand down towards the floor of the wardrobe. It was high, several feet off the ground, with drawers below, but she could not reach down far enough, the noose would not let her, jerked her back up.

She tried again, stretched her arms as far as she could reach, the noose choking her; her fingers touched a shoe, knocked it a few inches sideways, out of reach. She tried again, found it again, was just able to grasp it with the tips of her fingers. She had to fight for breath and for one moment thought she was going to black out. Then her fingers touched the shoe again and she lifted it up.

Holding on to it carefully, gripping it hard, she hammered the heel against the inside of the wardrobe door. She heard the tinkle of breaking glass, transferred the shoe to her left hand in case she still needed it, then cautiously raised her right hand up to the shattered mirror and felt around until she found a loose shard.

With her forefinger and thumb she broke it away, lifted it above her head and started sawing through the twisted silk.

The grip slackened, just a fraction. She carried on sawing, then suddenly the last strands snapped, and she fell forward on her face.

She lay there, shaking, gulping down air, lay there for several minutes before she was able to move, to crawl to her knees and turn on the bedside lamp.

Blinking against the brightness, she stared fearfully at the wardrobe. Part of her black silk negligee hung limply from the latticed carving on the top of the wardrobe. The rest was knotted around her neck.

She shivered with shock and with fear, as she realised what had happened, what she had done.

She had tried to hang herself in her sleep.

She had taken the negligee out of the bottom drawer, out of its carrier bag, had stood on the small chair Tom usually folded his clothes on, tied the top of the negligee around a carved scroll on top of the wardrobe, tied the other end around her neck, then kicked the chair away. It was lying on its side.

Going mad. Did all that in my sleep. Mad. I dig up lockets in my sleep. I killed a dog in a previous life. I try to hang myself. Maybe I am dead now. A ghost.

Can ghosts make people do things?

It's possible. There is evidence.

Her blood flowed slowly, so slowly it felt as if it had stopped; droplets fell through her veins one at a time like condensation from the roof of a cave. She put her hand out and stroked Ben, needing to touch something alive. He felt like a statue.

Steam came out of her mouth. The room was as cold as a deep freeze and getting colder. She walked across to the open window, pushing her way through the coldness as if she were walking underwater. She put her hand out to close the window and realised it was mild outside.

It was only cold in the room.

A creature shrieked in fear, its cry echoing around the darkness. It was half past three. Tiny ghosts glinted in the darkness above her, and the big moon ghost slid silently in the track it had long ago etched in the sky, coating the lake with a sheen, like ice. Fear etched its own track silently down her back.

She shoved the broken glass from the mirror carefully under the wardrobe so Ben would not tread on it, then

238

dressed in jeans, a fresh blouse and a sweater. Ben's tail wagged.

'No, we're not going walkies, chappie. Come on!' She spoke more cheerily than she felt, grabbed her handbag, walked out of the room leaving the light burning, and down the landing, snapping on lights as she went downstairs, picked up Ben's lead without stopping, opened the front door, went out, waited for Ben then shut the door behind her, walked over to her car and held the door open for Ben.

She scraped the dew from the windows, started the engine, and drove up the drive, fast, bounced along the lane, the car lurching, the suspension bottoming. Rabbits scattered as she rounded the bend past Rose Cottage and she noticed Hugh's Jaguar parked outside his barn.

She stopped at the end of the lane, the Citroën's feeble headlamps picking out the hedge across the road, and massaged her neck; the muscles were agony. She pushed the gear lever forward and pulled out into the silent road.

Chapter Twenty-Eight

A street-cleaning truck droned past, its brushes swirling against the King's Road kerb. The mannequins in the shop window opposite stood in arched poses, clad in street-fashion clothes in acid-house hues, glaring demonically out at the darkness through their Ray Ban sunglasses.

A trickle of crimson light leaked from the dark sky and dribbled down the grey precast walls of the high-rise block that towered above. Laura's windows were up there. Seven floors up. She tried to work out which they might be, but it was still too dark.

A spiky-haired girl in Gothic clothing, bombed out of her mind, stomped down the pavement repeating to herself 'Manic-manic-manic-manic', as if it were the key to the universe.

A police car drove by, the two policemen peering in through the Citroën's windows, and Charley remembered she had been drinking last night. The car drove on.

She climbed out of the Citroën, walked to the entrance of the apartment block, looked down the name panel and pressed Laura's bell. They might not be there; might be away for the weekend. There was no response. She was about to press the button again when there was a crackle, and Laura's voice, barely recognisable it sounded so tired: 'Who is it?'

'Charley,' she said.

There was silence, then the click of the lock and the buzz of the mechanism. Charley pushed the glass-panelled door and went in, across the foyer and pressed the button for the lift.

The lift door opened immediately with a clang that echoed in the stillness. The door shut and the lift moved upwards, clanking past each floor, and stopped at the seventh. She stepped out into the corridor, went to Laura's front door and knocked softly.

There was a rattle of the safety chain, and the door opened. Laura stood there in a limp nightdress, her hair dishevelled, her skin the colour of porridge.

'I need to speak to Tom,' Charley said.

'He's not here,' she said.

Charley looked at her disbelievingly.

'Want to come in?'

Laura closed the door behind them, and they went through to the kitchen. Charley looked down the passageway to the open bedroom door for a sign of movement, a sound. Was Tom hiding in there somewhere, silently?

'Coffee?'

Charley nodded. Laura switched on the kettle. 'He's not here, I promise.' The kettle hissed.

Charley sat down wearily at the kitchen table. Laura sat down opposite; they stared at each other in silence for a moment.

'I need to speak to him,' Charley said.

'I don't know where he is.'

'I thought —' Charley twisted her wedding ring. 'I thought you —?'

Laura wiped her face with her hands. 'God,' she said. 'I feel awful.' The water boiled and the kettle switched itself off. 'What a mess.'

Charley watched her, anger rising up now through

241

her fear and tiredness. Laura poured coffee and took a milk bottle from the fridge. Charley glanced around the kitchen, hoping she might spot some evidence of Tom; a pen or a tie or something.

'I don't know what the hell you must think,' Laura said, handing Charley a mug and sitting down again.

Charley did not reply.

Laura looked into her coffee. 'I'm sorry. I didn't mean it. I don't think either of us did. I don't know how I can explain it.' She rested a finger on the rim of her mug. 'I've been so unhappy recently — the last few months — everything's so bloody shitty. Bob's been a bastard, and the boutique's going badly.' She sniffed. 'I've made a real fool of myself. So's Tom.' She shrugged. 'Not much of an excuse.'

'Where is Tom?' Charley eyed her coffee but did not feel like drinking any.

'I don't know. We spent two nights — Wednesday and Thursday — after he — left you.' A smile crossed her face like a twitch. 'It was pretty disastrous. I'm sorry. I'm really sorry.'

Charley stood up; too much was whirring through her mind to cope with. She saw Laura looking at her neck, and turned away, examining a postcard of Tangiers clamped to the fridge door with a Snoopy magnet. She did not want Laura to think she could not cope, that she might have tried to — hang herself?

She stumbled on her own thoughts; could not think of anything to say. She did not want a row, not now, nor a confession. She felt a sense of relief that Tom was not here. Apart from that she was numb. 'I'd better go,' she said, and walked back down the passageway.

Laura followed her to the door and laid a hand on her shoulder. 'I'm sorry, Charley. I'm really sorry,' she repeated.

* * *

Charley pulled up outside the nursing home and let Ben out of the car. They walked into the park opposite under the crimson veins of the breaking dawn.

Ben ran happily around and she sat on a dewy bench, closed her eyes and hugged her arms around herself. The air was mild, but she felt a deep coldness that would not melt away. Her head dropped and she dozed for a while, and woke to find Ben's damp nose rubbing her hands.

Her feet were wet from the grass, her white slip-ons sodden through. She stroked Ben, lolled sideways and slept more. Someone walked by with a dog, but she kept her eyes shut, trying to rest, to savour the drowsiness which for the moment blotted out the fear and the pain.

At half past seven she stood up, clipped Ben's lead on, put him back in the Citroën and crossed the road to the nursing home.

The night nurse was surprised to see her, and Charley smiled back lamely, knowing she must look a wreck, then climbed the stairs with an effort, walked down the landing and went into her mother's room which was silent and dark, with the curtains still drawn.

She closed the door gently and stood listening to the quiet breathing, so quiet it sounded like the whisper of an air-conditioning duct.

She wished the bed was bigger so she could lie on it too and snuggle up to the old woman, the way she used to as a child when she was afraid of the dark, when she used to go into her room and sleep with her arms around her. Safe.

She sat in the chair beside the bed, breathed the familiar smells of freshly laundered linen and stale urine. Safe. She slept.

A tray clattered, Charley stared around, disoriented, coming awake slowly, her neck in agony, her back in agony too, stiff, so stiff she could barely move.

Bugger. The stove. She had forgotten to fill the Aga with coke. It would go out and she'd have to relight it; it was a bitch to light.

A nurse was propping her mother up in bed, the breakfast tray on the table beside her. The nurse turned towards her. 'You've come early,' she said breezily. 'Missing your mum?'

She nodded.

'My mum was in a hospice. I used to sleep in the room with her sometimes.' She smiled. 'You never think that time's going to run out until it happens. Would you like something to eat? I could get you some cereal, eggs.'

'Juice,' Charley said. 'Juice would be nice.'

The nurse held the glass of orange whilst her mother drank, tiny little sips. 'Nice having company for breakfast, isn't it, Mrs Booth?'

She stared blankly ahead.

After the nurse had gone out, Charley went through into the small bathroom and looked at her face in the mirror. Christ. Like a ghost. Her colour was drained, her eyes yellowy and bloodshot. She raised her head and looked at her neck. There were red marks and bands of blue bruising. Somehow she had been hoping that it was a crazy dream. That she'd wake in the morning and the negligee would be back in the carrier bag and everything would be fine and there'd be no marks around her neck.

She washed her face with cold water, dabbed it dry and turned the collar of her blouse up. Elmwood. She had fled from the house. Fled because of — madness? All part of the madness?

Poor thing; of course she couldn't cope with her husband leaving her; pushed her over the edge.

Must be a terrible way to go, to hang herself in a room on your own, like that.

Voices murmured inside her head, snatches of conversations as if she were sitting on a bus.

She went out and kissed her mother, stroked her downy white hair, tidied the loose strands. 'Talk, Mum, talk to me. Let's talk today, have a chat. It's Sunday. Remember we used to go to the country on Sundays?'

The nurse brought in a tray. 'I've popped some cereal and toast on, in case you're hungry.'

Charley thanked her, and ate a little and felt a bit better. She drank her juice, sat beside her mother again and held her hand. 'Who am I, Mum?'

There was no flicker of reaction.

'Who am I?'

There was a yelp outside, then another. Ben in the car, maybe. She would have to let him out soon. 'Who are my real parents?'

Silence. Another mournful yelp.

'What did you mean, *Lies death! Truth. Go back?* Did you mean you haven't told me the truth before?'

The old woman moved a fraction more upright. Her eyelids batted and her eyes widened. She opened her mouth, stared straight at Charley for a brief moment, then looked ahead again and closed her mouth, her jaw slackening, the way someone's might after they have finished speaking. She sank back against the pillow as if she were exhausted by the effort.

Charley wondered what was going on inside her mother's head. Did she in her confused state believe that she had actually spoken. 'I didn't hear what you said, Mum. Could you repeat it?'

But the old woman was still again, her eyes back to their normal intermittent blink; as if an aerial inside her had been unplugged.

Chapter Twenty-Nine

'I don't have an appointment,' Charley said. 'Is there any chance Dr Ross could see me?'

'I'm sure Dr Ross could fit you in, Mrs Witney.' The receptionist was a well-preserved blonde in her forties who always reminded Charley of James Bond's original Miss Moneypenny. She shook her wavy hair and gave Charley a warm smile. 'He won't keep you too long.'

Charley walked across the dark hall into the seedy opulence of the waiting room. A mother sat with a small boy just inside the door. The room had not been redecorated in all the years Tony Ross had been their doctor. The plaster moulding was chipped and cracked; an ugly chandelier hung above a mahogany dining table spread with magazines, and the walls, which needed a lick of paint, were ringed with a jumble of chairs that did not match. The open sash windows behind the grimy lace curtains let in the fumes and the clattering roar of the Redcliffe Road traffic.

'No!'

'Oh please!' The boy punched his mother's chest and she shushed him, giving Charley an embarrassed glance.

'No!'

'My friend Billy's got a four-foot willy —'

'That's vulgar.'

The boy giggled and looked across at Charley for approval. But she only noticed him dimly, her thoughts

246

closing around her like a cocoon. She felt grungy, still in the same clothes she had put on early on Sunday morning. She had not been home. Her jeans felt heavy and prickly and stuck to her legs.

She had stayed at the nursing home all Sunday, too drained to drive back home, to face the emptiness of the house; to face whatever it was that was in her mind.

Or in the house.

She had to go back, she knew that. She had to be strong right now if she wanted Tom back. He hadn't gone just because they only slept together once a month at the moment; maybe that was part of it, but there were other parts as important. Probably the most important was that he thought she was going nuts.

Her regressions irritated him, all her alternative treatments for infertility. Seeing the ghost of Viola Letters's husband had tipped him further over the edge. The stables. The car in the barn. The locket. He even felt her increasing mental instability was in some way contributory to Viola's dog being scalded to death.

If she moved out now and did not supervise the workmen it would be the last straw for him. *Sorry, Tom, had to move out, check into a hotel, because there's a ghost in the house which tried to hang me.*

She had to go back, stay there and brazen it out. She had to prove it to herself as well as Tom.

The receptionist called in the child and his mother. The staff at the nursing home had been good about Ben, hadn't minded him coming in, and the nurse had brought up a water bowl, then later some biscuits and a tin of food for him.

In the evening the night nurse had brought a camp bed into the room. It had been strange sleeping in the room, comforted by her mother's breathing; she could have been a child again.

She had wondered, all yesterday and all last night,

whether Laura had been telling the truth. If Tom and Laura were not together, somehow it made Tom's leaving her easier to accept.

She was glad he had not been in Laura's flat when she had turned up, glad in retrospect. It had been a stupid, dumb thing to do. Wanting to seem strong to him, to show him you did not care — and then turn up on his doorstep in the middle of the night. She was going to be strong, however tough that would be. She felt almost more bitter at Laura than at Tom.

Outside in the hallway Tony Ross was saying goodbye to the boy and his mother, his rich caring voice inflected with interest and enthusiasm; he put much effort into making his patients feel a little bit special.

'Charley! Great to see you! Come on in!'

He was wearing a grey Prince of Wales check suit, a tie with crossed squash racquets, and Adidas trainers on his feet. He had a lean face with twinkling grey-blue eyes and a mouth that almost permanently smiled. His hair was grizzly grey, cropped neat and short at the sides and almost bald on top, except for a light fuzz. He exuded fitness, energy, bonhomie.

'How are you?' He held her hand firmly for several seconds. 'Good to see you! It's really good! How's Tom?'

'Fine.' She swallowed.

'Great!'

She followed him across to his tiny office.

'Thanks for seeing me,' she said.

'It's been a while,' he said.

'We've moved to Sussex.'

'Yes, I got your note. Country life, eh? Lucky you.'

'We still want you to be our doctor.'

'Of course, I'd be delighted to carry on — although you should register with someone local for emergencies. So Tom's a squire now and you're lady of the manor? How are you finding it?'

She shrugged. 'OK.'

'Only OK?' His forehead crinkled and one eyebrow lifted.

'What's the problem?'

'There are several things.' She looked down at her lap. 'One is that I keep noticing a couple of smells, either a very strong smell of perfume — as if someone's come into a room wearing it — or a smell of burning, a really horrible smell of burning.' She frowned. 'I read somewhere smelling burning is a symptom of a brain tumour.'

His eyes studied her, giving her no hints. 'Any particular times when you smell these things?'

'It varies.'

'Do you get any dizziness? Blurred vision? Headaches?'

'Headaches.'

'Sharp or dull?'

'Dull. My head sort of stings.'

He took a silver fountain pen from his breast pocket and scribbled on an index card. 'What else?'

'It feels like my thermostat's gone haywire. I'm freezing cold one moment, then boiling hot the next. It doesn't seem to matter what the temperature is.'

He made a note.

'I also feel queasy a lot of the time.'

'Anything else?'

'I've had some very odd feelings of *déjà vu*.'

'Thinking you've been somewhere before?'

'Yes.' He had noticed the marks on her neck, and was leaning forward a fraction, studying them. 'It's quite strange. I've also been sleepwalking.'

'Have you had any change of diet?' he asked.

'Not really.'

'You haven't wanted to eat different foods to normal?'

The raw steak she had taken a bite out of.

The Chinese box. Why yes, Tony. I wanted to bury a tin full of maggots and to dig it up in two weeks' time and find one big maggot left. Yummy.

'Not especially. I go on and off tea and coffee a bit, I suppose.'

He made another note. His silver fountain pen glinted and a tiny white ball of reflected sunlight danced around the walls. 'How often have you done this sleepwalking, Charley?'

'I'm not sure. Three times, I think.'

'And do you wake up?'

'No.'

'Does it wake Tom up?'

She hesitated. 'No.'

He was silent for a moment. 'It's not in your imagination?'

'No. Definitely not.'

'How are you sleeping otherwise?'

'Badly.'

'Do you feel tired when you wake in the morning?'

She nodded.

'Afraid?'

'Yes.'

'Do you feel afraid in the daytime too?'

'Yes.'

'How are your bowels? Are they normal?'

'They're OK.'

'Are you urinating any more than usual?'

She shrugged. 'I'm not really sure.'

'How about your weight?'

'I've put on a little since we moved down. I haven't been going to my exercise classes, and I haven't bicycled at all.'

He smiled reassuringly at her. 'How are your periods?'

'The same.'

'Still as irregular?'

'Yes.'

'When did you last have one?'

Charley tried to think back. 'About a month ago.'

'Weren't you on pills at one time to regularise your periods?'

'My acupuncturist wanted me to stop those.'

'You've been having acupuncture?'

'Yes.' She blushed.

Ross smiled. 'Why not, Charley? Try everything. I've heard some very good reports about acupuncture.' He glanced through her notes. 'How many periods have you had over the last six months?'

'I'm not sure. Two — maybe three.'

'Are you and Tom still trying to start a family?'

Tom. Tom. The mention of the name was like a sting. 'Yes.'

'Are you going to try an *in vitro* implant again?'

'I don't know. I don't think I could bear the thought of another ectopic.'

'You were unlucky, Charley. The chances of a second ectopic pregnancy are small.'

'But I only have one tube left.'

'You've got some time still; you don't have to rush into any decisions.' He put his pen down and pushed his sleeves up his hairy wrists.

'You've been through a lot over the past few years, haven't you?' he said.

She felt weepy, suddenly, struggling to hold back her tears. She stared out of the window at the small garden, a lawn with a rose bed border beneath a high brick wall and the fire escape of the building beyond. It was quiet and she could barely hear the traffic.

Ross was looking at her neck again.

Tell him. Tell him.

Tom, it's Tony Ross here. Thought you ought to know that Charley's gone nuts; tried to hang herself.

'Moving home is a very traumatic thing, Charley. It's likely that these symptoms you are having could just be down to stress, but I'd like to have a few tests done. I'll take some blood and urine, and I think it would be sensible for you to see a neurologist and have a electro encephlogram — and EEG scan.'

'Tony,' she said, 'could I ask you something?'

'Sure, of course.'

She reddened. 'Have you ever had any patients who — who think they have been reincarnated?'

'Yes, I've had several over the years,' he said, replacing his pen in his pocket. 'I have a woman at the moment — bit of a fruitcake — who has back pains for no apparent reason. She's convinced it's because she was in a stagecoach accident in a previous life.'

'Do you believe her?'

'I'm a doctor of medicine, Charley, not a parapsychologist. I think it's a load of phooey. Why do you ask?'

'I — I'm just curious. Do you think there's something that could explain — medically — all these things I'm getting?'

'Yes, indeed, and a lot more convincingly than a past life.' He smiled confidently. 'It's not a brain tumour, you don't need to worry about that, but there's one possibility I'd like to eliminate. You wouldn't know if you have any history of epilepsy in your family, would you?'

'Epilepsy? No.'

'Of course not, you poor thing. These bloody adoption laws are so stupid. There are so many hereditary things which it might be helpful to know about.'

'Epilepsy,' she repeated.

'Trust me, Charley. You don't have anything serious to worry about.'

'Isn't epilepsy serious?'

'Not these days. I don't want to worry you, Charley. All your symptoms are consistent with stress and that's by far the most likely cause, but I have to eliminate other possibilities. You've always suffered from stress and moving house is bound to have made that worse. I think that's almost certainly all that's wrong with you, but some of your symptoms are also consistent with a very mild form of epilepsy — temporal lobe epilepsy. Temperature changes in the body, sensory delusions, olfactorial illusions — the perfume, the burning — *déjà vu*, your feelings of fear, depression, sleepwalking. Temporal lobe epileptics often carry out functions unconsiously, either sleepwalking or doing things when they are awake without realising it.'

Charley stared at him, her mind churning. 'Doing things without realising it?'

'We do things without realising it all the time. Haven't you ever driven down a motorway and suddenly found you've gone ten or fifteen miles without being in the slightest bit aware of it?'

She wiped some stray strands of hair off her forehead. 'Could you do something harmful to yourself without realising it?'

The corners of his eyes crinkled and he shook his head. 'The human body has a strong sense of self-preservation. If they're heading into danger, sleepwalkers usually wake up.'

'But not always?'

'There have been the odd instances of people falling down staircases or off balconies. There's no guarantee people won't hurt themselves. But it doesn't happen very often.'

'Have you ever heard of' — she hesitated — 'of anyone trying to kill themselves in their sleep?'

Their eyes met, his kind grey-blue eyes crystal clear,

as if he took them out and polished them.

'No,' he said.

'Do you think it's possible somebody could do that?'

'No, I don't.' He looked at her neck, more obviously this time. 'Why are you asking me this?'

'No reason. I was just curious.'

He stood up. 'Let's go to the examination room and do those tests.' He came round the desk and rested his arm on her shoulder. 'Is there anything wrong, Charley? You've got some nasty marks on your neck.'

'Oh —' she shrugged. 'I got it caught — a trunk — I was unpacking some stuff and the lid came down —'

He squeezed her shoulder gently. 'You'd tell me if there was something wrong, wouldn't you?'

She nodded but was unable to look him in the face, was unable to speak for a moment in case the tears exploded. She could feel his eyes on her neck again; she could feel them as if he were probing the marks with his fingers.

Chapter Thirty

Charley followed Ernest Gibbon upstairs, his feet plodding, the stairs creaking and smelling of boiled cabbage and scented air freshener. She looked at the familiar Artexed walls and the wooden plates with scenes of Switzerland whilst he paused to get his breath back on the first floor landing.

His skin hung slackly from his face, and his eyes, behind the thick lenses of his glasses, had sunk a little further into their sockets. He breathed in short wheezy gasps like a punctured squeeze box, walked across to his mother's room, rapped on the door and went in. 'Got a client, mother. I've put the lunch on, and locked the front door.'

They went on up, and Charley lay down on the couch in the attic room under the microphone. 'Thank you for seeing me so quickly.' she said.

He lowered himself into his chair, leaned over and checked his recording equipment, then made Charley do a brief voice test which he played back. 'How have you been?' he said.

'Not good.'

'Do you feel up to going through with it — all the way?'

'I need to.'

'Yes. You do.' He looked at her as if he knew exactly what had happened. 'You're going to have to be strong.

When you start screaming, that's when I've always brought you out before. I shan't bring you out this time. Are you happy with that?'

She tore at the skin above one of her nails, and felt a lump in her throat.

Gibbon switched out the overhead light.

She stopped, hot, tired and thirsty from her long journey, leaned against the brick parapet of the roaring weir, and gazed down at the house in the hollow, a hundred yards away below her. The house of the woman who had ruined her life.

She wiped the perspiration off her brow with the back of her hand and was grateful for the cooling spray that rose up from the weir as she scoured the property with her tear-blurred eyes for signs of life. She looked at the disused watermill, at the stable block, and warily at the barn with its silent empty kennel outside, and the brass ring beside it.

The black sports car was parked in the drive. Good. He was here. Somewhere. She slipped her hand inside her bag and felt the cold steel blade of the knife.

Talk. Just want to talk. That's all.

She stared again at the house, looking for movement in the mullioned windows, for faces, for the twitch of a curtain.

'Do you recognise where you are?' she heard a voice say, a flat distant voice.

The sun was setting directly behind the house, the rays of light stinging her eyes, making it hard to see, throwing long black shadows up the bank towards her.

'Are you in the same place as before?' The voice was faint, a distant echo. She vaguely wondered where it came from as she walked slowly through the gateposts on to the scrunching gravel of the driveway. The unborn child inside her kicked sharply, as if it could sense her fear, as if it were trying to warn her not to go on; she pressed her hand against her swollen belly, and patted it. 'It's all right,' she said. 'Talk. Just want to talk. That's all.'

She stopped at the bottom of the steps to the front door, and dabbed the perspiration on her forehead with the back of her hand. The house seemed much larger from here, forbidding. She looked up at each of the small dark windows in turn, and listened, trying to hear a sound in the motionless air of the warm summer evening that was not her own panting or the roaring of water.

She looked across the mill race at the stables, down at the barn, at the mill; and then at the car again. A thrush took off with a worm trailing from its beak. She heard the distant bang of a shotgun, then another, the bleat of a sheep, the barking of a dog.

She climbed the steps up to the front door and paused, nervously eyeing the shiny lion's head knocker which glared menacingly back at her. The door was slightly ajar and she pushed it further open and peered into the hallway.

There was no sign of anyone. She hesitated, then walked in, stopped and listened again. Her shadowy reflection stared back through the gloom from a spangled mirror on the wall. There was a staircase ahead with a passageway beside it, and doors to the left and right of her. The house smelled of furniture polish and a rich musky perfume; it felt feminine, elegant, alien.

There was a creak upstairs and she froze.

She stood for a full minute in silence, listening, but heard nothing more other than the tick of a clock and her own heavy breathing. She lifted the iron latch handle on the door on her left and pushed it open.

The room was empty. The diffused rays of the setting

sunlight through the French windows bathed the soft eau de nil and peach colourings. It felt so sumptuous, so beautiful; it almost made her turn and run out in hopelessness. The furniture was grand, graceful Art Deco, the pictures on the walls were mostly of elegant women in fine clothes, the lamps seemed to be ornamental. It was another world.

On the mantelpiece above the empty fireplace an alabaster court jester's face in a bronze bust smiled menacingly at her, as if he were encouraging her to turn towards the sofa, to look at the dents in the plump cushions. It seemed to be smirking at her knowingly.

There she saw a notepad on a writing bureau, with writing on it, a large feminine scrawl, in black ink.

Hector and Daphne, cocktails, Aug 20th?

Cow. Going to parties whilst she ... The handwriting was familiar. She had seen it before.

'Is it a woman's handwriting?' said the distant voice. 'Can you read me what it says?'

The voice faded. She went across the hall, down a dark passageway, to a kitchen with smart brown linoleum on the floor, bright yellow paintwork and an Aga set into a tiled surround. There were dirty plates on the table, and dirty dishes piled around the sink.

Slut, she thought, walking back down the passageway. Two places were laid on the large refectory table in the dining room for a meal that had been eaten and not cleared away. A half drunk bottle of claret, unstoppered, lay on the sideboard, two glasses, both with a small drop of wine left, were still on the table. The room smelled of cigar smoke. His cigars.

She climbed the steep staircase and stopped at the top, panting from the effort and fear, and listened. The house was silent. She looked up and down the dark landing, then turned to the right and went into the room at the far end.

There were two dressmaker's dummies on pedestals, one bare, with the word *Stockman* stencilled to its midriff, the other with a partially sewn dress in shiny turquoise taffeta pinned to it. There were four bald shop window mannequins in there also, two of them naked, two of them dressed in stunning evening gowns, one in a strapless black sequinned gown and wearing black gloves, the other in shimmering black moiré silk. She was awed by their elegance, awed because she'd never seen anything like them outside of a shop window in one of the smart London streets.

Her heart sank. London. The name itself brought a feeling of gloom. London. Where she lived, in the grimy building. London. A prisoner.

She walked down the corridor, past a second flight of stairs and hesitated outside a closed door. She opened it slowly, and saw a bedroom with a huge unmade bed, the sheets tousled. There were strong smells of musky perfume, stale cigarette smoke and scented soap. A shiny black telephone sat on a bedside table, an ashtray full of lipsticky butts beside it.

Slut.

She opened the doors of a huge maple wardrobe. Luxurious dresses were hanging there, coats and furs. Finery. The magnificence. Something she could never have known how to buy.

She went to the dressing table and stared in the mirror, ashamed of her own dowdiness, her dumpiness, her pudgy skin, her tangled hair, her cheap muslin maternity smock.

A thick crystal bottle of perfume was on the dressing table. She touched it, ran her fingers over the contours of the glass, picked it up, feeling its weight, pulled out the glass topper, tipped some on to each wrist and rubbed it in. It stung her finger and she noticed a slight graze. Must have cut it on the knife, she thought, but did not care; the pain felt good. She dabbed some on her neck as well, behind her ears, and rubbed more on her chest. The smell engulfed her. She shook more out, then more still, wiped her face with it, shook it over her clothes, her hair, shook it out until it was empty.

She took the bottle through into the en suite bathroom, stood and listened. Still silence. She removed the toothbrushes from a glass on the washbasin, lowered her knickers and urinated into the glass. Then, carefully, over the washbasin, she filled the perfume bottle with the contents of the glass, restoppered it, wiped it with a face flannel and put it back on the dressing table.

She felt a little better, stronger.

As she went downstairs, a horse whinnied outside. She hurried over to the front door and looked out. Two horses were tethered outside the stables, still saddled. Her heart pounded. They had not been there when she had arrived. One whinnied again; Jemma.

She ran down the steps, over the drive, across the grass and the ornamental wooden bridge over the mill race and up the slope to the stables.

There was another sound now, above the roaring of water, something that was half shout, half moan, coming from the stables. Another moan, then a woman's voice screaming out:

'Oh yes! Your dagger! Give me your dagger!'

She stopped. The sun had gone down further and a dark shadow hung over the hollow. She felt a chill spreading through her body and with it a sickness in the pit of her stomach.

'More! More! Oh God, more!'

For a moment she stood paralysed, unable to move. Then she began to run again.

'Oh God, yes! Your dagger! Your wonderful dagger. More! More! Give more! Oh! Oh!'

She reached the door and pulled it open.

'Dagger me! Dagger me! Dagger me.'

The woman's voice screamed out, echoing through the straw, the smell of horses, of petrol, of musky perfume. She went inside, into a dim tack room, with a lawnmower and a jerrycan and several smaller tins of petrol and paraffin, sacks of feed, a stack of hay, riding tack hung on hooks on the brick wall, and a pile of logs with an axe and a saw leaning against the wall beside them.

Through the doorway ahead into the dark stalls, she could see what she thought at first were two logs, then as her eyes adjusted she realised it was a man's legs sticking out from the end of a stall, his trousers and underpants down around his ankles, his shoes and socks still on his feet.

'Oh, oh, oh, that's so good!'

She felt something drain out of her. She began to quiver with rage, harder and faster, until everything was a blurr. She fumbled with the clasp of her handbag and slid her fingers along the blade of the knife.

No. She pulled her hand out and closed the bag. Talk. Just want to talk. That's all.

'OH YOUR DAGGER! OH! MORE DAGGER! MORE DAGGER!'

She walked through the doorway, past the first empty stall. She could see them clearly now, Dick's naked hairy legs and his buttocks, thrusting out at her, his shirt halfway up his back, the woman's slender white legs rising up either side of him, her knees bent, angulated, varnished toenails scrabbling against the loose straw, her head tossing wildly, her black hair flailing around, her fingernails buried into the base of his shoulders, Dick's bottom pumping, thrusting, faster, faster.

'OH! OH!'

She could see between his legs, the testicles flailing, the black bush, the red lips, the thrusting shaft. She looked at the woman's face, her hard beautiful face, eyes closed, hair thrown back, saw her eyes open suddenly, stare straight into hers.

For an instant time stood still. Then the woman's eyes flashed with a venom that startled her.

Dick suddenly sensed her presence as well and swivelled round, his hair tousled, his face, already flushed with exertion, turning puce with rage. 'Jesus Christ!' he shouted. 'What the 'ell you doing here?' He scrambled to his feet. 'You git out of here, you! Bugger off, you! You cow! You ugly cow! You hear me?' He staggered towards her, making no attempt to pull his trousers up, and slapped her hard across the face; then he slapped her again.

'No! Please — please we must —'

He shoved her, sending her tripping back through the doorway into the store room. She fell backwards and her head smashed into something hard.

'Go on, get out, you cow! Just bugger off, will you? Bugger off! Leave us alone!'

She stared up at him, dazed. 'Talk,' she mouthed but nothing came out. Talk. Just want to talk. That's all. We must talk, look at me, look at my stomach, eight months, please, you have to help me. Please —

The woman came out of the stall, wearing nothing but her unbuttoned silk blouse. 'If you ever come here again, I'll have you flung into prison,' she said.

She put her hand down to push herself up, and something gave. She felt a pain and heard the clatter of the lawnmower's blades rotating and fell back into the machine.

The woman laughed.

She staggered to her feet and spat in the woman's face, then in a sudden frenzy she threw herself at her and began pummelling her. The woman clawed at her with her nails and there was a searing pain as they tore through her flesh. Blood dripped from the woman's fingers, then she felt herself being dragged backwards by her hair. She wrenched herself free, rolled across the floor, hit a can, grabbed it wildly and threw it. It hit the wall behind Dick, the cap flew off and it fell to the ground with petrol gurgling out.

'You crazy cow!' he shouted, kicking her in the ankle, then in the hip, as she curled up throwing her arms around her belly, desperately trying to protect the baby. His foot slammed into her ribs, her shoulder. She scrambled away and somehow regained her feet, then grabbed the saw beside her and swung it wildly at him. Its huge jagged teeth dug into his neck, sending blood spurting out and knocking him to the ground. She swung at the woman, smashing it into her face, slicing deep through her cheek, cracking her against the wall.

Dick clambered up. The woman was on the floor, screaming, one hand pressed against her cheek, the other reaching for the axe. The saw sliced into her arm, then into her stomach. She saw Dick coming and took the axe, hit him in the chest, then she swung again, aiming between his legs, and he doubled up, screaming, clutching his groin, blood spraying like a burst pipe. She swung the axe again, missed him, smashed into the electric socket on the brick wall behind. Sparks shot out, there was a fierce crackle, then a *wumph* like a gas fire igniting and a trail of flame raced across the floor and into the hay, which exploded in a ball of fire.

He fell backwards into it, screaming, kicking his legs. The woman tried to crawl away, but the fire caught her silk blouse, ignited it and suddenly the whole place became one solid sheet of flame.

The horses whinnied outside. She ran to the door. Jemma and the other horse were rearing, pulling at their tethers, trying to get away. She dodged their hooves, untethered them, the reins whiplashing in her hands as they galloped down the bank.

The noise behind her was deafening. She stumbled down the bank towards the house, across the gravel, up the steps and in through the front door.

Phone.

She ran into the drawing room, stared around, could not see one.

Phone. There was one; somewhere. She remembered, staggered up the staircase and down the corridor into the bedroom. It was on the bedside table. She grabbed the receiver and tapped the rest several times. Please. Please. Quick. Answer. Oh God, answer.

She could hear the roaring and the crackling of the fire outside. Tapped the rest again. Please. Emergency.

She caught sight of her reflection in the dressing table mirror. Her face was streaked with blood and black smears.

A woman's voice said, 'Operator.'

'Fire! Elmwood Mill! Fire! Please come quickly.'

'I'll connect you with the fire brigade.'

Her vision was blurring. A figure came in through the door behind her. She smelled smoke; burning wood; burning straw. Charred flesh. She saw the eyes, just the eyes. Raw through the blackened skin.

There was a bang. The mirror exploded into spidery cracks. A large jagged shard fell away, landed at her feet.

She screamed.

'Stay with it, Charley.' A voice, dim, faint. 'Try and stay with it.'

She turned. The woman stood with a rifle, struggling to open the breech. Patches of her hair had been burned away to stubble. Her face was black, blistering; her blouse was stuck in smouldering blotches to her blackened flesh. A single wail like a siren was coming from her mouth. Blood dripped from her arm.

She dropped the phone and backed away.

The woman was struggling, swaying, could barely stand. The bullet rattled in the open breech then fell with a thud to the floor.

She scrabbled on the dressing table behind her for a weapon, knocked a hairbrush to the floor, knocked over the perfume bottle, then saw the shard of glass at her feet. She picked it up and lunged forward, smashing into the rifle, knocking the woman over and falling with her.

The woman's fingers gouged into her eyes, blinding her for a moment. The woman was stronger than she realised, seemed to get some new strength, tearing at her with her nails, spitting, pressed her hideous blotched, burned face down close against hers, and she smelled the foul stench almost as if it was coming from inside the woman's lungs. The woman climbed on to her, pinning her down, twisted the shard out of her hand.

She struggled, tried to free herself, saw the red eyes, crazed, saw a glint of the shard in the woman's charred hand. It flashed down and she felt an agonising pain deep in her groin.

'Baby!' she screamed. 'My baby! My baby!'

The flash again. The glint.

'Don't. My baby! *My baby!*'

The charred arm came down. The pain was as if a red hot poker had melted its way through her stomach and was now twisting around inside her.

A thin strip of white appeared in the blackness of the woman's face.

She was smiling.

The face blurred.

The pain blurred with it, then came searing back, and

she rose up and let out a scream she thought would tear out the lining of her throat.

She passed out.

Chapter Thirty-One

The interior of the ambulance shook and rattled. The boom of the exhaust drummed around the steel walls and the fumes that seeped in pricked the noses of the crewman and the policeman who were struggling to keep her alive.

Bottles vibrated furiously in the metal racks, a leather strap swayed above her head, hitting the stanchion each time with a soft smack like a boxing glove. She slid forward as the ambulance braked sharply, then up against the side as it cornered, the tyres wailing beneath her with their own pain.

Four minutes. After a pregnant woman dies, four minutes is all you have to get the baby out before the baby dies too. That's what the crewman was thinking. She knew because she could read his mind; she could read all their minds as she floated up near the roof of the ambulance, looking down at her body as if she were watching a play from a balcony. Everything seemed far away below and yet she could hear every word, feel every thought. Feel everything except the pain. There was no pain any more, up here, and that was good.

Don't bring me back, she thought. Please don't bring me back into the body. Save the baby, but let me go. No more pain.

The crewman held her pulse, stethoscope swinging from his neck. The policeman kept an oxygen mask pressed over her nose and mouth with one hand and a thick wad of dressing against her groin with the other. Strips of gauze lay across her chest, swollen abdomen and the top of her right leg, each with a spreading red stain, and rivulets of blood from the wound in her side ran into the bedding beneath her.

'Getting weaker,' the crewman said quietly. 'She's going on us.'

No pain, she thought. That was the best thing.

The policeman slackened the pressure for a brief instant and a fine spray of blood jetted on to his sleeve. He pressed hard again, startled.

The ambulanceman listened to her heart and placed another piece of gauze on a wound. 'How come she'd been left so long in the house? It's two hours ago we picked up the woman with the burns,' he asked.

'Didn't realise there was anyone else in the house until I searched it,' the policeman said. 'The burnt woman was in too bad shape to say much — she was lying at the bottom of the stairs.'

A contraction ripped through her and her eyes opened momentarily, stared up at him blank, unseeing, like the eyes of fish on a slab.

The policeman managed a weak smile. 'It's all right, love, you're going to be all right.'

'She's still fighting.'

Another contraction, then another, much fiercer, and water suddenly sluiced out between her legs. The ambulance lurched.

'Pail. Put the pail under,' the crewman said without taking his eyes from his watch. He leaned forward and put his head through the driver's partition. 'Contractions every three minutes and she's broken her waters.'

'I'm doing me best.'

He felt her pulse again and a surge of panic swept through him as he had to search several times to find anything at all. Her eyes were closed and her face was the colour of chalk. Going, he thought. She's going on us. The pulse was scarcely stronger than the tick of a watch; no blood, Christ, she was almost drained dry of the damned stuff. The ambulance slowed, stopped. The back doors opened; a trolley was already waiting.

She watched as they slid her body out and on to the trolley, and stayed above them, floating as if she were in a warm pool, as they wheeled her through into the pale green admitting room of the hospital.

'Stab wounds,' the houseman said. 'Some of them are very deep and she has heavy internal bleeding. She needs at least six pints.'

'We've only got two O negative cross-matched,' the sister said.

'That's all?' He walked away from the trolley, across the room. The sister followed him. 'She won't make it,' he said quietly. 'Not on that. Contact London and get some down. An ambulance or the police might bring it. Get the two in as fast as you can, and put her on a five per cent dextrose drip right away.'

The door opened and a man came running in, white jacket over his squash shirt and shorts. He stared down at her pale clammy body, his eyes wide open, caring eyes trying to comprehend for one brief instant, staring at each of the bloody dressings in turn. He carefully lifted the one on her groin and more blood spurted out. He nodded for the nurse to hold it while he examined her vagina.

'Breech presentation,' he said calmly, as if he were reading from a notepad. 'Baby's premature, a tiny mite. Breech presentation with breech impact into the pelvis, cervix four fingers dilated.' He put his foetal stethoscope to her uterus and listened. 'The baby's alive. Placenta posterior. The blade might not have pene-

trated, but we can't chance it. We'll do a full lapo-
rotomy immediately. She's very short of blood — she'll
need at least six pints before the anaesthetic.'

'We haven't got it,' said the houseman. 'We've only
got two pints. We're trying to get some more.'

'Anaesthetic will kill her.'

'So will the baby.'

'Can we have a word in private?'

She watched from above as the obstetric registrar and
the houseman went into the corridor and closed the
door behind them. 'I don't think we're going to be able
to save both of them,' the registrar said.

'What does that mean?'

'We have to make a decision. Between them.'

'The mother or the baby?'

'Yes.'

The houseman shook his head. 'At what point?'

'Now. If you want that woman to live, we've got to
terminate the baby.'

'We can't do that.'

'If we deliver, the mother's got an eighty per cent
chance of dying. You want that on your conscience?'

'Which do you want?'

Their eyes met and each knew what the other was
thinking. She's probably too far gone already. Let her
go. Let her go and save the baby. Except they knew that
they were not equipped to make that decision.

'Get the duty anaesthetist,' the registrar said.

The baby's bottom came out first in a film of membrane
and blood. The houseman clamped the cord and the
midwife sucked out the baby's mouth.

'Seems healthy and normal,' said the obstetric registrar. 'Doesn't appear to have been affected by the
mother's blood loss. Two surface cuts to be sutured
from the stab wounds.' He pointed to the gashes in the

270

left side of the baby's stomach and in its right thigh, then looked down inside the massive incision in the mother's stomach. 'More clamps, Swab.'

She became aware that the bleeding was stopping, and what was there was dark blue. Her body was starting to palpitate and her face changed colour, to puce then to deep purple. The surgeon looked at the anaesthetist, who shrugged. The purple was fading, turning to slate grey, the pupils of her eyes dilating widely.

'More blood. Another pint.'

It was too late.

The people below her in their green gowns and cotton masks stared at the level in the glass bottle, watching it sink down into the red rubber tubing that ran to her vein. The blood pressure needle fell against its rest and flickered, twice. It was almost as if the people in the room could feel her life slip out of her.

Free, she thought. Free now. No more pain. Darkness closed in, soft warm darkness like a summer evening. It became a long dark tunnel with a tiny pinprick of light at the end. The light drew her, getting slowly brighter, warmer, deep golden, filling her with an intense sensation of joy, of welcome. She reached out her arms, the light blinding her now, smiling, laughing like a child. Then there was a draught of cold air and she felt herself slipping back, felt something pulling her back down.

No. Please. Let me go.

A dark icy tornado swirled, spun her around, drew her hurtling down like an express elevator. Please, no. She was plummeting. The light above her shrank into a tiny spot, then was gone.

Fear rose up through her, froze around her, encasing her, blurring her mind. Light began to seep into her eyes, harsh blurred light, cold, hostile, filled with hazy green shapes, strange sounds. She felt a prick in her stomach, then another. She screamed in terror.

'There, there! It's all right! It's all right!'

Faces. Eyes behind masks.

'There, there! It's all right!'

Someone held a needle in the air. A man took it. Brought it down. There was a fierce stabbing pain in her groin and she screamed out again.

'It's all right! It's all right!'

The faces dissolved. They became one face. Eyes behind thick lenses. One face bathed in dim red light, motionless, unblinking, studying her. Ernest Gibbon.

It was as if she were underwater, miles underwater and the weight was pressing down on her. She tried to move, but her body was leaden. Dead. She was dead. He knew that she might die and she had.

He continued studying her motionlessly. She looked at him, the person that could make her undead, somehow. He knew the key, knew how to make her live again; knew the command, the nod, the twitch, the words that would bring her back, bring her out. He stayed silent.

She wondered what the time was. Dark, it seemed so dark. Her brain was fuzzed and she could not remember when she had come, how long she had been here. She wished he would speak, or smile, or nod.

It was a full minute before she realised that he was the one who was dead.

Chapter Thirty-two

Charley sat on the pew, at Viola Letters's funeral, sandwiched between Hugh and Zoe. Vic and his wife sat further along in the same row. Several other faces in the church looked familiar as well, from the cricket match, from shopping in Elmwood village.

She stared at the printed words of the funeral service and fought back a yawn. She'd had only two hours' sleep. Her dress, a navy two-piece she had bought last year was tight; she hoped it was sombre enough.

The particles in our bodies have electro-magnetic charges. When our corpses break down, either through cremation or burial, it all goes back into the earth and one way, or another, gets recycled. Each particle keeps its memory, like a tiny piece of videotape.

Hugh's words echoed in her mind.

Ernest Gibbon's face stared back. Motionless. Ashen.

She looked at the oak coffin with its brass handles and the flowers on top, wondering. Wondering if there was a connection between what had disturbed Viola Letters in the photograph and her death.

Ridiculous. Just an accident.

For a moment she was confused, thought maybe it was Ernest Gibbon in the coffin on the trestle in front of the altar, in the small church with its frescoes on the wall dating back to Norman times, someone had told her.

They were singing 'Jerusalem'. Charley held the hymn book and sang the words quietly. It was her favourite hymn; normally she found it rousing, but today it was as if they were playing it in another room.

The regression had started just after one p.m., and should have lasted two or three hours. It had been ten p.m. when she had come round, out of her trance, and seen Ernest Gibbon sitting there, dead. She had touched him and whimpered in fear, in the knowledge that she had been in a trance for an hour, maybe two, three, or even more, while he had sat there, dead. She had wondered if she was fully out of her trance and was still scared she had not been brought properly out.

She had gone downstairs and knocked on the door of his mother's room. There had been no answer and she had gone inside, and seen an elderly frail woman in bed, eyes glued to the television.

'Mrs Gibbon,' she had said, 'we need to call an ambulance.'

'He's with a patient. He must not be disturbed,' she had replied, not turning her head. 'Nothing must disturb him.'

'It's an emergency.'

'He is not allowed to be disturbed. It is too dangerous.'

The old woman was like her adoptive mother in the earlier stages of the disease; Charley knew the signs. She had gone downstairs, found a phone in the sitting room and called the ambulance. Then she had let Ben out of the car and was amazed he hadn't made a mess.

The ambulancemen had been disgruntled when they'd arrived. Ernest Gibbon had been dead for at least six hours and she should have called a doctor to issue a death certificate. Not them.

Gibbon's mother had come out of the room, one shrivelled breast hanging out of her nightdress, and told

274

them her son was with a patient and must not be disturbed.

When Charley had tried to explain to the ambulance-men that she had been in a hypnotic trance in a room with a dead man, they had thought she must be as barmy as the old woman and had called the police and a police doctor and left.

She'd waited for the police, aware that Gibbon's mother was beyond coping with the situation, and had to deal with the woman's hysterics when she saw her son's body and the truth registered.

A policewoman had turned up to handle the woman and Charley had finally left some time after five in the morning. It had been light when she'd got home and she had been glad about that.

There had been three messages from Tom on the answering machine. One early on Sunday morning leaving a phone number and a room number; a hotel, she thought. The second was on Monday morning. He was in the office all day, he said. The third was Monday night. He was going to Scotland on a custody case; he would call with his numbers when he got there.

She had gone to bed and tried to sleep, but the events of the past two days had replayed in her mind, over and over, and her regression had too, so vivid that each time she awoke, bathed in sweat, she was convinced it was still going on. Convinced that the woman with the hair burned to stubble and the blackened face was standing in the doorway watching her. Then convinced that she was in an ambulance and was dying, but they would not let her die, would not let her go.

Epileptic. *Some of your symptoms are consistent with* ... fine; that was all it was. Temporal lobe epilepsy. Delusions. Hallucinations.

The congregation knelt for the final prayers, and the service was over. The family came down the aisle first: a tubby elderly man, who bore a vague facial resemblance to Viola Letters led the way stiffly down the aisle, arm in arm with an elegant, ashen-faced woman. An assortment of age groups followed from the front pews, smart little children and pukka adults, different to the locals, who had come to say goodbye to a friend. The locals looked sad; the family mostly looked merely dutiful.

'Hallo, it's Mrs Witney, isn't it?' said the vicar, with a jollity in his voice that Charley thought would be more appropriate at a wedding. He shook her hand vigorously. 'You're new arrivals in the village, aren't you? I've been meaning to come and introduce myself.'

Charley stepped out of the porch into the dull grey morning, into the knot of people and the babble of voices.

'Rattled through the service a bit quickly, didn't he?' Zoe murmured to her.

She nodded absently, remembering Viola Letters's complaint to her about the vicar, and they joined the trail of mourners behind the pall bearers who were carrying the coffin up the path.

The sky was charcoal grey above them and a wind was blowing through the graveyard. The coffin sat on its ropes on the green baize carpet.

' ... we therefore commit her body to the ground; earth to earth, ashes to ashes, dust to dust; in sure and certain hope of the Resurrection to eternal life, through our Lord Jesus Christ; who shall change our vile body ...'

Change. Resurrection to eternal life. Eternal life here on earth. With eternal memories. Eternal change, eternal memories, eternally haunted by the past.

'The grace of our Lord Jesus Christ, and the love of God, and the fellowship of the Holy Ghost, be with us all evermore. Amen.'

Charley wandered away, thoughts drifting through her mind, away from the crowd, through the gravestones, past marble headstones with gravelled fronts, stones carved into scrolls, stones the shape of open books, stones with angels, new stones, bright and shiny, old stones, aged, stained, the writing barely legible, some leaning badly and some set in the ground and overgrown with grass and lichen. Some had vases of fresh flowers, or wreathes, some empty urns, forgotten, no one left to tend them.

She walked up the gentle slope, stepping around the slabs and the gravel, barely noticing anything except the occasional name or inscription.

'Ernest Arthur Lamb who fell asleep.'

'There's a land where those who loved when here shall meet to love again.'

There was a smell of autumn in the air; it suited the cold stones of death.

'John Rowe Buckmaster. Gentle in life, serene in death.'

'Barbara Jarrett. D. Aug 12th 1953.'

'Alice Madeleine Wells.'

Charley stopped. Stepped back, read the inscription on the plain tombstone again.

'Barbara Jarrett. D. Aug 12th, 1953.

The twelfth of August 1953.

She had been born that day.

She stood and stared at the plain headstone, dull, no other writing on it, so plain that she had nearly passed it without a glance.

Dear Rock, I love him. Please bring him back, Barbara.

The inscription on the locket. *D loves BJ.*

BJ.

Someone came up and stood beside her. It was Hugh. 'We're invited to the wake; they're having a little do at the George.'

'Right.'

277

'Would you like me to wait?'

'No. Go on. I might be a while.'

'Are you OK?'

She nodded.

'Can I buy you dinner tonight? Cheer you up?'

'I'll buy,' she said flatly, without taking her eyes from the gravestone. 'It's my turn.'

Hugh looked at the stone. 'Someone you knew?'

'Maybe.'

He walked away, and she shivered. Meaningless. Coincidence, that was all. She turned and watched as Hugh joined the last of the mourners who were filing through the lychgate. There was the scrape of a shovel and the rattle of earth. It sounded like a collection box. Mother Nature was collecting again.

'Know how to get there?' a voice boomed out. 'Follow us.'

Barbara Jarrett. D. August 12th, 1953.

There was grass in front of the headstone. No smart border to keep dogs off, no scrolls or cherubs or urn or flowers. No 'In loving memory of', no 'Beloved wife of'. Nothing. Just the name, the date.

Another time, dear, we'll talk about it, another time.

She thought of the old man in Saddler Cottages who had closed the door in her face. *Go away. Leave us alone. Go away. We don't want you here.*

Two old people. Viola Letters had noticed something in a photograph; Arthur Morrison in her face.

The stone suddenly changed colour, brightened, as if someone had shone a torch on to it. She jumped, then felt foolish. It was only the sunlight finding a hole in the cloud.

The electrician's rather dinky van was parked at the foot of the steps, and Charley was relieved there was someone in the house. White tapes were still stretched across the footpath; one had come free and jigged in a gust like a streamer. Constable Tidyman had told her at the wake that it was their responsibility to mend the bank. It was a public footpath and would have to be done soon.

It was hard to believe it was only four months since they had first seen the house. Since the excitement, the sense of peace, of hope. She could still remember the sensation that something was missing. The stables. Except they weren't missing any more. They were there, the other side of the mill race where they had always been, smart white stables. The head of a chestnut horse was looking out of one of the looseboxes. Jemma.

She blinked.

It was still there.

She whirled round. Her car was gone. The electrician's van was gone. The black Triumph was there instead, its roof down, its paintwork gleaming, its chrome shining. She looked up at the house. The window frames had been freshly painted, the brickwork repointed. She turned back to the weir. There were no white tapes, no chunk missing from the bank.

Her blood sifted through her veins like sand through a timer.

She closed her eyes, opened them again. A horse in the stables whinnied. The sand still poured but it was getting noisier and she could hear the faint hissing sound; then she realised it was the roar of the weir, that was all.

Come to the wrong house, she thought. I've come to the wrong house, took a wrong turning —

I try to do everything here in a controlled way. If you are getting uncomfortable or frightened, I can bring you back out, quickly. If you were to start regressing on your own, somewhere away from here, and the figure in the mirror took hold then —

Why should it? It's only something in my memory.
I don't know if it is just memory.

She blinked again. The black Triumph had gone. The stables had gone too. The white tapes were back, and half the bank was missing. The house looked old and tatty and plastic sheeting flapped over the builders' pile of materials. Two long ladders lay against the side of the house. Ben was barking inside.

She touched the side of the Citroën to steady herself; she was gulping down air as if she had just swum a couple of lengths of a pool underwater, scared, scared because Gibbon had not brought her back out.

You're OK, fine, came out of the trance naturally. You're tired now, that's all, tired and in shock; people often have weird hallucinations when they're overtired.

She went into the house. Ben came running up and as she bent to pat him she saw something move out of the corner of her eye, something coming down the staircase.

Her head snapped up. The electrician. It was the electrician walking slowly, strangely slowly, his face sheet white, his eyes open in shock; the short, chalky man who was normally so busy, so energetic, was treading his way carefully down the dust sheet, clutching on to the bannister rail like an old man. 'Was it you?' he said. 'Was it you what turned it on?'

'Pardon?'

He pressed his hand against his mouth. When he removed it, she could see a black mark running across the palm. 'The power,' he said. 'Did you turn the power back on?'

'I've just come in the door.'

'You in't been down the cellar?'

'No.'

'Some joker 'as. I turned the mains off, din't I, to rewire your bedroom sockets. Someone's switched it back on.' He held out his hand. 'See the burn.'

'God! I've got some dressings in the kitchen —'

'S'orl right.' His eyes darted around.

'Is it one of the builders who did it?'

'They ain't been here today.' He examined the burn. 'I dunno what's going on. I've changed all the wirin' and the fittins.' He sucked his hand. 'Let me show you somethin', Mrs Witney.' He walked down the passageway a short way and stopped by a wall switch.

'Take a good look at that.'

There were burn marks on the wall around the switch, and the plastic box had partially melted.

'It's the same in all the rooms. The wirin's melting again. Like last time. I thought it was the lad's fault before. Got a new lad and I left him to do most of the work. I thought he must have made a bodge-up, but it weren't him.'

'I left quite a few lights on over the weekend. I — I was away.'

'That shouldn't make no difference, leaving them on.'

He opened the cellar door and she noticed another smell above the coal and damp and mustiness, a faint acrid tang of burnt electricity. He turned on the light and she followed him down on to the damp brick floor and over, past the dark opening in the wall, to the fuse box. Several reels of wire lay beneath it and the large white box had brown scorch marks. There was a low-pitched humming sound.

The electrician gazed around. He went through the dark opening and she waited until he reappeared. The humming sound got louder and echoed around the room.

The electrician tapped the glass on the front of the meter. Inside a flat metal disc was spinning, so fast it was almost a blurr. Above it were several dials like miniature clocks; the hands of one were also rotating fast.

'See the rate the juice is bein' used?' he said. 'If you had every light and appliance in the house on, and then some, it wouldn't be using it at a tenth of this rate. And you haven't got nothing on. Just the fridge, and the timer for your boiler and a clock radio. Going to cost you a fortune on your bill — apart from the danger.' He reached up and pushed the master switch. There was a click and the cellar was plunged into darkness. He put on a torch. 'That's how I left it down 'ere.'

'Someone switched it on?' she said, her voice shaky. 'Are you sure it couldn't have thrown itself back on?'

The beam of the torch shone on the meter. The disc was slowing down now, the humming turning into a shuffling sound. 'I dunno what's goin' on.'

'You were going to speak to the Electricity Board. You thought there might be some cables or something, which were affecting —'

'I been had a look at their grid plans for this area. There ain't nothing round here.' He snapped the power on. 'We need an engineer from the Electricity Board to come down. Beats me. Never come across this before in all the years I been workin'.'

'What else can it be?'

He shrugged. 'I dunno. Maybe something to do with water — the lake — but I can't see what. Don't make no sense. I think to be safe we oughter switch off the power and leave it off until it's sorted out.'

'All the electricity?'

He nodded.

'I don't want to do that.'

'Could go up in flames, this place.'

'I thought you'd put in modern fuses. Tom said he'd asked you to put in the safest system.'

'I have. That's what I put in.'

'So why's there a risk of fire?'

'They're not tripping. And I dunno why not.'

'I've got to have some power,'

'You'd be best to stay in a hotel 'till we got it sorted.'

'I — can't do that. I need to be here. There must be something you can do.' She was aware of the desperation in her voice.

'I dunno what else I can do. I've checked everythin'. Rewired it, took it all out, rewired it again.' He grinned. 'Maybe you got a ghost.'

The grin dropped away and he looked uneasy, as if he had read something in her face that scared him.

'I'll try and get someone down in the next couple of days. Tell 'em it's an emergency. You'll have to be vigilant. If you're goin' out the house, turn the mains off. Have you got anythin' in the fridge or freezer what's going to go off?'

'Nothing that matters.'

'I'll have another try. But I dunno. I really dunno.'

'Thanks,' she said, her voice barely above a whisper. They went up the stairs. 'Would you like a cup of tea?'

'Ta very much.'

She picked up the small pile of post that had been dumped on the table and carried it through to the kitchen. It felt chilly in here. Because the Aga was out, she realised.

A late bluebottle buzzed by her. She filled the kettle and sat down, untied the blue and white scarf from around her neck and pressed the play button on the answering machine.

'Tom, you old bastard, what's all this about moving to the country? Got your very smart change-of-address card. Thought I might give you a good hiding at tennis one night this week. Give me a call. It's Tim — Tim Parker.'

'Er, good morning. This is Mr West from Fixit DIY, calling Mr Witney. The items you ordered are now in. Perhaps you'd be kind enough to let us know when would be convenient to deliver?'

'Darling, it's me. Please call me. I'm in Edinburgh. My hotel number is 031-556 7277. I'm in Room 420. You can get me in office hours on the same code, 332 2545. I'll be here until Wednesday.'

She let the tape play on without bothering to write the numbers down, a slight smile on her face. He was sounding increasingly anxious.

'Mrs Witney, it's Dr Ross's secretary here. Dr Ross would like to see you as soon as possible. Would three o'clock tomorrow afternoon be convenient? That's Wednesday, three o'clock. If we don't hear from you, we'll expect you then. Thank you. It's now twenty past two, Tues —' The voice stopped abruptly and the light on the machine went off. The power. The electrician must have turned it off again.

Tony Ross had not wasted any time getting the results of the tests. Was that because he had been more worried than he let on? Epilepsy? Or worse? Had he been lying about a brain tumour?

The bluebottle thudded against the window. The post was mostly bills. She tried to think what materials they had ordered from Fixit. Plans; she felt a wave of sadness as she thought about the plans she and Tom had made for the house. For their new life here.

Darling, it's me, please call me.

Sod you.

She ripped open the next envelope. It was another form from the General Register Office. Details of her adoptive birth certificate were required. Where was it? In an envelope with her passport, vaccination certificates and other bits and pieces. She had packed it somewhere safe when they moved. Shit. Her mind could not focus. In one of the large cardboard boxes. Which one? She thought for a moment. The attic.

Barbara Jarrett. D. Aug 12th 1953.

Who were you? Who were you, Barbara Jarrett?

Dear Rock, I love him. Please bring him back. Barbara.

You?

The kettle was silent; no power, of course, and the Aga was out. She went to the top of the cellar steps.

'Sorry, I can't make tea with the power off,' she called down.

'Be about ten minutes,' he shouted.

She climbed the stairs and pushed open the attic door. Just enough light to see by came in from a small window down at the far right end. To the left it became increasingly dark and shadowy. She could make out the water cistern. The holes in the roof had gone, and the light that had leaked in before was now sealed out. Dust tickled her nose and she stifled a sneeze. The ceiling was lower than she remembered and the walls narrower; the room seemed large and at the same time claustrophobic. She was acutely aware of the silence.

The wooden packing cases and large cardboard boxes had been dumped untidily by the removals men near the window, and it took several minutes of heavy work moving them before she found the one she was looking for. 'PERSONAL BELONGINGS' was written in marker pen across two sides.

She trod on something soft which made a crunching sound, and looked down. It was a dead mouse, its face partially decomposed. Her stomach churned, and she pushed it with her foot behind the packing cases so Ben would not get it.

The window shook in its frame in a gust, and something rolled down the roof. She ripped the tape off the lid of the box and opened it. The top half was full of old clothes, strange old clothes that carried with them in their plastic bags the smells of the past. They were neatly pressed, folded, with cleaning tickets attached

285

with safety pins, clothes she had not worn in years put away for — a rainy day? Fancy dress parties? Put away because they were her roots?

She found flared jeans, a miniskirt, a small wooden box full of beads and hippy bells, long white plastic boots, a corduroy cap, a plastic bag full of badges: CND, IMPEACH NIXON! LEGALISE POT! I AM GROOVY!

There was a sound like the scrape of a foot and she stared into the shadows at the far end of the attic, the dark end, with the silhouette of the water tank; but she could not see anything.

She rummaged deeper in the box and found another polythene bag, bound several times with an elastic band which was dried out and broke as she unwound it. She turned the package over, the polythene getting longer, until she could see inside. Letters and cards. One card was bigger than the rest, a valentine with a glum little man on the front holding up an enormous red heart. Inside, in Tom's handwriting, it said: 'To my eternal Sweetheart.'

The tears slid down her cheeks and she closed the card and slipped it back into the bag.

Something caught her eye in the shadows. A movement. She stepped back. Something was moving in the shadows.

Then she realised it was herself; she was standing in the light from the window, throwing the shadow.

It happened fast, without warning. A crack like a whip and her right leg plunged through the floor. She fell forwards, smacking her chin on to the hardboard. The floor sagged beneath her as she landed. Her right leg had gone through up to the knee.

She lay still, startled, trying to work out what had happened. She pressed her hands down on the floor and it sagged further; there was another splintering crack.

She was breathing fast, panicking now. She yanked her leg out then without trying to stand up, she slithered across the hardboard towards the door where the floor felt solid, and clambered to her feet. She rubbed her grazed leg; her tights were shredded.

She noticed the smell of perfume, suddenly. The attic reeked of it. Strong, pungent, musky perfume. A cold draught dusted her skin. Downstairs the electrician called out, 'Mrs Witney? I'm going to put the power back on now.'

Chapter Thirty-Three

A candle burned in a glass holder on the table. They sat by a large unlit inglenook with a grey marble surround like a tombstone. The small restaurant was quiet. Only two other tables were occupied, both by couples who talked in murmured voices.

Charley raised her menu to hide a yawn; tiredness came in waves. Hugh looked less world-weary, less beat-up than usual. He seemed to have made a special effort with his appearance tonight: his hair was brushed, his nails were clean and scrubbed, and his clothes were pressed.

She had dithered for half an hour deciding what to wear, putting things on and taking them off, wanting to look good. She felt better after she'd had a long bath and washed her hair, made up her face and put on a black halter top, trousers, a white satin jacket, patent shoes and a large chain-link necklace. She felt better, too, after another mouthful of gin and tonic.

'You're very quiet tonight,' Hugh said. 'You must be shaken finding your hypnotist dead like that — pretty horrific.'

'It was. And Mrs Letters's funeral.'

'Are you still blaming yourself?'

She nodded.

'I shall miss the old girl. I really liked her.' He picked up his glass and rattled the ice cubes. 'But it was an accident. Nothing more.'

She wished she could believe him.

'Where are records about graves kept?' she asked. 'If you see a name on a gravestone, and you want to try to find out about that person, where would you look?'

'On a recent grave?'

'Early fifties.'

'I should think the County Records Office in Lewes would be the place.' He looked down at his drink then up at her. 'Is it the grave you were looking at after the funeral?'

'Yes.'

His eyes watched her carefully, but she saw behind their studiousness something else, a warmth, an interest. For the first time since she had met him she sensed he was looking at her for another reason than merely to try to probe into her mind. She blushed and he grinned and raised his glass and touched her own with a light clink, and she drank some more and began to feel good, began to feel safe, to feel that maybe it was going to be possible, one day, to be normal again.

'Did you ever try to patch your marriage up?' she said.

He rattled the ice cubes again. 'Someone once said that marriage is like a glass. Once it's broken you can stick the pieces back together, but you forever see the cracks.'

'Are you ready to order yet?' The waitress was smiling; she looked informal, like a college student.

'A few more minutes,' Hugh said, returning the smile, flirting with her, and Charley felt a pang of jealousy. He studied his menu for a few moments. 'Will you and Tom get back together?'

She shrugged. 'I don't think I have any confidence in anything any more.' His large hand slid across the table and his fingers lightly touched the tops of hers. Then he gripped them gently but firmly.

'You have lots to be confident about.'

Strange emotions heaved inside her. 'Being adopted is an odd thing. You don't feel secure. You've been given away, for whatever reason, even if your parents have been killed, you have the knowledge that someone had to find you a home, give you away. It makes you feel all your life that everyone else in the world is going to give you away too. I think I fooled myself into believing that our marriage would be forever. Nothing's forever.'

He squeezed her fingers. 'That depends what you call forever.'

'Do you think that people meet again, in future lives?'

'Some believe that's what attracts people to one another. You know, you walk into a crowded party and you are immediately drawn to one person because it's someone you knew from another life.'

'But we're not aware of it?'

'Some people are. Not many.'

'And you believe it's possible?'

'Yes.'

She fiddled with her napkin. 'My doctor thinks I might be epileptic.'

'Doctors are good at thinking that sort of thing.'

Their eyes met and they both smiled.

'Did you find out who used to own the Triumph?'

'I haven't heard yet. I'm hoping to get her started tomorrow. I'm just waiting for some gaskets to arrive in the post. I'll take you for a spin.'

'That would feel very strange.'

'You know, somewhere like Edinburgh University might be interested in doing a study on you. They have a faculty of parapsychology.'

'No thanks,' she said shortly. She glanced down the menu. She wasn't hungry and did not care what she ate.

She searched for a new topic of conversation, one that would interest him.

'Tell me about ley lines,' she said. 'What exactly are they?'

'Narrow magnetic fields that run in straight lines. No one fully understands what they are. Ancient man used them as lines of alignment for sacred places. The Romans are credited with building straight roads, but they only built them along ancient leys. The electromagnetic fields seem to come from mineral deposits, ore seams and underground streams.'

'Can they affect electricity?' she asked, her pulse quickening.

'The strongest force fields are on junctions between leys. You sometimes get electro-magnetic disturbances on those.'

'What sort?'

'The Alexandra Palace in London is built over a junction of two leys. It's burned down three times.'

'Really?'

'Yes. The most common thing over these junctions is ghost or poltergeist activity. There seems to be some evidence that spirits get energy from these things. Ancient man built all his ancient places of worship — burial grounds, barrows, sacred stones — along leys. The most important ones are on intersections. Stonehenge is on an intersection.'

She frowned.

He looked at her in a strange probing way that reminded her of the first time they had met. 'So is Elmwood Mill.'

A full moon burned brightly above them as they climbed out of the Jaguar, and the water fell steadily over the weir. Charley listened for Ben's barking, but could hear nothing.

Hugh stood still for a moment. 'Do you know what I see when I look at the moon?' he said.

'What do you see?'

'Three bags of American urine.'

'Urine?' She picked up the large rubber torch she had left on the back seat of the Jaguar, and they walked towards the steps.

'That's what they left up there — the first men, when they landed. Three bags of urine.' He put his arm round her.

'Why?' her voice had a falsetto tremble.

'The official reason was to see what would happen to it. I often wonder if it was something different: like dogs and cats pissing over new places to mark out territory.'

She laughed. His arm was snug, comforting. 'So man's technology still can't nullify our base instincts?'

'Something like that.'

The roar of water seemed deafeningly loud against the silence of the house. She put the key in the lock, twisted it and opened the door. The sharp white light of the torch shot across the hallway, bouncing up and down the stairs, great shadows dancing with it as if they were clipped to the beam. No sound from Ben.

She swung the torch in a wide arc and saw his eyes glowing red out of the darkness of the passageway. 'Boy! Hallo, boy!' He did not move.

She hurried to him, knelt and stroked him. He was sagging on his haunches, cold and shaking; his hair felt almost prickly. 'I'm sorry, boy. Didn't you like the dark?' She hugged him, 'Come on, boy, come outside!'

He slunk to the front door, then seemed to perk up as he ran down the steps and across the grass. Charley unlocked the cellar door, felt the cold draught brush her face, and went down, glad that Hugh was with her. The mains switch moved with a loud snap and the overhead light came on.

292

Hugh glanced around, his head almost touching the ceiling. Charley looked up at the disc of the meter. It was barely moving, 'Do you know much about electrics?' she said.

'It's a good system you've got here. This is the latest, safest technology. I've got it in my own house.'

They went up the stairs and she closed the door. Hugh took her shoulders in his large hands and held them gently; his eyes were smiling; her own smiled back. They kissed. It was strange, wicked; a good feeling. His mouth was softer than she had somehow imagined. They kissed again, longer, much longer, for five minutes, maybe more, until they were interrupted by Ben who came running up to them, barking and jumping, and Hugh laughed and said it looked like Ben had made a pretty good recovery.

They kissed again in the passageway, in the chilly draught from the front door that was still open and she felt Hugh's hands slide up under her jacket, under her halter top and gently across the bare skin of her back.

As she worked his shirt tail out of his trousers and ran her hands up his warm powerful back, she did not hear the low humming that had started in the cellar.

Hugh lay, breathing heavily, cold sticky sweat drying on his body, sensing vaguely that he was at the wrong end of the bed. The moonlight beamed harshly in on his face, strong enough to tan him, he thought. He could hear Charley's breathing, deep, rhythmic, could smell her perfume, her sweat, her animal body smells, and he was becoming aroused again.

His mouth tasted vile, of stale garlic and brandy and cigar smoke. He tried to move but something was holding him down, pinioning him down, a weight across his chest. He put his hand out and felt something hard, smooth. One of her legs. Gently he lifted it and slid out from under it, padded across the room to the open window, and stood listening to the night, to the roaring water, the squeak of some creature, the solitary hoot of an owl.

He walked through into the bathroom and fumbled on the wash-basin for the toothpaste. He unscrewed the cap, squeezed some out on to his finger and rubbed it on his teeth. It tasted sharp, fresh, minty. He ran the tap and rinsed his mouth out, and out of the corner of his eye saw a figure coming through the doorway towards him, an indistinct, hazy figure through the darkness.

Charley. He was filled with a sudden energy and burst of lust as he saw a sheen of moonlight bounce on her breasts, saw her long naked legs. He wanted her in here, wanted to sit her up on the washbasin and —

She ran a finger down his back, tracing over his buttocks, down his thigh, then up, slowly up, took hold of his erection and began to rub it with strokes of her slender fingers, long light strokes, so light she was barely touching it. He smiled at her and she smiled back, a strange smile. A freaky smile.

Then he saw a glint of steel.

Saw the shadow as her arm came down and the knife sliced into his erection, sliced with burning agony right through it and blood sprayed like a fountain, agonising dark squirts in the darkness, spattering him in the face, spraying over her, covering her breasts, her stomach, her thighs, spraying over her grinning sick face.

The knife flashed again, seared into his stomach. Streaks of pain shot up inside him, and the knife twisted, tearing a scream of agony from his throat.

'Stop!' he bellowed, dropping his hands and grabbing the blade, but she tore it back, slicing open the skin of his hand, and bones of his fingers. The knife plunged again into his stomach, twisted, turned, lifted him upwards with an incredible maniacal strength, then he fell down on the blade and it cut him open like a filleting knife.

'Stop! Charley! Stop! For God's —'

He was howling, pummelling with his fists, shaking crazily, trying to back away. He smashed against the wall, except the wall was soft, cushioned him, bounced him gently.

Charley's face burned white, brilliant white. Moon white.

The moon.

He was staring out of the window at the moon, gulping down air. The room was quiet. Silence. Just as the roaring of the mill race outside and the thumping of his heart. He felt for Charley, but touched only an empty pillow.

There was a strong smell of perfume, a heady, musky perfume. Charley must have put it on, he thought, to freshen herself up. The smell seemed to be getting stronger, as if she were in the room now and coming towards him. But there was no one. He heard the door open and turned and saw Charley walking in, a shadowy figure in the moonlight.

Something was glinting in her hand.

His skin tightened around him. He pushed himself back, pressed the palms of his hands against the mattress, tensing his muscles, drawing his legs up, blind terror surging through him. He started moving across the bed, slithering across it.

'Hi,' she said. 'I've brought you a glass of water.'

He stopped, his heart booming, resonating inside him, and stared warily as she moved towards him, as the moonlight glinted off the thing in her hand. He did not relax until the hard glass touched his teeth, the fresh water washed into his mouth, and he drank gratefully, drank like a child. Then she removed the glass and replaced it with her lips.

They kissed, and she pulled back her head playfully, ran her fingers through his hair, and said, 'You taste nice and fresh. Did you brush your teeth?'

In the morning they made love again. Hugh lay on top of her and she felt his crushing weight, felt the warm strength of his body, the hairs of his beard tickled her face. He took some of his weight on to his elbows and she gazed into the blue-grey eyes that were so close they were blurred.

She felt safe. Safe with him here. Safe and good. A bird outside pipped. There was the clatter of the paper boy's bicycle and Ben, downstairs, barked. 'I'm going to have to throw you out in a minute,' she said.

'Oh yes?' He nibbled the end of her nose.

'The electrician'll be here soon, and the builders. I don't think it would be too good an idea if —'

'Can I see you tonight?' He rolled over and heaved himself up against the headboard.

She smiled, 'Yes, please.'

His eyes became serious. 'Charley, would you mind terribly if I did something?'

The change in the tone of his voice alarmed her. 'What?'

His face reddened. 'You know what I was saying last night, about ley lines — intersections?'

She said nothing.

'I — I don't know what it is exactly, but there is something very strange in this house — there's some atmosphere —' He smiled, but the smile failed to dismiss the worry that had suddenly etched into his face. 'It's probably what I think it is — a bit of electro-magnetic interference caused by the ley lines — and that's almost certainly what's causing your electrical problems.'

'Why have they only just started causing problems

now? Wouldn't they have done so before?'

'You don't know they haven't. Your predecessor here was mad as a hatter and she might not have been aware of the problems.'

'Or maybe they drove her mad.'

His eyes probed Charley's. 'Surveys don't reveal leys; not many surveyors believe in or are aware of ley lines. I know someone who is quite into these things, who might —' His voice tailed away.

'I thought you were the expert.'

'I know a bit about leys, but not —'

'Not what?'

He looked uncomfortable. 'He's a — what you'd call a sensitive.'

'What do you mean, a sensitive?'

'Well, he's like me, really, only where I tend to take the scientific view he takes a more paranormal view, I suppose.'

She frowned. He was being evasive and it made her feel uneasy. 'I'm not with you.'

He lifted a strand of hair off her forehead and kissed her. 'I think someone who knows about these things should have a look. And I don't think you should stay here on your own.'

'I have to,' she said.

'You can stay at my house. I'm sure I could get him to come round within a day or two.'

'Your sensitive?'

'Yes.'

A feeling of doom slid across like a storm cloud. Tom. Viola. Gibbon. Peregrine, the terrier. Hugh's semen trickled down her thigh. Betrayal. It had felt good a few minutes ago. So good.

'What would he do, this sensitive?'

'He'd be able to tell you.'

She bit at the hard skin below her thumb nail and

looked at the dressing table. The dressing table with the heart-shaped locket in the tin at the back of the top right-hand drawer. 'Tell me what?'

'Tell you what's going on in this house,' he said. 'Whether you have a presence here.'

Chapter Thirty-four

Charley parked in the pay-and-display below the castle walls, and walked up the High Street. She stopped at a signpost which indicated every municipal building except the one she wanted.

A man in a well-cut suit was striding briskly towards her, swinging his umbrella which was still tightly rolled in spite of the drizzle, and she asked him.

'County Records Office?' he said, swivelling on his metal-capped heels and pointing helpfully. 'Up to the top and round to the right, as far as you can go. The Maltings — got a blue door.'

She walked under a flint archway into quietness and climbed up a steep cobbled hill, past several well-preserved Sussex flint and red brick Georgian buildings, with the castle high up above. She was trying to think clearly, to sort out her thoughts, frightened, suddenly. Frightened to go on. In case . . .

In case she found —?

The drizzle was worsening. Part of her wanted to go back to the car park, forget about the records office. Another part walked on, head bowed against the rain.

Ahead was a low flint malthouse with a high roof and a blue door. A brass sign read 'East Sussex County Council. Records Office'.

Inside was a small entrance hall that smelled of furniture polish and damp umbrellas. The walls were lined with pockets of leaflets and a cheery-looking girl sat at the reception desk in front of a floor-to-ceiling rack of leather volumes marked 'Deaths 1745–1803'.

'Where would I find burial records for All Saint's Church, Elmwood?'

'Room C. Straight ahead at the top of the stairs.'

Room C occupied most of the roof space of the building. It was a long attic with small dormer windows and bright flourescent lighting. To her right was a low counter, to the left were metal racks of index files and a row of microfiche booths; the rest of the room was filled with flat tables and metal-framed chairs.

It was only half past nine, and Charley was surprised at the number of people already there. It bustled with an air of quiet urgency. People were scrolling through microfiches, leafing through binders of old newspapers, unfurling yellowing architects' plans, scribbling notes. At the far end, a group of students were clustered around a woman who was talking intently in a hushed voice.

Charley dug her hands into her raincoat pockets, went up to the counter and waited until one of the clerks looked up from her index cards. 'Yes? Can I help you?'

'I want to see the records on someone buried in All Saints' Church in Elmwood.'

'The burial register? Have you filled out a form?' She held a small pad up.

Charley shook her head.

'You need a seat number.' She pointed at an empty chair. 'That one'll do. Tell me the number on that.'

Charley walked across and came back. 'Eleven.'

The woman handed her the form. 'Fill that in, and

300

your name and address. Do you have a registration number?'

'No. Do I need one?'

'Are you doing regular research — or is this a one-off?'

'A one-off.' Charley took a pen out of her handbag.

'You're only allowed to use pencil here,' the woman said. 'I can sell you one for twelve pence if you haven't got one.'

Charley paid for a pencil.

'Is it a particular year you want to look up?'

'Nineteen fifty-three.'

'Write "Elmwood Burial Register, nineteen fifty-three" then go to your place and someone will bring it to you.'

Charley sat at the table opposite a smart businesslike woman in her late twenties who was scanning through a thick leather-bound volume and jotting down notes on a shorthand pad. Next to her a couple in their forties were poring over a set of house plans.

She wondered how long it would take. She needed to leave by twelve fifteen to make sure she caught a train in time for her appointment with Dr Ross.

A woman reached over and placed a cream leather-bound volume on the table in front of her and moved on silently. It had a gold embossed coat of arms, a typed white tag at the bottom and the wording, also in embossed lettering, 'Register of Burials'.

She stared at it. Forget it, she thought. Take it back. Leave it alone.

She opened it, turned the thick pages carefully, heard them fall with a slight crackling sound. The columns were spread across the width of both pages, the headings printed, the entries beneath neatly hand-written in fountain pen, the style of writing and the colour of ink changing every few pages. There were several church names she recognised, Nutley, Fletching, Danehill, and some she had not heard of. 1951 ... 1952 ... 1953. She stopped, glanced at the headings. 'Name'. 'Date of death'. 'Place or Parish where death occurred'. 'Place of burial'. Her eyes ran down the names. And found it.

'Barbara Jarrett. August 12th. Cuckfield Hospital. All Saints', Elmwood.'

That was all. She leafed on through a few more pages, but they were the same.

She read it again, disappointment seeping through her, then went back to the counter. The clerk looked up. 'Was that helpful?'

Charley nodded, not wanting to offend her. 'Thank you. I really want to find out a bit more about someone who is buried in Elmwood. She's in the register, but it doesn't say much.'

'What is it you want to know, exactly?'

'I — I — want to know who she was, see if I can find out a bit about her.'

'Do you know her date of birth?'

'No.'

'It's not on the gravestone?'

'No.'

'If you had that, you could go through the baptisms register, which would give you the names of her mother and father and when she was born. And you could go on from there and look up the electoral register and get their address.'

'I've no idea when she was born.'

'None at all?'

'All I know is the date of death.'

'There's probably someone in the village who might be able to help you, someone who might remember her. Have you tried that? Pubs are often a good source. Or some of the old shopkeepers.'

Viola Letters's face burned in her mind. The old man in the pub, Arthur Morrison, closing his front door.

'Of course, the announcements in the local paper might give you something,' the clerk said. 'You could check the deaths column. Do you know how she died?'

'No.'

'If it was in some sort of accident, it might well have been reported — that might give you her address and family.'

The woman's words resonated in her head. *Some sort of accident.* Her last regression. The burning stable, the fight. The ambulance. The room spun. Charley steadied herself against the counter; she felt a pounding in her chest. The entry on the burial register: Place or Parish where death occurred.

Cuckfield Hospital.

Hospital.

'Are you feeling all right?' she heard the clerk saying.

'Sorry,' Charley whispered. Hospital. Calm down. Nothing. Millions of people die in hospital.

'The *Sussex Express*,' said the woman. 'That was the local paper deaths would have been reported in then.'

Charley returned to her chair and waited, tried to relax, but her adrenalin was pumping now. The businesslike woman opposite gave her an irritated look; Charley wondered if the thump of her heartbeat was distracting her. It was loud. Like drums.

'There we are. It's heavy.' The clerk laid a massive volume down in front of her on top of the burials register.

Charley lifted the leather binder. A smell of old dried paper rose up from the yellowing newspapers inside.

'SUSSEX EXPRESS & COUNTY HERALD. Friday 2 January 1953.'

An ad in the top right corner read, 'Bobby's Plastic Macs — With Attached Hoods' and beneath were the headlines, 'KNIGHTHOOD FOR LEWES MAN!'

There were several columns full of the New Year honours list, then the rest of the news on the front page was local: a car accident. The success of a charity New Year's Eve ball. She glanced through, fascinated for a moment; the newspaper was so old-fashioned, its layout messy, its advertisements bland, its stories almost all local; there was something cosy about it. She turned several chunks of pages at a time, working through the months. It was a weekly paper. Local news always made the major headline, national or international had smaller prominence.

'CUCKFIELD WAR HERO WEDS.'

'Stalin Dead!'

'COUNTY COUNCIL DECISION ON BYPASS!'

'Rebel Fidel Castro Jailed!'

Friday 7 August.

'FIVE DEAD IN BOLNEY SMASH.'

She turned through the pages of news, advertisements, sports.

'Bobby's Beach Towels In Gay Colours!'

Then Friday 14 August.

The headlines said: 'NEWLYWED DEAD IN BLAZE HORROR.'

It took a moment for it to sink in. For her to realise she was not imagining it. She tried to read it again, but the print had blurred. She squeezed her eyes, but that made it worse. Then she realised it was blurred because she was holding it in her shaking hands, and she put it down on the table.

Beneath the headline was a black and white photograph of an unrecognisable burned-out building. The caption read: 'Remains of the stables.'

Inset beside was a smaller photograph of Elmwood Mill, taken from the side, showing the house and the watermill, with the caption, 'The historic mill house property.'

Then she read the story.

The charred and mutilated body of local man, Richard Morrison, 32, was recovered from the burned-out remains of the stables at his home in Elmwood village yesterday evening, after a frenzied knife attack by a woman believed to have been his former fiancée.

The woman identified by police as Miss Barbara Jarrett, 19, of London, died in labour as a result of wounds she herself received in the attack in Cuckfield Hospital. Doctors saved the life of her premature baby girl.

Mr Morrison's bride of less than two months, society couturier Nancy Delvine, 35, who was also savagely attacked was last night in a critical condition in the burns unit of East Grinstead Hospital where the police are waiting to question her.

The attack happened at Mr and Mrs Morrison's remote mill house home where less than two months ago they had hosted a glittering wedding reception at which some of the most famous names in British fashion, including royal couturiers Mr Hardy Amies and Mr Norman Hartnell, were present.

Mr Morrison, who ran his own livery business in Danehill, and was the only son of Elmwood farm labourer Arthur Morrison and his wife Maud, of Saddlers Cottages, Crampton Farm, married Miss Delvine after a whirlwind romance. They met only a few months ago, when Miss Delvine rented the idyllic Elmwood Mill for the summer.

Neighbour, widow Mrs Viola Letters, stated that she

had seen the heavily pregnant Miss Jarrett walking to the mill several times in recent weeks and that she seemed to be in an anxious and distressed state. Miss Jarrett, whose address was a hostel for unmarried mothers in London, came formerly from Fletching and was the only child of Hurstgate Park gamekeeper Bob Jarrett who was decorated with the DSO in the war. Mr Jarrett and his wife were too distressed to comment yesterday. (*Continued page 5, column 2.*)

Charley tried to turn the pages, but her fingers were trembling so much she could not grip them. She turned too far, flipped back, heard a page tear.

Then she saw the photographs.

The top one was a wedding photograph, a couple leaving Elmwood church, the bride in white, the groom togged in morning dress. The coarse grin on the man's tough face, the cold arrogant smile on the woman's. It was them. The two people she had seen in her regressions.

There were larger photographs of each of them beneath. The man sitting on a horse, the woman in finery, her black hair slanted over her eyes. The woman who had set the dog on her, the woman Dick Morrison had been making love to in the stable, who had come into the bedroom and shot at her and stabbed her with the shard of mirrored glass.

Then her eyes were drawn down to another photograph, smaller, less distinct. She stared in numbed silence.

'Barbara Jarrett. Jilted?'

A girl gazed out at her. A girl in her late teens. Pretty.

The heat seemed to go out of Charley's body. Prickles raked her skin.

The hair was different, long, curled, fifties style. But

that was all. That was the only difference.

It was as if she were looking at an old photograph of herself.

Chapter Thirty-five

Tony Ross was looking as fit and perky as ever as he squeezed himself behind his tiny desk. 'So, Charley, how are you feeling?'

'Very strange.'

'Oh?' He raised his eyebrows. His eyes were twinkling and she wondered for a moment if he was drunk; except she could not imagine him getting drunk. 'I have the results of the tests, the blood and urine samples I took.'

She nodded glumly.

'I want to do a quick internal examination, to make absolutely sure. I think you're going to be rather pleased with my diagnosis.' He jumped up and held the door open for her, then led her across the hallway to the examining room. Miss Moneypenny glanced up from her desk and she was grinning too. Charley wondered if they were both drunk, had just finished an after-lunch bonk, if that was why they were looking so inane.

He asked her to undress and lie on the couch. She kicked off her shoes, pulled down her cotton skirt, slipped off her knickers and unbuttoned her shirt, then lay down on the fresh sheet of paper on the couch. She watched him as he pulled on a surgical glove, squeezed out some KY jelly, felt his fingers sliding up inside her and winced at the coldness of the jelly.

She studied the concentration on his face, the movement of his eyes, looking for some trace of doubt or anxiety, but he just nodded and kept smiling. She sniffed to see if she could smell alcohol on his breath, but could detect nothing even when he leaned right over her. The fingers probed deeply, then he removed his hand, peeled off the glove and dropped it in a bin. He ran a tap and washed his hands. 'You told me you last had a period a month ago.'

'Yes.'

'Are you sure?' He dried his hands on a paper towel.

'Yes. Maybe five or six weeks. Things have been a bit chaotic, the move —'

'Put your clothes on and come back to my office.'

She dressed, irritated by this game he seemed to be playing. She went into his office where he was writing notes on an index card. He put the pen down.

'So you can't remember exactly when you had your last period, but definitely not longer than five or six weeks ago?'

'Definitely.'

He beamed even more broadly and leaned back in his chair. 'Well — you're pregnant!'

It took a moment before the word registered. Then it hit her like a breaker wave. Washed crazily over her, winded her. She stared back, speechless.

'It is quite possible for women to go on having periods well into pregnancy,' he continued. 'It's unusual beyond a couple of months, but it does happen. I'd say you are about sixteen weeks pregnant.'

Pregnant. Sixteen weeks. The words crashed about like surf inside her head.

'Everything feels fine in the uterus, all in the right place. We need to do a few tests, because of your age — but I really wouldn't worry. We'll arrange an ultrasound scan as soon as possible.'

'Sixteen weeks?'

'You haven't felt any movement inside you? You should start getting some soon.' He turned the index card over and tapped his teeth with his pen. 'Pretty surprised, eh?'

'How — how can it have gone on so long, without my knowing?'

'It happens. I had a very fat patient who got to seven months without knowing.'

Pregnant.

The word lay beached inside her. The sun beat down, drying it up, shrivelling it into a blackened carcass.

NEWLYWED DEAD IN BLAZE HORROR

'You don't look very happy. I'd have thought you'd be jumping for joy.'

'I don't understand. All these tests and things. We haven't been trying for months. The acupuncturist wanted us to wait until my body balance —'

The doctor waved his pen around. 'You know, Charley, medicine's a funny thing. It's a very inexact science. I can't tell you why you haven't realised sooner, any more than why you've got pregnant now instead of five years ago, or ten years ago. There are so many factors, psychological ones just as important as physical — sometimes more important.' He pulled a pad out of a drawer and scribbled on it. 'I'm going to give you some things to take, iron and some dietary supplements. Cut out alcohol completely and you must avoid all medication. You haven't been taking anything in the last few months, have you?'

'No.'

'I had a pretty good feeling what your symptoms were, but I didn't want to say anything and get your hopes raised.'

'You knew?'

'Not for sure. It could have been temporal lobe epilepsy, but I didn't think so. Tom's going to be pretty

310

pleased. Want to call him?' He pushed the telephone at her.

She shook her head.

'Tell him later, eh? Give him a homecoming surprise.'

She said nothing.

'Don't look so glum! I don't think I've ever seen an expectant mum look so glum when I've given her the good news.'

'It's not good news,' she said. 'Not good news at all.'

He frowned and leaned forward. 'Not good news?'

She bit her lip, then tugged at the skin on her thumb. 'Do you mean that *all* the symptoms I had are explainable by my being pregnant?'

'Yes.'

'So I'm definitely not epileptic, or anything else?'

'I'm absolutely certain your symptoms are due to your pregnancy — and, of course, not realising for so long would make them puzzling to you. Pregnancy causes hormonal changes which can affect women both physically and emotionally.'

She picked at a nail on another finger. 'Medicine is very convenient,' she said bitterly.

'What do you mean, Charley?' he said, surprised.

'You can explain everything, can't you? Neat. Pat.'

'It's what doctors try to do.'

She stood up, unbuttoned her shirt and pulled it open. She pointed to the small, barely visible ribbed line, three inches long, on the left side of her stomach. Then she hitched down her skirt and indicated the similar line on the inside of her thigh, below her groin. 'How do you explain these birthmarks?' she said.

He came round the desk and examined them closely. 'They're not birthmarks,' he said. 'They're scars.'

'Scars? They're birthmarks. My mother always told me so.'

'They've been stitched, a long time ago. You must have had an accident when you were very young. Quite neat lines. You might have been cut by a knife, or glass.'

She pulled her skirt up and sat down, rebuttoning her shirt. 'Are you sure?'

He sat down again himself. 'Yes. Old-fashioned stitching leaves marks like that; modern stitching is much better.'

She was silent, aware of his worried stare. 'Tony, are unborn children able to register what's going on when they are in the womb? What I mean is — could we — sort of — live our mothers' lives as they live them and remember things later?'

'Remember things our mothers did whilst we were in the womb?'

'Yes.'

He pushed himself back in his chair. 'What is it, Charley? Something seems to be really bugging you. Last time you asked me about reincarnation, now you're asking about pre-birth memories.' His eyes narrowed and he nodded pensively. 'Unborn children can respond to stimulae, yes; tests have proved that.'

She still picked at the nail. 'So there's nothing — supernatural — about perhaps remembering things — that maybe happened when you were in the womb?'

'A five-month-old foetus can hear a door shut twelve feet away.'

'Do you believe in ghosts?'

He grinned. 'Listen, I'm going to get strict with you. I know pregnant women have abnormal fears, but you're going over the top. You must relax. You're a normal healthy person and I'm quite certain you have a normal healthy baby inside you. You've been very wound up about these things that have been going on that you haven't understood. Now you know the reason for them, you don't need to be scared any more. You have

312

nothing to worry about. Just enjoy your pregnancy. Otherwise your poor child's going to be born a nervous wreck.'

She heard a voice somewhere inside her head, faint, as if it were trapped like an echo in a vacuum.

Seems healthy and normal. Doesn't appear to have been affected by the mother's blood loss. Two surface cuts to be sutured from the stab wounds.

She felt a chill blast of air down her neck. It triggered a feeling of fear, fear so deep and strong that the tiny creature inside her womb could sense it too.

It kicked.

It was dusk as she drove down the lane. She'd left Ross in a daze and wandered around, trying to put it all together, to find some meaning. The Citroën jolted through the deep pothole past Yuppie Towers.

There had been times in the past when her period had been late, when she had hoped ... When she had imagined the look on Tom's face as she told him the news. Happier times.

As she drove up to Rose Cottage the falling light seemed to change, to flatten. Viola Letters's Morris had gone from her drive. Instead there was an old black saloon. She was so distracted she almost failed to see the figure in front of her.

She stamped on the brakes, the wheels skidding on the loose surface, and was flung against the seat belt. The car lurched to a halt and she touched her belly gingerly, worried about the child inside and blinking at what she saw through the windscreen.

A man sitting at an easel, erect, with fine posture, in a white shirt, cravat and cavalry twill trousers. He tilted his head back, oblivious to her, raised his brush in the air, closed one eye and lined it up against the cottage then made a mark on his canvas. It was Viola Letters's husband.

He turned, as if he had become aware of her, and stood up stiffly.

Then he faded. Was gone.

The light brightened a fraction. She looked at the cottage. The black car was no longer there. The old woman's Morris Minor sat in the driveway.

Gibbon. Hypnosis. Still under. She was barely aware of where she was and wondered if she had imagined her visit to Ross, if that had been a dream. Then she felt another movement in her belly, faint, like a scratch.

'Hi,' she said lamely. 'How are you doing in there? OK, is it? What are we going to call you? You going to be a boy or a girl? I think you're a boy. I don't know why — you feel like a boy.' She patted her stomach gently. 'You want to stay in there for as long as you can. It's the pits out here.'

A smell of smoke and a haze of acrid blue fumes was drifting across the lane, and there was the droning staccato roar of an unsilenced engine. She was about to put the car in gear when she saw Zoe and her pointer walking towards her.

Zoe pegged her nose with her fingers. 'God, what a fug!' She flapped away the fumes. 'Bloody Hugh, honestly!'

'Is that where it's coming from?'

'Of course. Polluting half of Sussex! I don't know how on earth he can work in that — any normal person would be asphyxiated. I haven't forgotten about having you and Tom over. I'll sort out a date in the next day or so.'

Charley drove on, past Hugh's house. He was in his workshop, bent over the engine compartment of the Triumph, blue exhaust rising around him. He seemed to be engrossed, as if he were trying to tighten a nut, and she wanted to stop, run across and tell him her news but she drove on, afraid the news might put him off her.

314

Pregnant. Who wants to be lumbered with a pregnant loony?

Tom's child. Was Tom going to care?

Was Hugh going to believe her when she showed him the photocopies of the newspaper article?

The builders and the electrician had gone and she was relieved to hear Ben's bark. She hurried across the gravel and up the steps, then she noticed something off about the barks; they sounded muffled, intense, not like his usual greeting.

Angry.

She unlocked the front door and pressed the hall light switch. Nothing happened. Bugger. She sniffed. There was a smell of rotting meat in the house. Fridge, perhaps. She ran into the kitchen. Ben stood in the boiler room, barking at the ceiling, gruff barks as if he had made himself hoarse.

He turned his head towards her, whined, then looked up at the ceiling and barked again, desperately, as if he were trying to tell her something. She stared at him, then up at the ceiling, the black ceiling with the lagged central heating pipes. 'What's up, boy?'

He ignored her, then twisted round on himself and barked at the wall beside him, then snarled and ran out through the kitchen and down the passageway. She followed. He stopped at the foot of the stairs, glared up at them and growled.

'What is it, boy?'

He took two steps back, his hair almost rising straight up.

She climbed a few stairs. The smell of rotting meat was stronger here. She climbed on up to the landing. A gust of wind blew outside; something slithered down a wall. Her bedroom door was ajar; some of the floorboarding was still up and a coil of the electrician's wire was resting against the skirting board. The smell of rotting meat was stronger still; she wondered if it was a dead mouse, like the one in the attic. Except it seemed too strong.

She walked towards her bedroom, the loose boards rattling beneath her feet, echoing in the shadowy silence. She pushed the door further open and looked in.

The tin was on top of her dressing table. It was no longer rusty; it looked brand new. As new and shiny as when she had carried it up the hill in her first regression with Ernest Gibbon.

Someone had polished it.

Her head turned in short snapping movements; the room seemed to be closing in on her. She snatched up the tin and pushed off the lid. Then she screamed.

The locket was not there. Gone. Instead a real heart lay in the tin. It was small, fetid, rotting, and mostly covered in writhing white maggots.

She tried to back away, but the tin came with her, in her hand, the foul stench that had been released from inside churned her stomach like a pitchfork.

She backed into the wall and the tin jerked. The heart shook and some of the maggots fell off it. Others wriggled over the side of the tin and fell on to her hand, cold, dry, their feet pricking into her skin, trying to grip on her trembling flesh before they tumbled to the floor.

One crawled out, bigger than the rest, and perched on the rim. It see-sawed, then rolled on to her wrist, bit her as if in anger at having its meal interrupted, then tumbled through the air as her hand shot up and the tin flew through the air, hit the ceiling, then hit the floor with a bouncing clatter sending the rotten bloody heart rolling against a leg of the dressing table, scattering the maggots around it.

But she did not see it; she was already out of the room, running down the stairs, running for the front door.

316

Ben thought everything had changed into a game and ran joyfully beside her up the driveway. As they neared Hugh's house, the blattering roar grew louder; the engine was sounding uneven now, as if he were accelerating then decelerating, accelerating, decelerating, and every few seconds it missed a beat and backfired.

She paused at the entrance to Hugh's workshop and coughed violently on the fumes. Ben stayed back, not liking them at all. The roar of the engine was deafening inside as it echoed around, still speeding up, slowing down, but sounding increasingly uneven. The air was a dense haze of blue smoke. A powerful torch with a metal grill suspended on a long flex shone down into the bonnet of the Triumph, which was opened on one side, the cover in the air above Hugh's stooped figure. He was examining something in the engine, adjusting something, and seemed to be nodding to himself. A screwdriver was about to fall out of the back pocket of his boiler suit. She walked over to him, but he did not hear her, could not have heard her above the din. Exhaust and steam rose around him and she wondered how he could breathe in this hell-hole of a fug.

'Hugh!' she shouted. He did not turn round; he carried on with his head down, listening to his engine, nodding. She stood beside him and peered into the bonnet then pulled back, alarmed at the heat, the searing heat that sent up a shimmer through the fumes and steam.

'Hugh!' she shouted, panic in her voice. 'Hugh!'

She tugged at his arm, but it did not move. Still he kept nodding.

'Hugh!'

His arm was rigid as if it was set in a plaster cast. She moved further round the wide black wing, trying to see his face, but his head was low, inside the dark searing cauldron of hammering metal and spinning pulleys and

317

shaking wires and black concertina tubing that was vibrating, pulsing.

His tie was sticking straight down into the engine, taut as a hawser, the knot pulled into a tiny ball, his shirt collar bunched and screwed up around his neck. She leaned over further and could see the blade of the tie now, twisted around the fan pulley which was jammed.

Smoke was coming from his face, his hair. She grabbed his tie, but it was like steel. She pulled it upwards as hard as she could, but it would not budge, would not break. She dived for the Triumph's door, yanked it open and was conscious for a split second of the stale leathery smell, like fresh air against the fumes. She scanned the dash frantically, looking for the key, saw it, turned it off.

Nothing happened.

The engine continued its blattering roar. Through the windscreen she could see the back of his head. He nodded on, as if he was pleased, pleased that the engine was running, silently nodding to himself in approval.

As she ran back to him the engine coughed and missed, and his head jerked sharply. It coughed again, and then died. Smoke curled up, steam hissed and there was a purring rattle, a sweet stench of burning flesh, then a click and the gurgling of water. She looked around for a knife, for something sharp. A large screwdriver with a chipped blade was lying on the ground by her foot. She took it, hacked at the tie with it, and it bounced off. She scraped it across the surface but it barely made a mark and she threw it away, tears streaming from her eyes, from shock, from the smoke and the steam, from the horror.

Christ, there must be a knife in here. She tried to move him, tilt him forward so she could loosen the knot, but he would not move. A vortex of shivers swirled through her, tiny demon fish playing tag through her veins. She saw his blue metal tool box on the floor with several trays opened out, full of nuts, bolts, washers, ring spanners, a hacksaw. She grabbed the hacksaw and tried to pull the blade along the tie. It snagged. A row of threads came away, springy, like wire coils. She pushed the saw forwards then back and the bottom half of the tie fell away.

He slid a few inches only his head turning sideways towards her. His face was a mass of blackened pulp. His eyes were open, bulging, unblinking, almost out of their sockets. As she stared a strip of skin peeled away, curling upwards, like the skin of chicken that has been left too long on a barbecue.

Chapter Thirty-six

Charley ran out of the workshop, and threw up in the yard. Then she went to the front door of Hugh's house, a low moan of terror reverberating inside her, and turned the handle; it was locked. She went to the back and tried the kitchen door. That was locked too.

She stood for a moment in the stark white light that spilled out of the workshop into the falling darkness. Hugh's body still leaned over the bonnet of the car. Silence lay around her, pressed in on her. The taste of vomit made her stomach heave. She could hear herself panting. 'Hugh?' It came out as a whimper. An animal rustled the leaves of a bush behind her.

She took a step towards the workshop. The smell of roast meat came out strongly. She stared once more at Hugh's sightless blackened face, then ran back down the lane, Ben chasing along beside her, and burst in through the front door of her house.

She stopped in the hall, puzzled for a moment. It looked different; felt different. A menacing winged bust glared at her from the hall table.

Phone.

She ran into the drawing room, and stared, disoriented, at the colours, eau de nil and peach, rich and lush in the warm glow of the setting sun. The room was full of fine Art Deco furniture, Lalique lamps.

Phone.

She crossed the floor towards a walnut bureau, tumblers spinning in her brain, trying to hit the right numbers, to unlock the code. The room became dark, suddenly, empty, the floor covered in dust sheets; brushes sat in turps in an empty paint tin. The eau de nil colourings had gone; there was no furniture, no glow from the sun.

No phone.

She gulped deep gasps of air, smelling the dry dust sheets. Regressed. Just regressed. Relief pumped through her confusion. Hugh was fine. She had seen something that had happened a long time ago, someone who looked like Hugh. Freaked out, that was all. *Pregnancy causes a lot of hormonal changes.* Yes, good one, Dr Ross, sir!

A wall bumped into her, nudging her gently. It did it again, and she moved away, irritated, trying to concentrate, to get the image of Hugh's face out of her mind. So vivid, it had been so vivid. As vivid as the fetid maggoty heart in the tin. The polished tin.

Imagined that too. The tin was in her dressing table drawer, where she had left it. Sure it was. Pregnant. Everything's fine. Going to be fine. She climbed the stairs almost jauntily, Ben following her, and went into her bedroom.

The drawer was open. The tin lay on the floor, empty, the lid near it. Both were pitted with rust and caked with mud. No one had polished them.

As she took a step forwards she felt a lump under her foot, heard a crunch and looked down. It was the locket, on the floor. A fine uneven crack ran through the enamelled heart.

She knelt, and something clattered against the chain. Something she was holding in her hand. Oh God, no. She froze, closing her eyes. Opening them again, willing it to go, not to be there.

But it was still there in her hand. The hacksaw with the red and green threads in the teeth. The threads from Hugh's tie.

She ripped the cordless phone off the hook, dialled 999 and put the receiver to her ear. Nothing happened. She punched the numbers again, three electronic pips, then nothing. Dead. Electrics. She had not put the electrics on. Maybe the cordless phone wouldn't work without electricity?

There was a vile smell of stale burnt wood. Something moved in the mirror. A shadow in the corridor. Someone coming in the door.

As she turned, the phone fell from her hand, clattering to the floor. She backed away in terror, crashing against the bed, sidled her way around it, trying to get further away, staring in disbelief at the figure, naked apart from an unbuttoned silk blouse, her face blackened, her eyes red, raw, her hair burnt to stubble.

It was Nancy Delvine. Standing motionless, staring in pure hatred.

Charley's ears popped as if she were going up in an aeroplane. All sounds vanished except for the dull thuds of her own heartbeat.

I believe in ghosts. But I don't know what they are.

Shivers rippled through Charley. It was getting colder. Vapour poured from her mouth.

I don't know whether ghosts have any intelligence, any free will — whether they can actually do anything other than keep appearing in the same place, going through the same movements, like a strip of video replay. Hugh's words drummed inside the soundproof box that was her head.

I'm not sure whether a ghost could really harm someone, apart from giving them a fright by manifesting.

The apparition raised one of its arms. Something glinted in its hand. Charley covered her stomach protectively, backed away, tripped, fell and hit her head. She heard splintering glass; shards from the mirror fell around her.

Nancy Delvine's hand raised further.

Charley fought against her own fear, breathing in short bursts, fought her urge to scream, to turn away and curl up helpless in a ball.

You are just a ghost. A trace memory. You are nothing.

She got back to her feet without looking away. Manifestation. She took a step towards it. You are just a manifestation. The apparition did not move. Its hand stayed in the air. Ben was snarling. Another step.

It was getting colder with each step. She felt her skin creeping, lifting. A band tightened like wire around her skull, and it felt as if a million maggots were crawling over her head, their feet pricking into her scalp. She stared the apparition in the eyes. Nancy Delvine's livid eyes stared back.

Manifestation. You cannot harm me.

Everything blurred, frosted. Her pace seemed to be slowing down; each step took an age, as if she was pushing through a great weight, like a diver walking on the floor of the ocean. It was cold, so cold. Terror swirled inside her, wind blew her hair, her face, blew inside her clothes, inside her skin.

Must not scream, she knew, must not show fear. Most not stop.

Then suddenly she was out on the landing. The pressure had gone. She kept on walking, faster, down the stairs, across the hall, out of the front door. It was dark. Cold air blew on her back. Her skin was still crawling.

God help me. She cradled her stomach. OK, she mouthed silently to her baby. It's OK.

It was just the bedroom phone that was dead. Dead

because it was cordless, needed electricity; the kitchen phone would be all right. She stared into the blackness of the house, listened, then went down the passageway to the kitchen. The table was nearer than she realised and a chair slithered across the floor as she bashed into it, its legs screeching. She grabbed the phone, held it to her ear.

The line was dead.

She tapped the rest, looking at the doorway, fearful that at any moment the apparition might come through. The light on the answering machine was off. Electricity. Did phones use electricity? She ran into the hall and picked up the torch from under the table. Then she opened the cellar door, shivers pulsing through her, and clambered down.

There was a low steady hum. She raked the darkness with the beam, then shone it on the fuse box. The master switch was in the OFF position, but the disc was spinning in the meter. It should not be turning. She pulled the switch down with a click which echoed around the cellar. The humming grew louder. She tried to turn it off, but it would not budge.

Something on the wall hissed at her, there was a ripple of sharp bangs and the wiring erupted into blinding flashes, vivid as a lightning storm. Acrid smoke filled her nostrils. Something hit her hand that felt like a wasp sting; a tiny piece of burning plastic. She shook it off, coughing on the smoke. Then the crackling and flashes stopped as instantly as they had started.

She shone the beam back to the master switch. ON. There was a fizzle and a weak flicker as the ceiling light came on, a dull yellow glimmer like a candle in a draught. Again she tried to push the master switch off, but it was too hot to touch. She folded her handkerchief over it and tried again. It would not move. The humming was getting louder.

She staggered up the steps and into the kitchen. The answering machine light was winking. She grabbed the telephone receiver.

It was still dead.

She tapped the rest up and down. There was a hiss behind her, and a curl of blue smoke rose from the light switch; a brown blister spread outwards along the wall around it as she watched.

She ran into the passageway. Dense smoke was billowing out of the cellar, so dense she could not breathe. She smacked into a wall, blinded by it, flapping it wildly away with her hands, coughing, choking, trying to think.

Up the lane to Zoe, use her phone? Too long. Got to stop the fire first. Must stop it. Must get it under control. Water. Must get water. She raced into the kitchen, turned on the tap, and took out the pail from under the sink. The wall around the switch was burning fiercely. Water dribbled into the bucket. She looked frantically for something she could use. Got to get things out of the house. Possessions, save things, documents, valuables —

Ben.

'Ben!' she screamed, her throat in agony, running into the hall. 'Ben!' She flung herself up the stairs, down the landing, into the bedroom.

He was cowering behind the bed.

'Come on, boy! Have to get out.' She tried to pull him. He would not move. 'Come on.' She patted him gently, then tugged his collar. He looked up at her, whimpering.

The floor jolted as if someone had thumped it from below, and wisps of smoke rose through the floor-boards. She yanked his collar, but he sat resolutely, frozen in fear. She pulled harder and his paws skidded across the bare boards. 'Come on!' she screamed.

325

A sheet of flame shot up the wall and blackened the window. The glass exploded. Ben broke free of her grip and bolted into the landing. She ran after him then stopped in horror.

Flames were leaping up the stairwell.

Ben turned in panic, snarled at the flames, at Charley. The sound of the fire was deafening, the heat scorching her face. The bedroom erupted into flame behind her and Ben fled up the attic stairs.

'Ben! No! No! Down, we have to go *down*!'

Tears streamed from her eyes as she went up after him. 'Come back, you idiot dog!' she bellowed. He was at the far end of the attic, barking at the small window. Smoke rose up through the hole she had made when she had put her foot through the floor. 'Ben!' she shouted. Then the whole house seemed to move, to twist, and the landing floor below fell away into flames.

She slammed the attic door shut, ran over to Ben and pressed the latch of the window, but it was rusted. She put more pressure on it and the lever snapped off. She rammed the glass with her shoulder and it exploded outwards, the rotted frame snapping with it, and she nearly fell. She grabbed the sill, steadying herself, feeling a draught, the air cooling her face. She gulped the fresh air greedily, then coughed; it was thick with smoke. She looked down but the smoke and the darkness and the tears in her eyes made it impossible to see anything.

Ben had his paws up beside her, whining, scratching. She leaned out, cupped her hands over her mouth and screamed: 'Help! Help! Fire! Help!' Her voice petered into a hoarse croak drowned by the crackling and splitting roar of the flames below.

The floor lurched and she was thrown off her feet to the boards. They were hot. Plaster and rotted wood rained down from the ceiling.

Out. Got to get out. She scrambled across the

slanting floor to the packing cases, dug inside the one she had opened. A pair of jeans, another. She knotted the legs together, tested them. It was getting hotter. She rummaged for something else, something strong, her old combat jacket, pulled that out, found an arm and tied it to a leg of the jeans.

Ben ran to the doorway, barking. Someone was standing there, just a silhouette through the smoke. It was help. Fire Brigade. She was OK, they were both OK. Relief flooded through her. 'Over here!' she shouted. 'Coming ov —' The smoke choked her voice, swallowed up the figure.

She dropped the clothes and ran to the door. Then she stopped in stark terror as the smoke cleared enough for her to see that it was a woman standing there, smart, elegant, in riding gear, hatless, her black hair hanging carelessly across her face.

Nancy Delvine.

Smart, elegant, Nancy Delvine.

Ben whined, pawing at the ground as if he was trying to back away but could not. Smoke jetted up around him. As she moved towards him, she felt the floor sagging. 'Ben!' she yelled.

There was a loud crack, then the sound of splintering wood. Ben looked at Charley for a brief instant.

'Ben!'

He lurched, drunkenly, one step towards Charley, then plunged through the floor into a volcano of flame.

Charley threw herself forward. 'No! Ben!' The floor dropped several inches. Flames leapt into the rafters, raced along the beams and streaked over her head, showering hot sparks on to her.

The floor rocked, sagged more, as if it were suspended on slender threads. Nancy Delvine was gliding towards her, the flames eating up the floor behind.

Charley yelled out in fury and in agony. 'My dog. Get my dog, you bitch!' She pushed herself on her hands and knees away from the flames and thumped into the wall. She scrabbled to her feet, crouched in terror, staring up into Nancy Delvine's eyes, hard, venomous. Even over the smoke and flames she could smell the sweet musky perfume.

Manifestation. Apparition. You are nothing. Nothing.

Nancy Delvine smiled, came closer.

'What do you want?' Charley said.

Closer.

Nancy Delvine spoke. It was the same cold arrogant voice she had heard before, in the doorway of Elmwood, in her regression. 'You killed my dog.'

Closer.

'And my husband.'

Closer.

'You destroyed my life.'

Pins and needles surged over Charley in agonising ripples, worse than the heat, much worse. She gritted her teeth against the pain. 'It wasn't me. It was my mother.'

Nancy Delvine came closer. 'You are your mother.' She smiled again. Then the flames swallowed her, and she was gone.

The floor tilted, tipping Charley forwards. Frantically she grabbed the window sill, hung from it. Flames stung her flesh like whiplashes.

She heaved herself on to the sill, her eyes bulging in terror at the ground, now lit by the glow of the flames through the smoky darkness. It was a long way down. Her clothes were smouldering. Gripping the sill with her hands, she began lowering herself down the outside, trying to shorten the fall. Her feet dangled, scrabbled, trying to find a hold on the rough walls, but there was nothing. The sill was hot, crumbling; she closed her eyes. Any moment she would have to do it.

Then a voice yelled. 'Charley! Wait! Darling! Don't jump. Hold on!'

Tom's voice.

Her fingers were slipping, her arms hurt, the pain, the burning, the choking smoke. Easier to let go, to drop, easier to die. Her grip slackened.

She heard the clatter of a ladder and Tom's voice again. The sill was burning her fingers. The ladder vibrated from his footsteps. She felt his hand on her leg, guiding it across and down, on to the top rung. Flames burst out of the window above her, leaping into the darkness as if they were searching for her, but she did not notice. She could see nothing except Tom's face in the flaring light.

Epilogue

Alice Hope Witney was born on February 14th. Charley and Tom decided on the middle name Hope because, in a way, her birth had given them both hope for a fresh start.

Alice splashed in the bathtub and gurgled. Charley lifted her out, dried her, and dressed her in her sleep suit. Then she carried her downstairs into the kitchen.

The kitchen was smart, high-tech. Charley had made it as different as possible from the kitchen she had planned for Elmwood. Everything had gone in the fire, every photograph, item of clothing, piece of furniture, book. It was as if her past had been eradicated. She did not mind. In a way, she was glad.

The insurance payout on the fire had been good and they had sold the land to a property developer. Their new home was a large semi-detached house in a tree-lined avenue in Barnes, close to the river. Neither Charley nor Tom had any hankering to live in the country again.

She switched on the television in the living room, sat on the sofa and gave Alice her bottle. Alice had Tom's hair and his seriousness; at times too serious as if she were already, at eight months old, trying to work everything out. Charley wondered if Alice would ever one day remember things from the past, the way she herself had.

It was a year now, almost exactly. Some days it seemed a long time ago, just a faded dream; others, it felt like only yesterday. Little things triggered off the memories: the smell of a pipe; a man under the bonnet of a car; the colour of a tie.

She often wondered in quiet moments like now, as night fell outside and the television flickered, what had really happened and how much more there was inside her, locked away, that a hypnotist could get out. But it would have to stay there. Where once she had been so curious to know, now she must try hard to forget.

Some nights she awoke from a nightmare screaming, reliving a part of the horror. Ernest Gibbon might be sitting at the end of the bed, holding Viola Letters's yellow sou'wester in his hand. Or Hugh, in his sawn-off tie, with an agonised expression on his blackened face. Or Ben padding towards her and, as she reached out, he would plunge through the floorboards into an inferno. Sometimes she saw Nancy Delvine through flames, and as the fire engines roared down the drive, she would clutch Tom and scream, 'Don't let them! You mustn't let them. Leave it; let it burn down!'

The inquests had been the worst part: Viola Letters's and then Hugh's. The same coroner both times. Viola Letters's death he had concluded was an accident. On Hugh's he had been less positive and recorded an open verdict.

Alice finished her milk and burped, then lay sleepily in her arms. Charley carried her upstairs and tucked her up in her cot. Alice woke up and stretched her hands towards the mobile that hung out of reach above her, plastic bumble bees and butterflies. Charley gave it a twirl and Alice watched the pieces swinging, light glinting off them. She was fascinated by anything that sparkled.

Charley switched on the pink night light and the baby alarm, and went downstairs to make supper. Tom would be home soon. She took some lamb chops out of the fridge and put a knob of butter in the frying pan. There was a crackle of static through the receiver of the baby alarm, a gurgle, then Alice's breathing, steady, rhythmic. Asleep.

The garden lit up suddenly. Harsh bright light. The intruder sensor. Charley's eyes scanned the lawn, the neat flower beds, the greenhouse. A startled cat jumped the fence at the bottom, and she smiled in relief. Butter sizzled in the pan and wisps of steam rose. She glanced out at the garden again; the light was still on, and she felt strangely comforted by the ordinariness of their garden. Normality. Elmwood had never felt normal and maybe that was part of it.

She wondered whether she had really seen the ghost of Commander Letters that day, and the ghost of Nancy Delvine in the burning house, or whether they had been trace memories of people her own mother had seen, that had been passed on to her. This had been Hugh Boxer's theory, and there had been an article in the press Tom had cut out for her, with a programme on television on the same subject. Science, it seemed, was favouring that same argument.

And yet. You never knew in life; you never really knew. She had been to a couple of libraries and read all she could find on reincarnation. But the more you searched, she began to realise, the larger the riddle became.

Forget it, Tom had said, and that was the right advice. Maybe nature was helping her in its own way. Life had been good the past year. The balance; always a balance. Positive and negative. Yin and Yang. The good seemed to have followed the bad. Tom was doing well in the partnership. Their marriage had survived, although Hugh had been right when he said that a broken marriage was like a broken glass: you could stick the pieces back together, but you would forever see the cracks.

Laura was getting married again. Their friendship had never recovered. They had exchanged Christmas cards with Julian and Zoe and Zoe had scribbled a note inside saying she would give them a call in the New Year and invite them down for dinner. She never did. Charley was quietly relieved to have had the last link with Elmwood severed.

There was another crackle of static through the alarm, then a sharp clatter, as if someone had given the mobile a push. Except that it was out of Alice's reach; safely out of reach.

There was a splintering crack. Alice cried.

Charley sprinted out of the kitchen, up the stairs, and into Alice's room, snapping on the main light. The mobile had broken and was dangling down into the cot. Alice was screaming, panicky, windmilling her arms which were tangled in the cotton threads and tiny opaque shapes.

As Charley leaned over the cot saying, 'OK! It's OK, Mummy's here,' Alice's right arm jerked straight up in the air. Charley felt a searing pain in her face and pressed her hand to her cheek, startled. She took it away and saw that her fingertips were smeared with blood.

Alice was motionless in her cot, staring at her. For one fleeting moment Charley saw something in those eyes that terrified her. It was in the blackness of the tiny pupils. As if they carried in them an evil that had come down generations, that had travelled through all time and had brought with it a cunning and a hatred and a sense of victory.

333

The room went cold as if the baby had drawn all the heat into herself. Claws spiked Charley's skin; someone stood behind her, pushing her forwards, to the cot. To the thing that was inside it.

'No. Let me go!' she screamed, turning.

There was no one. Just the wall. Perspiration fell from her skin as if from slabs of melting ice. Alice's eyes closed and her head lolled to one side; her tiny balled fist opened and a shard of splintered plastic fell on to the sheet, marking it with blood.

Fear held Charley's throat and she stood for a moment before she was able to move, to reach down and touch her baby. Then she took Alice's hand, terrified it might reach out and grab her like a claw. She examined it carefully, but it was unmarked. She picked up the shard, disentangled the remains of the mobile and pulled it free. Alice was sleeping again as if nothing had happened, her breathing settling back into a steady rhythm.

Charley went through to the bathroom and dumped the bits in the waste bin. In the mirror she saw a ribbon of blood trailing down her face. And she saw the fear that was in her own eyes. The disbelief.

She had imagined it.

Tony Ross had said the shock would go on, would manifest itself in odd ways, and strange symptoms, for years to come.

Imagined it.

She pressed a towel against her cheek and went back into the bedroom. Alice was sleeping, her lips curled into a contented smile. There was a calmness and serenity about her. As Charley watched, her expression altered, then again, her eyes blinking busily, her tiny mouth changing from a smile to a frown to a question, her face like an ever-revolving kaleidoscope, as if she was reacting to things going on deep inside her mind.

334

Trace memories in her genes. That was all.
Charley hoped.